WOMEN
OF
KARANTINA

NAEL ELTOUKHY

TRANSLATED BY
ROBIN MOGER

The American University in Cairo Press
Cairo New York

First published in 2014 by
The American University in Cairo Press
113 Sharia Kasr el Aini, Cairo, Egypt
420 Fifth Avenue, New York, NY 10018
www.aucpress.com

Exclusive distribution outside Egypt and North America by I.B.Tauris & Co Ltd., 6 Salem Road,
London, W2 4BU

Dar el Kutub No. 23356/13
ISBN 978 977416 662 4

Dar el Kutub Cataloging-in-Publication Data

Eltoukhy, Nael
        Women of Karantina/ Nael Eltoukhy;—Cairo: The American University in Cairo
    Press, 2014
        p.   cm.
        ISBN: 978 977416 662 4
        1. English Fiction
        823

1 2 3 4 5   18 17 16 15 14

Designed by Adam el Sehemy

Printed in the United States

I've got no problem with the nasty stuff, swear to God. It's the other way around. It was her who always had a problem with the nasty stuff.

—Inji

THE SWEETEST NEWLYWEDS

Two characters set in their proper place by fate.

1

The dog, which was in the habit of rummaging through the trash, could not find the trash it was in the habit of rummaging through.

It was March 28, 2064. For many reasons, to be related herein and hereafter, this day was the grimmest in Alexandria's history. Everyone suffered its sting, but the one who felt it most was the dog that couldn't find the trash. He hunted along the Metro station's wall where the great heap should have been, with clouds of circling flies hovering above it, but found nothing. Not even the wall itself. The neighborhood was strangely exposed to the sun. Like a desert.

The dog was hungry. He trotted the length of the station wall, or where the wall should have been. He wagged his scabbed tail. Gazed into the distance. Rolled in the dust and rubbed his body against the wall. He was famished and frustrated, despondent and hot. Darkness gathered over the scene and there was nothing, not a single thing, to be found anywhere. He began to bark, and far away he saw a length of piping move. He gave another bark and it was then, with this second bark, that something struck his leg, something hot and hard, exactly like a bullet. For sure, a bullet. One leg lamed and one leg gunshot, the dog continued to sweep the neighborhood with his eyes, hunting for some other heap of trash and careful not to make any sound that might bring another bullet his way. Feeble, bleeding, he hid behind a dirt pile. Suddenly, his body bucked beneath a rain of gunfire.

We see him now, dead on the bloodstained dust. A little while later a passing woman picks him up and chucks him into a deep trench. Maybe it seems to her the best way—the most seemly—to bury him.

Some unhappy thing has happened here. A life has come to a close, and with it a great tale.

Fate will play its games, will bring together what belongs apart. A man may have standing, wealth, and honor, and all at once be left bereft, without standing, wealth, or honor. Fate may bring two together—two colleagues, two neighbors, two dogs from the same pack of strays—and with love bind them; then all at once, in one heartless stroke, deny each one the other. How wondrous the whims of Fate.

The tale began long ago. It spread through generations, circled above sites from the south of Egypt to the north, and encompassed many a homily and moral lesson, much profound philosophy concerning man and his desires and qualities. It is of that type so rarely found in the history of mankind, a tale in which pleasure, yearning, profitable fact, and precious counsel are conjoined.

Were we obliged to describe the proceedings of this tale in a phrase, it would be "divine providence." Divine providence it was that set each and every character in his or her proper place and inspired him or her with the right thoughts at the right time. And should it fall to us to derive a lesson from this tale, then it would be that nothing is impossible; that provided his intentions are sound, then man—by the grace of his Lord, exalted and gloried be His name before and above all things—is capable of anything.

The day the dog was killed, another dog, a bitch, was over on the other side of Karmouz, although she, unlike him, was rooting through a fat heap of trash. The bitch, with suppurating hide and patched with bald spots, with swarms of fleas about the bits that still held hair, hid as the gunfire swelled, then bolted. The bitch was waiting for the dog, but a powerful presentiment came to her that he would not come tonight, would not come any night. Her heart was downcast, her soul despondent, and the omens were not shy to show themselves: the trash contained little food, and the sounds of explosion and gunfire took away her appetite for anything.

The tale of the dog and the bitch began three months back, on a patch of wasteland. He saw her rump wiggling in front of him and jumped her. They started rubbing their bodies against each other and the fleas made

4

their way from his pelt to hers and vice versa. Her hide was full of sores, and his too, but that did not prevent them taking their pleasure. They fell in love and resolved to devote themselves to one another, unto death. Now she bore his babies in her womb and all the signs were telling her she would give birth today. And all the signs were telling her that she would give birth alone, without her mate.

Frequently, the tale is greater than us. It might be the tale of a mother and father who loathe each other, or of a family, or of conflicts and interests we've not the strength to fight. And it might be the tale of a nation taking shape. The tale here is a tale of a nation taking shape.

In no wise is it a tale of dogs, not even one of men, who remain, however high they rise, mere motes in the ocean of this boundless nation. We are just numbers here, not because we're nothings in ourselves, but because there are so many others besides, better or worse than us, warring with us or against us, and the nation is the sum of all. All these little tales, these bonds of love and hate, of marriage and divorce, of kin and conflict, of inheritances affirmed by wills and deeds of ownership, of ownership without deeds and inheritance without wills, of composers' tunes and authors' works, of engineers' accounts, and of the decisions of leaders and the strong arms of the poor—of all these things is the nation made. The nation is all these things. The nation is us.

Faint and weary, the bitch moved slowly on. She walked and walked. She passed military checkpoints and soldiers, puddles of blood and piss, shell casings and Molotovs, corpses and torn scraps of flesh and fabric. At a certain point she started to sniff. She caught the scent of her life partner all around her. She looked in every direction, but could not see him. Suddenly she turned to a vast pit in the ground, a pit that had not been there yesterday, and there at the bottom of the pit she saw the body of her dog. The bitch didn't hesitate: heedless of the pups she carried in her belly she leapt into the depths. Perhaps she died. For sure, she died.

Many tales are born and die this way. Many tales God does not wish to see completed. Entire stories perish every second in every place around the world. Many tales require no more than their telling to be told. Alone of all of them—and in order that we might understand it at all—our tale requires that we tell it entire: in other words, from at least two generations back. Alone, it warrants us taking our time, probing the background; it alone demands a little patience of us, in the telling and the listening. The tale began more than sixty years ago. A very distant day indeed.

2

I n that distant time, the sun was ever beaming down over Egypt, the nights were quieter, the days more joyful, and the Nile flowed by all the while. Everything was wonderful in Egypt. Or that was how Egyptians felt about their country. The truth is what people feel, not objective, physical facts. Who cares about physics?

We shall now relate a charming love story: a story that brought together two young hearts as they started out through life.

Ali, thirty-two, with a little fixed-rent apartment in East Ain Shams—twenty-five pounds a month—and powerful prescription glasses, lives with his brother. He had, regrettably, failed to complete his university education, studying two years of law, then dropping out to work in a clothes store owned by him and his brother next to the apartment. And life goes on.

Inji, twenty-one, recent graduate of the Faculty of Politics and Economics, a promising young woman, with small, dainty spectacles, a small, dainty body, and an American accent to top it off, lives alone in an apartment in Medinat Nasr. Her father passed away in Abu Dhabi, and as his only child she came into a more-than-respectable sum. She dresses simply. She loves buying clothes from pavement sellers and third-rate stores.

Ali and Inji's first encounter wasn't earth-shattering. A girl in glasses walked past the shop and he said, loudly, Over here, Doc. She stopped to inspect the goods and he turned to his friends and said, Honor enough she's stopped at my place. And indeed, she did end up buying a pair of trousers. Inside the place she smiled and looked into his eyes and said, How are you, Ali? Her name was Inji, she told him, and he recalled a distant cousin living out in Abu Dhabi. He asked if she was Uncle Suleiman Abdallah al-Aleili's girl. She smiled and told him, Yes. For a few seconds he was tongue-tied, then he asked after her health, and that of her father, and How's the weather in the Emirates? And off she went and he forgot her. She wasn't a first cousin: her father was his father's cousin. She came back a second time. And a third. She was the one who didn't forget him. And bit by bit he began to take notice of her and ask her things that weren't to do with clothes. He wasn't shy, it was just that he couldn't quite believe it. Real classy, speaks English and all that, as he put it to his brother, Mustafa. Bolder, he took her number. When he asked for it, she smiled. Asked him, Why do you want it? as she prepared herself to—yes, really!—read it out to him. He was unnerved, but he pulled himself together and adjusted his thick specs: To ask after your father, miss.

Events moved along and they were powerless to stop them. Events out-stripped them both. He called her up next day and told her about a new blouse just come in. She stopped by, bought the blouse, and said why not go for a little walk? The two of them. He opened his mouth. She said, We could go to Medinat Nasr, you know. It's not far. She said, How can you live here in Ain Shams and never go to Medinat Nasr? She said, When's your day off? She said, What time do you get off work? He didn't answer. His mouth was still open.

The first few times they met he didn't speak much. It was she who spoke, who suggested stuff and asked him questions, and he would respond in monosyllables. He just couldn't credit it. The whole thing was like a dream. But gradually he started to join in, to open up and play the fool—you know, things like Inji asks him how he takes his tea and he closes his eyes, rests his top teeth on his lower lip and tells her, Hot . . . scorching . . . and she smiles and looks at him and her eyes shine. And he's tongue-tied.

They were in love. That's what it looked like to his brother, who was watching from a distance. But Ali didn't get it.

Suleiman Abdallah was still living in Abu Dhabi when his daughter decided to return to Egypt. He died two years later. From the outset he had known the best thing he could do was to take his wife and get out of Ain Shams and its shit. He traveled to the Emirates and had a kid there, even as his cousin, Mohamed Sayyid, was killing himself for pennies in Ain Shams. Which of the two paths was the better? Mohamed Sayyid knew all about real life; with the sweat of his brow he opened a clothes shop next to the family home, got married, and had a family. True, Suleiman had done a bit of manual labor at the beginning of his sojourn in the Emirates, but he was soon able—with his brains—to make a living bringing Egyptians over. He had an in with relatives in Sohag and contacts in the Emirates. It was penny by penny at first then the dirhams began spontaneously proliferating in his bank account. He bought an apartment in Medinat Nasr, then he bought the apartment above it, and the one in front of it, and the one beside it, and by degrees became the owner of two whole floors. And Inji inherited the lot. She rented out the top floor and kept the bottom.

That was the situation when Ali met Inji. She was the girl of the guy who'd gotten out, and he was the son of someone who had become more and more entangled in his country. They were not a man and woman who had met as Destiny looked the other way. They were two opposing principles, two views of the world, and together constituted—in those naïve times— what we might term a Clash of Cultures, a harbinger of clashes to come.

Ali told her how his father had died. He dredged up distant, painful memories. He spoke to her of the South, of taar, of TV thrillers about Southern honor—*The Fugitive Light* and *The High-Country Wolves*—and he spoke of his father, found slain outside his shop, of the rattling groan that had issued from his throat, of the blood that drenched the clothes, of the store, that closed down for a full two years. Not a single customer would come near us. . . . Swear to God, right, I swear to God, I'd be walking in the street with my brother and I'd feel people trying to avoid us. When I was really fed up I'd go to the mosque to pray and you'll get an idea when I tell you nobody would pray with me. And all Inji did was close her eyes, in sympathy. Then she patted his shoulder. He enfolded her hand between his palms and began his approach. He held his left leg against her right leg. He reached his hand behind her back and began moving it around under her T-shirt. She was considerably put out. Ali! she shouted, Are you out of

9

your mind? What are you doing? Ali was not sure exactly what it was he was doing, so he was put out too. He said, Miss, don't get me wrong. You're like a sister to me, honest. She looked at him with outright scorn and left the store. Two days later she sent him an SMS: I feel something for you, Ali, but I need to keep my distance for a bit to make sure of it. Don't be angry.

Inji was an exceptionally complicated character, if the expression serves. Living alone in Medinat Nasr and having her adventures. In her first year at university she said she was going to be a top diplomat. She studied hard. But at the same time she met a young man and fell in love. She was just off the boat from the Emirates and didn't know anything about anything. The young man was using her for her money, that much she knew, but it didn't bother her. All the same, he dumped her, and for a long while afterward she was a nervous wreck. She failed her first year. Then she abandoned her high-flying dreams. She'd pass with mediocre marks and every year would have another fling, or more than one.

The most beautiful thing about Inji was that this did not break her. She remained a sunny, delightful girl, still prepared to place her trust in the world around her, unreservedly. One day she decided that she had to get to know her family. She asked Daddy about his cousin in Ain Shams and he told her he was dead. I know, she said, I mean his kids. Her father told her how to find the store, as well as he could recall, and she set her mind to spring a big surprise on her distant cousins: this flip side of Egypt she knew nothing about. Inji the Egyptophile.

But greater than her passion for Egypt was her passion for her roots. Her passion to discover her roots, to be exact. A single daydream came to her like clockwork, every day for days on end:

She's in the Congo, chatting to a tribal type, when out of the blue she speaks her father's name: Suleiman Abdallah. The African doesn't understand. She says it again, and he nods. Abdoolaa! he exclaims, Abdoolaa! then leads her to the chief. The chief's half asleep. She asks him about Abdoolaa and he doesn't understand. The first African speaks to him in their language, and then the chief turns to her and says, That's right. There was a boy here, a drummer, whose name was Abdoolaa, but one sweltering day they led him away to . . . to . . . . He leaves the sentence unfinished, but with his hands he sketches the shape of pyramids. To Egypt? she asks. Yes, yes! comes his excitable reply: To Egypt! She gets to her feet, in the center of the tribal council's circle, and dances: I've found my roots! I've found my roots!

So it was that Inji's deepest desire was to visit the South, if only once, just once, to search out that fugitive, elusive root, lost in time. Just once, Lord, then I can die happy. Thus she addressed God, then pulled the blanket over her body and slept.

Ali couldn't let it go. He admitted as much. Even though this job of his had taught him to be patient. I'll be straight with you, brother, there's not much wrong with the girl. It's not that she's my cousin, that's not it. She makes you feel like she's a professor or something. I'm furious with myself, to be honest.

Ali remained furious with himself for two weeks, unwilling to forgive himself, Inji unwilling to answer his calls, and his brother throwing him reproachful glances all the while. Ali learned to wake early, to smoke on an empty stomach, to bite his nails and fiddle with his balls and turn customers away, especially the college girls. Ali opened the shop each morning with a curse to heaven and a gobbet of spit to the ground. He had turned into an animal.

A full month later, Inji sent him a message. A one-liner: I love you. Ali collapsed onto a chair and started weeping. At that moment, it seemed to him that his pain was over, that it was goodbye to the moonlit vigils, the torments, and the endless nights. But it was only the beginning.

Taar—a debt of honor to be avenged—is a story of its own, one from which Egypt has suffered greatly, particularly in the poor and ignorant South, and all the government's persistent attempts to uproot the idea from the heads of its inhabitants have been in vain. The people have clung to their obduracy in the face of any effort to enlighten them. And so it is that what we might call a culture of honor killing has remained powerfully rooted, first and foremost in the South, though there is nothing to stop it feeling its way downriver to the rich and educated North.

It was something along these lines that Ali was trying to explain to Inji as he told her of his father. An old debt of honor, its origins a mystery to all, had flared up between the al-Aleili and Amin families in Akhmim Sohag and claimed the life of Mohamed Sayyid al-Aleili. Your uncle was the best of men, Inji. Don't you believe anyone who tells you different. He had nothing to do with taar and guns. They're the ones who followed him up here from the village. Ask your dad. He'll tell you.

Oh, I'm so sorry, Ali. You must have had people saying you had to take revenge, right? Ali fell silent. After a moment: Everyone. And don't go thinking that your own father didn't have people telling him the same. Everyone was saying it. Till I couldn't take any more. My brother and me we don't want trouble, but I swear to you on this cigarette, not one of them will get away in one piece. Inji patted his shoulder. Her hand lingered for a moment. She stared at him for a full minute, smiling. Her leg touched his and when he pushed back, when he tried to play along, she said, Ali! What are you doing? and got all upset. The world is unjust; has long been so.

Ali took her around all the sites: the Citadel, the Pyramids, City Stars Mall, the Nile. She wanted to see Egypt. That's Egypt, sweetheart. Happy now? She wasn't just happy; she spent the whole time delirious with joy. Most of that time she was hanging off his arm in a sleeveless T-shirt and sunglasses with a camera suspended around her neck, all of which made her look like a tourist. As for Ali, he looked like an idiot. He insisted on stuffing his shirt into his ancient jeans and keeping his striped sleeves unrolled and buttoned at the cuff, and with his faint mustache and bottle-top glasses he failed, overall, to make a good impression. But they didn't care, and that was the most beautiful thing about their relationship. Perched on a pyramid's stone block she rested her head on his shoulder. His armpit stank of sweat but such trifles did not bother her. Suddenly she asked: Ali? Is what you said true? What did I say? You were saying you didn't want trouble. Look here, Inshi—that's how he pronounced her name—me and my brother, we keep to ourselves, but on one condition: that no one starts with us. Treat me nice, I'll treat you nice. You so much as think of hurting me, I'll fuck you right up. So what about your dad? You'll just let his blood go unavenged, Ali? Let his blood go unavenged! I swear to God, those kids won't get away from me. I'm the one who'll take his taar, you hear me? Not anyone from your lot, not my brother, even. She smiled. Promise me, Ali. What's that? I said I swear to God, isn't that enough for you? She grabbed his hand and rubbed its palm on hers. She looked at him and her smile grew wider. You're my sweetheart. Have I told you that?

But that wasn't everything. Ali wasn't looking for trouble, and Inji knew it—but Inji was. She knew that right is right and wrong is wrong and she knew she would have a long, hard road with Ali. Sometimes she would take refuge in romance, as in the scene above, and sometimes she'd become more brutal. She lit a cigarette and gave it to Ali. They were sitting in Beano's café.

Ali! The waiter's taking his time. You noticed?

Yes, my love.

Well, could you hurry him up?

He'll be here any moment, my love.

Ali! (Tensing) We've been here half an hour. It's really unacceptable. Tell him it's unacceptable.

(He gestures to the waiter to speed things up.)

(Silence.)

That's it?

Eh?

(Nearly shouting now) Ali! Do something! Tell him it's too much. Tell him it's unacceptable to leave us hanging just because His Lordship isn't happy with the tips from his last table.

(Not a word.)

(Scornful) Ali, you quite sure you want to avenge your father?

Back then things weren't set in stone. Here's this character who might do this thing, say, and then you find out they were aiming at something else entirely. Or take another case: there's this character who might be thinking of two things at the same time, in pursuit of a third thing, and it's impossible to say which of the two he wants more. Is it the first or the second? It was a mysterious time. Its motives were mysterious. Ali and Inji decided to spend two days in Sohag. Ali spoke to someone he knew and told him he would be staying over for a couple of days. He didn't say a word about Inji. Let God look after it.

They enter Ramses Station dragging a large bag behind them, two tickets already purchased. What made Inji decide to travel to Sohag? What made her spend two days trying to convince Ali of her decision? Was it the desire to see Egypt? Was it the desire to set eyes on the backdrop to the things he'd told her about his murdered father, with Inji still clinging to her right to revenge, her taar? No one knows, and maybe it was a mix of these incentives and influences. It was a mysterious time. But no matter the motives, the events are what count.

Inji lights a cigarette and Ali gets angry. Not in front of everybody. Inji gets angry. I'm free to do as I please. He gets angrier still. Free is when you're by yourself, not with a man. She swallows the insult and plots revenge.

Know what, Ali?
What?
I've no idea why you're going to Sohag.
Wasn't it you who said I should introduce you to my family?
Ali, don't be silly. Your family's my family.
(Irritably) What is it you want?
You said you wanted to go back to avenge your father.
Sure.
What do you mean, "Sure"? Yes or no?
I don't know.
Ali. You're not a man.
(No answer.)
What I call a man isn't scared of responsibility.
(He looks around. Exhales.)

They stand on the platform. He takes out a cigarette and finds he hasn't got a lighter. He moves off a couple of paces to look for one. The sound of a screech issues from the spot where he was standing. Inji's voice: How dare you! A man's rough tones: But I wasn't anywhere near you. Ali leaps. In one bound he's beside them. He grabs the man hard by the shirt. You'll be settling up with me, here and now. Today's the day I fuck you up good and proper, with God's help. The man flails out, trying to get away. There is no god but God! You've got it wrong, sir. But Ali, right or wrong, does not hear him. He kicks him in the shin and at the same time the man's shirt rips in Ali's brutal grip. The man loses his composure. Beneath this unanticipated hail of blows he manages to land a slap square on Ali's face. For two seconds, Ali is still. The gathered crowd, which was trying to pull them apart, falls nervously silent in turn. Wary now, and waiting for some terrible comeback, the man backs away. Ali lunges forward, punches him in the belly, in the head, he does not let up. The man tries to squirm free, and the people restrain Ali. A massive specimen comes up to clamp his arm. Ali gives him a sharp shove and Inji rushes to free her lover. The man bats her away. She gives him a shove. Ali gives him a powerful shove. Suddenly this happens: the man falls onto the tracks. Right onto the tracks. The Southern Train is pulling in. Now the man is mincemeat beneath its wheels.

The platform is completely empty. Everyone has run off. Alone on the platform, Ali takes Inji in his arms, the two of them very tall, very splendid, upright and full of rage, clothes torn: two gods. Striding confidently, they leave the station. On the opposite side of the square outside, Ali stops a taxi. They ride along in silence. Utterly silent. Silent, aside from a worn and weary, "Ain Shams, driver."

Mustafa watched his brother enter the apartment with Inji and the pair slump down on the big couch in the front room. Mustafa was making a cup of tea. Mustafa emerged from the kitchen.

Blood and sweat and grime cover their clothes. He questions them. No one answers. After three minutes have passed, Ali speaks: I killed someone. Inji experiences a moment of machismo: I killed him with you. Mustafa lights a cigarette. He hands it to his brother and his brother speaks. His gaze is unwavering, his tone robotic. For half an hour he speaks. Mustafa can do nothing, has nothing to suggest. After a bit he goes back to the kitchen, where he calls somebody. He ends the call and returns to Ali. You two are coming with me, now. You'll sleep in the street tonight. Tomorrow

15

morning you'll catch the first bus to Alexandria. A guy called Sheikh Hassan will be waiting at the station. I've spoken to him. He's someone I know from the army. I helped him out and he'll help you. Any plans you've got floating around in your heads, forget them. Taar or otherwise. We've got enough shit to deal with.

Ali, Inji, and Mustafa spend the night on a wooden bench in Tahrir Square, Ali resting his head on the big suitcase and Inji resting hers on his shoulder and Mustafa keeping his distance. At first light they get up and make their way, a humble convoy, a knot of kin borne away by the sin in which they flounder, to Ramses. A bus to Alexandria is still empty. Four or five seats are taken. The three of them drift off, each on a different course, and when the bus's horn sounds, when it has filled up, they return, and Ali and Inji sit on the back row and wave farewell to Mustafa. The bus drives off. Only then do they sleep, deeply.

3

'm Sousou. My name's Said, but call me Sousou. I prefer it.

. . .

   You scared of me, or shy, or what?

. . .

   Don't be scared. I've never hurt anyone in my life, and I never will, God willing.

. . .

   We do good by God's grace alone.

. . .

   Where you two from, anyway?

. . .

   Didn't I tell you? You're scared of me. What, I'm asking you because I want to hurt you?

   We're from Sohag.

   No finer folk, my friend. Cigarette?

Sheikh Hassan is a kind man, the kindest man Ali has ever met in his life. A truly righteous man. He's made the pilgrimage to God's House ten times and has never given an evil look to anyone, not a lustful glance, not a gaze of envy.

   Ali's working in a clothes store in Camp Cesar now. Most beautiful place in the world, Camp Cesar: taste and style; a working-class neighborhood and a tourist hangout at the same time. Ali lives there with Inji in a little apartment owned by Sheikh Hassan and they pay the rent together, a thousand pounds a month deducted from their salaries, plus one further condition: I'm a God-fearing man. On the Day of Reckoning I don't want Him going through His books and telling me I've brought two together to live in sin. If you want to be together you've got to marry . . . and it won't cost you a thing: just a piece of paper to buy God's goodwill and may He bless you with a pure and noble progeny.

And so it came to be: Ali married Inji. They lived in Sheikh Hassan's apartment and started working at his store, Way of Truth Clothes, with Inji on the till and Ali as Sheikh Hassan's right-hand man for everything from pulling in the customers to sealing deals for new orders.

The days come and go. A month passes, two months, three. Inji is pregnant.

How did each one learn to live with the sin they bore about their necks? How did they cope with having become, in mere seconds, in the blink of an eye, killers on the run? Ali had previous: long ago he'd slashed a man's face with a knife. He had gone to prison and since then had avoided fights. He liked to say of himself that he wasn't the argumentative type. Inji, of course, had no criminal background of any kind. Both, it seemed, treated their situation as a temporary setback. They were on the run right now, but a time would come when they'd stop running, when they would return to their new home in Ain Shams, and when they did, the crime would disappear from history, would be wiped from their memories, the dead man would return to life, and they . . . they would awake from the nightmare. For nights on end their conversation turned about this point.

I'm scared.

(He puffs out cigarette smoke. Says nothing.)

Ali, we have to go back.

Go back where?

Our home. Your home. You have to tell the police. It's a murder in defense of honor. You won't get anything for it.

And people?

What about people?

When they find out I killed someone . . . .

(Correcting him) That we killed someone . . . .

When they find out we killed someone . . .

You killed him by mistake.

(He smiles sourly.)

(In agitation) You don't want to do *anything*!

(The sour smile.)

You've no sense of responsibility!

(The sour smile fades. He puffs out smoke.)

You're always afraid of confrontation. It's always me who takes the decisions.

(He turns to her. Grabs her hand. He squeezes her wrist hard. Violently. He looks her in the eye. His eyes are bloodshot.) I killed a man for you.

(Correcting him) We killed a man.

(Shouting) I'm the one who pushed him in front of the train because he was bothering you. I'm the one everyone saw murdering him. You were just the little lady who poked him in the belly, but it's my future that's down the pan. My future and my son's.

(She turns away. After a while she looks back at him and her eyes are trembling with tears) I don't love you anymore.

(The same sour smile returns.)

Sousou was smart. He worked a liver cart outside the store. Ali got to know him eating there. Soon after, Sousou started to drop in at the Way of Truth and a friendship, a special kind of friendship, grew. They spent almost the whole day together. Ali, new to the neighborhood and trying to make himself agreeable to those around him, gave him a pair of Levis, which he paid for out of his own pocket, and Sousou could not think how to return the favor. Sousou came to Ali's home and made himself a friend to the family. Almost her friend as well. Not a great friend. Inji didn't like him much. Inji didn't like anyone from the neighborhood. She was fed up with her life, with everything. Sousou made himself a bet that she'd come round, but he lost the bet. She didn't come round. And this did not hurt Sousou's feelings.

Sousou had a feeling for people. He was in his twenties, short, with a husky voice, and he limped, one leg longer than the other. Perhaps this handicap was why he was so sensitive to the plight of others. The moment he saw Inji he knew there was some secret here: an educated girl, cultured, come with her husband to work a cash register in a clothes store, revolted by everything around her, and her life and that of her husband a mystery to all. Sousou had no desire to harm anyone. It was knowledge he sought, knowledge alone, a knowledge innocent of power. Time and time again he took the liberty of inviting Ali to his place, a small rooftop shack, and there he introduced Ali to his brothers, Adel and Abu Amira (the oldest of the three and the homeowner), as Bashmuhandis Ali: the man we're to show a good time. And Adel did not skimp. Beer and hash till sunup. But at ten, Ali made his excuses. Abu Amira grabbed him by the arm and said, Over my dead body, brother, you're staying with us tonight. Respectfully, Ali replied that the wife might worry about him, that she was in her first month of pregnancy. Abu Amira swore a fearsome oath and solved the problem: So you call her now and I'll send the wife to keep her company. Us men can relax. Ali called Inji to tell her and Abu Amira went off to negotiate with his wife who left the shack fifteen minutes later, and the men sat up till morning.

Ali didn't talk too much, just spoke of Ain Shams and Cairo, from which Sousou gathered that they had not, in fact, come from Sohag. He asked him what he had done before he came to Alexandria and Ali spoke of the clothes store. He asked him what had brought him here and Ali almost spoke . . . and was silent. He was silent a long time; then he said that only God knows what's best for us. The answer did not convince Adel, who, though not partaking of the hash, had drunk nine beers. This made him punchy. He drew closer to Ali and asked if he had a hundred pounds on him so he could go downstairs and settle up with the owner of the bottle store. He'd pay it back tomorrow. Ali fell for it. He took out his wallet and Adel snatched it away and extracted the ID. Before he could glance at it, Ali had jumped on his back and brought a knife to his neck. You want to ask me something, then ask nicely, otherwise I'll hurt you.

Sousou had drifted away under the influence of the hash. Suddenly he came to and went over to try to calm Ali. Ali shoved him away. A full minute, then Ali got to his feet and made for the door. Before walking out he took a hundred pounds out and tossed it in the air. That's for the beer. I won't have any man invite me over and think he can shame me. Abu Amira watched it all unfold. He did not intervene to defend his brother.

Ali went home. For a week afterward a question kept returning to Sousou's mind: Who is that man?

Adham Sabri. This had been Inji's idea of a hero ever since reading of his exploits while in the Emirates, and after she was back in Egypt, too. It was then that her obsession with the secret service started. She imagined her life as one long adventure in which everything combined: action with drama, patriotic fervor with burning desire. She would dream—in some part of herself—of heroism. For this reason, perhaps, deliverance from this secret life was her only wish. The hero doesn't hide from the cops, because the hero is the cops . . . so she saw it. She was young and knew nothing of life.

The evening Umm Amira came to visit her and they talked together till two in the morning, Inji discovered that there were some subjects she couldn't speak of and others she must first work out with Ali how to talk about, before either of them, individually, could speak of them with someone else. It struck Inji that there was an area of her life that had become secret, and she wept. Umm Amira cried out, What's up, sister? I upset you? and Inji began to dry her eyes. No, I'm sorry, Umm Amira. It's me that's upset you. Forgive me. At that very moment Ali came in. Umm Amira was at a loss. She stood up, making for the door, to leave. Inji pressed her to stay the night with them, and she stayed. Inji made up a small couch in the hall for her and Ali went off to sleep beside his wife.

At five in the morning Ali felt thirsty, after his sleepless night the day before. He got up, opened the fridge, and gulped down a whole bottle of water. He made his way back swaying and as he swayed he saw Umm Amira with her robe hitched up off her legs, a little stout but never mind. He started to scratch his cock, his hand in his trousers. He drew closer. Bent down . . . and almost fell, then suddenly she was holding him steady, her finger to her lips. Don't make a sound.

Never before had Ali slept with a woman he didn't know—with the exception of whores, of course—and since marrying his wife had never once betrayed her. His devotion to her was forged in fire.

That day, however, a number of factors worked together to inspire in him a lust for Umm Amira: first, the beer that filled his stomach; second, that he sought, by sleeping with her, to revenge himself on her husband, after his brother Adel had tried to take his ID from him by force and he had failed to intervene (this, then, is the purest revenge: revenge for the sake of revenge); third, that he wanted to immunize himself against his ill will, in the event that Adel had seen something on the ID card—that he was registered in Cairo or was a bachelor (this is procedural revenge: revenge with a purpose and function); and fourth and finally, that he really was aroused. She was filthy, and smelt disgusting—the reek of rot and cheap booze—and this just aroused him all the more.

From the start of their marriage Inji had only permitted him to sleep with her at the beginning of the week. Later on the bouts of depression and revulsion started, and Ali was only human, blood and neurons, from time to time subject to his base needs, among them sex.

In two hours Ali had given her one three times, none of them up to scratch, it's true—poor hygiene can put a man off his stroke—but he was pleased with himself and his self-satisfaction carried him into his bedroom on tiptoe. He emerged and handed Umm Amira fifty pounds, told her tenderly, Buy something nice for Amira, then went back into the bedroom. Three hours later he awoke, showered swiftly, and left with Inji to open up the store.

Thus ended the most important day in the lives of the young couple, Ali and Inji. The days that followed were simply the payoff.

Sousou, Adel, Abu Amira, Umm Amira: a family of three brothers and one wife inhabiting the rooftop of an ancient building in Camp Cesar. Like many other families their roots were in Sohag. Sousou worked a liver cart and Adel had a spot on the sidewalk in Ramleh Station from which he sold boxers and vests, as well, lending Abu Amira a hand. Abu Amira was a doorman, if we must use that word.

Adel was a dud. Ali saw it from the way Abu Amira looked at him the time he snatched the wallet: petty, adolescent, no class. Sousou was smart. Abu Amira depended on him for a lot of things. He'd hear about the kids looking to rent apartments and he'd hear of landlords in the area looking to rent out their apartments, and he'd bring an even greater number of young men and women to the second-floor apartment that the building's owner rented out by the hour to those in need. Abu Amira was an estate agent too. And a pimp, if we must use that word.

Abu Amira was preparing Sousou to take his place. He loved him. He was the only one who reminded him of his own youth and he liked to fancy himself his father and not just his brother, a sentiment that made its way down the chain to Umm Amira. She treated him like she was his mother.

The night Ali slept with Umm Amira he told her, Buy something nice for Amira. She did not answer him, because she was a wise woman, and not so dizzy as to tell him the whole tragic tale, the tragedy of Amira, who had died aged ten. People had gone on calling her mother by her name. She heard them, suffered, held her peace, and took herself away. She swallowed her pain and took herself away.

Inji. We would be doing her an injustice if we said that all she did those days was feel revulsion at the world around her. She was fashioning her baby in her belly as well—the mother's sacred role, and also, perhaps, the chief cause of her revulsion. Ali did not take this in. He was young and inexperienced. Killing a human being is not an experience of great importance. He asked her once, D'you want us to go back to Cairo and give birth there? and she turned her face away. God rot you, he whispered to himself and let her be.

It was around this time that Inji was getting to know a customer who would come and visit her in the shop. Hagga Itemad was her name. The hagga took the initiative. She told her she looked like a stranger to the neighborhood, by which she meant the foreign accent. Inji told her she'd studied politics and economics, and the next day Hagga Itemad returned and shyly asked if she would help her daughter with her English. The girl's struggling with her English, and as for you, there'll be a car to pick you up and bring you back, and whatever you ask for you'll have. I won't haggle. Inji agreed without even asking Ali. She informed him of it once, speaking rapidly in the tone of someone who's made up their mind, and he didn't object. He hadn't the courage to object.

Hagga Itemad knew Sheikh Hassan. Distantly, as she put it. He was the one who advised her to speak to Inji when she complained to him about her daughter's English grades. The first time Inji visited her at home, the hagga made her mulukhiya with chicken and stuffed vine leaves, and vowed by all that was holy that Inji would eat with them. Inji could not refuse. She didn't speak a lot at first. Gradually her appetite grew, for talk and food, and the hagga nudged her shoulder. Relax my dear, she said, and brought a drumstick up to her mouth: Come on now. Eat that.

Inji didn't tutor the girl that first time. Didn't see her at all. She ate and ate and ate. At last she found herself sitting alone with Hagga Itemad in the living room, the hagga—legs stretched out on the floor, head resting on the armchair—in her nightgown, her arms formidable, her chest tremendous and whitest white. The contrast between the white of her bosom and her brown neck seemed absurd to Inji. Inji propped herself against the couch facing the hagga and pressed her knees to her breasts. The hagga rolled a joint and handed it over and Inji smoked and stared at the buzzing fan.

The pair of them were out of it. After a bit, the hagga turned to her. Inshi, my girl. Slowly Inji looks round. The hagga goes on: You killed someone in Cairo, didn't you, my dear?

The narrow circle in which Ali and Inji moved knew the story of Ramses Station. The murder tale. With a few embellishments: the accident became deliberate homicide and Ali and Inji were killers with no one to take them in. And yet it was precisely this that caused them all to rally round, including the two examples now before us: Abu Amira's family and Hagga Itemad. They had a general and nebulous outline, but the details were sorely lacking. Perhaps it was for this reason that Hagga Itemad called on Sheikh Hassan with her daughter as a pretext. We can conceive of the people of Alexandria as a vast gang, stupendously vast, a gang that is always striving to recruit new and powerful and important members to its ranks. And by the people of Alexandria we mean Abu Amira's family and Hagga Itemad.

This generalization is a touch misleading, true, but life is impossible without generalizations.

It is extremely difficult to pinpoint Inji's reaction to the hagga's question, but we have clues to work with. Subsequently, when she told Ali what had happened, she would say, I didn't know what to tell her. I felt everybody could see me. And then I found myself laughing and saying, Yeah, I killed someone and anyone else speaks out of turn to me, I'll kill them too.

Where did Inji get such strength from?

Life in Alexandria teaches many things. Very many things indeed.

Life in Alexandria has no time for feelings.

Hagga Itemad broke down Inji's walls. In the hagga she found someone to be close to, away from the store and home. And for her part, the hagga was lovable, a businesswoman born and bred, who treated each and every person as they wanted to be treated. She knew everyone and everyone knew her and she made sure that everyone knew everyone else. Inji loved her and the hagga in turn never held back any advice the girl might need, whether it concerned pregnancy, life in Alexandria, life on the run from the police, or life on the run from guilt.

The last point's an important one. The hagga suggested they pray together in the mosque. She suggested she put on the hijab. You think the hijab will make you ugly, but you're a fool. My girl, you'll be a picture. And Inji put on the hijab and took to reading the Quran daily. She cheered up, and at long last her heart opened to her surroundings. She permitted Ali to invite Sousou round and she cooked for them. And then, one by one, all the members of the Amira clan dropped by: Umm Amira, Abu Amira, and finally, Adel.

The thaw had set in at last.

Inji tutored the hagga's daughter Minnatallah every day. A bright girl, but pig-ignorant at the same time. True, she got the hang of things quickly enough, but she knew zero English. So Inji had to start from scratch. Minna, stick your tongue out when you say *th*. Minna, there's no such thing as *he walk*. It's *he walks* or *he is walking*. Minna, there's a difference between *b* and *p*. Minna, will you concentrate, please, and stop gaping at the ceiling.

But Minna was bright. She picked up words in English in a flash, in Inji's American accent, and could repeat them back. Not well enough to hold a conversation, of course, but enough to pass the exam. Day after day Inji would enter their home life, would see it from within. A simple home for simple people. Not rolling around in money, sure, not speaking foreign languages all the time, it's true, but they had something straightforward about them, something intimate and honest. Inji had always felt this kind of honesty was the hallmark of the bona fide common man, and she saw it embodied in the hagga's family.

But where was the hagga's husband? The question revolved continuously round Inji's mind, with no answer forthcoming, and she had been too shy to ask. She'd been frightened. Minna had once mentioned something about Daddy the heroic martyr and something, too, about Sheikh Hassan, who ensured they never wanted for anything. Minna said no more and Inji didn't ask.

The hagga did not question Inji about the murder again. It seemed that she was trying to piece together the details of the incident through her own private channels. She never despaired. She collected fact after fact until she'd put together a bulging file. This file did not make an appearance just then. It would have its day. Hagga Itemad left nothing to chance.

Ali's affair with Umm Amira continued in his apartment. She talked a lot, was always talking. She told him every little thing about everybody. Under him, on top, beside him, and behind him, she would tell him every little thing about every single person, and Ali heard nothing. Quite the opposite was true of Abu Amira, aglow with some tremendous energy, which had been evident from the first and was only growing stronger with time. Ali tried talking to him, tried proving himself before him, but subsequently he was content just to watch him. He watched him as he lit cigarettes, as he stared into the distance, as he sipped his tea, tied his laces, slipped money from his wallet, as he pissed into the café's urinal. Abu Amira's every movement seemed freighted with some special philosophy. He said little but Ali hung on his every word. There was much he didn't understand. He was young, and back then he had yet to come to terms with life. The Fates had appointed Abu Amira to teach Ali everything.

For days at a time Ali was silent. And Abu Amira shared his silence, lighting a cigarette and giving him a drag, drinking tea and giving him a sip, scratching his balls and looking at Ali and laughing and, suddenly, speaking. He said: Things aren't like they were. There's no good in the world. And Ali stored this sentence in his head and stored the winks and nods that preceded it and came after. Only in this way did Ali become an adult.

We cannot say for certain just when it was that the prospective friendship between Ali and Abu Amira metamorphosed into a relationship of a different kind: an apprenticeship; adoption, adoration . . . something like that. Ultimately, all we can do is relate a seminal circumstance in this transformation. We all remember that Ali had slept with Umm Amira about five times, and these five times had given him the idea that he could take liberties with Abu Amira.

They are playing backgammon at a neighborhood café. The game's outcome is more or less a given now. Abu Amira will take it. But Ali seeks vengeance for his slighted dignity. He narrows his eyes and says, Okay then, friend, but I've got you beat in something much better than backgammon. Abu Amira smiles. He shuts the board. He orders tea for Mr. Ali. Crosses his legs. Scratches his mustache and plucks out a long black hair dangling from his nose. He looks at Ali. His voice changes. It becomes charming, smiling, indulgent. Beautiful. And just who, my dear Ali, has really got the better of the other? You, is it? Fine, you're quite right. But which time do you mean?

Now Abu Amira turns his whole body to him. He brings his face up to his. His voice is low, unsmiling, and deadly: So the wife likes to enjoy herself. That's nothing for her to be ashamed of. Doesn't hurt anybody. It doesn't hurt me. I couldn't give a flying fuck either way. But when the man she's with isn't a man, well, that makes me very upset indeed. Upset for her. Upset for him as well. Especially if he's going about acting the big man. Abu Amira chops his words out, parcels them up. Gives them bite. Abu Amira stops talking. He gestures to the waiter: Mr. Ali's check is on me. The man's our guest.

Abu Amira did not hold in disdain the things that are commonly disdained by most people. Certain things did not shame him. Others did. That's how he was. Perhaps that's what made him strong. More than once Ali tried to wound him with a taunt, to find that he was unwoundable. What can you do with a person that can't be hurt? Nothing at all. Step by step, Ali entered the fold of Abu Amira's family, not on equal terms this time, nor welcomed openly, but listening, asking, seeking counsel. Everyone starts off small. This lesson was needed to bring it home to Ali that things had changed.

At their next meeting Ali asks Umm Amira if she's told Abu Amira what had happened between them. Well, of course, she shouts, he's my husband! Ali doesn't understand these people. He grabs her by the arm. Your husband or not, he doesn't concern me. He's nothing to me and I couldn't give a fuck either way. A little pimp and I couldn't care less about him. What I do care about is that what happens between us stays between us. She frees her arm from his grip. Stares at the floor a while, then back at him. Shame on you, Mr. Ali. Abu Amira's not a bad man. It's not right for you speak of him like that. The man gave you everything. Ali is incandescent with rage. He rants and raves. Hits her. Gave us everything how, you whore? He kicks her in the stomach. She holds his gaze and doesn't make a sound. When he's done she gathers up her things and leaves. She gives him one long look, a look he doesn't understand.

When he is alone again, he will remember the monthly sum that Abu Amira sends to his apartment—a helping hand for the newlyweds—and the many gifts, from meat and fruit and hash all the way through to the television and the living-room furniture. He weeps for a bit. He remembers everything: his double-crossed father, his debt of vengeance cast aside, Ain Shams, his brother Mustafa. Today, it is Mustafa he remembers in particular; Mustafa, without whom they would not be here. He gets up to call Mustafa. For the first time since leaving Cairo, he calls him; with no plan in mind, he calls him from his house phone. He whimpers, asks him how things are in Cairo. Mustafa barks at him. Don't think you're coming back now. Concentrate on making a living and when things have calmed down, I'll call you. Ali replaces the receiver. Ali continues to weep.

The next morning he drops in on Abu Amira. Hands him a cigarette. They laugh together. They slap their palms in resignation and when the opportunity presents itself, in the course of their conversation, Ali gets up and kisses his shoulder.

It was a hard lesson, but there you go: the true lessons, the ones that teach us truths, are always hard.

4

I n those days Alexandria was simmering.

The seaside city had engaged in many struggles in defense of its independence and that of its citizens. Indeed, the only way to describe Alexandria's struggles against the Egyptian authorities is as a manifestation of the margin's struggle against the center. The authorities against which Alexandria struggled were not just the Egyptian authorities; they were local as well.

One day, Alexandria awoke to news of a young Egyptian's murder— a young man called Khaled Said—at the hands of police informers. The young man was tortured, beaten up, and his head staved in. That same day a page was set up on Facebook entitled "We are all Khaled Said," with nearly a hundred thousand subscribers joining within the first day, a number that swelled in the days that followed to reach half a million on the eve of the 2011 revolution. Alexandria was filled with demonstrations of every stripe: thousands thronging the Corniche, black-clad in memory of Khaled, and violence too. Then there was the dramatic elevation of two icons of the opposition, ElBaradei and Ayman Nour, to challenge the iniquitous dispensation of Mubarak and his family. But all that was just the tip of the iceberg.

Alexandria is a cosmopolitan city. At least, that is what it was before the revolution of July 1952, which was followed by the systematic expulsion of foreigners from Egypt, and thus from Alexandria, in which were concentrated the country's largest European communities. From that moment on, one felt a sense of loss in Alexandria, a sense of glories past and dissatisfaction at the wretched present. This feeling curled through the air, carried along on the waves of the sea, by birds in the heavens, by men on the sidewalks.

Three governors the Alexandrians fought tirelessly against: Ismail al-Gousaqi, Abdel Salam al-Mahgoub, and Adel Labib—and since the struggle against reformist authorities is always fiercer and more vital than that against reactionary authorities, the battle with the last two was bloodier by far. When, for instance, al-Mahjoub decided to confine all microbuses (what the Alexandrians call "ferries") to a single station in Karmouz, away from the two rail hubs of Sidi Gaber and Masr, the drivers assembled at their accustomed stops, pulled up the handbrakes, and refused to move. In the end, the police were forced to intervene. They fired shots into the air. Only then did the strikers disperse, and then only after one of them was killed.

This incident was a rehearsal for a bigger show. One autumn day in 2004 a fishmonger called Fedda Amin al-Madawiya persuaded the municipal council to order the demolition of a villa in Laurent once owned by a former ambassador by the name of Mofeed Aboulghar, after he had sold it to her—to Fedda—by a properly registered contract. The vast majority of Alexandrians took a different view from that of the municipality. For weeks they had been following the reports written by a dynamic investigative reporter—and member of the independent Future Party—called Amal Sabour; reports that made much of the villa's aesthetic, historical, and architectural merits while at the same time shedding light on Fedda al-Madawiya's attempts to force Aboulghar to sell it to her, which had culminated in falsifying charges (among others, prostitution and drug dealing) against some of his relatives. One and all, the inhabitants of Alexandria massed in front of the bulldozer that had come to knock the villa down on the orders of Fedda, the building's legal owner. The scene concluded with the bulldozer halting before the mob that sat in solidarity with the former ambassador. It came back to complete its task another day, but only after the case had received its share of publicity, the scene with the stationary bulldozer having taken on a significance equal to that of Rachel Corrie singlehandedly facing down the Israeli bulldozer.

This tale went hand in hand with another, also significant. Alexandria's governor ordered the banning of shisha from the city's cafés, part of a plan to ban the sale—the consumption, even—of cigarettes, itself part of a plan to turn Alexandria into a "smoke-free city," itself part of the governor's plan to become Director-General of UNESCO. Yet free-born Alexandrians remained unmoved by such lofty considerations. The café owners announced their objection and the governor ignored them. They announced a strike and he ignored them. They openly declared that they were ready to engage in acts of violence within the city limits. He ignored them. They set a date—Thursday, July 22, 2005—to cast the city into darkness. They gathered in small groups in various locations from Bahari to Miami and started smashing the streetlights along the Corniche by hurling pebbles, while those with firearms shot out the bulbs. The police arrested a few of them. They interrogated them and got nothing. In the end they let them go and the governor overturned his decree. The free-born Alexandrian knows that truth is worthless without the strength to protect it.

As numerous historians have observed, the Alexandrians have not won a single decisive victory in all these battles. A victory on the ground, we mean. All their victories have been spin or symbolism: dramatic, stirring scenes rather than actual victories. We are borrowing here from the Alexandrian cartoonist Hassan al-Basha who, in the local newspaper *Sea and Seagull*, depicted a meeting of an Alexandrian cell headed by an armed man, gazing at a blackboard marked "Chronicle of the Victories of the Sea" (by which is meant: Alexandrian victories) and saying in disgust: It's just one "stirring scene" after another. Aren't there any proper victories?

Some two decades earlier, in the mid-eighties, the city of Alexandria saw the opposition strike a blow that was, back then, quite unprecedented anywhere in Egypt. It was in a number of summer theaters—where troupes would put on plays starring comedians of the first rank, like Sayyid Zayyan, Mohamed Nigm, Waheed Saif, and a very young Mohamed al-Heneidi—that the seeds of Alexandria's first political protest against its oppressors in the modern era took root. Audiences took to whistling at and applauding any scene that bore a trace, however faint, of political subversion. And if we bear in mind that these were family theaters first and foremost—since throughout the eighties and nineties Egyptian families would spend the summer months in Alexandria—then we can add to this the fact that they raised a generation of children who received their first political lessons there and later, as tumultuous youths, would put them into practice.

In the first days of the 2011 revolution, one of the original "instigators" was arrested, a man called Hani Samir. He was brutally tortured, and after his release was invited onto a famous TV talk show, on which he said, word for word: It was my dad who taught me politics. Not politics exactly, but he taught me to love Egypt and to understand that if something happened to my friend it might happen to me later. When I'd see him and his friends at *The Green Soldier* (a famous play starring Sayyid Zayyan), shouting and clapping and whistling, it would make me shout and whistle too.

In those days, Alexandria was the brightest chapter in the chronicle of Egyptian resistance. All of Egypt's other provinces were keeping their heads down. No one knows precisely why. A short while ago we referred to the Alexandrian mentality, always alive to a former glory that had slipped through its fingers when the July regime took over back in 1952, but there are other factors too.

From the moment the city was founded—well, a century after it was founded, to be precise—the unmistakable traits of the Alexandrian had started to take shape. Rage, for instance, is a seminal trait, the rage which is sometimes referred to as "ill temper" in Egyptian dialect. Your Alexandrian's a nice enough fellow most of the time, no one disagrees with that, with the exception of those instances where he senses some outside threat, particularly—if we're aiming for precision—a threat directed at his Alexandrian identity. Small wonder, given that Alexandria is the only Egyptian city to have evolved a clear communal identity of its own and to have developed rites for the veneration of this identity—and rites for rage, should this identity be harmed. Alexandrians learned this from their former European neighbors, so proud of their consulates and foreign privileges, but they also take it from their current neighbors, the Bedouin, the desert Arabs of Matrouh. The revolutionary Bedouin of Matrouh was—and remain—the neighbor with whom the authentic Alexandrian feels most at home, not the slack-jawed Delta peasant foisted on him by geography.

The year before "The Year of Khaled Said," a blogger wrote a post on Alexandria, a satire, more or less, whose Alexandrian protagonists were given mocking nicknames. Thousands of Alexandrians were up in arms, on blogs and Facebook. The blogger's Facebook account (we've no desire to mention his name) was shut down for one year and its reactivation—which further enraged the Alexandrians—coincided with the flare-up of the Khaled Said affair. This might unravel for us the reason behind the unbridled anger with which news of Khaled's murder was received. It was not directed at his killers alone, nor at the police, but at anyone who took it upon himself to mock the city, let alone spill Alexandrian blood. One famous image from the protests was of a young woman, lip bleeding after being assaulted by policeman, and carrying a sign on which was written "Alexandrian blood does not come cheap."

For all these reasons, and in the midst of all the fighting and fire, the blood that flowed for freedom's sake, Ali and Inji surfaced in the City of the Sea. In other words, just as Alexandria's yearning for a savior burned brightest.

A new phase of Ali and Inji's life began with the birth of Hamada.

A fat boy, four kilos. Eyes wide like his father's and green like those of his grandmother, Inji's mother. He laughed a lot and cried little, looking about him in astonishment. The infant was passed from hand to hand. He seemed like a divine compensation for the injustice suffered by his parents, exiled, dispossessed, forlorn.

The infant brought Ali to his senses. For a while, he stopped sleeping with Umm Amira. He turned into a proper father. He grew a big mustache and started speaking slowly. His sources of income proliferated: the shop, the little scams practiced on his customers, and the passing of some of these customers—the ones after sex and hashish—on to Abu Amira's house and so getting paid twice over. Ali knew how to talk to the customers. He trailed Adel to Ramleh Station, to Saad Zaghloul Street and the street named after Saad's wife, Safiya, and slowly but surely he accustomed himself to sitting at the bars downtown. He didn't drink much. He watched the drinkers. Talked to them. Led them by the hand to Camp Cesar. Handed them to Abu Amira. Abu Amira would narrow his eyes at him. Sometimes he'd smile and sometimes he wouldn't. So what? People smile at times and at other times they don't. But Ali was yet to learn this and was unsure how to interpret these smiles, just as he was unsure about the meaning of anything to do with Abu Amira. And so he went on. He walked his path and never looked back.

But there's more. Back then, everyone would smile at Ali. People who knew him and people who didn't: taxi drivers, shopkeepers, café waiters, even the junkies and johns. He sensed something circling him, drawing closer, but he couldn't touch it. Forever about to attack. Inji felt something similar. Minna would bring her students so she might teach them too, and in these students' looks there'd be a spark, a passion, a longing, but for whom she couldn't say. If we might be permitted to interject, we would have to say those looks were looks of adoration—for her. Unquestionably.

Inji fought the feeling. She put up considerable resistance, a violent resistance, because it filled the air around her, it hemmed her in wherever she went, even though she had no proof that it was there. At the end of the day, there isn't one of us capable of believing that everyone adores them and, moreover, that he can discern this purely from their looks. Like he's a hero. Like he's Raafat al-Haggan. It was two months after giving birth before Inji got her hands on tangible evidence for her suspicions. Hamada was in her arms and one of her students was telling her about an emotional tangle she was going through—the boy had spoken to her several times of his desire that they should split up—and the girl was crying, so Inji put Hamada on the couch and took the girl in her arms. And as her tears reached their peak the girl cried out, Oh miss! If only I could be like you! The miss said nothing, then, after a bit, hesitantly asked, Why do you say that, Shaimaa? The girl pulled her face back and wiped her nose with a shirtsleeve. She stared at the floor for a moment. Because you're strong. If there's a guy you don't like you kill him.

Ali too was beset by looks of wonderment. How is it that their reputation has spread through the entire population of Alexandria in a year or less? No one can say. The amazing thing was that Ali was a coward. Little things still frightened him. The government, for instance. He still believed in little things too. The bond of brotherhood, for example. And he still avoided little things. Like talking about *that day*. Until, that is, the most important event in his life occurred: a little phone call from Cairo. His brother Mustafa on the line, asking if he could pay a visit. Ali assented. Mustafa had lunch with him in his apartment in Camp Cesar.

They're not leaving me be, Ali.

. . .

Every ten minutes it's the government at the door, asking about you.

. . .

Keep clear, Ali.

. . .

I'm begging you, keep clear, man. The police will have you.

And do what?

Look here. The store's yours. It's your father's store, Ali. I just want you to sign over your rights. It's only temporary, Ali, I swear by the Book, and then when the good Lord's sorted everything out, it'll go back to how it was before.

. . .

The government will get you, brother. By all that's holy, they'll have you.

. . .

Look, Ali. I brought you here. I made a pledge before God that I'd get you out of this mess and I kept my word. So now I'm promising you that I'll bring you back again and I'll cancel anything you sign, but please, on your son's life, you have to get me out of this. This way, if anyone comes and asks me I can say I don't know anything about you. The store'll be mine and you'll be in the clear. It's for the government's benefit, that's all.

The following day Ali signs the rights over to his brother. He tells Abu Amira the whole story. Abu Amira gazes at him for a long time then says, Your brother's cheated you, my friend. And Ali is certain that his brother has cheated him. But he needs to cling to some kind of hope. Abu Amira asks him to call Mustafa. He calls. No answer. Abu Amira persists: Call him, brother. Call him tomorrow, the day after, a month from now. He won't answer. Ali calls him the next day, the day after that, a month later; he punches in the number like a lunatic and no one answers. Everything is shifting beneath Ali's feet: the shop, the precious bond of brotherhood, his father's memory. He goes back to Abu Amira. He tells him that he has lost everything, that his life is in danger and that he's fed up with it all. Abu

Amira breathes out cigarette smoke and says firmly: See here, brother. You've been made a fool of. You've been cheated big time, and a brother that cheats a brother is no brother at all. He leans in. He's a brother who wants to die. Right? Right, Ali replies uncertainly: Right. And Abu Amira continues: Your brother's going to be killed, Ali, and we'll kill him here, in Alexandria. Isn't that God's justice? Ali doesn't answer. He stares into the distance. Abu Amira's voice is the only thing that is surefooted now. And I don't ask for a thing. You'll have your inheritance, and no one will say a word to you, but anything you take I'll have my share. I won't say to you, I want such-and-such, and so on. These things belong to you. You have to settle it with your conscience. Right? Ali doesn't answer. Abu Amira goes on, tenderly: Answer me, Ali. Am I right or am I wrong? And Ali's voice comes back unsure, a whisper: Right, Abu Amira. Right.

Ali's relationship with Mustafa was not a strong one. After their parents passed away, Ali suffered from the stubbornness of his brother, who always refused to sell the store—which at that time was not doing so well—and hand him his share, even when Ali's need was greatest. When he fell in love with a girl who lived next door and wanted to propose, his older brother refused to buy Ali's share of the business and he refused to stand by Ali. Worse, he repeatedly asked Ali to find himself a rented place so he might have the Ain Shams apartment to himself. Ali recalled Thana, the girl he'd once loved, telling him that Mustafa had met with her and asked that she encourage him to look for an apartment or otherwise get out of his life for good, and that if she didn't then he, Mustafa, would have no obligations when it came to the pair of them. Even smuggling himself and Inji out of Cairo—the black thoughts streaming into Ali's head—had been to that same end. Mustafa had taken over the apartment, the store, everything. Is this what your father would have wanted, Mustafa? Ali muttered to himself as he unfurled the rug to pray. When he had finished praying he was smiling at last. A great weight had shifted off his shoulders.

Umm Amira's in Cairo. She returns, bringing Mustafa with her. She leads him by the hand, like a dumb beast. Riding with her in the train, he seems pleased.

36

Looking forward to a nice little fuck when he gets to Alexandria. In the apartment in Karmouz she hands him over to Sousou, who offers him a joint and asks after Ali's store. Mustafa senses a trap closing about him. He replies that the store is his and in his name. Sousou leans in toward him, smiling: See here, brother. You're going to be killed. You're not here for us to pussyfoot around. I want you to sign over your rights to the place right now. The bell rings. The lawyer enters. Mustafa signs. The lawyer exits. Sousou goes downstairs with Mustafa. They take a ferry to Sidi Gaber Station. The train is pulling in. Sousou chucks him under the train. He turns. With complete self-assurance he leaves the station. With complete self-assurance he calls Ali. It's all good.

Before dawn prayers. Ali is performing the two sets you pray on entering the mosque, and Sheikh Hassan is praying some distance away. The prayers over, he approaches. The sheikh opens his Quran and starts to recite, but Ali has something to say:

I want to make a confession, Sheikh.

Yes, my son. Yes, yes.

I am a man weighed down with grievous sin.

God's mercy encompasses all things, my son. All things.

I'm a murderer. A killer.

Ah! Ye are brought to slaughter though it be hateful to thee.

I've killed my mother's son. I've killed my father's son.

(He breaks down. Sheikh Hassan pats him. Sheikh Hassan recalls Mustafa, his old army comrade. He recalls his duty and fights back a stubborn tear.)

What do I do now, Sheikh?

(The sheikh is silent.)

The uncertainty is killing me.

Okay, do you want the truth? Or will you get upset?

(He looks at him.) The truth never upset anyone.

Keep to your path, young Ali. Keep going. Our Lord has chosen you. Will you tell him no?

(He looks at him with tear-filled eyes.)

No! Don't you dare cry! Anything but that, Ali. You'll upset me! That's what's known as disrespecting the Almighty and All Wise! Just suppose, for the sake of argument, your boss says I want you to work for me and help me out. You'll scurry away and do what you're told, won't you? So what about when the King of Kings comes calling? Right, Ali?

A dawning light spreads across Ali's face. The mosque's servant gives the dawn call. "Prayer is better than sleep" swells through the room and Ali's heart is filled with joy. He stoops over Sheikh Hassan's hand and kisses it.

No one can say for certain just what took place in the days preceding this conversation, that is, the period between Mustafa's murder and Ali's confession. The best guess is that something is frightening Ali. Inji comforts him; murmurs that Mustafa had it coming. A crook, and he had it coming. But he is not so sure. She whispers that each and every Alexandrian is proud of him. She hears it and she knows. He hears it too, and he knows. But he weeps in front of her. She asks him to visit Abu Amira. Abu Amira makes you feel better. Go to him, baba. But he puts off the visit, day after day. This one time, Inji comes home. She doesn't see him. She goes out onto the balcony. She finds him standing by the balcony wall measuring it against his leg. What are you up to, Ali? and he says nothing. Comes back at her with a piercing stare.

No one can say for certain just what happened in the months after Ali spoke with Sheikh Hassan. The pennies started to flow through Ali's hands, who gradually grew from plain Ali into Miallim Ali: a boss. Being a miallim is not a question of what you wear. Ali still dressed in shirt and trousers. At root it's about independence, and Ali had long ago left Sheikh's Hassan's store and opened a new place nearby, which he filled with CDs of Quran recordings. He sold the store in Cairo, rented out the apartment in Ain Shams on the sly, and bought two adjoining apartments at Abu Amira's. This let him bring the customers and girls back to his place instead of the apartment owned by the landlord (kept sweet with a monthly handout). Ali had a firm grip on the future now. All that remained was to secure the path that led there. Using the money Inji made from selling the two floors she owned in Heliopolis, Ali converted a ground-floor apartment in his building into a prayer room, and appointed some young sheikhs to teach the Quran there.

They were both determined to start from scratch. Inji left the store and now taught young Muslim girls to memorize the Quran in the mosque, and gave lessons in computers and English.

Inji and Ali are now satisfied that their path is secure. True, they haven't much money to hand, but they have everything they need to generate it.

All right, and what of that second pillar of the nation, its beating wing? What of those fully empowered Egyptian citizens, their patriotic spirit a byword down the ages? Ali did not for one moment forget the Copts. He built a little church for them in the street—unlicensed, sure, but no one dared touch it. Ali, with his working-class roots, was never known to show any bigotry toward the Copts. He would always say of them: Our Lord, Exalted and Glorified be His name, exhorted us to do good by them. For He smooths the idolater's path in this world that He may torture him in the next. My role's to pave the wrongdoer's path with gold, until he gets it in the neck later. The street was a rare and authentic instance of religious tolerance, whose like Egypt had not known in recent decades. It could be claimed, without exaggeration, that Ali and Inji had brought Egypt back to itself.

Ali's relationship with Abu Amira did not change. The latter remained the boss, the leader, the leading light, though Ali was now the one employing him, rather than the other way round—a development of the last few months. It was not in Ali's nature to throw his weight about with anyone, let alone the one who'd taught him everything. But it is hard to point to details, even here. Abu Amira taught him to charm the customers, taught him how to make a customer pay without uttering a word—with just a smile, or a fierce look followed by some affectionate phrase. And he taught him how to speak to the prostitutes, too: That sort needs tenderness. She might be a whore, she might lack class, but she still needs tenderness. Ali took the lesson to heart. Abu Amira took him on a tour of all the places, gave him women's phone numbers, explained to him where they would sit, and the things they did that let you pick them out. You can tell, brother, you can tell. And Ali trailed behind Abu Amira, lighting his cigarettes sometimes, and never ashamed. Abu Amira was like his older brother, and who among us is ashamed of his older brother?

Umm Amira. Ali had long since lost his desire for her and, to be honest, had come to despise himself for sleeping with her all those times. Umm Amira's a great girl and all that, but she's old, she's ugly, and I'm a young guy. I want to enjoy my life, as he put it.

So Umm Amira tried to catch his eye.

Inji is asleep and she calls him on his cell phone. She flirts and reminds him of their secret code ("rabbit," for instance, was their word for the male member). Scowling, he responds by asking after her husband, so she decides to play dirty. The doorbell rings and he opens up to find her there, and without warning the volcano erupts. What, I don't do it for you anymore? A snort. Lord have mercy! The times you used to charm your way into getting a feel when I said no. You pimps! Ali tries to shut her up. Inji wakes. Abu Amira climbs the stairs. Umm Amira looks at her husband and the tears fill her eyes. This faggot, the man you gave a start in life, he's mocking me. He said I'm ugly, that no one would give me a second glance. But Abu Amira has heard everything. He seizes her. Holds her in his arms. A powerful stench of booze wafts from her mouth. He pushes her down the staircase till she falls. He kicks her. She rolls and tumbles to the ground floor. With both hands he grabs her and thrusts her in the direction of his apartment. She refuses to come along. She falls down and he clutches at the collar of her house robe and drags her over the asphalt as her legs kick in the air. Her robe is ripped to shreds as she's hauled along. She screams shrilly as she's hauled along. She addresses Ali: Faggot! She addresses the neighborhood: Pimps! You think he's a sheikh? He's scum! He's turning this place into a brothel. And he's a kiddy-fucker too!

Umm Amira was prey to frequent nervous episodes. Perhaps this explains Ali's revulsion toward her. She drinks and drinks until she's blind drunk, then starts acting up. And Abu Amira heard what she said. Her thing with Ali didn't bother him that much. He knew. She told him, and Ali told him. But the drunken cameos and the public scandals he couldn't take. Abu Amira endured a long night once his wife had finally surrendered to sleep. Didn't sleep a wink. When the dawn call sounded he arose, washed himself, and walked to the mosque, dripping water. After prayers he approached Ali.

40

Ali looks at him with reddened eyes. Abu Amira's eyes are turned to the ground. For the first time, his eyes are looking down. You're like a younger brother to me, Ali. But this time what you say goes. Whatever you tell me to do, I'll do it. Ali doesn't answer. He is looking away. Abu Amira watches a drop of water fall to the mosque's matting. Ali tears up. By the spotless soul of my departed mother, Abu Amira continues, you're dearer to me than Sousou or Adel. I can't bear to see you like this. Whatever you tell me, Ali, my friend. Ali looks at him. His eyes shine with tears but they are unforgiving. His voice is firm, steely, chopped up into brutal chunks: Divorce her, Abu Amira. If I see her again I'll kill her.

The scandal didn't end with Abu Amira divorcing Umm Amira. The scandal was laid bare, before Ali, before Inji, before the neighborhood, before all Alexandrians, each and every one. Inji disappeared. No one knew where she had gone, and Hamada too, the little boy. Suddenly they both vanished, evaporated. Where were they and what were they doing? No one knew. The Alexandrians, who had previously given Ali unlimited support, seemed to have vanished too. If one of them saw Ali now, he turned his face away. And the customers . . . There were none. There were no customers any more. The customers, too, had vanished.

Alexandrians are a sensitive people. There's no one easier to win over, and yet neither is there anyone easier to lose forever. If the people sense that the one in whom they've placed their trust has let them down, then they shall go away from him and shall not return. For an instant, Ali had betrayed the Alexandrian's trust in him. Sheikh Ali, who built the mosque, who made his living from God's Book, had been having a relationship with that filthy Umm Amira—and a kiddy-fucker into the bargain. (For the sake of accuracy, Ali had never been a kiddy-fucker. Just where Umm Amira pulled that from, as she was being dragged along the ground, we've no idea.) Rumors beset Ali on every side.

Some clarification is needed. It wasn't the things Umm Amira had screamed out as she was dragged along that were the source of the bother, not exactly. The scandal was the problem: filthy Umm Amira, sleeping in the street, dead drunk, and rousing the whole of Camp Cesar with details such as these. And who are the residents of Camp Cesar? They are respectable families when all is said and done. The middle class: so hard-done-by in the Egypt of today. The odd outrage might occur in Camp Cesar from time to time, and that's something one has to live with, an inescapable evil. But for things to become so public, for a woman to shout them out in earshot of kids and women and young ladies—well, that's something the neighborhood's conservative residents could not abide. The neighborhood's residents respected Abu Amira and they held Umm Amira in contempt. Abu Amira himself had always held his wife in contempt.

Ali abandoned his apartment and went to live with Abu Amira. He told him: The customers are boycotting me, Abu Amira. Abu Amira told him: We haven't done anything wrong, brother. Go out there and tell them. People need to know what you're thinking. And Ali buried his face in his hands. Moments passed. Long moments. Then he looked at Abu Amira and delivered his soliloquy:

You know, Abu Amira, back in the day whenever anything would happen to me I'd tell myself it was just a nightmare and that would make me feel better. But now I'm tired. Thinking tires me out and God doesn't want to take it off my hands. It's a son-of-a-bitch world. I told myself it would get better, but it seems like it's got no intention of getting better. Even the woman, she left me alone in the house and fucked off. The world's become such a hard place, brother.

Abu Amira hands him the joint. Have a puff, Ali. Have a puff and don't think so much. Thinking tires you out.

And Ali has a puff. He puffs and puffs and suddenly he looks up at Abu Amira and his eyes are red. Whoa! You spiked this hash?

They rock with laughter. They flap about on the floor and beat the walls. They walk on all fours like dogs. They chase each other through the house. They make like lizards and try to scale the walls, and fall. They make like birds and try to fly. They stand on the table, one then the other, and tumble down. Then they laugh. One mounts the other and they keep on laughing.

Sheikh Hassan was not much help to Ali in his current crisis. Sheikh Hassan was himself one of those who steered clear of Ali. Peace be upon you and

Upon you be peace, and that was it. Ali tried approaching him but he made excuses about needing to wash for prayers. Sousou and Adel kept their distance too. This was suggestive. Sousou and Adel knew almost everything there was to know about Ali before the scandal broke, so it's not as though they can have been shocked by the failings of that pristine angel called Sheikh Ali. What was it, then, that made them avoid him during this time? It gave Ali the idea that something was afoot: like directions or orders to avoid him, to fence him off and cut him loose. Was Umm Amira government? For a long while the question nagged at him, as he rolled hash into joints, counted floor tiles in the apartment, played games on his cell phone, slapped flies with the swatter, squashed mosquitoes between his hands. And when he could keep it in no longer he asked Abu Amira if Umm Amira was government and Abu Amira replied that she wasn't cut out for it. Was Abu Amira government? That was the next question.

No. It wasn't a question. It was a fact. Sitting on the balcony of his apartment, Ali goes over everything again. Who was it who'd opened his arms to him from the moment he'd arrived from Cairo? Who had made sure everything went smoothly for him in Alexandria? Who had urged him on, made him grow up, and made a human being of him (thus, bitterly, did he accede to Umm Amira's charge)? Who'd set his own wife on him, for him to sleep with? Who'd set his wife on him, in order to disgrace him? And who had known everything about him without having to ask? Ali scratches his cock. Spits into the street. Then he goes downstairs to sit with Abu Amira on the bench outside the building. He gives him a cigarette. Lights it for him. Falls silent. Then he turns to him and says: You're government, Abu Amira. I know it and I'm not upset with you. But why didn't you tell me, brother? Abu Amira doesn't answer. Suddenly he turns to Ali and slowly says: I'm government, Ali? You're saying I'm government? Ali gives a tight smile. I'm not angry with you. I swear I'm not. Abu Amira's voice swells. He shakes Ali's shoulder. I'm government, Ali? I'm government? After everything I've done for you? And Ali tries to free himself. And as he struggles, he knees him in the chest. What have you done for me, you stinking piece of shit? Abu Amira looms over him. Ali shrugs him off, stands, and screeches: No one's done shit for me. I've made myself. I don't owe anybody anything. It's you who owe me, all of you. Ali's voice rises. He is almost screaming, and now he's standing on the bench. He continues to screech: It's me who got you lot started and if anyone thinks I owe him, come and show yourself!

Ali's nerves were in swift decline, and it was suddenly apparent to the inhabitants of Alexandria that the young sheikh in whom they'd placed their faith was bound for madness. And no one has the power to alter destiny.

5

And why couldn't Inji be government?

Who was it who had appeared in Ali's life out of the blue, with no prior warning, convinced him to travel to the South, and got him mixed up in a murder? Who was it who had resurrected an ancient debt of honor and plotted to turn him from a clothes seller, minding his own business, into a criminal? Who had been so keen on Ali's decision to kill his brother?

It's true that Inji did all this, but if we are to accuse her of being government, we must first exercise a little caution. Examine the details.

Inji is a woman, and a woman can forgive anything—anything—except an affront to her dignity. The spectacle of Umm Amira being dragged through the dirt as she disgraced her husband tore her apart inside. She gathered her clothes together, took her young son, and decided to go to the home of Hagga Itemad. She said, Hagga, the man's an animal. Doesn't know what's good for him. Just imagine, he goes and sleeps with bald Umm Amira (Umm Amira's hair was thinning at the front) and in my own home. My own home, which I bought for him with my own money. The hagga started to console her, saying things like: Men are all the same. But Inji wasn't satisfied. She said that she wanted to make a new start away from all that filth. She said this, and burst into tears. The hagga was quiet for a bit then mentioned an apartment in a building she owned in Karmouz. Nobody knows about the building, my girl. Go and sit yourself down there for a couple of days until you've calmed down and God will provide.

In Karmouz, Inji encountered a new kind of life. She started over, surrounded by the kindness of goodhearted native sons, stand-up guys, who helped her get over her ordeal in no time. Her only possessions were the hearts of those around her, unlike Ali, who had lost nothing but their hearts. At first, Inji went back to giving children Quran lessons in the mosque, as well as courses in English and computers. It wasn't money she lacked exactly, but a future. She wanted to become part of the neighborhood. She wanted to become something: of the people and for the people.

And love was never far away. Sheikh Khaled also taught the Quran at the mosque. They would meet after evening prayers, he with his short beard and she in the niqab she'd worn since coming to Karmouz.

They walk together to Manshiya. They sit by the sea. They eat corn on the cob, her nibbling under her niqab and him over his beard. The bits of corn catch in the niqab's cloth and beard's brush, and they take this to be a test sent by God, a test that binds them, and should they confront it with steadfastness, God will reward them by bringing them together. Thoughts race through their minds and each looks at the other and smiles in gratitude.

Lovers have their own way of thinking.

Inji had been through a lot since she had gotten to know Ali and had her life turned upsidedown: travel, the kid, indignities and filth. But her body was still the same. Pure fire. Could still the storm. And, despite the niqab, she still liked to turn it on: in the way she walked, the way she took the arm of the man next to her when she crossed the street, her speech (the intimacies she used with everyone: Take care of yourself, I've missed you, Make sure you let me know how things are going . . .). And Sheikh Khaled had noticed all these things. And said not a word. Just . . . she takes his arm as they cross the street, so he lays his hand on her shoulder when they aren't crossing any street. As they sit together he wants to tell her something important, so he grips her thigh. He takes advantage of their position behind a rock by the sea and lifts her niqab a touch and kisses her cheek. And she trembles.

In the beginning she would only tremble. Then, she began to tremble and take the initiative. Inji needs emotion. Inji's a human being. And what Sheikh Khaled's after is no sin. He wants God's sanctioned pleasures. They met in the mosque over a shared love of God's Book, and Khaled, when

46

he kisses her cheek (she doesn't allow him to go further) whispers, You're my licit thrill. And she has taken to putting his hand on her shoulder, to stroking his chest and brushing his nipple with her fingertip should it be erect or, if it isn't, pinching it so that it springs up, then brushing it with her fingertip. Nothing to stop her having what she wants.

Inji spoke to Hagga Itemad. She told her everything. She was very embarrassed, but the hagga decided to pay her a personal visit in Karmouz. They laughed together for a bit, then Inji's tongue was loosed: she was still Ali's woman and was scared that she might anger God. The hagga lit her a joint and settled down to listen. I won't lie to you, ya hagga, I've become scared of God's anger and everyone makes mistakes. Sheikh Khaled's always at me and I don't want to make a move until I've spoken with you. Hagga Itemad listened gravely, then asked how things stood with Ali. I'll ask him for a divorce, Hagga. The man's a pimp, plus he cheated on me. The hagga listened, then said, And you, my girl? You're going to carry on denying your- self a life until the court tells you whether you can divorce? Inji didn't reply. The hagga leaned in. Look after yourself a little, Inshi. God knows, you're like a little sister to me, and Sheikh Khaled's kind and doesn't do wrong.

Inji's heart radiated joy. The advice came from the person dearest to her. Next time Sheikh Khaled whispered that she was his licit thrill, she would look him longingly in the eye. Really? She'd ask. And he'd smile benevolently and kiss her neck, and for the first time she'd permit him to kiss her on the mouth. No, it's not a question of her permitting him. It was she who'd take the initiative, she who'd gnaw and suck his lips, she who'd push her tongue inside his mouth, who'd bite his tongue when he tried to slide his forward, who'd lap at his saliva and brush hers across his tongue. It was she who'd hail the ferry and lead Khaled to her apartment in Karmouz.

Hard times and protracted deprivation had ensured Inji would get aroused at the slightest thing. Song lyrics, even. Even the words Sheikh Khaled murmured, gazing up at her as he kissed her nipple—I want to sin with you—or lightly bit her neck or scratched her back . . . All things that left her wider and wider open to this stranger.

And in the end? She grips his hand. Pulls it roughly to her straining nipples. See what you've done to me, she whispers and he gets hornier and hornier. On top of her he pants that he'll split her in two and she gets hornier still. She clutches his cock and brings him inside her. She is not totally satisfied.

During her separation from Ali, and following her niqab phase, Inji had not submitted to a regimen of total continence. She had become addicted to the secret habit. Addicted meaning addicted. Five times or more an hour—or call it an hour and a half.

This prevented her from attaining full satisfaction the first time. She didn't get there, you might say. She enjoyed herself at first, then resorted to using her fingers in tandem with his penis, then her enjoyment ceased for good. Things began to turn around the second and third time out, till she was able to do without her fingers altogether, as, she observed, had Khaled. For the sum of Khaled's previous sexual experiences—and this is a fact we reveal here for the first time—had been beating himself off.

Anyway. These were the two lovebirds' first nights together, and like all first nights, nobody was thinking of the future. It was all tease and gasp. The only problem with first nights is that they pass. They wouldn't be called the first nights if they didn't: the Only Nights, perhaps, or the Amazing Nights, the Arabian Nights . . . anyway. The first nights passed and Sheikh Khaled disappeared.

Inji searched for him everywhere. He had vanished: from the mosque, from Manshiya, from Karmouz, from Alexandria. She asked Hagga Itemad, who insisted she knew nothing. Inji nearly went mad. She chewed her nails and cut her hair and when she caught sight of him for the first time three weeks later, riding the tram, she launched herself at him. Where've you been, Khaled? she whispered in his ear. I've been worried about you. And he pushed her out of his way. She went on whispering. It's me, Inji. He pushed her hard. She lifted her niqab to show him she was Inji. He shoved her off the tram and rode away.

Inji told the whole story to Hagga Itemad. The hagga thought for a bit, then called her daughter, Minna. Minna heard her out with great interest and, grateful to the woman who had taught her English in mere months, decided to take a stand. She sent an email to Sheikh Khaled. She added him to her list of contacts and chatted to him endlessly. Night after night after night she sat up chatting to him. Time after time after time he asked her to set up a webcam and after the camera was set up he asked to see her, and after he'd seen her, and she him, and after he'd begun to see himself as the alpha and omega of Don Juans, she made her request: that he deliver her to the train station. She was going to visit her aunt in Damanhur.

At the station they stand together, alone. From nowhere, Inji appears. She greets Minna. He pretends not to know her but she isn't hurt. After a while he tries to leave. He's got an appointment. But it's too late now. Behind him, behind Minna, the train is pulling in. She sees it. One push and Sheikh Khaled's sprawled beneath the train. One push and he is turned to mincemeat. They walk, Minna and Inji, out of the station. People are horror-struck. Screams swell. Everyone clears a path for them. Minna is terrified. She holds her breath. It's the first time she's done something like this. Inji crossed that bridge a long time ago. Inji's in pain, that's all. Suddenly, she remembers the dead man at Ramses Station. She remembers Ali. Nostalgia slays her. She bites her nails all the way home. Nostalgia makes her bite her nails.

With time the business with Sheikh Khaled came out. The good people of Alexandria had no idea who the perpetrator was. They wound around themselves, wheeled about, questioned, second-guessed, and floundered, and had no idea who the perpetrator was. Until, that is, Hagga Itemad took it upon herself to pass the information on to the doorman of the building in Karmouz. And the people began to play.

Historically, a significant portion of Alexandrian recalcitrance has been directed not only against authority, but against the purveyors of medievalism and backwardness as well. Alexandrians are an enlightened people by nature. One example should suffice: Karantina. The fact is that from the days it housed British barracks, this neighborhood in the Qabbari district of West Alexandria had always been an important center of Alexandrian resistance against the fundamentalism that swept, slowly but surely, through society. Before the revolution, it had served as a base for certain Alexandrians, agents of the British, who'd witnessed the gradual rise of the Muslim Brotherhood and Young Egypt movements and had chosen to fight them both with the democracy of the Allied Powers. So they traded in news and information and passed it to the British and, in the end, got what they wanted. The Allies won the war and the curtain was brought down forever on Nazism, Fascism, and all the twentieth century's totalitarian creeds. Simultaneously, and somewhat ironically, the curtain was also brought down on the British presence in the Middle East. The revolution came and they departed. The revolution transformed the dwelling places of Karantina into government housing for the poor, and it was from these humble shelters that the true legend of Karantina sprang up: tin shacks, backroom stores, jackknives, swords, and drugs. The poor of Alexandria decided to settle there and merge into that sprawling Egyptian structure called "the shambles."

Shambles is an unjust term, for these were not merely homes for those below the poverty line, for criminals and registered offenders. No, these shambles played a central role in the rebellion against authority and the mores of conservative Egyptian society, into which crept, slowly but surely, the hitherto unfamiliar practices of Wahhabism and fundamentalism. As crime took root, as anarchic practices like drinking alcohol, smoking weed, and gangsterism took root, the inhabitants of Karantina were able to take on the conservative, and sometimes Wahhabi, values of the Alexandrian middle class. And so the blows fell, one after the other, dealt by the inhabitants of Karantina to the allied forces of the authorities and encroaching fundamentalism. And this, of course, the status quo would not stand. Karantina's shacks were razed, a violent measure taken by the governor in the early years of the new millennium, and a school complex set up in their place. The inhabitants were scattered to the winds, but in their hearts they still carried the legend of Karantina and their dream: an anarchist Alexandrian society dead set against the powers that be.

Sheikh Khaled, on the other hand, represented everything Alexandrians loathed. He completed his studies at the Dar al-Ulum in Cairo, then set out for Alexandria, bringing with him the extremist ideas he'd acquired in the city of a thousand minarets. No sooner in situ than he became the model of observance: growing out his beard and clad at all times in a white robe, a sweater worn over it in winter, and a toothpick in the top pocket. At first he would attend the mosque to pray five times a day, and then he started to teach the Quran. So far, so unremarkable. Inji did the same, for instance. But what the Alexandrians could not forgive was his stopping people in the street and urging them to pray at the mosque, and packing phrases of a fundamentalist, extremist bent into his Friday sermons. And when one local resident voiced his objection, Sheikh Khaled grew most severe, his "God said" and "the Prophet said" his trusty weapons, something most abhorrent to the tolerant nature of Alexandria's inhabitants, who began to look askance at this intruder from Cairo and tried to keep him in check. But he swelled into an ogre and with him swelled the specter of fundamentalist Islam, and the victim in all this, as always, was the people.

For all these reasons, once the knowledge that she'd murdered Khaled got about, Inji became a hero of a very special kind, and the greetings and congratulations rained down upon her in every street she entered—something she had only ever experienced with Ali, long ago, in her old life in Camp Cesar. No one let her pay for anything. The residents would send their kids to study the Quran, English, and computers at the mosque. She was asked for by name now, and little gifts arrived wherever she was. And big gifts. And middling gifts. And requests, too. Like: the municipality's confiscated the stock of a pavement vendor in Saad Zaghloul, and we don't want to bother you, Sheikha Inshi, but if you could do whatever God puts in your power . . . . And Sheikha Inshi goes in person to Captain Amr. She speaks to him in friendly tones. She says that she's responsible for the kid whose stuff he took. He says, But after all, we've got to do our job, Sheikha. She says, Do your job anywhere else, but by God's glory if you come near my patch, you jumped-up little shit, I'll have you sent to Sidi Gaber Station in an eyeblink. The allusion to the murder frightens the officer. The confiscated stock is returned to Saad Zaghloul and for many days thereafter—for years, to be exact—the municipality's iron grip around the pavement sellers loosens. Of course, that's not what took place between Inji and Captain Amr, but it is what people talked about between themselves. Until now, no one knows exactly what transpired.

All right. So, the loosening of the municipality's iron grip in Saad Zaghloul Street had another direct consequence. One of the permanent pavement vendors there was Adel, Abu Amira's brother. Adel was one of the most enthusiastic peddlers of the account, outlined above, of what took place between Inji and Captain Amr. He whispered it to all his fellow vendors, to all his fellow bon viveurs, to all his relatives, and to Abu Amira, until it reached Ali. Ali was as before: rolling joints and counting tiles and playing games on his cell phone and swatting flies and squashing mosquitoes.

Adel went to visit Sheikha Inji. He told her that he had nothing to do with any problem between her and Ali. He told her that he had sided with Ali at the outset, because Ali was his friend, but now he sided with her and he'd be honored to be one of her boys. Inji was firm. That Ali you're taking about, my friend, his name's Sheikh Ali and he's my husband and father of my child and he was never your friend nor ever tried to be. Ali's friend is Abu Amira. Crushed, Adel fell silent. She went on. Look here, Adel. Tell your friends that they're family now, and you're like my little brother. Anything happens to them, I'm here. She gave him a light pat on the shoulder and he almost wept. He returned to Camp Cesar. He didn't tell them anything. He kept it to himself, kept it shut up inside him where the light of mystic peace began to dawn.

Every day, Inji sits with her son Hamada teaching him the Quran and talking to him about his family's history. Talking to him about his father. And Hamada understands. He's two years old now: bismillah, mashaallah, what a lovely boy. She tells him she's here because of something that happened long ago. A day long, long ago, when something happened in a place called Sidi Gaber, something called a man murdering his brother. Then she corrects herself. No, no, she says. This thing happened in a place more distant still, called Cairo, and the something is called a man avenging his honor. Then she corrects her correction and says, Brother, the place is the South and thing is taar. And little Hamada laughs, chirps garbled sentences, and she takes him up and kisses every inch of his face. Oh, I'm such a little darling! I'm mother's little man!

Business. Hagga Itemad introduced her to Madame Nadia, a Karmouz grandee with a couple of pennies to rub together and a desire to invest them. Hagga Itemad advised Inji to open an English and computer center. Where? The two floors beneath hers in the hagga's building. The running of it would be left to Inji: she knew about things like that. Inji embraced the idea. She had not forgotten her past as a member of the intelligentsia and she saw in this a chance to return to her roots. And Madame Nadia had heard about this woman, a newcomer to Karmouz and to Alexandria, and rising fast, whom people spoke about from time to time. She decided to sit with her in person. And Inji spontaneously reverted to her original manner, mixing Arabic and American-accented English and careful, at the same time, not to seem too green. Inji impressed Madame Nadia. She recited the Fatiha and said mabrouk.

Madame Nadia only had one reservation: the niqab. She spoke to Inji about it, who smiled and told her she had no problem with other girls, whether they were in niqab or not, or even totally naked, so long as it was their own *free choice* (in English). As far as I'm concerned, Madame Nadia, it doesn't bother me what others wear. Honestly, *it doesn't matter*. What really matters is that people are happy with what they're wearing, that they're okay with it deep down. Believe me, anyone can get away with their style and their clothes, anywhere they like, so long as they've got *self-confidence*. Inji was able to impose her logic on Madame Nadia because her logic was loaded with a great deal of *self-confidence*.

Inji took over the running of the center and her presence brought young men and women flocking to study there. This impressed Madame Nadia, who realized that she knew hardly anything about Inji, and so she asked about. A few people told her a few things, but the important detail was relatively late in arriving: Inji's a killer, Madame Nadia. Inji killed in Cairo, she killed in Camp Cesar, and she killed in Karmouz. God knows if that's the lot. There was no intention to slander her here—quite the opposite: it was pride, pride in a daughter of Karmouz. And it was in this spirit that the news reached Madame Nadia.

Inji paid her a visit at her office. It was daytime, in Ramadan. She lit a cigarette. Inji made no comment. It was Madame Nadia who commented: Cigarettes don't break the fast, Inji. Were there cigarettes in the Prophet's day, to break his fast? Inji was silent. Madame Nadia stood up. I want you to come with me on a quick errand, Inji. We'll be back before you know it, don't worry.

Madame Nadia drove Inji to her home in Gheit al-Enab. An apartment she owned on the ground floor. In they went.

Utter darkness. Madame Nadia walks ahead and Inji follows. The room within is darker still. Inji can barely see a thing for all that it is day outside. She hears the scrape of Madame Nadia's footsteps on the right side of the room. She hears her whimpering. Then the sound cuts out. Inji wants to call out to her but her voice is gone. The scattered facts string together in her mind. Sheikh Khaled's murder. Madame Nadia's taking her revenge. She's cut off completely, in a darkened room, no one knowing where she is. Suddenly, from her left, she hears her voice. Maybe you don't know much about me, Inshi, but I know every little thing about you. Don't think you're working with me because I like the way you talk to me. You're working with me because of what people say about you. She's the one, I said to myself. I want her with me. But you need to know something first.

You never ask for anything, Inji. My girl, you should have. I'd have helped you. There's many before you have tried to do what you're doing but they've all failed. These things are in God's hands. He's the one Who sees His servant through or sees him fail. And take care: there could be hard times on the way.

See here, my girl, you're young. The tale I'm going to tell you took place twenty years ago now. You were just a child when it happened. And no one knows a thing about it. The papers never wrote about it, and never a peep on TV.

The Hagga Itemad you know, the one you see me such good friends with, she was my husband's second wife once upon a time, and we couldn't stand each other. But the wheel turns, Inji my girl, the wheel turns. Could you imagine a couple of wise old birds like us still fighting over a man? Of course not.

The man's no stranger to you. He's been dead fifteen years. Maybe you won't know him, but you know his brother. Sheikh Hassan. The man who set you up when you first came to Alexandria. A good man, right? And his brother's the one who, twenty years ago, set Alexandria alight.

A mysterious figure, his roots most likely in the South. He appeared one day in the sky over Kom al-Shuqafa. Mohamed Harbi was his name, but he

54

was only ever known as Harbi. He wasn't known to have a trade. It was said that he was insane, and it's true he did do strange things. He started with perfectly reasonable stuff: holding a guy up with a sword and taking everything he had on him, fighting with a store owner and coming back at night with his friends to burn the store down, assaulting underage girls (and legal girls). All par for the course. Most of us have gotten up to one or the other in our tender years. What was new was the unreasonable stuff. Such as? In '92, Harbi stood in the middle of the Corniche Road in Miami holding a deck chair, which he set up and sat down on, staring scornfully at the advancing cars. By some miracle, the cars managed to miss him. Two cops came up and tried to drag him to the pavement. In an instant he'd pulled a sword out from under his robe (where he'd strapped it to his waist) and thrashed it about in the air, wounding one cop in the arm. They both backed off, enough for Harbi to take off running—despite his slight limp—and catch a ferry on the seaside lane heading for Chatby. Where he unfolded his chair, smack-dab in the center of the road as before. Five minutes and he was bored. He folded up the chair and went home.

For those who don't know, for those who don't remember, this was the period when Egypt was under assault from terrorism, and so it was possible to pin a charge of terrorism on Mohamed Harbi. This was because Mohamed Harbi had another specialty: releasing livestock from quarantine. He did this on two occasions, at the head of a mob from Kom al-Shufaqa. They released the beasts and passed them on to traders, who led them, in turn, to Amiriya where they sold them. It was claimed the animals were infected, but Harbi took a different view, that the animals enter quarantine in good shape and come out sick, and so it was to save them from this fate that he mounted his operation. In any case, that was the moment that Harbi became a terrorist in the government's eyes, and no greater sin can man commit than terrorism.

It was then that he met his first wife and married her, Inji: the same Itemad you know. But he wasn't happy with her. And I knew who he was. From a distance. Between you and me, Inji, I had my eye on him. And he had his on me. He'd give me a wink from time to time. But I didn't like to get between him and his wife.

He was at the end of his rope with his wife and I told him to leave her so she wouldn't suffer either, but he said, No. I'll marry you and stay married to her too. Between you and me, I was young. Life was still a game and everyone was talking about Harbi. He was like the big boss in Kom al-Shufaqa. Anyway, I agreed. Mohamed, I told him, Promise me you'll divorce her later And he said, I promise.

Was Mohamed Harbi insane? No one ever said so out loud, though many thought it. Whatever the case, the time for that reckoning had not come. What mattered were the many people who believed in him and followed him; was that for years (not many, true, but they made their mark) he had created and sustained a myth for Alexandria: the myth of the city's conception of itself. The man who defied the government and led one of the largest spontaneous protest movements ever to be formed by a single individual (single and also unlettered, disorganized and with no experience of protest movements); the man whose primary motivation was not wealth or women or revenge, but to stand up to the authorities, to challenge their settled ideas about themselves . . . this is the true history of Alexandria.

And that, my girl, is what you need to know. You can march around with your tits in everybody's face, but if you don't know anything, it won't get you anywhere. If you want to finish what old Harbi started you have to first understand what it is he did. Am I right? You're an educated girl and speak languages and, God willing, it'll be through you that God delivers us. And that is why, Madame Nadia explains, Inji is here, in Harbi's old den, surrounded by his things: his swords and switchblades. God willing, this room and everything in it will go to you, or rather, to those close to you. But only if you live up to my expectations, Inji, and I know you won't let me down.

Mohammad Harbi's death had been one of the most influential scenes in the film reel of Alexandrian history:

So the government, as they say, was looking for him and he was staying with a friend of his, a guy in the Young Muslims who later became an informer. I'll tell you who I got this from in a minute. I never say a false word about anyone. This friend of his was winding him up. He sat there filling him with poison and telling him, You aren't the Harbi I used to know, sitting inside like a woman because you're scared of the government. Harbi was hot-blooded. He couldn't take it. He straps a sword to his side and goes out. Soon as he steps outside he sees the street full of cops and officers. It was a trap, see, and they'd made a deal with this friend of his. The man runs and keeps running until he reaches Fouad Street and crosses over, still running. And guess what? They've got a car waiting for him. The car drives up and smacks into him.

For a minute she is silent.

You know, Inji my girl, it was like his body was pasted onto the car. And the car keeps going until it reaches this pickup truck coming out of a side street and they crash into one another.

She is silent for a long time. The memory is painful. More than anyone could bear. The sight of Mohamed Harbi's body, jammed and folded between the two vehicles. Madame Nadia remembers something else. A cry, lingering and dramatic, like the mourner's wail—Harbi!—the *bi* drawn out until the sound began to fade: Harbiiiii! And as it died, Harbi heard it and saw his death before him. Who cried out? The driver of the Peugeot? Of the pickup? One of the soldiers waiting for him outside the house? And at what precise instant did it ring out? And, more important, how was it she recalled its very tone, to this day, when she had not witnessed the incident herself, but only heard about it? Harbi! Warning. Harbi! Deadly, fatal. Harbi! Mysterious, cut off from every possible context. Harbi! With the *bi* drawn out, drawn out to no purpose.

Suddenly, the breeze claps the shutters. The shutters swing open. From between the slats a dust cloud storms the room, and more important than the dust: the light. The room fills with sunlight. Its features materialize. Inji coughs lightly, then opens her eyes. Two long swords hanging on the wall, and a machine gun, and a nine-millimeter automatic, and a collection of knives embedded in the desk's cracked surface. Madame Nadia is over on the far left-hand side of the room, seated, weeping, wiping at her tears with her fingers, wiping her snot, which she flicks to the ground with forefinger and thumb. The floor's awash with snot and tears.

The Inji Center pulled in new customers every day, customers who came to study, customers who came to play games, customers who came for online chat in the small cybercafé, and customers who came for love. A small room on the center's second floor had started life as a cafeteria, at first relatively laid-back when it came to certain maneuvers—certain postures—between young men and their girlfriends, then openly laid-back, then unreservedly laid-back, until it ended life as a spacious apartment set aside for sex. Inji never took a single unpremeditated step, and all with the full knowledge of Hagga Itemad and Madame Nadia. Planning the project started at around the time Inji found out about Mohamed Harbi's story; in the middle of Ramadan, in other words. Hagga Itemad did not oppose it; she just asked that the whole thing be put off till after Ramadan, and Madame Nadia said the same. Inji was the only one dying to get started. She started mulling and calculating and going back over her time with Ali in Camp Cesar. To Madame Nadia she said that she wanted it to be something different, something respectable, not like the filthy holes elsewhere: Our customers are high-class and we've got to be high-class too. In response to this statement, Madame Nadia announced her wholehearted consent.

Madame Nadia's old dream had been to get out of Karmouz. The years went by, she accumulated her fortune, and she still hadn't managed to get out, and so she replaced her old dream with another: to create a new Karmouz, with cybercafés and coffee shops on every corner. She gave all her sons and daughters lessons in English and computers. The fact is that much of Madame Nadia's personality becomes comprehensible to us if we would just recognize her obsession with modernization, and Inji did. She drew her out with the dream of the high-class customers who would frequent the center because of the new apartment: Gulfies, army officers, and cops. I know them from my Camp Cesar days. Madame Nadia smiled, and Hagga Itemad smiled, and Inji continued to rise.

Harbi was utterly forgotten. Madame Nadia didn't talk to Inji about him anymore. Hagga Itemad made one solitary reference to him: she asked if Nadia had spoken to her about anything. Inji said nothing. The hagga pressed her. She bluntly asked if Nadia had told her the story of Harbi and Inji inclined her head. The hagga went on. He was just her lover. He wasn't her husband. He never married anyone but me or had any children apart from my girl, Minna. If you ask her she won't deny it. She's just ashamed to admit it.

For a long while this was the only reference made to the story of Harbi, but Inji did not forget.

One night she dreams of him. He is at the head of a strung-out column of humanity, with a black beard and thinning hair, screaming wildly, like Russell Crowe on posters for *Gladiator*. In among this straggling army is Ghada, one of the girls who work for her at the center. Ghada sees her and waves happily, then takes her by the hand to introduce her to Harbi. Inji wakes up, sweating. Her sweat dries and she smiles. She calls Ghada. She tells her that she misses her. Inji is always scrupulous when it comes to her relationships with her workers. She doesn't call them whores, but rather "teachers" or "waitresses," depending on the jobs they do, and these things make a difference. These things make a big difference.

Another recurring dream: she and Ali, sitting together in their old house in Camp Cesar. Ali is playing with Hamada, murmuring to the child and feeding him his finger, and he looks at her. And he smiles. So she smiles, and gets up and goes into the bedroom. He follows her. He fondles her and feels her up and she responds: she starts to get wet. She wakes before she comes. Consoles herself that the journey is often better than the destination and, drawing on the dream, turns to her secret habit.

The night after Harbi's murder, his wife Itemad had a nightmare. She was walking along a road, a road like a tunnel, a tunnel lined with sheikhs reciting the Quran. She looked at one of them. His eyes were fixed on his lap. Suddenly he lifted his face to hers. He was blind. His eye sockets were completely empty, so empty that he pushed his forefinger into his left socket and began to laugh. His mouth, devoid of teeth, gaped. Itemad tried to scamper off but the tunnel was narrow, or rather, it had become narrow, lowered. All of a sudden she realized she would have to crouch, so she crouched. Another sheikh was reciting: Say: I take refuge with the Lord of the Dawn, and hysterically repeating the word "Dawn" over and over, the low and narrow tunnel bouncing back the echo of his voice and the tunnel's walls transforming into a vast mural, a mural filled with human body parts, with arms and hanks of hair and blood and legs, with genitals, both male and female, the genitals spreading till they took it over, and the cry Harbi!

59

echoing, echoing from every side, and it was then that Itemad knew she was dreaming and tried to wake and couldn't.

She tries to stir her arm, her leg; her whole body's numb. Harbi! Harbi! A hand reaches out to her body. The hand of one of the sheikhs. She jerks up in terror. Her daughter Minna is waking her, shaking her by the shoulder. In desperation Minna cries, Mama, wake up!

The days that followed Harbi's murder were terrible for Itemad. She gave in to depression. She refused food and drink, just chopped away at her hair and snorted cocaine in a tiny apartment in Chatby. It was in these dire circumstances that she met Nadia. Thanks to the coke Itemad wasn't all there, and when this woman turned up and introduced herself and said she was her husband's wife, Itemad didn't get it. Nadia sat with her and laid it all out, from her first meeting with Harbi to their relationship and his promise that they'd be married. Itemad pounced: So you were his bit on the side! How does that make you his wife, you dirty bitch?

That was the first meeting. Later, a friendship would grow. They were bound together by memories of the departed and their dreams of him: rising up out of the ocean's depths; descending from the heavens; standing outside the bus station and opening fire on everyone coming into Alexandria; limping as he runs and yet, despite his limp, the government on his tail unable to catch him; pouring kerosene into the sea and igniting it with a match, the fire devouring the whole Corniche; Alexandria is a city aflame with fire and splendor; Harbi emerging from the flames' midst, gigantic, powerful, his leg healed, and suddenly: Harbi! They each awake, sweating. Each drinks a glass of water, says, *In the name of God, the Compassionate and the Merciful*, and goes back to sleep.

The night before Harbi's murder Nadia woke at dawn. She was thirsty. She went to get a drink, picked up a glass, and it fell from her hand and shattered. She bent to gather the broken glass and cut her hand. She left the glass for the morning and washed her hand and went back to sleep. Asleep, she dreamed of broken glass: glass and spilled water and blood and an angry face, scowling and grim. The dream was a nightmare. What is it that makes a dream a nightmare? Nothing, not its story nor its atmosphere nor its protagonists:

it just becomes a nightmare. Some point, some critical moment, when the dream decides to transition, to make the sex change, to switch back on itself. Its inner eunuch surfaces, mocking and scornful, and the Devil's face leans out. Nadia screamed.

The next day she called Sheikh Hassan. She went to see him at the mosque. Told him about the dream. She told him that she was set on Harbi heart and soul, burned for him, yearned to go to him and see him, if only for one minute. A tear fell, single and solitary, then another. She did not wipe them away. She tried to fight it. In a voice that shook she said, If I could just touch his body. Her resistance crumbled. She sobbed, and her face darkened, frowned, grew ugly. Hideous. She fastened her eyes on the mosque's matting and the sheikh was at a loss. He wasn't sure if he should touch her in front of everybody or not. He brought his palm up, made as if he were patting her, then his hand came back to his side and all her defenses fell away.

I couldn't take it anymore. I'd had enough, Inji. My heart was raw, my girl. I spoke to your Uncle Hassan and told him, but what to do? God had spoken. (A moment's silence. She gazes out of the window and moves her lips. She readies herself to utter something, rehearses it inaudibly three times, then turns to Inji and releases it in one go, no faltering, no stammer:) God had spoken and His sentence was being carried out and if you didn't like it there was nothing you could do.

At the time of Harbi's death all Alexandria was asleep. Alexandria had already forgotten its champion and was beginning to return to its daily routine. There was a universally held belief that Harbi's fire had gone out, that he was finished, that, as his friend put it, he wasn't the same. Three young bucks made ready to mount a raid on his symbolic legacy: Sayyid, Sika, and Sultan. The acts of petty gangsterism they engaged in here and there led them to think they were ready to take Harbi's place at the vanguard of Alexandrian history, but their exploits, aside from being petty, did not endure. Harbi's death came to put everything in its proper place. In no time Harbi's legend was abroad, setting Alexandria alight, and anyone who'd once dared, by word, or deed, or gesture, by even the slightest hint, to disrespect him, was cast out, cast into the trashcan of history. Alexandria entered a time of darkness. Black shirts and trousers and gallabiyas came out of closets, the stores and cafés doused their lights at night, and fathers sent their sons to smash the streetlights with bricks. From that moment, Alexandria became a black city.

The tale I'm going to tell you, you won't find written in books or taught at school. It's a tale only we know. If you ask around, there's a thousand who'll tell it to you, but no one will ever write it down.

6

The only one who didn't steer clear of Ali during this period was Abu Amira. Despite everything. Ali was suspicious of everyone. Beyond a doubt, all that time sitting at home had negatively affected his nerves, and the departure of his wife and child had only made it worse. But Abu Amira stuck with him.

Ali walks the streets these days and no one knows him. Abu Amira smiles and says, Good. Let them forget you for a bit. That's better for you. The translation of which, as Ali understands it, is that no one in the neighborhood knowing who he is, is better than them knowing and spitting at him—and he gives a bitter smile. He's forced to rent out his apartment, and with the rent money he resumes operations at the CD store. He fills the place with even more Qurans, grows a trim beard, wears a gallabiya, and sets aside a corner stocked with prayer beads, gallabiyas, and white skullcaps. Ali is a clothes seller at heart and part of his stock he gives to Adel to sell on the pavement in Ramleh Station. What hasn't been mentioned is that Inji's intervention on behalf of the vendors in Saad Zaghloul was in his interest too, as some of their stock belonged to him. Ali watched all this from afar and stored it away. Ali was getting back on his feet, painfully slowly and by no means surely, but what counts is that he was getting back up. Another source of income opened up before him. When pushed, a man can do anything.

It began at home.

At three a.m. the door bell rings. Major Akmal. He comes in, drinks his tea, and broaches the subject: We want you to be our man. . . . There are things that you might know that we don't. We want specific information. We might need it now, but expect us to need it at any time. And of course, Sheikh Ali, anything you need or want, we'll do it for you. Ali has one condition, a red line, if that's the phrase: Abu Amira. That man's welfare is my concern and I don't want him hurt. Major Akmal smiles and places his hand in Ali's.

Ali had lost much of his power back then. And that was for the best. It made him more secure: no enemies; no one on his case; people happier with him. True, he was less involved, but he still knew things: petty dealers, big traders, stores where drugs were hidden, brawls with knives and swords, where and when someone would be and where and when he wouldn't. And so, like this, he was able to expand his store and pull in customers once again.

Major Akmal's home visit was his first and last. Careful to meet somewhere far away from everywhere, Ali and Akmal (in plain clothes, of course) would chat, smoke shisha, have a laugh, and make merry every Thursday night at an upscale tourist café at the beginning of the Cairo Road, by Carrefour. Plus the extra SIM card Ali owned, specifically for calling him. Ali began to emerge from the depression that had claimed him, and rub shoulders with people. The customers began to increase and the Gulfies timidly showed up at his apartment. Ali resumed his activities in the apartment he'd set aside for encounters between the Gulfies and the girls Akmal pointed out to him. He'd lost the passionate backing of the public, sure, but he'd gotten official protection, and with official protection he started to win back a little public backing. It's started to drizzle, as he told Major Akmal, who smiled and said: Because you're doing the right thing, Ali. We only want what's best for you. And he patted Ali's shoulder tenderly. And Ali laughed from his heart.

Like any man, Ali was jealous of his wife's success, and like any man he never admitted it. A part of his life that was over and done with, that's how he saw it. One of these days he'd recover his full strength, his customers, his son, and then and only then would he send Inji her divorce papers. This was the gulf that could never be bridged. The deep and hidden wound in the game of Snakes and Ladders that he played. Once, Adel told him that Inji had defended him (Ali) in his presence and he smiled, but his ill will didn't fade. Before going to sleep, he'd think of Inji and his son. He'd say, She loves me still, I know it, but I'll never forgive her as long as I live. And having reached this conclusion, having convinced himself that it was she who yearned and he who didn't, sleep could claim him, smiling, contented, placid as the angels. When he awoke he'd play with a blue tracksuit she'd left when she walked out and that he'd come across dumped at the bottom of the washing machine. At first he'd sniff it, and when the smell was gone he got in the habit of fondling it with his fingers. He'd never liked the blue tracksuit, but things had changed. A day may come when a man is forced to like what once he hadn't. Such is life.

Ali never said a word to Abu Amira on the subject of Inji. He knew what he would say: Hamada's mother's not in the wrong. If anyone's done wrong it's that dog's daughter, my wife. That's what Abu Amira would say, skirting the unspoken corollary, the fact that he had married a whore who'd sleep with anything that moved. No one brought it up. Ali was grateful to Abu Amira, not because he hadn't killed him on the spot, but because he'd never made a single reference to it. He hadn't put their friendship to the test. Abu Amira understood the true meaning of manliness. Another thing Ali did not speak about to Abu Amira: after his first visit to Major Akmal, he longed to tell his best friend about the confusion he felt. Longed to hear what he had to say, if only one word, a shake of the head. But Abu Amira was as unconquerable as conscience itself. Ali wasn't up to a showdown. Courage is for some.

Listen up and listen good, Sheikh Ali, begins Major Akmal, dragging on a cantaloupe-flavored shisha: We know almost everything about you, and believe me we've a lot of respect for you. I'm not talking about myself here, I'm speaking for the entire Interior Ministry. As far as we're concerned you're the perfect example of a man who makes his own luck—ambitious, knows where he going—and that's rare enough these days.

Ali signals to the waiter to bring a new plug of molasses tobacco for his pipe. Major Akmal leans forward. How's Hamada these days? Ali does not answer. He stammers something. Major Akmal goes on: Don't you want to see him? Ali gives an uncertain smile. He fingers his beard and stares at his nails, says: Is there anyone who wouldn't want to see his son, ya basha?

How lovely. Of course, Sheikh Ali, you know your ex-wife's news better than I do. . . . The atmosphere crackles. The major goes on: Or is she still your wife?

Still, ya basha.

Okay. That's excellent. We want information on her.

How do you mean, information?

Information, Ali. What she's up to, her activities, who's backing her. Get close to her. Grit your teeth and get in there. (He grins.)

. . .

Sheikh Ali. Believe me when I say this isn't a favor for me. It's nothing to do with me. It's a favor for a friend of mine, and in return your son will come back to you and you'll get back to how things were before.

. . .

You know the guys she's slept with? That she's got everyone laughing at you? What she says about you? I didn't want to mention any of that to you and I don't want to tell you any more.

Ali gets the check. It comes and he pays it. He gets up with Akmal and they leave the café.

Ali leans against his car, facing Akmal.

What I understand you to mean, ya basha, is that you want me to inform on my wife. Is that it?

Well, not exactly. You could put it like that.

(Louder) Get close to her and bring you information? You want me to inform on my wife! There's no other way to put it!

Ali . . .

(Shouting hysterically) You want me . . . me! . . . to inform on my wife . . . on my own wife . . . !

(Passersby stop; the café's customers stare.)

Major Akmal walks away. Ali follows him. He grabs his shirt. Akmal reaches for his hip to pull out his gun and Ali beats him to it, whips a jackknife out of his sock. He unclasps it, screaming: You'd shoot me? Me? He swipes with the knife and cuts his shoulder. You've forgotten yourself! You're insane! The name's Miallim Ali, if you've forgotten. Another swipe: another cut in the other shoulder. You want me to start informing on my wife? Me? Major Akmal is running down the middle of the fast lane and Ali after him, and suddenly:

the End that Comes to All. Major Akmal is spread out on the asphalt, sur-rounded by his blood, centimeters from his gun, and the car is driving off. The café's customers are all gathered outside. Ali looks at them. What? he bellows, What are you looking at? and gets into his car. He wheels it round and heads for home, pedal to the metal, knees trembling and heart thumping.

Abu Amira had once told Ali: Let them forget you for a bit. That worked well for Ali, for a time, and under cover of obscurity he got things done, got bigger in his own time and without fuss. But now the opposite is true: remembrance leaps out of its hiding place and is everywhere. The line You want me to inform on my wife? spreads through Alexandria. It's on everybody's lips: businessmen, undersecretaries, taxi drivers, drug dealers, housewives, nurses, and doctors. Ali is back, growing bigger and bigger in people's eyes. They retell the old stories, and the new one. They retell the story of Inji. The first chapter of his history runs into the third, the second utterly effaced, and together we see that people's forgetfulness was not for-getfulness at all, just a slight break in memory, a pause as the historian sets down his pen.

Young Hamada, Hamada Ali Mohamed Sayyid, becomes the star of his class at school. One of the students whispers to Miss: His dad's Sheikh Ali, who killed the cop. Miss is well aware. The teachers try to cozy up to him, to make small talk. What's he thinking, this tight-lipped, chubby child who rarely speaks, whose mother is Inji and whose father is Sheikh Ali? Does he have any conception of what he was destined to become? Hamada gazes at them all and does not speak, disdainfully it seems, and goes home to his mother and tells her all and she hugs him. She tells him about his fore-bears, about his father, about herself. The child asks her about Papa and she answers that they're both upset with one another. Upset why, Mama? And she answers that long ago they fought, then grows flustered and stops.

At that time, as we have mentioned, Sheikh Ali was Alexandria's star in the eyes of all, with the exception of one group: the cops. A taskforce from the vice squad raids the apartment he owns and rounds up the bed-sheet-swaddled johns, and on their way out of Camp Cesar they're fired upon from various positions. It happens without warning: gunfire from everywhere. Ali, who was asleep at the time, wakes up. He dresses and rushes out to join the battle. Standing in his doorway he sees a tall young man. The youth comes up to him and roughly tells him: Stay out of this, Sheikh Ali. Go back inside. No one's going to take your customers and if they try they'll never leave the neighborhood. Ali retreats, the gunfire still spitting back and forth in that little street in Camp Cesar. Under cover of the gunfire the johns take to their heels. The cops lose their heads. They loose off shots in all directions, hitting Abu Amira in the arm, wounding another in the leg, and killing a woman who is standing on her balcony to watch. She falls to earth from the third floor. Only then does the captain, the taskforce's commander, order his men to withdraw.

An uneasy calm descended on Camp Cesar in the days that followed. Life was elsewhere: on Facebook, blogs, and in the independent press. Someone (was he put up to it?) managed to take photos at the scene of the woman's shooting and her fall from the third floor, and the news spread throughout the country. The police raided a safe house (the patrons fled) and when local residents tried to defend themselves, the police killed another woman in her own home. Without any great show, without unsettling the daily routine, unfamiliar types began to fill the street. Tall men carrying automatic weapons were everywhere. The street became an armed encampment, smoldering, preparing for another assault by the police. It had become clear that another piece of lunacy on the part of the cops would end in a massacre, particularly now that Egyptian public opinion was inflamed against them. The day after the battle, Ali himself received a visitor. The visitor, a man of few words, was adamant: There's a chance they'll summon you for the investigation into the major that was killed. Don't go. Don't leave your house to go anywhere. We can protect you here just fine, and nobody can get close. Before he left, the visitor added, briefly: By the way, Sheikha Inji says hello. Ali smiled.

Ali did not leave the house. He watched the weapons flood the little street, the banners hung up over storefronts. A code was fixed on. "Zamalek" meant the government and "United" was our team, us: Sheikh Ali and Abu Amira, Madame Inji and Itemad and Nadia, the ferry drivers, Sheikh Hassan, falafel vendors, whores, and political activists.

Welcome One and All to Camp Cesar . . . All Except Zamalek
Alexandria Is the Graveyard of Zamalek
United Rule the Land . . . We're Your Lords and Masters, Scum

And so on and so on, and on every sign a portrait of Sheikh Ali.

Abu Amira with his injured arm visited Ali at home. Ali rolled him a joint and passed it over. Abu Amira asked Ali why he hadn't told him that he'd worked with Major Akmal. Ali didn't answer: he was busy trying and failing to capture the ball in a cell phone game. He tossed the phone. He was quiet for a moment then he looked at him and said: I couldn't do it, Abu Amira. I was ashamed to tell you. Abu Amira nodded. He picked up Ali's phone. He opened the game and started playing. He played for a minute, then pressed pause and started sucking on the joint.

The neighborhood can't cope, Ali.
(Ali looks at him.)
The guys protecting the neighborhood aren't from here, and those who are don't know anything about guns.
. . .
The government will take control in no time. You need another spot.
Leave, you mean?
You'll leave, and I'll leave too. Don't get me wrong. There's a guy who wants to take your apartment. Sell it and move to another neighborhood. It's no big deal.

Ali got up. He went into the bathroom. He sat on a chest and buried his head in his hands. He raised his head and spat on the floor. From the other room came the sound of Abu Amira's voice:
Your wife Inji wants to see you. I told her to stop by tomorrow. She'll bring the kid.

Feverish preparations swept through the neglected apartment. Ali asked Abu Amira to send him a girl, who got the apartment spick and span in mere hours. He sent his clothes to be washed and brought in a supply of cake

69

and soda, which saw at least part of his fridge stocked at last. He played the Quran for three hours straight, hoping that it might still his beating heart, but of course, nothing worked.

At seven the doorbell rang. Inji walked in wearing a black niqab and a baggy black cloak, Hamada in her wake. She said hello and Ali, hearing her voice, remembered everything: the eyes, the delicate nose, Ain Shams, the train at Ramses Station; the old days. He attempted to approach his son but the boy shrank back and sought refuge with his mother. Inji sat on the couch and in firm tones began to talk:

You have to move, Sheikh Ali. The people here won't cope with what's coming. They're with you, but that's not enough. The folk in Karmouz are better prepared and they'll be better able to protect you; plus, over there it's more secure. Abu Amira told me there's a buyer for the apartment and that he's made a decent offer. Sell it and come to me in Karmouz. Take the floor above my center. It would be the best thing for you and me both.

Perhaps you don't know what it is you've done, Sheikh Ali. What I can tell you is that there's a war on and that it won't do to back down now. If we don't strike hard we could be crushed, and we won't know how to strike in a neighborhood that's not secure.

There's going to be a war in Alexandria. And it won't do to have you fighting this war on your own. Your chances would be slim. I might join in myself—a brief, snatched laugh. Picking on something my own size, you might say.

Inji is silent for a long, long time and suddenly, in a voice that shakes: Ali . . . Ali looks up. I'm sorry, Ali, but I really can't forgive you.

Forgiveness is something that God grants. God.

Everything comes from God. No one disputes this. No one has the strength to dispute it. Forgiveness, though, is the only thing that man has no hand in at all. God is the Forgiving, the Pardoner, and by His grace alone shall he for whom thou harbored enmity be as thy closest friend, and of course all those who figured in Alexandria's history back then were believers. Ali was unable to defend himself before Inji. He turned his face away and rose to make her tea. When he returned she'd unfastened her niqab.

She looked as she had four years before, her face filled out a touch, faint wrinkles upon her lips, and black kohl tracking a tiny line down her cheek. The boy sidled up to him. He reached his hand out to Ali's beard and Ali tried to hug him but he shrank back once more into the arms of his mother, who this time pushed him away. Won't you give Papa a kiss? The child sidled up to him, kissed him quick, and returned to his mother. Inji smiled, a tearful, radiant smile. He'll be used to you in no time, she said, and patted Ali and took him in her arms. He said: I've missed you so much.

Hagga Itemad agreed to sign over ownership of her building's second floor to Ali, and for a reasonable price. Bit by bit she was losing her foothold in her own building, but it didn't worry her. She was, like all Alexandrians, ever eager to feel the winds of change even if those winds might blow—at first—against her.

No one ever does anything to win God's good graces alone. Even in moments such as these, so charged with grand patriotic hopes, everyone was looking for what they could get in return, and it was this, the return, that made the difference and determined how things ran. The hagga asked Inji to hang a large portrait of her over the building's entrance and Inji agreed. The hagga sensed that history was being written, and a single line on her was fair. This was the return she asked for. She asked nothing for herself, no creature comfort; everything she asked for was in order that she might see her children honored after she was gone.

A pickup carried the furniture from Camp Cesar to the home in Karmouz. What little furniture there was (Ali had begun to sell it off in recent months) was transported in a single load, seen off with gunfire; banners of farewell; song, dance, and tears; livestock sacrificed in the street and blood-dipped palms printed on the walls.

The Suzuki pickup moves along the Corniche, Ali standing on a sofa on the back with his gallabiya, his beard, his headscarf fluttering in the breeze, and a machine gun. Before him stretches a line of cars, another line behind, and one and all are firing in the air, while Ali and three other men loom over everyone with a gigantic tape deck: Emad Barour warbling for all of Alexandria's inhabitants, the sea, and its spray to hear: Ali ya Ali ya Ali Ali ya Ali Ali ya Ali ya Ali Ali ya Ali . . . and when he gets to Where's that Ali? there are gunshots and the men cry out, make flames spurt from gas canisters, and the pedestrians along the Corniche point up at Ali as they dance. Nothing matters. The sheikh and his three men standing there in the face of all-comers, the government and their foes. Today, a new history begins and the residents of Karmouz greet the newcomer with palm branches.

What's up with my sweetheart?
What's with him, tell . . . .
What's up with my sweetheart?
What's with him, tell . . . .
He caught me!
Oh my!
He caught me!
Oh my!
On the balcony, saw me standing,
Tossed a lemon as I stood there.
I decided it was rash and stupid
To pledge my poor heart to his care . . . .
To pledge my poor heart to his care . . . .
He scared me and I said, I'll leave him,
But how can I go back and get him?
One day perhaps he'll just ignore
The people when they stop and stare.
The people when they stop and stare . . . .

Be as spoilt as you like, take your time, take your time,
Light my fire and make me burn, take your time, take your time . . . .

Ali ya Ali ya Ali Ali ya Ali
Ali ya Ali ya Ali Ali ya Ali

You know your eyes, dear, they haunt my heart, dear,
Your love's a thing apart, dear: no cure.

You know that I know: how could I leave you
So soon, dear? You're my life and lord . . . .

Oh . . . Uncle, my uncle, uncle of them all,
King, oh my king, oh king of them all.

Ali ya Ali ya Ali Ali ya Ali
Ali ya Ali ya Ali Ali ya Ali

At Manshiya the car takes a left and ululations start to ring out. The streets
grow narrower and the Suzuki spends most of the time stationary, the men
dancing in front of it, alongside it, with their guns, the approaching tram
pulling to a halt, the passengers, driver, and conductor piling out to join the
procession, and . . . Ali ya Ali ya Ali Ali ya Ali.

At the entrance to Karmouz Ali gets down and proceeds on foot, ringed
around by his men and friends and loved ones: Abu Amira, Sousou, Adel,
Sheikh Hassan, and everyone else, those he knows and those he doesn't.

At the entrance to the building a banner has been hung up in welcome:
The Inji Center welcomes Alexandria's finest son, Sheikh Ali al-Sayyid. Ali
goes in, Abu Amira and Sheikh Hassan at his side, while the rest of them
party on outside. A large portrait of Hagga Itemad that hangs in the lobby
catches his eye. Abu Amira looks at him. Ali makes no comment. On the
third floor, at the door to the apartment, he stops. Ghada opens the door.
Ali doesn't know her. Ululations start up inside. Hagga Itemad, Madame
Nadia, and other women are sitting there, Inji among them in her niqab.
Her face is turned to the floor. Ali comes up to her, takes her right hand,
kisses it, and—softly though audibly, in a voice everyone can hear—says:
I'm sorry, my lady. Inji looks at him. Behind the niqab her eyes smile. Play-
fully she says, Whatever for, Sheikh Ali? and he laughs. Just let it go. And
everyone laughs. Ghada and the girls dance and the men withdraw to rejoin
the party down below. Only Ali remains. Inji takes off the niqab. She ties it
round her waist and dances. Carole Samaha is playing—Oh Ali, cousin Ali,
who runs through my veins—and Inji gestures to Ali, leans over him, teases,
and the women grab his hands. Dance, Sheikh Ali! Go on dance, ya sheikh,

and he rises, Hamada on his shoulder and lifts his headscarf and drapes it over Inji, knots it round her head, moves her back and back again, and she moves with him. He leans toward her and she leans toward him. He binds her head and his together with the headscarf and kisses her behind it and the boy's foot drums on his mother's shoulder. He laughs from on high, and claps his hands.

The loveliest people.

7

Of course, things didn't go quite so smoothly at first. Ali and Inji took a while to get used to one another. Certain incentivizing factors were in place to set the old familiarity flourishing between them: a shared interest in the boy, in TV serials, in petty squabbles.

After everyone had departed Inji was silent. She didn't speak. The boy slept and she fell silent and her silence dragged on for hours: nothing but the plainest pleasantries. Ali assumed that she was shy. He asked her where the kitchen was and impassively she answered, Right next to you. He didn't understand and she snapped: The door behind you, brother. . . . What's wrong? he asked and she said, Ali, I need you to understand. Ali, things between us aren't like they used to be. Things have changed.

Meaning?

Meaning we have to take care how we treat each other in front of others, you especially.

(He pats her hair and she thrusts his hand away.)

Today of all days you shouldn't have joked with me like that. What do you mean by telling me to let it go?

. . .

You could have said that you regret it, that you're angry at yourself, but how could you make everyone laugh at me like that?

They weren't laughing at you. They were happy.

Oh yeah? So when the girl who works for me says, Let it go, for his sake, and laughs, she's just happy, too? Why was it so hard for you to say, I'm sorry?

I said I'm sorry.

Say it again.

You wish. Sweetheart, if I did wrong to the president himself I'd never say it twice.

(Shouting) So you did wrong? Or didn't you? Which is it?

No, I didn't.

Eh? What's this? So it was my mother who did wrong then, is that it?

Keep a civil tongue in your head.

(She twists her mouth.) I'm civil enough, no thanks to you.

The conversation is over. She gets up to open his luggage, bag by bag. She takes out his clothes and throws them on the couch. Suddenly, a flea bites her. She looks in disgust at the open bag, then, with suppressed rage, at him. He looks at the floor, embarrassed at the dog's life he's been living: no cleaning, no care, no bathing, no laundry. Then, from nowhere, he's looking her squarely in the eye and bellowing:

No, no. I didn't do anything wrong. You're the one who didn't take care of my needs, who forced me to turn to that woman.

And why was that, do you think? You were like some rutting bull—more, always wanting more, till I had to make my excuses. I couldn't take any more.

I don't think so, sweetheart. Miss High-and-Mighty here was fed up with all the nasty common people and wanted to go back to Mommy and Daddy. She couldn't stand me and she couldn't stand the people here.

Where was this? How can you . . . ? You piece of shit, I was sleeping with you the day before you started with her.

Three days, missy. I worked it out. And anyway, I always had to ask for it. You never once came to me of your own accord and told me you missed me.

The day before. Focus, baba. I came to you and you sat there joking around and said, I'm tired.

I don't think so. Plus, you were wearing the blue tracksuit and you know I don't like it.

First off, I'd lost that tracksuit. When I walked out I left it with you. I don't even know where it is.

(Mocking) And secondly?

(Turning away) I don't know. There isn't any secondly.

So shut your mouth. Don't make me insult your religion.

And don't make me insult yours, sixty times over.

(Roaring with rage) Sixty times over? What's that supposed to mean? There's no such thing as insulting my religion sixty times over in the first place.

(She stares at him defiantly and suddenly hears what he's just said, and laughs.) Know what? You're unbelievable.

(The look of rage lingers in his eyes. Seconds pass and he smiles. Seconds pass and he laughs.)

A word here and a word there, all helped sweeten the atmosphere between them. But unity in the face of dangers did its work as well. The government had planted spies in the neighborhood, a lot of spies, more spies than Inji's men knew about, planted in the café across the road from the Inji Center. When an informer was unmasked it was like a holiday. One of the men would pick a quarrel with him and, in the middle of it, expose him, and the man's existence in the neighborhood would become a living hell. Sometimes it would end in blood. A small nick to the face would end an agent's operations in the neighborhood. The massacre was yet to start, though all the signs suggested it was near.

A minor clarification: the time that Ali had spent isolated, from life, from people, from his wife and son, had not been wasted. He had listened to stories about Alexandria and its inhabitants, had roamed the cafés and sat and struck up conversation, and had memorized the histories of the streets he walked: as if making up for a lack, not only in his education, but in his own less-than-irreproachably-Alexandrian roots. He had begun to create these roots for himself. He was like a schoolboy, struggling and sweating over his books, his heart a university of popular lore. The tale that stood out most from that period was the tale of Karantina: a fully formed Alexandrian community uprooted from its native soil and scattered into an exile that spanned the length and breadth of Alexandria itself.

Where had Karantina's residents gone after they had been plucked out of their shacks and a school complex had been built in their place? How had they been absorbed into the many tributaries of Alexandrian life? Had they been absorbed at all? Was it still possible to bring them back into the fold of their original habitat? How might that happen? Ali consulted Inji about calling the café that faced the Inji Center, Karantina. He went further, suggesting that the Inji Center itself be renamed the Karantina Center. Inji, who did not discount the possibility that spousal jealousy lay behind the desire to efface her name, refused. At first. But Ali was persuasive. He outlined his idea:

I've been reading a lot, Inshi. I've read a ton, about everything, and I know everything. Karantina was a big deal. A really big deal. The people there were solid folk; lovely people. I sat with some of them. They want the best for us and they love you. They really love you. And they're handy. They can turn their hands to anything. When we name our center after their neighborhood they'll come. They'll come and gather round us, and anyone who hasn't heard of you yet will hear. Inshi, there's a war coming and we need men to stand with us. Men and guns.

Inji is silent. She looks on the verge of being convinced. Ali seizes the chance and drops another bombshell.

And there's the picture on the front of the building.

What picture?

The portrait of Hagga Itemad. It has to go.

And why is that?

Fine, my girl, leave it up. But we'll put another picture next to it. Abu Amira's done a lot for us and he deserves a portrait.

Ali, I'm not going to discuss this!

. . .

You'll drive me crazy. Isn't that the pimp who got you to sleep with his wife?

He divorced her when he found out.

No. He divorced her when you told him to divorce her. He knew from the beginning.

Abu Amira's my friend, Inji. Don't talk about him like that. I won't hear a word against him.

Your friendship's between you and him. Hagga Itemad made me promise. She told me her portrait had to stay up there by itself.

And wasn't it Hagga Itemad who turned you against me?

She helped me grow up.

And what's it to me? I don't owe her anything. She wants to flatter you and charm you away from me. And just so you know, it's not just Abu Amira's portrait we'll be putting up. Sheikh Hassan's too. One entire floor of this building is mine: my property; I own it.

Ali, please don't make such a big deal out of this.

(In disgust) It's you that's making it a big deal.

And that is how things really were; that was the situation, with the massacre approaching and the government plotting to intervene and destroy the happy family from within. On the surface, the situation facing the government appeared to be complicated: weapons on the rise, men multiplying, and Ali and Inji's popularity sky-high. But nothing is impossible. It only needed one informer sitting at the café, striking up a conversation with some newcomer (he wouldn't dare try the regulars), and asking about the owner of the computer and language center in the building opposite. A man and his wife, the man replies: two saintly sheikhs who work for the good of the neighborhood and those who live here. The conversation meanders and the snoop utters the golden words: I know them. They're our neighbors in Akhmim. His father was killed in Cairo and the son hasn't taken his taar. Where I come from, no one will respect the man you can say that about. Where we come from, my friend, in the South, taar's something fundamental. Anyone who hasn't taken his taar gets no respect from anyone.

A rough voice behind him threatens to blow the deal: Who's the sweetheart who doesn't like the sheikh? Alarmed, the snoop ends the conversation, but the news travels rapidly. The news spreads. The news can't be controlled. This is the way the world has always been. Ali starts hearing things. A word here. A word there. He tells Inji, who turns her face away and says, Ten years we've been here and you haven't taken your taar. How long do you expect people to wait? Ali starts to panic. He's caught in a cleft stick: he either risks losing his good standing with the people or he wastes valuable energy in the South, in a place he knows nothing about, a gamble that might cost him his life and at the very least—for certain—will leave the Alexandrian front unguarded, so the government can raze the entire neighborhood.

The massacre, then, isn't approaching at all. The government's playing a smarter game than blood and bullets. A distinguished journalist writes in a national daily about one "Sheikh Ali," the man with Southern roots who leads a gang of thugs in Alexandria while incapable of taking his own taar, thus failing the first question in the Southern test of honor. In the bathroom, Ali plucks a few white hairs from his beard. He remembers it all. His whole history, black and white, leading up to this moment. He punches the mirror over the sink. It breaks, and he cuts his chin. A terrible cry rings out, its echo bouncing, bouncing: No one will break me! . . . Rake me! . . . Ake me! Did the cry come from Ali's mouth or had it echoed inside him? No one knows, not even Ali himself. For sure, no one heard it but him.

He dresses quickly, glances at his wife's sleeping body, and descends. By the time he reaches Camp Cesar the dawn call has sounded. In the mosque's washroom he spies Abu Amira. The two of them fall in step together, water dripping from the rolled sleeves of their cloaks. Ali leans in and says: After prayers we should sit together for a bit. I need to ask your advice.

At Abu Amira's apartment they sit together. Ali lays out the problem and Abu Amira nods. When Ali finishes talking he makes no comment. He is silent for a long time, ten minutes or so, then says: Tomorrow, after the afternoon prayer call, God willing, I'll be at your place and I'll have the solution to this problem of yours. Ali's eyes gleam. He goes up and pats his shoulder, but Abu Amira draws back. Two minutes later he resumes: I've never once asked for anything in return for a favor. But this time I will.

Long story short, Abu Amira wants to take the mission on himself. Ali cuts him off, saying that he needs him here in Alexandria. Abu Amira continues. He won't be traveling to Sohag: his brother Sousou will. Sousou's been involved in things like this before, but this time he'll have the starring role; plus, it's an opportunity for Abu Amira to bring his brother on. Is Ali still the Ali of old? Is Abu Amira still the Abu Amira of old? Fine, so why stand in the way of our sons and younger brothers growing up and being like us? Am I right? Abu Amira leans back on the sofa and speaks on:

I'm thinking of bringing the kid Sousou on a bit. He'll do things just as you want them in the South. If you tell him, Kill the governor, he'll kill him. All he wants is a stall in the street. Liver and sausage sandwiches, snacks, stuff like that, and he can look after you at the same time.

Ali was clipping his nails. He clipped all his nails and there was just one left, hanging from his little finger. He bit it off and spat it into the bottom of a tiny coffee cup on the table. He gathered all his clippings in the cup, drew a toothpick off the table, and started scraping his teeth clean. He was talking as he scraped and his words came out unclear:

No, Abu Amira, not just Sousou. You'll come here too, and I'll open a clothes store in your name. It'll be for you and your brother Adel, once he gets out of jail, God willing. Plus another little store for Sousou. I want you three by my side. But there's a condition. Just like I found my dad lying dead outside his store, I don't want to hear that there's a single member of the Amin family still alive. I don't want one of those faggots saying that Sheikh Ali doesn't know how to take his taar. Right, my friend?

Right.

From today, you're one of my men. You and your brothers are my most important men.

. . .

Maybe I wasn't able to tell you that before, or maybe the time wasn't right. Maybe I was just waiting for the moment. But I'm telling you now. I don't know what I would have done without you, Abu Amira.

. . .

If God took me back in time, maybe I'd do everything the same. (A moment's silence.) Maybe none of us chooses his fate. But that's why God gives us the good and bad, and the smart man's the one who praises Him for the good and puts up with the bad.

. . .

Could be everything in my life has been bad. Could be I've been caught up in things that are too big for me. But it's enough that God brought you into my life.

. . .

(He tosses the toothpick aside and, with a nail clipping, hooks a scrap of meat from between his back teeth.) You might be one of my men, but the truth is I learned it all from you. The truth is that I was always the youngster and you were the older man.

Sheikh Ali . . . .

(He places the scrap of meat at the bottom of the coffee cup.) Speak to your brother, Abu Amira. Make sure he travels to Sohag at the beginning of next week. If this business gets sorted it'll be a debt on my honor, and I won't forget it.

Sheikh Ali . . . .

I'm off to bed now, Abu Amira. (He smiles.) Forgive me, my friend, I haven't slept for three days straight. You stay just where you are, but turn the lights out when you leave.

What Abu Amira wanted to tell Ali, but couldn't, was an old tale that dated back to the time the two first met.

We will tell you here a short tale, a tale of Fate and Signs, of children who meet their deaths, of fathers of a spiritual bent, and of young men who believe only in what they can see with their own eyes.

On June 15, 2005, Amira passed away: Abu Amira's daughter, and the reason he was known by that name. She had never been ill in her life. She just played with the junction box beneath the house and died. Electrocuted. Abu Amira wasn't a fanciful man—he never had the slightest suspicion of foul play, for instance—but nor was he naïve. When it happened he realized that his daughter's death was more than just the death of his child; it represented the possible fate of thousands like her. Who leaves a junction box lying open, for example? Wasn't it more than likely that this oversight might claim dozens of victims in the street, and that other similar oversights might claim dozens more? Okay then, so what was it had driven the little girl to play in the street when she should have been at school? Was it not the crumbling education system, the system that drove thousands of young learners to drop out every year, and the crumbling economic system that left thousands of fathers unable to pay their offspring's school fees?

Who was responsible for his daughter's death? To his mind, everything indicated that this business was more than just a child meeting her death due to some unfortunate oversight. The story here might easily become the story of all the nation's children, exposed to death at any moment. These ideas never occurred to Abu Amira in this form. They were just intimations. With every passing moment he felt his wretchedness redoubled: his, and that of those about him; the wretchedness of his work and theirs, the wretchedness of his life and theirs, of his family and their families. It was hard to take, to know that people like us had no way to live or raise their kids right. So he said to Umm Amira, in the course of a candid chat some months later. She gave him a pat on the shoulder and he was sure that she felt exactly as he felt, if not more so.

On June 15, 2006, he saw Ali for the first time. Sousou brought him home. Introduced him as Bashmuhandis Ali. It was the first anniversary of Amira's death, but Abu Amira locked his grief up in his heart. They drank and smoked and Abu Amira asked Ali what he thought of the neighborhood. Ali didn't hide his dislike: the neglect, the trash on every side and, most dangerous of all, the open junction boxes wherever you went. They could kill the small children who played in the street. That night was the first anniversary of Amira's death and Abu Amira believed in signs.

A few days later, Adel needed a plastic bag to keep his tapes and T-shirts in when he was out and about. He searched the whole apartment and found nothing. Abu Amira spotted Amira's old schoolbag, forsaken, dusty, and dumped beneath the couch. He said that Adel could use it for the time being and, to help him, began emptying out its contents: notebooks, a textbook, a pencil, a pencil sharpener, an eraser, and a sheet of paper. Abu Amira gave the bag to Adel and began to examine the sheet of paper. There was a drawing on it, a man and a woman, and between them a small, chubby child. When he saw the drawing something thumped in Abu Amira's chest. Something called Ali. The man his daughter drew at least three years before she died was the man he'd met just days before. He didn't speak about it to anybody. He kept quiet. When Inji gave birth to her son the sketched-out scene was complete. Before her death a little girl had drawn the family that would avenge her blood. You could almost say she'd prophesied. For sure, you could.

Later, Ali would take it upon himself to repair the open junction box, yet another sign to add to the album of signs that Abu Amira kept in his head and that would lead him to say to Sheikh Hassan, as he chatted to him one evening after prayers, that Ali is one of God's saints, then tell him the following brief tale:

Last night I saw the Prophet, Sheikh. He approached me and there was this little kid with him. The deceased. I asked her, So you don't miss your dad then, Amira my girl? That's why you didn't come and celebrate your birthday with us this year? Dad, she says, God willing we'll all celebrate together. But you take care to look after Sheikh Ali, now, if you want God to look after you. And I look at the Prophet and I see that he's laughing and his teeth are strong and shining. When I woke up I went to pray two rakaas to God and my mind was perfectly at ease.

8

Taar, or honor killing, is a story of its own, one from which Egypt has suffered greatly, particularly in the poor and ignorant South, etcetera, etcetera, and Ali did not know much about it, about taar in the Old South. He welcomed Sousou into his home and told him about the Amin family, about a taar that dated back some twenty years. Not a word more than any child in Akhmim could have told you. This made Sousou's task all the harder, but a job was a job. Before he left, Ali said, smiling, Ask after my family when you're there: the al-Aleilis. See how they're doing, good or bad, and how people view them.

Sousou's train for Sohag leaves in two hours' time. He'll arrive today and over the next couple of days his men will all follow him down. It's dawn, mid-January. Sousou's dressed in jeans, a thick leather jacket, and a headscarf. Before he leaves the house he ties the headscarf across his face and for days afterward Ali won't be able to recall anything but this face—this half face—and his slight limp as he departs. He will spend much time trying to recall Sousou's real face and will not succeed. In this, perhaps, there is something of the divine, for the Sousou who leaves will not be the Sousou who returns. He will disappear utterly and someone else will take his place. Time changes everything.

Half an hour after Sousou departs, Ali goes off to attend the dawn prayers. When he gets back he's swaying slightly. He puts himself to bed and sleeps. Collapses, is more like it. Inji senses his presence. She gets up and looks at him and finds him deep asleep. She smiles. Tender Inji. So very tender.

*

What was it Ali meant by saying, "Ask after my family when you're there, the al-Aleilis. See how they're doing, good or bad, and how people view them"? The words sounded most peculiar to Sousou's ear, and more generally too, given their context, if we were permitted to examine them from a distance—without our being involved, I mean; without our being part of the scene or one of its protagonists.

The night before, Inji spoke with Ali. Smiling, she said that she was jealous of Sousou. Why, my Nouja? I wanted to go to the South. (A pause.) Ali, haven't you ever wondered about your forebears in the South? Your family there, I mean. How long have those people lived there? Who was your family's founder? Naturally, Ali had never given any of these things the slightest thought, but he narrowed his eyes and said he'd thought of little else from boyhood on; then, sensing he was being less than sufficiently convincing, he tacked on some details: When my father would leave me alone in the store I'd stare at this portrait on the wall. Just stare and stare. It was a portrait of your father standing next to mine, as kids, hugging one another. And I'd sit and say to myself, I wonder, their father, my grandfather, what did he look like? What did he do and where did he live?

He was in the South, of course!

Yes. You think I don't know that? What's the point of saying that?

It's not that you don't know, it's just . . .

It's not that I don't know, it's just that you know everything . . . isn't that right?

No, it's not.

Of course it's not right. You don't know anything. You think you understand the South? Okay then . . . your family, and not so distant either, where did they live before they came to Akhmim?

Well, of course I don't know. What kind of question is that?

(A short, mocking laugh.)

You don't know either, if it comes to that.

(A brief silence, then he lifts his gaze to meet hers.) That's right, I don't. But at least I don't say I know when I haven't a clue.

(A short, mocking laugh.)

(He gives a snort of contempt . . . but silently.)

A Savior. . . .

The truth is that all the peoples of the world, at one time or another, have put their faith in a savior, most especially in those eras of decline when no hope remains but hope itself. The burning desire for a savior is a well-documented anthropological phenomenon, with its own religious symbols—Jesus Christ; the Mashiach, deliverer of the Jews; the Mahdi; al-Hakim bi-Amr Illah—and secular symbols too: Nasser, Guevara, Mao, even Abdel Halim and Elvis Presley. It is hope that makes people—tottering beneath the yoke of injustice and tyranny—turn their thoughts to salvation. In those days, a song by a Lebanese singer, one of those video-clip hits, was being widely played. The lyrics of the song ran, Yes, my love, there's hope, when we're together in the morning, pet me and say sweet nothings. . . . .

In one of Alexandria's bygone eras, at ten a.m. one Friday, an individual by the name of Abu Khaira made his way to the mosque of al-Morsi Abul Abbas in Bahari. With him were two fellows who'd stayed up with him the night before popping pills, and as the sun rose all three had become convinced that the time had come, that all this injustice would now pass away. They reached the mosque's locked door and pounded on it. No one opened. They kicked it and one of them fetched a mighty hammer with which they battered away until it burst asunder (two of them performing this operation while the third stood at a distance to threaten anyone thinking of coming closer). The three of them entered the mosque. Abu Khaira ascended the minbar and, moved by curiosity, the people piled into the mosque. Abu Khaira gave the call to prayer, then chanted, God is great, God is great and to God be praise, and looked out at the congregation: Enough, Alexandria. We've had enough. The crowd started to swell as Abu Khaira launched forth on his Friday sermon, an hour and a half before its appointed time. He said, first, that Friday sermons were a heresy; that he'd gone to Saudi Arabia and seen a Friday sermon there that had lasted no longer than five minutes and that the people there had been talking, the whole way through they'd argued and talked—everyone just chattering away, he said, chat chat chat and no one did a thing about it. The Prophet's example is wonderful, he said, but the people don't follow it, and then they wonder why their Lord won't help them. . . .

The night before, Abu Khaira had mixed a variety of chemical substances with booze, and as he delivered his sermon he felt dizzy. He swayed forward until he nearly fell, staggered back, fell silent for a minute, then heaved up his guts, the puke falling on some of the congregation. Then he resumed. Enough! Enough! It's time for this dawn to sing! Children of Mohamed, hear me! I say now that I've had enough and if anyone speaks to me out of turn, by my mother's womb he'll regret it. Enough, Alexandria, enough! Then he passed out. He tumbled down the minbar's steps and lay there, wedged halfway down, asleep.

It is hard to pinpoint with any certainty the signs foretelling that two persons would appear one day to restore glory to this forgotten city by the sea, but we are aided in our task by interpretation, just as interpretation aided the inhabitants of Alexandria, too. Sheikh Abu Khaira's sermon, the Lebanese chanteuse's song, the people's dreams—all pointed to the fact that Alexandria had entered the Age of the Savior. And the Savior, charged with giving voice to the people's dreams, with leading his people to the light, must be someone. Someone, meaning not just anyone—someone of good stock; though he be poor, though modest, his pedigree must be established, rooted in history; rooted, moreover and most especially, in Alexandrian history. The city's savior must be a son of the city. Ali and Inji were nonesuch. And this was no small problem. Let us see how things pan out.

The phone line between Sheikh Ali and Sousou was always open in the days that followed.

Bored or busy, Sousou makes his calls, asking more or less meaningless questions to dispel, perhaps, the sense of isolation that he—born to the stink of brine and fish guts—feels in the arid South. Each day he charges the phone with twenty pounds of credit and talks. Sometimes Ali's at the center, sometimes at the café, sometimes he's left his cell phone at home or in the office—and sometimes Inji picks up instead. Okay, well, this happens a lot, not "sometimes."

One day Inji answers and Sousou tells her all about the place, about the good-hearted people there, about the links and bonds between them that he's trying to puzzle out. He tells her about the old man, her old man, her grandfather's father, Bekheit, the man they all talk about down there. He owned farms and villages, land and livestock, but God denied him children. Inji says, Denied him children how, Sousou, if he's my great-grandfather? And Sousou is at a loss. Yeah, well the guy who told me the story put it like that, but look here, I'll ask him to explain tomorrow, because he skipped that bit. Silence, then he goes on: Maybe your great-grandmother already had kids when she married him. A lot of people do that. The South has changed a lot, you know. And he talks and talks, he burbles on, and Inji listens. She butts in to set him straight on something, or lets him finish without setting him straight. Sousou's a talker and he's entertaining and Inji spends hours with him in back-and-forth. Has there been some kind of softening between them? Time will tell. We only know what time sees fit to tell us. We're just the messenger.

And with time, the tales that Sousou passes on—to Ali and Inji both—grow more detailed. No sooner does he hear a new tale than he rushes to the phone, charges it, and speaks. Is Sousou soft in the head? No, he's just a carefree young man who loves to talk and Inji knows it. Inji loves to hear the stories of Bekheit, the great forefather, the sacred source, and Sousou, as we've established, is entertaining. He tells jokes, skips smoothly from one subject to the next. Nothing checks him. Inji engages, and Inji wouldn't engage if there weren't some softening there. Time tells.

While this is taking place, Ali is with the workmen. The nature of their operations is gradually changing. The Inji Center for Computers and Languages becomes the Karantina Center, and the Karantina Center is dominated by its café—formerly the cafeteria and cyber center—as the center's role in teaching computers and languages slowly shrinks. The café spreads out like a spiderweb, a snake, a serpent; it commandeers two floors and the language courses are either filled or, increasingly, not filled. But, customers fill the café. They smoke shisha, drink and play, watch soccer matches and the chosen few are taken up to the center's girls on the second floor. Abu Amira's portrait is hung over the building's entrance next to

Hagga Itemad's, plus one of Ali with his beard and Inji in niqab beneath the legend: *Say, I take refuge with the Lord of the Dawn*. Karmouz, it is clear, has entered a new phase. With just one café, designed and built with the very latest techniques, you can bring modernity to an ancient, indigent neighborhood. It is the dream of modernization all over again.

Do you love Egypt, Sousou?
It's my country, Sheikh. It's where my people come from.
Do you love your people then?
They're my people, Sheikh. They're the people who live with me in my country.
Ah, Sousou. My good fellow.
I love you, Abu Hamada.

Conversations between Sousou and Ali were, in addition to their practical benefits, studded with many delightful sallies and pointed merriment.

Bekheit. Bekheit was the secret that Sousou brought to Ali in the days that followed. Great-grandfather Bekheit had been no Southerner born and bred; he was a newcomer from the North. By God's grace, Sousou added, I'll get hold of a piece of information that will make you very happy. You'll say prayers for me when you find out what it is, but be patient. Ali waited patiently and then, a few days later, Sousou called again. I've discovered all, Sheikh Ali. This Bekheit of yours was Alexandrian, from Bahari no less. What do you think of that then, boss?

Ali had never trusted Sousou. He didn't think he was a traitor, but he didn't hold him in great esteem. He didn't see in him the man he saw in Abu Amira, for example. He recognized his talent for assassinations, for seducing kids with drugs or sex, and for outwitting the government—anything involving action—but there was something critical that Sousou lacked: a level head. Sousou was a sucker for the juicy detail, not plain facts. A fatal weakness in a job like this, said Ali to himself.

On this occasion the facts were on Sousou's side and, more important than the facts, the narrative: a coherent story. The great-grandfather had been an officer, a yuzbashi, transferred from Alexandria to Sohag, where he married and started a family. Sousou did the rounds, asking after the family's origins. No one knew further back than Bekheit. One old woman could recall the day he'd come to Akhmim, a radiant youth with tarboosh, mustache pricked up, and gleaming brass buttons. The young Bekheit, exceptionally charming as he was, soon endeared himself to the locals and one of them in particular took his fancy: Ahmed Zaki's daughter, Fatima. He sent a letter to his parents in Alexandria, telling them he'd found the life he was looking for down there in the South, that he was fed up with life up there—they preferred his younger brother over him, one of his many insecurities—and that he had vowed to his Lord that he would never again set foot on Alexandrian soil, even if it were for work, even if it meant the hangman's noose. His father replied with a letter in which he stated that he no longer considered him a son and that he gave him over to God's care, but that this would not prevent him—as a Muslim and a man who feared God—from granting him his share of his inheritance. When the father died, Bekheit's brothers visited him at his home in Akhmim and gave him what they called his share. And he accepted. He didn't argue. He didn't protest.

In the conversations between Sousou and Inji the information came thick and fast, but the details were different, from encounters with quite different people. The Alexandrian great-grandfather wasn't from Bahari, exactly, but Kom al-Dikka. And he hadn't severed his ties with his family, of whom none, in any case, were left, except his elderly mother. Quite the opposite: she sent him letters, written, it seemed, by one of her neighbors, telling him that she missed him and was waiting for him to return, mentioning sums of money that she needed and the father's tomb that needed a new coat of paint, asking him to sort it out, first thing, when he arrived in Alexandria. All right, then. In one of these letters the mother brings up Bekheit's nephew, the one with the eye problems, and asks him to come back quickly and examine him. Therefore great-grandfather Bekheit was a doctor, not an officer. Let's look at what we've got:

The two stories differed, contradicted one another on some counts, yet this is the nature of the truth that we are unfolding before you, drop by drop, attempting as we do so to attain it whole and undivided, to seal its

91

fissures agape with contradictions. And even this final truth—complete, endorsed, and thoroughly checked—is not free of contradiction, so what are we to make of these conflicting facts, gathered together from here and there, from who knows who? Nor was Sousou, perhaps, entirely committed to this quest. He interviewed very few individuals, twice each: after the first interview he called Sheikh Ali straightaway, and called Inji after the second. Inji asked him about the letters Bekheit's mother had sent to Bekheit and Sousou said he'd seen them with his own eyes. She asked for the address recorded in the letters and he read it out to her. The thing was bona fide, then. Likewise, Ali asked him about Bekheit's father's letter to Bekheit, and Sousou said he'd seen it with his own eyes. Sousou wasn't lying, by the way. Sousou wanted to lend further credibility to the truth that he was slowly arriving at himself. Sousou was a sucker for the juicy detail, not plain facts.

Suddenly, without warning, Ali dreamt of his great-grandfather Bekheit. This was a quite extraordinary event: Ali had never been known to show any great interest in his forebears; moreover, and significantly, Bekheit was a newcomer to his memory banks. Ali had only heard his name from Sousou, and his appearance in the dream conformed to what Sousou had told him. He was tall (My height times your height squared, Sheikh Ali, cubed: that's Bekheit for you), handsome, and plump (A nice little belly he had, Sheikh. They say that when he walked along it was like a mountain striding the earth: the ground would shake beneath him).

Captain Bekheit, at the head of a police squad sent to chase down a vendor from Saad Zaghloul Street . . . but the vendor—who resembles Adel, Abu Amira's brother—takes to his heels. Bekheit, sitting in the passenger seat to the right of the driver, commandeers the steering wheel and takes off after Adel. Adel, running and running. Alexandria's sea drains away to reveal tribesmen, robed, with staves in hand, singing: The full moon's risen afore our eyes. Adel thinks they sing for him and petitions them for help but they refuse to help him—they know his abject origins—and then Great-grandfather Bekheit arrives on his horse, and they shower him with salt and ululations, and all at once we see that they sing for him.

When Ali awoke he told the dream to Inji: I was beside him and he was placing Alexandria in my care. I'll carry Alexandria in my eye, Great-grandfather, I said, and then he brings you up. Your wife in one eye and Alexandria in the other, Sheikh Ali. If one falls, they both fall.

Naturally enough, this did not please Inji. First of all, her husband was hogging the great-grandfather to himself, and the great-grandfather was her great-grandfather as well. Second, her husband was hogging Alexandria, and Alexandria was her city as well. There were dirty games afoot in Ali's dreams and dreams were a weapon that Inji had in plentiful supply. She dreamed of Bekheit herself.

Bekheit is placing his possessions from Alexandria into a small cloth bundle, which he ties to a staff and slings over his shoulder, and heads south.

She awoke and told Ali her dream: He was sitting there in his clinic reading my palm. Soon, Alexandria's going to be cleaned out top to bottom, and all because of you, he told me. He told me, I'm so happy I can't tell you. But pray for me, Great-grandfather, I said, so the Good Lord blesses me. I've already prayed for you, he said, and I want to tell you that you must take care of Ali. Share everything with him and don't let your good standing tempt you to do him wrong.

Ali didn't like this. He looked at Inji and kept quiet.

Sousou stopped with the endless phone calls. He began to get serious. His experiences on Southern soil consumed him like fire. The phone calls became sentences of telegraphic brevity:

Lost half my weight. They don't feed me here, Uncle. Your folk are misers. Grown a little mustache.

If anyone saw me wearing Southern clothes they wouldn't know me. I swear it. Wouldn't know me. What do you think of that?

No problem, Uncle. Two days, God willing, you'll see: the Amins will be chopped up and chucked in the Nile.

That last line was the most important, naturally, but even so, Sousou made little reference to his attempts to hunt down the Amins. He left Ali and Inji hanging. They knew he was up to the task, but a hint of anxiety crept in. Anxiety's only human.

9

nji does what she wants. Always has done. She goes where she will, from the time she made up her mind to return to Egypt from Abu Dhabi, to pushing Ali to take his taar, to building up her empire in Karmouz, brick by brick.

Inji decided to track down her departed great-grandfather herself. She turned to Ghada, asked her if any of her clients came from Kom al-Dikka, and Ghada said no. All right then, Ghada. What I'm going to ask of you now I want you to consider a personal favor, and there'll be a very generous reward. Inji produced an address in Kom al-Dikka and handed it to Ghada. Great-grandfather Bekheit's house was long gone, sure, but it had been established that a tea stall faced the old plot, manned by a fellow in his fifties. The man was the son of an old man, and the old man was the sheikh's son, and the sheikh might have known Bekheit. All Inji wanted was information and she was quite clear: more information equaled more money, and by more money she didn't mean a thousand, or two thousand, or even three. More money meant twenty thousand. Ghada, I know you might well take off and leave us once you've got that much in your hands. It's up to you. I won't stand in your way. But for me the crucial thing is that you bring me accurate information on this man I told you about. Is that clear, my love?

Ghada's thinking went far beyond the great-grandfather, beyond the twenty thousand pounds. That month Ghada had turned thirty and, to be quite honest, was fed up with her life. Ghada hadn't been born this way. Which of us has? Ghada had completed her education at the Faculty of Commerce and by rights should have become a big-shot accountant, but a disastrous affair had led her, as it does, to a café in Maamoura where she took her first steps on the path to iniquity. Hagga Itemad scooped her up and set her to work as a babysitter in a number of homes, and it was in the homes in which she served that Ghada continued along her path. Iniquity's exquisite, but only at first; thereafter it's all torment and anguish, tear-filled nights—so she believed, and sought some sum to keep herself covered. She considered a number of projects—a fish stall, cigarette kiosk, banking the cash and spending the interest—but the one she took most seriously was becoming Inji's partner in the café. This was the one best suited to her ambitions. Ghada took herself off to Kom al-Dikka, determined to succeed.

Impossible was not in Ghada's dictionary.

Impossible was not in Inji's dictionary.

Impossible is not in the dictionary of any searcher after truth.

Inji was not searching for her truth alone; she was searching for a nation's truth. Ali, for the period Inji left him, had researched and studied the history of Alexandria, something that had not been an option for his wife, who was busy at the time establishing her center, her fortune, and her formidable reputation. So Inji wanted to make up for this by attaining her truth, her roots, by which means she would be able to understand something of what had taken place in Alexandria over the course of the last century. An old dream of hers returned: she is watching a puppet theater, cheering and clapping along, when the man next to her exhales in irritation, disconcerting her. He points in the air and she looks up to discover that she is a puppet herself, that a long string reaches up to the ceiling where the man manipulating her is standing. She tries pulling on the string but it won't budge, so she tries climbing it. It's very tricky: one step forward, several steps back. In the background music plays—*Evening of beauty, seduction and roses, the finest there are*—and Inji ascends, and the song rises with her: *Search for the true source* . . . . Inji plummets from the puppet theater's ceiling. Inji falls off the bed. Inji is unable to search for the true source. For all these reasons, Inji decides to do in reality what she has failed to achieve in the magical world of dreams.

Ali knew nothing of Ghada's trip, and it should be said that he was about to undertake a trip of his own, one that Inji knew nothing about. He decided to go himself to Anfoushi, to the address that Sousou had described to him. He ran his eye over the place—a working-class café—then dropped in at the Anfoushi police station, where he sat with Lieutenant Colonel Kamal.

They chatted together about the state of the nation, and in the course of the conversation Lieutenant Colonel Kamal said: Sheikh Ali, don't think that I'm against you or Madame Inji. On the contrary. You could say the whole Interior Ministry's with you; it's just that we don't make the rules. Ali made no response to this flattery, which he knew to be untrue, resorting instead to a preemptive strike: And we all love you, I swear it. Any officer asks us any favor at all, we've never held back. The Interior's the shield of the nation. He received a call on his phone, canceled it without answering, and turned to the lieutenant colonel. I hope the girl we sent you last week was to your liking, ya basha? And so it was, in practice, that with these words the records of the Anfoushi police station were placed at the disposal of Sheikh Ali. The oral records, of course. Lieutenant Colonel Kamal told him all about the station, about its officers, troopers, and beat cops, about its history and the history of the neighborhood, and Ali began to probe and sift his words for any trace of a yuzbashi named Bekheit who'd been transferred to Sohag. For hours on end he heard him out. There were three Bekheits. The first, one Major Ahmed Bekheit Abdallah, a serving officer; the second, Suleiman Bekheit, who'd served in the mid-nineteenth century, rising from yuzbashi to saagh before the trail went cold (the lieutenant colonel said nothing more about him, and Ali didn't like to come right out and ask); and the third, a Colonel Bekheit Abdel Samad, who'd left the force back in the 1980s.

The second: *Suleiman Bekheit, who'd served in the mid-nineteenth century. . . Suleiman Bekheit, who'd served in the mid-nineteenth century . . .* Ali replayed Kamal's words to make sure of the name, to make sure of the details, and in his mind began to weave a tale.

Despite making this brief visit, which seemed to promise further visits, more leisurely and scrupulous, Ali did not let on to a soul. Each morning he'd stand in the bathroom brushing his teeth and combing his beard before the mirror, and Inji would walk past and he'd remember his trip; he would remember that there was something he had to tell her, just a little hint, you know, so she wouldn't later accuse him of hiding things from her. Each morning he'd eat breakfast with her, two loaves, cheese, and tea, and she would stare at him and he'd remember his trip, he would remember that there was something he had to tell her. He would go to the café with her and go over the accounts and he'd remember, he'd remember, and yet in the end he chickened out. Ali wanted to forge links with his Alexandrian forebears. Ali, scholar of every aspect of the city's history, envisioned this history as an unbroken chain—the founder of old Alexandria, Suleiman Bekheit, linked to its modern founder, his great-grandson, Sheikh Ali. Alexandrian history was a history of rebellion: the great-grandfather had rebelled against the authority of the state and fled to the South, where he founded a family outside the law, and the great-grandson had returned to Alexandria, fleeing his family, to found another family, also outside the law. But pay attention: outside the law, not from any hostility to the concept of law in general, but rather from hostility to the law as it stands, the law of the corrupt state, of dynastic rule. Ali's concern was with justice, not the law, if that makes sense. And all of this would come to nothing if Inji found out. Not because Ali wanted to keep the glory for himself—the last thing Ali cared about was himself—but because Inji was what you might call an interfering, obsessive wench, or more correctly, she was nuts. She'd stick her nose in everywhere, down to the smallest detail. One day he would tell her. For sure, he'd tell her. He was just waiting for the right moment.

Taar is a story of its own, from which Egypt has suffered greatly, particularly in the poor and ignorant South.

A group of strangers attacked the big mosque in Jezirat Mahrous, a village in the municipality of Akhmim, Sohag governorate, beheading the imam and a couple of worshipers during the evening prayers. Panic-stricken, the congregation scrambled to escape the mosque. The strangers' first act had been to shoot out the neon lights, plunging the mosque into darkness and making it impossible to identify them, before committing their crime and beheading the three men. Mohamed, Abdallah, and Abdel Rahman: Abdallah Amin's three sons. The bodies they left in the mosque. The heads, however, they dropped off the new bridge, to be found, hours later, bobbing in the Nile.

At dawn the next day, Said Ragab Shehata, better known as Sousou, left the apartment he'd been renting in Akhmim and returned to Alexandria. Let it be noted that Said Ragab Shehata had grown a thin mustache and let his belly sag down appreciably during his stay in Akhmim, and let it be noted, too, that no sooner had he stepped onto the platform in Alexandria and taken a deep draught of Alexandria's briny air than he, without thought or calculation, kneeled down and kissed the ground. Let it be noted that the man who came home to Alexandria loved Alexandria.

Karmouz: the ground is carpeted with roses, every inch burns bright with lamps lit day and night, and on all sides the Ninety-Nine Names of God, the invocation *In the name of God, the Compassionate and the Merciful*, the refrains of "We start tonight," thundering out from giant speakers and a DJ's deck. And through it all steps Sousou, astride a strong white charger, a white gallabiya and black cloak on his back, dispersing salutations to the people and making for a storefront on which, in shaky lettering, is inscribed: Karantina Liver, Propr. Said Ragab Shehata, Sousou, and his sons after him, God willing.

Sousou dismounts and the people gathered watch as Ali and Inji advance to meet him from across the way. Ali embraces him and bestows a kiss, gesturing to the street's new liver outlet, while Inji greets him and laughs, right in his face. The crowd can't hear what was said; the music drowns out everything. Until, that is, Hagga Itemad is spied coming up the street, and Ali signals for the music to stop, climbs up beside the DJ, takes the mike, and begins:

I'd like to salute Hagga Itemad. Hagga Itemad, who stood by us when we were starting out, to whom, saving God's presence, we owe so much. God set it in the balance of her blessings. Hagga Itemad . . . it's not business or financial interests that keep us so close, as God's my witness—the woman's like a mother to us, never slow to pass a wise word on. . . . And so I'd like to say that any good fortune we enjoy is all thanks to this dear lady, and any evil's our own doing. . . .

Hagga Itemad has grown old. She has knee problems. She comes on, one arm leaning on her daughter Minna's shoulder, the other on the shoulder of her lifelong companion, Madame Nadia. She taps her palm on her chest and bows her head in acknowledgment, and Sheikh Ali goes on:

98

And now we salute one of the neighborhood's best men, the finest man in the whole neighborhood, the pride of Karmouz, Miallim Sousou, who defended his family's honor, who wouldn't stand for us to be put down. Miallim Sousou, brother of Miallim Abu Amira, who was by our side as we built Karmouz up brick by brick and never denied us anything. Miallim Sousou, who I think of as a younger brother, who I hope sees me as his older brother from a different mother, and who's grown up now and become a man. I swear to God, if I had a daughter I'd go straight to Abu Amira and ask Sousou to take her hand, may God bear witness to what I say. But we say, What God wills is best, and as He joins good men to good women, who better than Miss Minna? Miss Minna, daughter of our mother Hagga Itemad, daughter of the martyr, the God-fearing son of Alexandria, Hagg Mohamed Harbi, the man who never faltered, who never backed down, and all for the sake of the neighborhood and its people. Hagga Itemad, we're asking for the hand of our pretty little mademoiselle, Miss Minnatallah, for Miallim Sousou. I swear by God that there's no worldly interest here, no love of wealth or power, just love for this blessed union.

Hagga Itemad can't raise her voice as once she could. She laughs shyly and leans into Madame Nadia and whispers in her ear. Madame Nadia doesn't let her down. She lets rip with a tremendous ululation and then the ululations come in waves. Everyone there, men and women, ululate and dance. Only Minna stays put. She glances bashfully at her future groom. The female of our species is a beautiful creature, characterized by bashfulness.

The romance of Minna and Sousou did not start that day. It was fully two years old already, from the time Sousou had first caught sight of her at her mother's apartment, where he was dropping off a few deliveries. From that moment, despite the cultural and social gulf that separated them, they started to exchange the sweetest words. A pure and innocent romance flourished beneath the watchful gaze of the hagga, who only ever intervened to pass on invaluable and kindly advice. And beneath Madame Nadia's gaze as well. She took a view from the outset, one which she hesitantly voiced to Hagga Itemad: I mean, sister, why not set your girl up in her father's house?

The hagga felt a sense of foreboding. Hagg Harbi, the man they'd fought over upon a day, was on the table.

Which house would that be, Nadia?

Her father's house, sister. The one in Gheit al-Enab.

That's not her father's house, Nadia! That's your house.

Shame on you! What were her father and me, then? Weren't we one?

Whether uttered in good faith or bad, these last words left the atmosphere electric. Oh no, my dear, Itemad shouted, not one at all! One's what you say when they write your name in the register. You, my girl, were his bit on the side. It was me he'd come home to at the end of the day.

She said this and got to her feet. It would take her another two weeks to set straight the damage done by these words. Relations between her and Nadia had always been a matter of give and take. However poorly one treated the other—and Harbi was ever the wellspring of their strife—they would return to one another in the end. On this occasion, their rapprochement, or Nadia pardoning Itemad, required the latter to consent to a condition laid down by the former, to wit, that her old apartment in Gheit al-Enab, the apartment where Harbi had spent most of his time in her company, would become Minna and Sousou's marital home.

Nadia, too, had a vision of Alexandria's history. Of history as links forged in an unbroken chain. The city, which had formerly been the center of Harbi's resistance against the Egyptian authorities, had now become the center of another resistance, mounted by the Karantina generation, the generation that had plucked the banner from Harbi's hand and proclaimed its fight against injustice. We should really think here about the significance of this metaphor's appeal—Alexandrian history as links forged in a chain—to Nadia, Ali, and everyone else. They hadn't come up with it, though. The copyright was held by Harbi. Immediately after his death, Itemad told a story about him. He was sitting with her, smoking a shisha in the dead center of the living room, a bare expanse with a couple of chairs and a television on a table. She was persuading him how important it was for Minna, just one year old at the time, to get a proper, upmarket education; how important it was she go to a nice school so she wouldn't turn out like them. He took a pull on the pipe and asked her: And who told you I want her educated, woman? I want her to continue my work. I want all Alexandria to continue my work.

In any case, the decision to send Minna to school won out. But Harbi's words remained, deathless. Itemad repeated them to Minna when she was older, she repeated them to Nadia, Nadia repeated them to everyone she knew, and everyone she knew repeated them to everyone they knew. The words became a slogan, inscribed in golden letters within the pages of Alexandria's oral history. Alexandrian links are forged one to the other, no link alone. Sousou and Minna shall dwell in the apartment where Harbi fought his battles. Ali and Inji are the living and perpetuated embodiment of Harbi; Harbi the living, perpetuated embodiment of yet others, lost in time, and so on, since the beginning of creation, since the moment Alexander of Macedon stumbled across Alexandria: a neglected plot of land by the sea.

What do you know about crocodiles, Sheikh Ali?
They're scary animals?
All right, so what's scarier: them or snakes?
Well, snakes are pretty scary too.
All God's gifts to us are scary.
You're quite right, Sousou.
It's you who taught me, Sheikh.

Inji was looking for her roots somewhere else: in Kom al-Dikka. She had heard nothing from Ghada for days. It put her on edge. She almost told Ali—he was a man, he'd sort it out—but at the last minute she backed down. Ghada's first phone call took two weeks to arrive. She said she was on her way.

In the office at the café Ghada told Inji what she'd learned. Three men, or two men and a boy, among them the owner of the tea stall Inji had directed her to herself, who said they knew things about Great-grandfather Bekheit. She'd had a bad feeling about them. She slept with the lot and they gave her a bad feeling. Ghada knew an honest man from a liar. And that was that, until she bumped into a strange woman who grilled fish in the neighborhood. It was the woman who approached her and invited her to her home, a small room under the stairs, and there she got her drunk and asked her why she was searching for Bekheit. Ghada, who still had her wits about her, said it was just this whim she'd had, you know, and refused to say more. The woman then asked her straight out if she was searching for him for the sake of that two-faced bitch, Inshi? Ghada gave no answer. The woman said: I know her well. Go and tell her, sister. Tell her I've got what she wants. The man she's after is an old, old story and I know it by heart. Just tell her Auntie Umm Amira says hello.

Her name's Umm Amira, Ghada went on, but the people there call her Umm Amira the Melon: her hair's all fallen out. She looks a fright, Madame Inji, I'm telling you.

Inji appeared unaffected. She asked how Umm Amira might be reached and, more important, how come Ghada trusted her when everyone else had let her down. Reaching her was simple: they would go together to the stall where she grilled fish. She was there twenty-four hours a day. Why she trusted her was a long story:

I didn't believe her at first. What gave me doubts was that it was her who chased after me. She came to me, not me to her, and that's the biggest sign that there was something in it for her. But then she gave me a photo of Bekheit.

Inji's heart pounded.

I said to myself I wouldn't show it to you until I'd told you the whole story. She took it out. The photograph was old, dating back to the early days of the twentieth century: the great-grandfather with his vaselined mustache and tarboosh. Lord above, Madame Inji, the man's the spit of you and Sheikh Ali. Isn't he meant to be great-grandfather to you both? I couldn't believe my eyes when I saw it, I swear. Never thought people could look so alike!

Inji let her prattle on and lost herself in the portrait. Her heart pounded. She was gazing at the birth of the legend. Year one.

For a moment she was lost in the portrait, or so it seemed. Through the niqab's slit, Ghada saw her eyes shine damply. Inji excused herself and shut herself in the bathroom for a few minutes. When she returned her face was more radiant than ever. Her eyes were smiling: See here, Ghada. You've done everything I asked of you and more. The last thing I want you to do is introduce me to this Umm Amira woman. Wouldn't it be great if she could come here to the café?

Umm Amira, of course, couldn't come to the café. Ghada suggested it to her and she flared up: By all I hold sacred, I'm not setting foot in that neighborhood of theirs. It's a filthy spot. If they want to come and drink tea with me, they're more than welcome. I'll be sitting here happy as a queen. Inji resolved to go with Ghada to see her.

Umm Amira had lost all the hair from the front of her head and she didn't wear a hijab. She sat at her stall, smoking and sipping from a bottle of liquor she stored down the front of her robe. Despite the niqab, she knew Inji the second she saw her approaching with Ghada at her side. Welcome to the loveliest girl in town! she cried thickly: Come and say hello to your auntie, my precious bride. Inji didn't much like this welcome—she was a girl and bride no more, she was Sheikha Inji, Madame Inji, the Queen of Karmouz. It was this Inji who extended her fingertips, but Umm Amira jumped on her, hugged and kissed her, and led her and Ghada off to her little room. She refused to talk until they had eaten a bit of fish she grilled for them with her own two hands. They ate, and Umm Amira began to talk:

It's like this, my girl. Because of you I've spent years and years cast out here like a dog. No one knows me, no one asks after me. Let it go, I say to myself: I'm not going to stoop to the level of a little madam no older than my own kids. Right? Even if it was you that got between me and my husband, and even if you were the reason I've been treated so shamefully. Forgive and forget, that's me, but now the time has come to pay the check. I want to be compensated, and compensated well, and in exchange you'll know everything you want to know about your great-grandfather.

What is the nature of the compensation that Umm Amira, Melon Head, is asking for? Not much: Just justice, and not a penny more. She wants a fish stall next to Karantina, no less than Sousou got, that rat brother-in-law of hers, plus ten thousand pounds cash in hand, all up front, no installments or checks. Inji, who'd removed her niqab and was smoking a cigarette, looked at Umm Amira and agreed. But on one condition: the fish stall would have to wait a year, while Inji checked her information against what other people said. When the final announcement was made—the unveiling of Bekheit, Kom al-Dikka's old doctor, as the founder of Sheikha Inji's family—then Umm Amira would get her stall.

Wonderful, sister. So today I'm going to tell you a few things and then tomorrow you and Mademoiselle Ghada will honor my humble home again and give me my cash and I'll hand you a few pictures and papers that the dear departed wrote with his own hand.

Inji agreed.

It was a long story. It started back in Umm Amira's childhood. At the end of his life her father had lost the plot. He was always talking about them, the ones casting spells on him and his daughter, and about Sheikh Hamed, the man with the cure for everything. The booze had completely destroyed his mind; that, the heroin, and old age.

I had no idea who this Sheikh Hamed was, so off I go and ask Mother. Mother had a hard life, so did we all, but she still kept the clothes clean like they say, never saw me go without, and to this day I'd take her over the fattest cat in Alexandria. Anyway, it's her told me the story. Sheikh Hamed was a fellow who spent all his time at the mosque, and he had five kids. I still remember their names: Hassan, Abdallah, Fadia, Bekheit, and Hussein. Now this is an old, old story. It all happened long before I was born. My mother told me the story of these people. They were a lovely lot, every one of them, all except Bekheit. He was no good. (She looks at Inji. Checks her reaction. There is no reaction on Inji's face.) So, as I was saying, this kid Bekheit, after his own father's spent good money on raising him, has coughed dust to put him through school, he up and says, I'm off to see the peasants! (Inji corrects her: The South, Umm Amira.) He fucked off, sister, what do want me to say? South? Peasants? Who's counting? He just says, I'm going to be a doctor and I'm going to set up with the peasants. So my father works for this Hamed—he'd bring him deliveries, make sure he had everything to hand—and he overhears the guy fighting with his son. Filth! Scum! Son of this and that and the other . . . Not nice, if you get me. I've spent good money on you and you want to abandon me when I'm old and tired. And the son, well, he's made up his mind, hasn't he? Nothing you could say would make a difference.

Before Sheikh Hamed passed away, his faithful servant stole from him a great chest in which he kept his money: fifty-four pounds on the nose. The money he took care of quickly enough. What he couldn't take care of were the letters he found in the chest from Bekheit to his father and the photographs of the five children, Bekheit among them. The chest remained in the possession of Umm Amira's father. He held on to it until he died and it was the root of the guilt complex he felt toward Sheikh Hamed. This chest, and all it contained, was now the property of Umm Amira, and Inji could have it for the price of ten thousand pounds and, later on, a fish stall.

Inji was crying. She took tissue after tissue from her bag and dried her tears. When she'd heard her out, Inji looked up at Umm Amira:

The letters and pictures are ours, Umm Amira. You stole them from us.

Take them, sister. Take them if you're so sure and then you'll be the sheikha you claim to be, and not the petty crook you act, and I won't be Umm Amira.

Inji shut up.

The next day, Inji dropped in on Umm Amira. She handed her the sum requested and took away a plastic bag containing a number of ragged papers. When she'd left, Umm Amira went to buy her liquor. The man gave her a bottle of brandy, which she drank. She drank the entire bottle in her room, then doubled up in pain. She clutched her stomach and tried to vomit but she couldn't. She fell to the floor, gripped a chair leg and bit it, and for a half an hour she stayed there, kicking her legs in the air.

That same day, before any of the neighbors could catch a whiff of the corpse, two young men raided her room. They took the bag with the ten thousand pounds and brought it back to Inji. Inji opened the bag, counted the money carefully, then gave the men their due.

Hey, Sousou!

Right here, Sheikh!

How did the world begin, Sousou?

The world began when God, may He be praised and exalted, created Adam.

That's not the point. I know that. You think I don't know that? The point is, what did people wear? What did they drink? What language did they speak?

People ate till they were full, Sheikh Ali. They wore clothes and they spoke our language.

I'll catch you out one day, Sousou.

(Laughing. Crying with laughter. Smacking his palms together.) You're a honey, Abu Hamada, I swear by the Good Book. A sugar cube.

Just who was Yuzbashi Suleiman Bekheit?

Ali quite wore himself out in search of this bit of information.

By this time, there were long lines of women from Karantina at the Anfoushi police station. Ali had formed many friendships within the station. It was the golden age of relations between Karantina and the government. Ali stayed up with the officers every night. He got to know them all by name, from the lowliest recruit to the station commander, the colonel himself. And of course, it was all on his tab. The favor he asked was a simple one: to find the slightest trace of Suleiman Bekheit. But the trace was nowhere to be found. One meeting—in a room in Karantina, attended by Colonel Ahmed Omran, Lieutenant Colonel Kamal, and Second Lieutenant Medhat—sparked a glimmer of hope in his heart. Colonel Omran had the most to say:

See here, Sheikh Ali, I don't know who put this story into your head about some officer called Suleiman Bekheit who served in Anfoushi (Ali looks wordlessly at Lieutenant Colonel Kamal), but it's a load of nonsense. No one here can give you that information, my son. You have to get a permit and take it to the municipality, then another permit and take it to the ministry, then a third permit to search in the National Archives. It's a tricky business. Not easy. (He looks around him, at his men.) Not easy at all. Right?

It was indeed a tricky business, but not, in Second Lieutenant Medhat's opinion, quite as tricky as all that. They were all drunk. Strict military etiquette, respect for the views of higher ranks, was out the window.

If you'll permit me, Omran Basha, Medhat said, this thing needn't be so difficult. It's just a single permit from the National Archives and the guy you're after's filed under eighteen hundred and something. . . . There you go, Sheikh Ali.

Lieutenant Colonel Kamal, leaping to the defense of his account: But Omran Basha, I got this Suleiman Bekheit stuff from General Abdel Hamid. That man was a walking treasure trove of police history.

Colonel Omran: What's all this about General Abdel Hamid, son? The man's not a credible source. You know I graduated with him, don't you? (Kamal nods.) Ali, my boy, fetch us a bottle of whiskey, would you?

Medhat: You know, General Abdel Hamid taught me in police college. You know . . . (He winks. Seems wary of saying anything he could be asked to account for.)

Omran: Lord help us. And how did you manage to put up with him, Medhat?

Kamal (trying to extricate himself from the hole he's dug for himself by bringing up the general): You a bit tightfisted then, Sheikh Ali? Didn't you tell us we'd be nibbling on pigeon and shrimp?

Medhat: Yeah! Where's our pigeon, Sheikh Ali?

Kamal: And the shrimp!

Omran, warbling drunkenly: O Sheikh Ali, where's the pigeon . . . ? (Cries of delight) O Sheikh Ali, where's the shrimp . . . ? (Cries of ecstasy) Why so cruel to your companions, you wretched man?

Thunderous applause, then they chant along, one voice composed of many tuneless voices: O wretched man, O wretched man, who promised us the shrimp . . . .

Chorus: O wretched man, O wretched man, O Sheikh Ali, you wretched man.

Second Lieutenant Medhat was the first person to call Sheikh Ali and let him know they were back on the scent. The scent in question had a name: Suleiman Bekheit. The vision had turned out to be true, after all. Medhat traveled to Cairo and examined the records in the Police Museum, the records in the Interior Ministry, and the records in the National Archives, and returned with something approaching the full story. Yuzbashi Suleiman Bekheit had left Alexandria in 1890 and traveled to the South. All Alexandria was of one mind back then, and he was a bright young officer who loathed the English too. Some said he'd been transferred to the South because of his support for Orabi, when such support was considered the height of treachery: High treason, Sheikh Ali. And Medhat started to relate the dead yuzbashi's exploits: standing at Orabi's right hand and shouting out before Khedive Tawfiq, I swear by the Almighty we shall have no more kings after today!

Suddenly he leaned in: Now then, Sheikh Ali. I couldn't have done any of this without signatures from Colonel Omran and Lieutenant Colonel Kamal. They're asking you for their share. Ali replied that a sum of fifteen thousand pounds would be deposited in the accounts of both of them, tomorrow, and in the second lieutenant's too. The second lieutenant smiled: Lovely. And my present?

Sheikh Ali didn't understand. The second lieutenant explained: I want a present, just for me. Not money. I'm taking a holiday. A week on the north coast. Now that girl who works for you—Iman. I like her. What say you send her with me? It'll be a nice change for her and you'll get her back all rested and happy. Now that's a little gift just for me, because I haven't told you everything I've got.

What the second lieutenant had gotten was more precious than a hoard of gold. He pulled out an ancient clipping on which was printed a report of Y Suleiman Mohamed Abdallah's transfer to the city of Sohag. Ali read the report through twice, then asked where "Bekheit" was, and Second Lieutenant Medhat smiled: You'll find that name on his pass, but his three-part name's just Suleiman Mohamed Abdallah. They're not going to write out five or six names, are they? What, you want them to include an interview as well, Sheikh Ali?

The second lieutenant laughed. Sheikh Ali laughed. He took the clipping. He read it through dozens of times while the second lieutenant looked on. He was smiling as he read. His eyes filled with tears as he read. He wiped away his tears as he read. And at the back of his mind the strains of a sad song played—*Evening of beauty, seduction and roses, the finest there are* .... *Search for the true source, search for the true source, for the true source, search on* ....

The next day was a day of celebration for Ali. He told no one that he had found his great-grandfather. It would a surprise for everyone. In the morning he awoke while Inji slept on. Unusually for him he put on his suit. For the first time in years he stuffed shirt into trousers, struggling with his vast gut. He polished the cracked lenses of his glasses and went downstairs to the office. He phoned Abu Amira, Hamada, Sousou and Minna, and Madame Nadia, and asked them all to come over quick as they could. They came, one by one, and he began to outline his idea:

It would soon be the twentieth anniversary of their arrival in Alexandria—his and the madame's—back on January 1, 2006, and an occasion such as this called for a celebration. Now, look around you: Is Alexandria the same Alexandria it once was? Is the Alexandria whose people have suffered injustice, hunger, homelessness, and deprivation throughout the course of history the Alexandria you see today, so self-assured, so strong, so defiant, writing its own destiny in history's pages? Does this not call for a modest celebration? The floor is open to suggestions.

Abu Amira proposed a zikr, a swaying, chanting circle of pious mindfulness; Madame Nadia suggested festooning the neighborhood with lights and hiring a microbus to drive through Alexandria blaring out the story of the past twenty years; Minna said, Take out an advertisement in *Al-Ahram*, and Sousou supported her. None of the suggestions impressed Ali.

He looked at them. That's it? Nothing else? No one answered, so he spoke himself.

Karantina is not just some excrescence on the history of Alexandria. It is a child of that history, of the history of Egypt itself. When our pharaonic ancestors wished to honor men for their deeds, they built pyramids that once made were never forgotten. Even the Greeks and Romans built wonderful and valuable things. What Ali was proposing was a vast statue, set up outside the Karantina Café, in which immortal memory and pleasant prospect might be united, a statue to give voice to the struggle, not only of the people of Karantina, but of all Alexandrians. Ali fell silent and no one said a thing.

They stayed like that, utterly silent, for two whole minutes, then Madame Nadia broke the spell and cried: A lovely rose!

Everyone looked at her. For a moment she was unnerved, but she overcame it and explained her idea: Karantina is a beautiful rose in the heart of Alexandria. There, people breathe sweet air and find ease of mind. The statue would be a gigantic rose, erected in the middle of a little garden, twenty meters square. Something like revulsion passed over Abu Amira's face as he listened to Madame Nadia's suggestion. Roses and ducks and swans, he said by way of observation, are for children. But we built Karantina with blood and sweat and steel. The earth parting to reveal a hand holding a machine gun: that's the symbol their struggle deserves. We gave our all, my friends, and the younger generation has to understand that nothing comes easy these days. It's by force of arms alone.

Sousou started to speak in support of Abu Amira—his brother, his father, his teacher—but reached a different conclusion altogether: If we gave our all, then we should be giving the younger generation hope. I'd like to propose making a great big statue of a laughing, happy face with "The Young Generation" written across it. Minna seconded him.

Hamada was no ordinary person. Deep down he was an artist. Everything inside him told him so. He'd suckled at art's very teat: the stories his mother told him as a toddler, the drawing lessons where he excelled; and he was a nature lover too, sitting by the drainage ditch for two or three hours every day, staring at it wordlessly, a torrent of emotions pulsing through him. Hamada had not uttered a word during the conversation. Only now did he deign to speak: considered and calm and soundly reasoned.

Sousou's on the money. We have to give the younger generation hope. And Papa's right too: we're not alone. We're a piece of Alexandria, and Alexandria's a piece of Egypt, and Egypt is our country. All of us.

He turns his face from one to the other. Then he rises, pacing the office floor.

From the day Mama and Papa came to Alexandria they were thinking of Egypt, all of it. (He comes to a halt beside his father, facing them all.) I'm proud that this man here (he points to his father), my own father, comes from Cairo, that my great-grandfather came from the South and that I myself come from Alexandria. What I'm saying is that we have to think of all of Egypt. Egypt: the beautiful hen who keeps her eggs safe and warm, who hatches chicks, whose chicks are Egypt's youth. (He swivels his whole body toward his father.) That's our statue: a hen. A hen gazing heavenward. To the future, I mean, and sitting on her eggs. And a lamppost. A lamppost with a great sun hanging off it, and that sun is Karantina. And it's that café, (looking to his father now) and it's you. It's you and me and all these good folk here, each and every one.

Ali rises from his chair. He folds Hamada into a bear-like embrace, then looks out at the others. He asks to them bear witness to the artist he has brought into the world. He claps his back. Then they read the Fatiha.

So it was that work began on building the gigantic Egyptian Hen and the Sun of Karantina shining down on all and sundry.

Today, and for the first time in the history of humankind, Ali and Inji are free as birds. Hamada's with his friends and the café's closed for Friday. At eleven a.m. they step outside and catch a horse-drawn carriage that takes them from the beginning of Anfoushi to Montazah and back.

Ali asks the driver to pull the canopy up: the madame wants to show her face. Under cover of the canopy she reclines in his arms. Ahhh! How long has it been since she lay back in his arms and felt so safe and secure? And he, like a teenager now, rather than the husband of long standing that he is, slips his hand beneath her black cloak, fingers the edge of her bra and gives her a wink as she writhes wilder and wilder in his arms. He moves his hand lower; his fingers touch her breast. He feels her nipples stand proud and, one then the next, swift and deft, he fondles them, and she looks up well pleased and murmurs, Oh my, Sheikh Ali! Enough, I beg you!

Ramleh Station. Ibrahim Pasha Mosque.

Lying in his arms, him toying with her breasts, she gazes up at him: Know what? Long as I live, I'll never forget that you wanted to leave me. He smiles: Could I ever leave you, love of my life? Inji was holding fast to a bad memory from the old days. When she saw Umm Amira again, that bitter history had come flooding back. She holds her smile: No, no, don't act dumb. You wanted to leave me for that mangy bitch Umm Amira. He holds his smile: You really want to make a fight out of this? She starts to frown: No, Ali, what fight? The woman's gone for good, it's over.

You haven't heard anything about her?

About who?

Umm Amira.

(Silence. Then:) She's dead.

. . .

(An even longer silence. Then:) Ali, you know everything. I killed her, Ali, and you know it.

All of a sudden Ali bristles. He pushes her off him. Stares into her eyes, looking for the slightest hint of mockery and finding nothing. You killed her? What are you talking about? She tries to recapture the untroubled mood that had prevailed not a minute before, and fails. Ali, she was a filthy old bitch. She wanted to come back and open a store in the neighborhood. She was trying to blackmail me, Ali. She wanted to come back and make a fool of you again, the disgusting woman.

Ali doesn't understand a thing. She is forced to explain it to him: the story of Bekheit that she heard from Umm Amira; the woman's exploitation of the situation. Just imagine, Ali! Her only claim to fame was that her father stole my great-grandfather's letters and she was using them to exploit me.

Azarita, entering Chatby.

The Chatby Casino is being demolished. It's been being demolished for twenty years now. Ali says nothing for a minute. He buries his head in his hands, then lifts it slowly: Look here, love. Everything you think you know is complete trash. For starters, that woman was ripping you off: there weren't any letters. My great-grandfather—your great-grandfather: I've found out who he was. He was an officer up here and he went off to the South, and that's that. There was never any need for all that trouble. That's for starters. Secondly . . . .

Secondly, what you just said is wrong! I've got some of his letters and I've seen his pictures. He looks just like us.

(Shouting) Secondly, what I'm telling you is right, and you'd better stuff a shoe in your mouth and shut up!

You can't talk to me like that!

Can and will. You're chasing something you've made up out of thin air and now you've killed a crazy old woman and you'll cost me the dearest friend I ever had.

Who's your dearest friend?

Abu Amira's my dearest friend.

Oh no, Abu Amira's not your dearest friend.

He is. He's my dearest friend.

(Sensibly, sagely) No, no, Ali. No, my love. That Abu Amira of yours is a son of a bitch. You know that it was him who killed your brother.

Killed my brother? Killed my brother? Sure, Abu Amira killed him, happy now? But he was also there when we needed him.

He stood by us all right. Not because you gave him and his brothers work, though. Oh no. Not because they were making more money than they'd ever dreamed of.

(To the driver) Driver! (To Inji) It's Abu Amira who got us where we are now. (To the driver) Driver! Turn round and go back if you please. (To Inji) The man did his duty without reward or thanks. (To the driver) Driver! Captain! You up there! I'm kissing your hand here, sheikh. Can't you turn round and take us back?

The hack wheels about. Ali relaxes a little.

Look here, Inji, my love. From the day we were married you've always done as you see fit. You do what you want, like there's no point to me at all. Isn't that right? Well, this is the first time I'm going to ask you to do something: I want you to forget this business of your great-grandfather. It's something that woman cooked up to cheat you, and now you've exercised your right and killed her. Do we agree? Can we leave it there? Isn't that enough?

No, Ali, we can't leave it. You're the one who's being messed around by those police officers. I know all about that. I was following all that very closely. The whole Interior Ministry, which you've been chucking our money at, is laughing at you, Ali.

I'm being made a fool of and you know everything, is that it? Business as usual, then.

He returns his face to his hands, and seconds later raises it, the tears wetting his beard with its scattered white hairs. He looks up to the sky: One trouble-free day. Just one trouble-free day in my life, O Lord. Give me of Your Mercy, Lord, for You are the most merciful of all.

The Friday prayer call starts up in the distance.

Sometimes man needs to look around him. Man, in his ignorance (God, may He be exalted and glorified, says of man: *Verily he is unjust and foolhardy*) moves forward down his path, bent on traversing the great distances ahead, and never once pauses to look around him, behind him, above him, beneath him, to see where he stands in that vast void called the universe. Called history. We shall not make the same mistake. We shall look around.

No one claims to be able to change history wholesale, once and for eternity, with a single gesture. History proceeds at its own pace. To check its progress is to sow the seeds of its evolution. This is what Ali and Inji had been doing ever since they came to Alexandria: sowing seeds, some of which were good to grow, others which weren't.

A short while ago we saw how the Chatby Casino was being demolished before the very eyes of Ali and Inji as they passed by in their hack. For decades now this casino had been the cradle of the hopes and dreams of Alexandrians old and new, a breathing space in which the Alexandrian, and the Egyptian in general, might send forth his complaint to the raging sea that swelled behind it. What this means is that Ali and Inji's reformist drive in Alexandria did not bring about wholesale change. Capitalism, with help from the government, still had the power to rob people of their contentment. Does this mean that nothing had changed? Of course not. And here for your perusal are the facts:

One day, the governor of Alexandria decided to declare his city "smoke free," in the wake of which decision the smoking of shisha was banned in cafés, the ones by the shore at first, then moving inland. The decision was thwarted by the café owners, so the governor donned the velvet glove: shisha wasn't being banned in Alexandria; shisha was disappearing of its own accord. And this would have been very bad indeed had it not been for Ali and Inji.

Ali, who was addicted to rough-cut molasses tobacco, didn't buy this smoke-free city thing: It's your right to smoke and my right to breathe clean air, and all that tripe. He would descend on some café with two or three of his men, where they would smoke till dawn, and in no time their table would be crammed with the poor and honest citizenry of Alexandria: those who wanted favors, those who wanted to debate some issue or other, and those who, plainly put, wanted nothing other than to sit with Sheikh Ali himself. His company was conditional on shisha: if you weren't smoking, then you could shove off home to your mother. Sarcasm is an unfailingly effective weapon against puritans. Other such sessions would be convened by people like Abu Amira, Miallim Sousou with his wife Minna, Sheikh Hassan, even Madame Nadia, in various spots throughout the city. The numbers of those ordering shisha grew, and the never-ending demand for molasses tobacco slowly but surely left its mark on the cafés' bank balances. Even as the government, politely and respectfully, tried to claim its unearned cut, the men of Karantina, polite and respectful in turn, held it back, without a shot being fired. This was a supremely clean fight, though there were others that were not so clean.

"What is it they are fighting to defend?" wondered a national daily well known for its regime affiliations, atop an article whose tone was, to put it mildly, skeptical. They claim that they are defending religion, this man who calls himself "sheikh" and his niqab-wearing helpmeet, Inji. Yet they run a brothel and sell alcohol. Honestly, what is this?

All right. Ali and Inji were most assuredly not partisans of an extremist Islam, just as they held no candle for moderate Islam. Islam as a whole, despite the great respect we hold it in, was not the banner beneath which they fought. Their struggle could be characterized as liberal in tendency; it just so happened that it was being led by two God-fearing believers. The whole thing is perfectly simple. The liberalism of the thirties and forties, that was what Ali and Inji were endeavoring to reintroduce to Alexandria. Alexandria before the soldiers took over, the Alexandria of foreigners and laissez-faire, Alexandria the international city, Alexandria before the rise of the new puritans. Ali and Inji had never thought about things with this degree of clarity, and the word "cosmopolitanism" had certainly never entered their heads, but thus is history when viewed from afar. Its protagonists never speak for themselves. It is history that speaks. We are the ones who speak. We are history.

In response to the newspaper's query—both entirely incomprehensible and inexcusable—three young men raided its head offices in Cairo. Two of them burst into the editor-in-chief's office and the third stood by the door menacing anyone who tried to approach. Then they departed. This sally had two contradictory results: First, an increase in the public's sympathy with

Ali and Inji, who had revenged themselves, on behalf of all ordinary Egyptians, on the lies and fraud of the press; and second, it prompted Ali and Inji to clear themselves of the charge that they had planned the raid in person. On the Internet, a gathering tide of voices claimed the paper itself had carried out the deed in an attempt to create an illusory enemy for itself. And Ali and Inji continued to rise.

But success was not their constant companion, not all the time. The fight over Chatby Casino was one of their best-known ongoing battles and neither party—Ali and Inji on one side and the governor's office on the other—could claim an outright victory. Businessmen had approached the governor with offers to buy the casino and reports of this had thrown the press into a frenzy. From certain women in the café, Inji heard certain reports, and made up her mind to take action. Capitalism shall never be allowed to win, she told herself. She spoke to Hamada on the phone. She asked him to leave school and come home immediately. In the office she outlined the story to him. The casino doesn't belong to the businessmen, it belongs to the people, and this country still has laws. Right? And over and above all that, the casino was a source of income: some of the Karantina girls would go on the prowl for customers there and bring them back to the café. Which is better? A businessman buying a public venue to satisfy some whim, or good-hearted people bringing pleasure to the working man in exchange for a modest fee?

Hamada—a towering, full-figured youth, a sight to make the eye dip coyly down, and a high school student too—set about hiring a number of his friends. They went to the casino and set up a huge banner outside, which read "The casino belongs to the people, not to some of the people." A guard spotted them and asked them to leave. They jumped him and a body of passersby joined in on the side of the guard, seeing as he was an old man, like their fathers, and the anticipated massacre was set in motion. Two passersby were wounded, and the guard had his right eye gouged out. The police turned up and led Hamada and his friends off to the cells. They received sentences of varying severity, with Hamada picking up a mere two months. He saw them out and emerged even stronger. The people feared him even more and for several months no one was prepared to go near the casino. People were scared.

But the fight flared up again when the businessmen resumed their demolition of the casino. Hamada orchestrated another battle, in which one of the laborers was killed, and he fled. No one stopped him. For months the work was halted then it started up again and so on and so on . . . The only thing standing in their way now was this bestial desire to continue with the casino's demolition, this monstrous alliance between the authorities and the wealthy. And the acts of terrorism no longer terrified anybody. The laborers would refuse to go on for a few weeks, then they'd go back to work. But Ali and Inji did not give in so easily. The fight went on.

All of which served to increase the self-belief of Alexandrians. Here were individuals defending them. Disturbances and acts of civil disobedience were on the rise. Victories increase the Alexandrian's self-confidence and defeats do not trouble him. Sheikh Hassan, with his spotless reputation and status as a martyr's brother, made his refrain at Friday sermons (as other sheikhs did, too): *If ye suffer hardships, then they suffer as ye suffer, yet ye have hope from God and they have none.* At other times they would recite other verses: *Fighting is prescribed for thee and it is hateful to thee, yet might it not be that ye hate that which is best for thee?* And others besides.

All that, and then there was the government, which received nearly its entire budget from Ali and Inji, yet still insisted on describing them as gangsters. The government—the true thug, the true terrorist—was calling *them* gangsters. All this was the cause of an unshakable sense of bitterness on the part of Ali, Inji, and Hamada.

One day, Inji had a nervous breakdown. News reached her that one of her girls had been arrested in an apartment in Hanoville. She screamed aloud in the office, What do you want from me? What do you want? Grim-faced, niqab off, she went downstairs. She sprinted to the Karmouz police station. She tried to force her way in. The troopers at the door stopped her. She slapped her uncovered face and chopped off hanks of her hair. What did we do to you? Just leave us alone! Leave us be! She sank to the ground and heaped her hair with dust. Is it right what you're doing? Is it right? Ali came himself and held her tight, pushing her into his car. He stroked her head and made her swallow a tranquilizer. Ten minutes later she passed out.

All that people remembered about this incident was Inji's face, the face they'd never seen before: old, wrinkled, the hair starting to turn gray.

In that instant, Inji's face was the face of a madwoman. That's what the inhabitants of Karmouz remembered.

Ali never had a nervous breakdown. He kept his wits about him, wise and sharp, although his glasses, with the thick, cracked lenses that he never tried to replace, might have given a somewhat different impression.

He was sitting at home, smoking shisha and eating an apple, and all of a sudden he remembered something. He rang Hamada, who arrived half an hour later. He handed Hamada an apple, started fiddling a toothpick in his teeth, and fell silent. He was silent for a good while, looking Hamada in the eye. The youngster didn't understand what was being asked of him, but he likewise held his tongue. After ten minutes, Ali spoke. Your mother, Hamada. Your mother's gone mad.

Hamada bowed his head. His father continued: Your mother wants to kill me. And he stopped.

The father had no hard facts to offer his son. He had a feeling. He felt it in everything: his wife's glances, her movements, her conversation, the hatred that declared itself in every word she uttered.

Maybe she wants to kill you too.

He added that he had washed the apples—his apple and Hamada's apple—fifteen times. He only ate from the edge of the plate now, for fear of poison. I want you to keep your eyes open, my son. I'm not saying this because she's a bad person; it's just that she really hates us. She doesn't love us.

One day, Ali had come across an old book lying on the chiffonier in her bedroom. The book discussed various types of poisons and their dangers. There was a folded piece of paper inside it. It marked her place. Where she was reading, I mean. The page was about African snakes. Your mother wants to poison us with an African snake, Hamada.

Hamada loved his mother. He didn't like to hide from her any questions he might have. He asked her why this book had been on her chiffonier and she gave a bitter smile and said: Ask your father. The book belongs to

Sheikh Ali. Inji paused, then added: He's spent his life thinking about this one thing. Always wondering how he's going to kill us. And we just take it.

An African snake, Ali? Is this what it's come to? So muttered Inji to herself as she sobbed, head buried in her hands.

Hagga Itemad died.

Before she died she had visited her daughter Minna at her house in Gheit al-Enab. She was worn out and sensed the end was near. She told Minna that she was soon to die, that she had dreamt of Hagg Harbi walking ahead of her down a darkened street and stepping into an abandoned building, then leaning out from a first-floor balcony and pressing her to come up. What are you waiting for? Come up, my girl! The hagga smiled understandingly and told her daughter: Now, I'm not upset. Please don't think I'm upset. I just wanted to let you know something.

The hagga had signed over the building's two remaining floors to Sheikha Inji, to add to the floor that the sheikha owned and the floor belonging to Sheikh Ali. Minna couldn't believe her ears. Her mother must be senile. But the hagga confirmed it was the case. She asked her daughter not to be upset. I weighed it up carefully. They're the ones who have worked the hardest for this city, and Inshi is like your big sister. I've made her promise to take care of you, my girl. Don't be angry at her, sweetheart.

Sousou was sitting with them. He shot to his feet: What's that you say, woman? He made as if to attack her, but Minna held him back. He went to his room, unwillingly. Hagga Itemad stowed the insult away inside her and left. Ten days later she died.

It was Ali who held the aza for her, not Minna and Sousou, neither of whom attended. This seemed very like a declaration of hatred, of enmity, of the deluge of blood to come. Karantina, it seemed, was on the brink of catching fire.

THE STORY OF A KILLER

The severed finger suffers no sores.

1

Art is fire.

No one knows just when it first afflicted man, or how. How many successful men have been thus stricken, have seen their souls consumed and become the lowest of the low? How many complete unknowns have been seared by Art's flame and raised to fame? Art is an affliction from God, and divine afflictions may bode ill, or well.

For a long time now, Egyptian cinema has been bewitched by the idea of Art. We all recall that scene with Anwar Wagdi and Fairuz in the patched cloaks and pointy hats of sorcerers, singing *The heron of Art and its nightingale can find no one to feed them*. And we remember the quarrel between Abdel Wahhab and the poet Bairam al-Tunisi, with the latter's words, "You people of song, our heads hurt: A minute's silence, for God's sake," elegantly rebuked by the composer, thus prompting him to pen the poem that ran, "Art, O you who hold love dear, is soul addressing soul in their souls' tongue. . . ." Such confusion when defining the precise nature of the concept proves our point: Art is a curse, a conflagration, a consuming flame. Art is man's heaven or his hell.

From childhood Hamada had been afflicted with the curse of Art.

His silences, his keen eye, his surging emotions: these things were not of this world, the world of men, but belonged to another altogether, a world in which philosophers, great thinkers, authors, artists, sages, and saints roamed free. His mother once told him the story of his grandfather who lived in Abu Dhabi. The boy was stunned, not because his grandfather was so far away, but because he had never imagined there was a place called Abu Dhabi. He had started to learn what words meant, so he knew that Dhabi meant "gazelle," and he knew that Dhabi sounds like sabi, which means "boy," and armed with these two facts, pictured his grandfather in the shape of a child, a child with a long white beard squatting beside a gazelle, and like this he loved him.

Such literal imagery attended Hamada in all sorts of situations. One day he overheard his mother tell Aunt Nadia, We are building Alexandria, and at that very instant he saw Alexandria as a vast stone edifice and his mother and father standing there, building it up block by block, then sprawling out atop it, panting from the heat and drenched in sweat. His teacher once asked him what Mama and Papa did for a living and he told her they were building Alexandria, and the whole class roared. A classmate asked him what they were building, since Alexandria itself had all been built years ago. Later, the class would learn that this was the Hamada whose father had killed the officer and Hamada would tell this classmate, smugly, See? but the boy's skepticism remained unshaken. He said that if his father had killed the cop then that meant he'd killed a cop, not that he was building Alexandria. Hamada kept quiet and didn't answer. He stowed it in his heart. And ten years later, on the university's steps, the answer came to him: the kid who'd challenged him was a lackey of the regime. Hamada called him, reminded him who he was, and asked him to meet up at a café in Karmouz. The kid arrived in Karmouz, and as soon as Hamada saw him he signaled to Sousou. Bullets lashed the boy's body. His body was shredded into a thousand million pieces.

Art knows no boundaries. Hamada discovered his gift in primary school, in art class. He loved to paint roses, the sun, gardens, then his talent expanded to encompass people, buildings, and cars, expanded further and further still, till it outgrew the bounds of picture making and encompassed music, too. He would croon to himself in the street coming home in the evening, croon in the bathroom and driving his car. He would croon as he drank. This one time he went into a cafe in Manshiya. He ordered a Pepsi and, when the Pepsi came, added a slug from a bottle of whiskey he'd brought with him then began to sing "His eyes taught the art of love" in a loud voice. The waiter came over to tell him it wasn't allowed: alcohol wasn't allowed in the café and causing a disturbance wasn't welcome. Hamada was blind drunk, he couldn't see in front of him, but he submitted gracefully. He settled his tab with the man, tipped him well, and apologized. And left. Two hours later he returned in a pickup. He got out with a number of men. He burst through the café's door, whipped a machine gun from under his sweater, and opened fire. The men with their clubs spread out, smashing the place up. Five were killed during this operation and nine wounded, and Hamada went home. Thus was the artist within him moved, the artist jealous of his art, who would war against those who stopped him singing. At home he set about stripping down and cleaning the firearms and resumed his humming of "His eyes taught the art of love": Bring it . . . Briiiing it . . . dum diddum diddum diddum . . . . The song was stuck in his head.

Unlike his parents, who only ever drank in moderation, Hamada had become addicted to booze from a young age. From the age of twelve, to be precise. He was in the first year of high school when he tasted his first drop of alcohol. He downed three bottles of beer on that occasion and vomited copiously, after which he would drink almost every day, ascending to the Karantina bar and drinking what he pleased, or else buying the stuff and going to drink by the sea. Maybe alcohol was the cause of his huge bulk. He was tall and burly, with pale skin and dead eyes, yet he never had any negative feelings toward his body. Or rather, the feelings were stored up inside him, never revealed to anyone. (Contrary to popular opinion, artists—the more sensitive of them in particular— only rarely give voice to their true feelings.) Hamada mocked his body and accepted its mockery by others. At a particular point, however, the extent of the pain that this caused him would become clear: when the mockery went too far. And it was in that moment that he might do anything, no matter how crazy. He once gouged out a classmate's eye in high school and once he fell upon another and bit his face till it bled and once he controlled himself and did nothing and when he got home wrote a sad poem that began:

Oh my days, am I no good or is it the world that's at fault?
Why treat me so unkind then tell me it's the world?
To see me, friend, you'd say, A killer, most uncouth,
but I'm a poet of exquisite sensibility, and that's the truth.

A single glance into Hamada's bedroom reveals his inner nature: a large canvas of a sunset over the bed and another of a beautiful waterfall; romantic music floating up from the computer's speakers; the scent of roses; the bedroom window opening out onto the most stunning artwork of all time—a statue of a heaven-gazing hen sitting on its eggs while overhead shines down a sun on which is written "Karantina"; a book—*The Nightingale's Most Beautiful Songs*—lying on the bed; a pillow, a red velvet heart, with golden lettering that reads, "O heart of mine, how long shall you be empty?"

Hamada's room was one of the most important of the influences that shaped him, the key to understanding his personality. An introvert from childhood, he kept to his bedroom morning, noon, and night, seeking refuge from the privations of the world outside; morning, noon, and night he played chess against his computer, solved Sudoku puzzles in the papers, drew, or drifted through waking dreams. His father and mother failed in their attempt to connect him with the world. Ali offered to accompany him to the mosque, but he refused. At sixteen years of age his only desire was to sit at the bar, swill booze, and look at women, and so it stayed until he fell in love with Sabah.

At first he'd no idea who Sabah was. All he knew was that his heart was hers. She'd turn up in her revealing outfits and sit with her young man, and the following day she'd sit with her other young man. Sabah was a whore. (In his mind he heard his mother bawl him out: You're the whore! It's called a waitress, you dozy bullock . . . .) He drained the glass until his face turned red, then approached her. She was waiting for her friend. He sat down and asked her about herself. He asked her if she knew he was the owners' son. He didn't wait for an answer. Told her he liked her. And she didn't answer him. She glanced fearfully at the bathroom door from where her boyfriend would emerge. Hamada picked this up; he swallowed his pain and withdrew unbidden.

Those who claim Hamada forgot about Sabah, even for one day: they lie. He wrote dozens of poems about her, sung her thousands of songs, bought a guitar and composed a million melodies in her name. For her sake he fought battles by the hundred thousand. The number of battles was never tallied up, of course; we're talking in round numbers here. He injured men and was injured in turn, he killed, he burned, he stood at the head of armies and shut down streets from end to end. And he felt no remorse. Mama spoke to him. She told him a young man called Haitham Ragab had asked for Sabah by name, to come to his villa in Muqattam, and she'd traveled to Cairo, where he and his friends had slept with her and then refused to pay a thing. He'd hit her and threatened to kill her, too. Hamada went mad with rage. He started sweating, his face turned puce, his pulse raced, and from his depths he cried out, Noooooooooooooo!

At the villa he spoke calmly and reasonably to the young man who, sur- prised, told him he'd paid the girl her full two thousand, that the girl had taken a fancy to his new Samsung phone and that he'd given it to her as a "cadeau." Hamada was smiling. The instant the word cadeau was out of the young man's mouth he smashed him in the jaw with his left fist, scream- ing: Ca-what you son of a whore? The young man fell off his chair. He fell onto his back. Hamada loomed over him and began unzipping his fly. Now I'll show you who's the man and who's Sabah. The young man got up and Hamada beat him to it with another blow from his ring-laden right. Terrified, the kid retreated to the kitchen and Hamada rushed after him. He plucked a whiskey bottle from a sideboard and with a single blow broke down the kitchen door. At this juncture the right-hand pocket of his jeans began to tremble. His cell phone warbled out a snatch of a mawkish old- time poem: The companions are bemused; maddened, they mull things over, mutter back and forth . . . but he had other, more important things to take care of first. The kid had grabbed a large kitchen knife to defend him- self, but Hamada was quicker. He brought the whiskey bottle down on his head, then picked up the knife and plunged it into his heart. That done, he pulled the cell phone from his pocket and returned his mother's call. She ordered him to return to Alexandria immediately without carrying out the mission. The kid had paid Sabah her money and the girl, wanting to keep it all, had invented the story. For a few fleeting seconds Hamada's heart was assailed by a crisis of conscience. He sat down next to the corpse and buried his head in his hands. The corpse moved. He glanced at it, raised the knife aloft, and stabbed it five times more, then continued his crisis in the car. A thousand verses as he drove along: Because of you I've killed a man,

I suffer and no one gives a damn, Because of you I've roamed from land to land, And in my heart grief's seed expands . . . .

This was one of the first of the battles that Hamada fought for Sabah's sake and that allowed him to bind his destiny with hers, so that together they might create the most beautiful love story ever told.

Each morning the hen would gaze up at Hamada's bedroom. And he would sit by his window and think.

And one day he decided to take action. He went downstairs. He sat by the pedestal of the statue that coddled its four eggs and with a thick board marker wrote his name on the first egg—"Hamada"—then Sabah's name on the second, on the third, "Hamada and Sabah's children," and on the fourth, "Our children's children, God willing."

In mere days the writing had been wiped off by winter downpours and Hamada wrote it up a second time, and it was erased a second time, then a third time, then a fourth. Of all these scribblings, what remained, what held fast and true, unclaimed by the rains, was what they signified. In Sabah, Hamada saw the woman fated to be his future wife. Not only this—he saw himself as a continuation of Ali and Inji's family, gazing out at a future in which he would be patriarch of his own family, sire of offspring who would shape Egypt's fortunes. At no time did Hamada picture his parents' history as just the fleeting career of a couple of revolutionaries. Uncoupled from the nation's history, the life story of an individual (of two individuals, in this case) can have no meaning. Hamada knew this from an early age.

Hamada was brought fatherless into this world. He remembered little of Ali from his early days. All he remembered was Inji, coddling him and telling him her story, her many stories, of Ain Shams, Medinat Nasr, Sidi Gaber, Camp Cesar, Ramses Square, Abu Dhabi, and Karmouz. When she spoke of Papa she didn't speak for long. Papa's far away. Papa loves you. Papa will come back soon. Papa will come back but not just now, he might be a little late. He might be very late. You've a devil on your back called Papa! Forget it: your Papa's gone to hell. Happy now, you son of a dog? And beneath the deluge of distorted facts Hamada's personality sprang up, spurning coherent facts and viewing all creation as wide open to possibilities—as befits the personality of an artist.

When he saw his father for the first time he was afraid. The sight of the man, with his beard and thick, cracked, filthy glasses, made him cling to his mother, but once he came to live with them, Hamada began, slowly, to draw closer. He asked him about the whole story: what and why and where and when and how. And Ali told him other stories, about a character called Uncle Abu Amira, about Sousou, Sheikh Hassan, and Adel, unjustly imprisoned. He told him about cell phone games: when you get three balls of the same color next to one another they spontaneously explode. That's why we're all so far from one another, Hamada. You, me, and your mama are here, Mister Sousou and Miss Minna are in Gheit al-Enab, and Sheikh Hassan's in Camp Cesar. That day Hamada learned an important lesson, which would help him in the future; just as he learnt another lesson from the games: when you get three X's together you can destroy the isolated blocks. That's why we all stay close together, me and you and Mama, Uncle Abu Amira and Sousou's store. Unity is strength, Hamada. Older now, Hamada regarded the Hen of Karantina as the symbol around which everyone could gather. The hen was more than just a hen; its four eggs more than just four boiled eggs of stone. His father parked himself on the couch and spoke on:

Once upon a time, Hamada, the world was simple. Understandable and clear. Good was simple and evil was simple. Back then, there were two people who tried, with their humble powers, to defy the injustice that was everywhere. They owned nothing. Nothing but their faith in truth and justice and good and beauty. But God does not forget his servants. God had placed the railway at their service. In those days, train carriages disposed of wrongdoers; carriages traveling in all directions, from Ramses to Sidi Gaber, from Sidi Gaber to Ramses, from Ramses to Sohag. (He shuts his eyes for a long time then opens them.) The days passed, the days came, and motorcars appeared, microbuses, tuktuks, and all God's soldiers joined to rid the world of His enemies. Now we hear tell of marvels: machetes, switchblades, swords, and automatic weapons. God has set modern science in the service of the people, Hamada.

None of this fazed Hamada. He proceeded on his way with force and fixity.

He would sit facing his papa and mama, record their stories on his phone, and plan to write a vast verse epic of their tale. It began with a folk couplet: The sweetest thing, people, is to pray to the Prophet; The Prophet is sweet, his remembrance is sweet, and prayer is sweet . . . By the Prophet.

Hamada's at university now: Faculty of Commerce. He writes poems and reads them out to his fellow students. Just to them. He doesn't bother with poetry competitions like his shallow fellow students and neither, of course, does he bother with student unions. Art's not commerce, my friend. He does not try to peddle his art, not to anyone, and those friends who ask him for poems to send to their girlfriends get nothing at all. The dedicatee of Hamada's poems is a mysterious girl called Sabah. No one knows who she is, nor why the plump poet loves her so, nor why he's scratched her name on the side of the huge guitar he brings with him to campus. Nor why the following scene took place:

Strumming violently, Hamada conjures a heavy-metal track from his guitar and screeches, Sabah! My love! Light of my eye! Sabah! Soul of my soul . . . . And his voice swells, he screams louder, he sweats, until he topples off the lecture-hall bench. For a week, Hamada stays home: asleep at night, awake during the day. Once he wakes up to find someone beside him. He tells Hamada his name's Farouq and that he's come to see how he is. Hamada grasps his shoulder and asks him if he'd been talking much in his sleep. You were snoring, Farouq replies. Tenderly Hamada says, While I was unconscious I uttered the dearest name there is. I spoke the name Sabah. Did you catch it? And Farouq nods.

Farouq became Hamada's closest friend. His only friend, more like. He took him all round Karantina. Showed him its people. They sat together on the hen's plinth. On one of the eggs Hamada wrote: "Hamada Ali Bekheit— Farouq, Karantina, 16/3/2021, Eternal Friendship." Then he went upstairs with him to have a drink at the bar. As they entered, Hamada came to a sudden halt. He grabbed his friend's hand and asked him: Hear how my heart's beating? Farouq nodded and Hamada pointed over at Sabah, sitting inside with two men.

Sabah is first and last a body. A magnificent body: fat and lean. Two great bare thighs, one resting on the other; two giant teats; and an exposed stomach on which, below the bellybutton, a long tattooed line of blue dots reaches down until it ends in the cleft of her short skirt. Only natural, therefore, that any man who saw her would touch his cock. This is what Farouq did, and Hamada saw him do it and said nothing. They drank, got drunk, had fun, and halfway through their session Hamada assaulted his new friend. Gave him a terrific kick in the balls, then another, then another. Then screamed: Touching it in front of me? On your mother's life I'll snip it off for you next time. The kid had fallen full length on the floor. Hamada seized him by the collar and dragged him outside the bar. He tossed him into the stairwell and returned to his seat, asking for a shot of tequila. He looked at Sabah and in a low and dreamy voice that only he could hear, he said: For your sake I cast my women free, and lost, of all my friends, the one dearest to me.

Hamada's friendship with Farouq did not end with this incident. The following day Hamada met him after lectures and informed him that he'd written him a poem to say sorry. He read it out to him then swore, by God!, that they'd pay a second visit to Karantina that very day. They paid it a second visit, and a third—without the kid spending a penny from his own pocket, naturally. Hamada saw his friend as a glorious project. I want you to be my right arm, he told him once. When I read you poetry I want you to clap and when I sing you'll sing along. I want to be in your heart, my friend. And Farouq nodded. Confidently, Hamada patted him on the shoulder.

The next day Hamada spoke to Papa. He told him he'd made a new friend and was recommending this friend to come and work with them in Karantina. The kid's solid, totally trustworthy, and God willing he'll pick it up in no time. That's the first thing. The second thing is that he was feeling something, a quite unfamiliar feeling. The first time he's felt this feeling. It's like . . . something wonderful, like . . . like . . . . Then he dropped the bomb: I want to marry Sabah. Sabah who? Papa inquired, and he became flustered. His father played with his beard. Sabah the whore? he asked. To himself, Hamada said, She's a waitress, you oaf. . . . and nodded. Ali made no response. Only, a little while later, he said, Lay out the prayer mat and fetch me the shisha. Hamada did not understand this reaction, but he took it to mean his father was blocking his path to love, so he got to his feet. He decided to leave the house forever. He spoke to Farouq and told him he'd be staying over at his house that night. He went downstairs into the street, walked a couple of hundred meters, then remembered he'd left his phone behind. He went back to get it, and when he arrived he was tired out from walking. He slept for ten hours and on waking had forgotten the whole business.

Like any young Egyptian male in similar circumstances, Hamada looked on his parents' inheritance, his future property, with an unquiet eye. For this reason he had tried to prove his loyalty in more than one way: wading into battles, evangelizing for Karantina, settling accounts, and passing updates on the employees to Ali and Inji. It was just a different way of doing things, that was all. Ali and Inji were politicians at heart. They'd managed to achieve what they had with the barest smidgen of blood and a great deal of maneuvering. But this had changed. The world had become a very tough place indeed and everything, as Abu Amira once put it, came by force of arms. And this is why Hamada had come to believe in revolutionary violence. Not believe in it exactly: the revolutionary violence had forced itself upon him, because life had become so hard and people's hearts had changed.

When Hagga Itemad died, Hamada was still studying for his degree in commerce. His father sent him to Sousou, to find out what Sousou intended to do: Where would the aza be held, for instance; did he and his wife need anything? These were Ali's questions, but the way we frame things is what makes the difference, always; more important than the question of what we say is the question of how we say it. Hamada wanted to add a few words of his own, to prove that he'd become a man and was wise in the ways of his elders. To Sousou he said: See here, Sousou . . . my dear Sousou . . . I don't want you to be all upset because the old lady put the building in our name. You're a believer, you know that's how God crumbles the cookie, and I'm positive you never had your eye on your wife's inheritance. Sousou looked at Hamada with disgust then said: Let him do the aza. We don't have any money to put one on. Furthermore, I've never in my life so much as glanced at a penny that didn't belong to me, but what's right is never upsetting. Your father knows full well that he has no right to all that. Got that, you little shit? Hamada—so delicate, so fine of feeling—was wounded by these words. Sousou hurled an ashtray in his face and bellowed, You'll speak politely! Hamada leapt at him but Sousou was quicker. He beat him to it, cracking him on the head with his staff then shoving him back out through the front door while he screamed, On my mother's womb I'll teach you your place, you moron, you son of a pimp!

For many years afterward Ali would blame his only son for being the cause of the war that broke out between himself and Sousou and Minna. But Hamada was stubborn and quite unmovable when it came to his convictions. Times have changed and the diplomacy of the past no longer works. Our world has soured. And even if we were to suppose that Hamada hadn't provoked him, would that have turned the tide of Sousou's hatred? Sousou, who had never wished them well in his life? Hamada's style was based on rushing into war in order to win it. Ali and Inji's style was based on delaying it, delaying it and delaying it and delaying it, until, sweet Lord! Enough already!

We're in the age of speed, Farouq, and they're just plodding along the same old timeworn tracks.

It's always trickier to hold the summit than to scale it. This lesson made a forceful impression on Hamada and he worked hard to put himself through all the toughest training routines. Mental conditioning in particular. The age to come will not be one of brawn and physical force but of the mind and information. He spent his free time solving crosswords and Sudoku, and playing Monopoly with Farouq. Farouq never won at Monopoly. Hamada always won, and characters like Hamada are never content to win; quite the contrary, because defeat teaches us new things and victories keep us where we are. Hamada would tie his money up in major deals and Farouq wouldn't notice. Farouq would fall into traps and fail to spot the simplest plays. And Hamada would tell stories. He had managed to develop this talent of doing two things at the same time—playing and talking—and even though his conversation during play did tend to revolve around the play itself it hinted at a future time in which he'd be able to buy Aleppo, say, while talking about Sabah. So far he hadn't managed to pull it off, but he would one day.

Know what your problem is, Farouq? I'll tell you. You're an idiot. Don't get upset with me, my friend. I don't want to upset you. You're a beautiful person, a great artist, but art's not everything, friend. You have to be clever too. Take me, for instance. I'm an artist, I play music, but I've never been beaten at this game. From here on out anyone who gets beaten at Monopoly doesn't belong with us. Karantina needs brains and art together. I'm telling you now that you're no use to me. You don't teach me anything new. Who taught you to buy that square, Farouq? Who taught you to put a market on Benghazi? Who taught you what's written on the cards and what isn't? I taught you everything Farouq . . . and you? You're nothing. You're an idiot, Farouq.

Farouq was a forgiving man. He didn't respond to his best friend's insults. He looked at him, smiled, and put a silly little house on an even sillier little city, and that was what drove Hamada over the edge, who this time grabbed the board and chucked it at his friend's face. The cards and dice and banknotes scattered across the café floor and Farouq, with matchless forbearance, started to gather them up. Hamada was trembling. He hid his face in his hands, muttered, You fool, you fool, you fool . . . over and over in a hysterical tone, and Farouq put every banknote back in its place on the board, looked up at Hamada, and patted his shoulder with a bewildered hand.

The soul is always vulnerable to deception. The body is tangible and can be trusted; what's lacking is evidence for the soul's existence. Artists in particular are prone to psychological instability—what psychologists know as the correlation between mental instability and creativity. All the artists who have touched our lives with their beautiful creations suffered from addictions to drink and drugs, from extreme nervous conditions, from depressive and suicidal tendencies. And Hamada was an artist to the core.

Hamada never understood why his mother treated him that way. She relied on him for many things, but for many more she avoided him. For instance: Hamada was an expert in all manner of insects and reptiles. He'd spent his life teaching himself all about snakes. He bought a profusion of books dealing with this arcane and profitable field of knowledge. Left them all over the house in the hope his parents might one day notice them and ask his assistance in some enterprise grander than turning over a coffee shop or beating a girl senseless because she took a job behind their backs. Hamada was forever sad because his mother never sought his help in ridding the house of insects.

The house was constantly being raided by Persian ants and cockroach hordes, especially in summer. Hamada would sit across from his father, telling him about the difference between the various types of ant, about African snakes, how cockroaches hatch their eggs, about the attributes of the winged cockroach. And even so, each summer Inji would call out the exterminator. The employee would spray the house and its inhabitants would decamp to their new apartment in Agami. This pained Hamada. Not just his lack of involvement in ridding the house of cockroaches, but the lack of faith shown in him for all such operations. Once he told his Mama that he felt like a zero before the decimal, like something worthless. He wept and held tight to his mother's arm. The doorbell chimed and in walked Farouq, smiling as usual. Hamada's eyes were still teary. Farouq's astonished expression left his friend no choice but to explain his problem, so Hamada told his tale in a choked voice, glancing at his mother so she might witness what he was telling Farouq and glancing at Farouq so he might see what he was telling his mother. Inji looked disgusted, or at least uninterested, in the dramatic scene unfolding before her. Suddenly, in a cold voice, she spoke. Hamada, sweetheart, there's no one called Farouq. There's no one here but us. You're talking to thin air, my boy.

Hamada shuddered. His terrified cry rang out: Shut up! Shut up! Then he looked over at Farouq and grabbed his arm. He could feel the arm between his fingers. But only the arm. Bit by bit, Farouq was vaporizing. His head went first, then his neck, then his belly, then his legs, then his right arm. The left arm alone remained, suspended in Hamada's hand, until it too disappeared: shoulder, elbow, fingers. Hamada sat down on the couch, and broke down and wept.

This incident—Hamada's discovery that Farouq was just a figment of his imagination—did not affect the relationship between the two of them. They remained loyal friends, with a hint of reproach in the gaze Hamada directed at his dearest companion. Why didn't you tell me, my friend? Why did you deceive me? Why leave me prey to doubt? Why, why, why . . . ? And Farouq would look at him and smile a meaningless smile.

2

nji had a soft spot for Sousou. The only member of Abu Amira's family
she still had a soft spot for and whose company she still enjoyed. Soft spot
here means soft spot, nothing more. In his troubles he'd come to her and
ask, What shall I do, dear lady? and she'd complain to him about Ali. The
man's an idiot, Sousou. He doesn't see things right. The soft spot started,
as we know, with Sousou's lengthy phone calls from the South, and as soon
as Sousou had returned, as all the residents of Karantina knew, he'd married Minna, and it was no longer possible for the soft spot to grow into
anything else.

Sexual intercourse between Ali and Inji was scheduled: once on Thursday and once mid-week. The act itself was fine, on the whole, aside from a
degree of listlessness to be expected of any long-married couple, and ever
since Sousou had left for Sohag, Inji frequently thought of him as she lay
beneath Ali. When he came back, with a new mustache, a new body—full,
not fat—his face would come to her each and every time. She consoled herself that perhaps a day would come in which the world would treat her fairly
and she'd leave Ali and marry Sousou. But Hagga Itemad spoiled everything
when she signed what was left of her building over to Inji. She made people
hate her, lit the fuse of Sousou's rage and that of his wife, Minna, and ruined
forever the possibility of any dalliance between her and Sousou.

For some reason or other—we can't but put it down to the fact we sometimes confuse one person with another—Inji was confusing herself with Ali
when she imagined that her husband was the cause of the break between

themselves and Sousou. Although the building—the true source of all the problems—was signed over to her and not to Ali, she continued to reproach him with her glances, and when the war between Ali and Sousou broke out, she chose to play the part of a fifth column, in league with the enemy: acting the zealous patriot while playing down his danger. Fuck the world and Ali with it. Fuck Ali most of all, who wants to deny her the thing she wants so bad.

We can't say for certain that these feelings were reciprocated. Sousou had no time for love affairs and romances and the like. Sousou was building himself up, building his empire, and destroying the empires of other men. When he and his men moved out of his store and opened another in Gheit al-Enab where he lived, it was the trumpet blast that signaled the start of the war. Ali saw this, Inji didn't, and Hamada boiled with rage for five whole hours. Sousou's men took to sitting around Ali's building, the very men without whom the job of protecting Karantina would have been impossible. Sousou didn't abandon his old store; rather, he rented it out to one of his men, Ramadan Maadoul. Ramadan Maadoul wasn't just one of Sousou's men; he was a government informer as well. Sousou was well aware of this and said nothing. The day might come when we need even the informers: for their characters, for what they bring.

And Ali did not forgive this step. Three of his men drove Ramadan from the store and tipped the oil and liver on the ground. A minor operation, but Sousou required it in order that he might respond and assert the new status he claimed for himself. Ten of his men attacked the Karantina Café. They climbed to the top floor and turned out men and women in their underwear. The lot of them, paraded through Karmouz stark naked, with Sousou's men behind them toting weapons. And when Ali tried to respond to this strike, he found no men: they were all in Gheit al-Enab now, with Sousou. And Inji was against shooting Sousou, and Abu Amira's word was mud. The only person Ali found when he looked around was Hamada. Hamada, it doesn't bother you seeing Sabah walking naked in the street? Rage ignited inside Hamada. His father was at his side now, every step of the way. Hamada would be an army, a weapon, to replace the weapon called Sousou, which had blown up in their faces. In addition to logistical guidance, related to events on the ground, Ali gave his son guidance of another sort, all of it historical, concerning Sousou's forebears and the wellsprings of his influence. For instance, it's true that rounding up the men and women and ejecting them bare-assed from the café was Sousou's doing, but it wasn't his idea. In carrying out this operation Sousou had mimicked another operation, buried in the past, which had been carried out by one of Alexandria's most notorious characters of recent decades: Sika.

As we all agree, Alexandrian history is links forged in a chain, and the loss of one means not just the loss of a single, solitary link, but the loss of all the links before and after. And so it is beholden on us to tell the tale of this most important link in Alexandria's history, the tale of Sayyid, Sika, and Sultan, or the Three Esses, as they became known, for short.

The tale began one winter, beneath the rain. Sika appeared. A huge mustache, hair thinning on top and a ponytail behind, a striped shirt open to the waist, and a gold chain suspended across a hairy chest. He smiles and bares his teeth, abscessed and irregular, a look of frightening evil in his eyes. One day in the mid-nineties. Alexandria was wintering hard: thunder, lightning, sheets of rain, and other special effects. A police car entered a narrow street in Abu Suleiman. Sika lay in wait. He bombarded it with bricks and Pepsi bottles from a rooftop and, in a moment of madness, leapt down. The officers and troopers found him in their midst. They watched him butcher an officer with his sword, then suddenly, miraculously, he vanished. For two weeks no one saw hide or hair of him and then he returned. Sika was in love with a girl from the neighborhood. Her father was a primary school teacher. He spoke to her father, who told him that the girl was too young, still in high school. But Sika was a criminal. He abducted the girl's brother, hid him away, and told the father that he was quite capable of doing to young Iman what he'd done to the officer; was capable of doing other things besides: acid, rape, murder. In the end he married her. After butchering the officer, he married her. In those days his popularity was at its height. He stayed at home for a month after the wedding, and then was on his way again. It had got into Sika's head that he was the legend of Abu Suleiman, of Wingate, of all Alexandria. Harbi's legend had begun to fade. Harbi had disappeared; no one knew where he was. His initial appearance had confirmed that Alexandria was in need of a folk hero and Sika was ready and willing to fill the gap—though he was to prove a disappointment, let it be said. He assaulted underage schoolgirls, sold adulterated drugs, broke into apartments and robbed their owners, and to force residents to show him loyalty he sent his men out through the neighborhood and took protection money off them on the first of every month and on holidays. And that still wasn't enough. Prices were through the roof and money scarce. The protection money increased month after month until one entire family refused to pay. With five of his men, Sika entered the building that had refused to pay. They spread out through the four apartments. They forced everyone in the building, men and women, to strip. They ejected them naked from the building, bringing up the rear with machetes, switchblades, and automatic weapons. He was a heathen, a man without faith. This didn't frighten the people. They waited for the chance to bring him down. It was at this point that all the residents of Abu Suleiman turned into police informers, informers with a single purpose: to inform on Sika. And when a police squad raided his home he stood up. He opened fire, and was fired upon. It was raining once again. The curtain came down during another winter—beneath the rain. Sika was killed.

When this tale took place, Sousou was still a little boy. He heard a lot about Sika's life. It both repelled him and spoke to him. After he'd grown and found his footing in Camp Cesar he'd gotten to know one of Sika's lovers at an Agami disco. He heard her story and put her to work in the Camp Cesar apartment. She told him intimate details: Sika was the one who made me happiest. He never said no. Stayed up all night. Time after time: never spent (a lewd glance) and neither was I . . . . If history be of two types—official history and alternative history—then it was official history that described Sika in terms of thuggery and crime, and alternative history, history according to his lovers, that described Sika in terms of sexual vigor. Sousou had never believed in official history; he believed in the history of the people, in scattered facts, little details, micro-history, and Sika was a hard man, not a thug. That's how the people told it.

Among Sika's men was a thin, neat young man named Sayyid. Small, neat half-frame glasses, a thin, finely drawn face with a jutting brow, no mustache, and a chin that looked like it had never sprouted. Like he was fresh from university. Sayyid witnessed his boss being killed and fled. He left Abu Suleiman completely, afraid of the people's anger. He had been one of the perpetrators of the incident when men and women were ejected onto the street and was responsible for stripping one girl in particular of all her clothes, removing her panties and bra with his own hands as revenge for her refusing to marry him days earlier. He couldn't stay in Alexandria so he traveled to Matrouh for two months, and then returned to the neighborhood, his Bedouin kinfolk in tow. At that time, the Matrouh Bedouin held sway in Abu Suleiman. Sayyid, with his family, with what remained of Sika's henchmen, managed in mere months to forge a legend to match his boss's. The neighborhood went into total shutdown. Everywhere young men were smoking hash in the street and in the cafés, and any police car, were it to venture in, would be ripped into sixty pieces. In those days, one slip meant death and Sayyid's slip was not long in coming: a certain individual whispered into his ear that Miallim Ragab in Wardiyan was selling his stuff to a miallim in Qabbari called Sultan at a discount, because the two men were connected by marriage. The blood began to boil in Sayyid's brain and he decided to buy off another miallim in Wardiyan as a challenge to Ragab. This coincided with the surfacing of a megalomania that afflicted him as it had his predecessor Sika. He ratcheted up the payments imposed on the people of Abu Suleiman and murdered a family who'd tried to wriggle out of paying: a man, his wife, his elderly mother, and two children. Under cover of night the men of Sultan—who was working for Miallim Ragab—attacked and killed him, and the people hailed Sultan: a harbinger of hope, the turning of a new leaf.

When this took place, Sousou was at high school. Now he knew three guys: the first hooks him up with the second, the second with a third, and then the third with the first. It's a small world. One time, Sousou hung out with one of Sayyid's classmates from the Faculty of Arts. The guy talked to him about Sayyid's academic prowess at university, about his passion for psychology and his keen eye for anything to do with how people's minds worked. Once more we arrive at the sticky issue of official and alternative histories. The official says, "drug dealer" and the alternative says, "top student" and "keen eye." Sousou's preference was always for alternative history.

It was a year, year and a half, since Miallim Sultan first showed up in Qab-bari. Miallim Sultan, a true boss: gallabiya, coarse features, big mustache, a bald spot. A fierce but kind expression with a certain inborn nobility about it. His rise to fame was unconnected with that of Harbi. Harbi led a number of operations to help out Miallim Sultan, and to help out Miallim Ragab too, and when Harbi vanished, Sultan did business with others. Sultan and Ragab both belonged to an important family from Qena. The family emi-grated to Alexandria in the seventies and settled in Qabbari, then Ragab had moved to Wardiyan while Sultan stayed in the neighborhood to which he'd grown accustomed. Given all this, it was only natural that Sultan should marry Ragab's sister. They'd been raised together; had known each other for ages. Same roots, same neighborhood, same destiny, God willing, for good or ill. At first Sultan was that classic type of good-hearted miallim: he never made trouble for Ragab and kept himself to himself. Only ever did things that served the people's interests: like killing Miallim Sayyid, for example. So far, so good, but Harbi was hugely influential. People everywhere chattering about Harbi. It drove Sultan crazy. What had the kid done that he hadn't? And, like his predecessors, he was aware that a change was taking place in Alexandria and with the inborn sense of the true Egyptian he'd scented this powerful yearning for change among his own people. And he put himself for-ward for the role. He stopped taking care of the cops and supplying them with drugs. This was the first phase. The second phase was to murder any of his men who were dealing with the cops behind his back, and the third phase was to murder any of his men who had dealt with the cops, if only once, even if it had happened in the distant past. In other words, anyone whose history bore any trace of dealings with the cops. Miallim Sultan initiated a sweeping purge in Qabbari, a campaign whose slogan ran: The severed finger is never abscessed. He resolved to cut down all his henchmen who were suspected of the slightest connection with the Interior Ministry, to kill those of his customers suspected of the slightest connection with those henchman who were suspected of connection with the ministry, to kill those customers sus-pected of any connection with the first lot of customers, and so on. Every day, Miallim Sultan would discover a new candidate for murder. And the purge reached further still. Dealings with the cops took on a broader, more elastic, definition. For instance, anyone who entered the police station to apply for an ID card now had to prove he hadn't cooperated. Even former prisoners were required to prove they hadn't been brainwashed on the inside and that no one had asked them to sell out. Miallim Sultan neglected his work and gave himself over to making his prophecies come true: "Qabbari: The First Liberated Neighborhood" was the slogan he daubed on Qabbari's walls in a crude, black-lettered hand. And as the purges followed, one after the other, he lost much of his power. He lost his henchmen and his henchmen's henchmen, all of whom he decided to kill himself. And despite his appearance of weakness his soul was growing ever stronger and firmer and more radiant, and at the end of each day he would repair to his bed and murmur softly and contentedly, The severed finger is never abscessed. When the inevitable Judas bullet struck him, as he was carrying out one of his periodic executions, he fell to the floor and murmured the same line, in the same tone, a tone of contentment, of conviction, of tolerance: The severed finger is never abscessed.

At this point, official and alternative histories came together. By which we mean Miallim Sultan in his capacity as a reformist rather than a drug dealer, as a person who tried to take on the authority of the Interior Ministry and to found an Alexandrian utopia, but who, given the casualties of his reform program (and just as happened in 1841 and 1967) was unable to complete his task. All these voices, the voices of Sika, Sayyid, Sultan, and those like them, fell still at Harbi's death. The latter's murder in public view was proof to the people that the king was still the king. Everything returned to how it had been pre-Harbi: there were drugs, thugs, and terrorism, but without any thought of change, without grand words, without Messiahs or false prophets. In the end, the individual most closely associated with that discourse of change was Harbi. That time was Harbi's time and the rest rode on his coattails.

Now, after that quick glance at the mid-1990s, a return to our present era, the 2020s: Sousou is studying the history of his forebears, the Three Esses. Sousou is boning up on all these details precisely so that no one can accuse him of ignoring them and jumping straight to generalizations. And after boning up . . . Sorry, so sorry, forgive me, Sousou says, but Harbi was a filthy character. Crazy, or rather: he didn't know what he wanted. The ones who really made Alexandria were the Three Esses.

In this way did Sousou recast the history of Alexandria in his head, did he read back between the lines and confront the original narrative with a narrative of his own, with "his own" very much in the possessive sense: Sousou saw himself as their fourth, the Fourth of the Three Esses and the one who would succeed where they had failed. The links of Alexandrian history are bound one to the other, as we've said a million times before.

This was the tale of the Three Esses, and Sousou thoroughly internalized it. He hung pictures of them all around his home in Gheit al-Enab. Now pictures of Sika, Sayyid, and Sultan were everywhere around the Karabantina of Gheit al-Enab.

Sousou hadn't had much by way of an education—sixteen and that's your lot, not even a diploma—so it was only natural that his enunciation lacked sufficient precision. From the beginning Sousou didn't pronounce Karantina right. He shortened it: Karatina, and sometimes Karasina or Karatsina or, spoken in jest, Karabantina. And something or other selected the last for immortality. When he split with Ali he took the name with him. He named—or renamed—his store Karabantina Liver, and on his house hung the sign Karabantina Buildings. Gradually, his wife Minna started pronouncing the name this way and his men pronounced it this way. We are now witnessing the transformation of Karantina into two neighborhoods, the seeds of different dialects taking shape for each. One neighborhood, lying along the tramline and called Karantina, belonging to Ali and Inji and Hamada and filled with portraits of Harbi; and a second in Gheit al-Enab, called Karabantina and filled with portraits of the Three Esses and their Fourth, Sousou. It wasn't therefore a matter of two individuals facing off, or two neighborhoods, but of two philosophies, two histories, two languages and value systems, each of which claimed to be the founder of modern Alexandria. In matters such as these, a definitive answer is a very tough call. Completely impossible, in fact.

The split had become severe. Everyone could see it, even old, sick Abu Amira, visiting his younger brother in Gheit al-Enab. He got out of the car to find Sousou waiting for him in a tuktuk. They tootled off together through the streets of Karabantina, Abu Amira gesturing at the pictures and asking Sousou:

Who're they, brother?

That's Sika, that's Sayyid, and that one's Sultan.

The criminals?

The heroes.

The criminals, Sousou?

The heroes, ya hagg.

You're hanging up pictures of criminals, Sousou?

Hanging up pictures of heroes, ya hagg.

At home, Sousou prepares the shisha. He brings it to Abu Amira, who begs off—The doctor says I really shouldn't—then takes a seat. Look, brother, I've become an old man now and I don't want to see you fighting with Sheikh Ali and me in my last days, as you might say.

He's the one who started it, ya hagg. Make him give us back our rightful share of the building.

That building's in his wife's name by right and law, Sousou.

By right and law? Right and law? It's rightful and lawful to sign a building over to a criminal?

Sheikh Ali's a hero.

It's rightful and lawful to make an old lady sign over the building to a criminal?

The hagga signed over the building to a hero.

And it's right and lawful that you, Hagg Abu Amira, are standing up for a criminal?

I'm standing up for a hero.

Sousou offers Abu Amira a half chicken from his own hand while they are eating lunch. Taste this, ya hagg, you'll love it. All God's gifts are sweet, Sousou. Abu Amira's health is not what it once was. He eats a sliver of breast then looks at Sousou.

You know, it wasn't right of you to throw those men and women out naked, Sousou.

Come on! Was I chucking them out of the mosque? It's an unclean place and those inside are worse.

I don't want you dicing words with me, I want you to go and apologize to Sheikh Ali and tell him, I'm sorry, my brother, and I won't do it again.

Okay then . . . .

Praise be to God.

But who told you I won't do it again?

(No answer.)

With God's help, it's going to be me and me alone who teaches him some manners.

(No answer.)

See here, brother. He's like my little pet monkey. We'll have our fun with him and when we're bored we'll have that truce you want. But as long as I'm not bored, let's play.

(No answer. Abu Amira is busy picking the sliver out of his teeth.)

Where are the pictures of Harbi, Sousou?

Harbi?

Harbi. You've forgotten Harbi, boy? Your wife's father, whose house you're sitting in? Miallim Mohamed Harbi?

Sure I know him, but forgive me brother, terribly sorry, it's just that I don't put up crooks' pictures in my neighborhood.

So Harbi's a crook now, is he?

A crook, yes.

So Hagg Harbi, Sheikh Hassan's brother, you're saying he's a crook now? Is that it?

That's it. A crook, ya hagg.

So Hagg Harbi's . . .

(Cutting in, his voice growing shriller) A crook, ya hagg. A thug. A filthy human being. Everything he did as filthy as him. (He falls silent for a while. Calms down.) Get you some tea, ya hagg?

Just a touch of sugar, brother, bless you.

The tray has a cup of tea on it and a shisha pipe. Abu Amira raises no objections this time. He's sitting on the floor, puffing away, and leaning his head back against the couch.

So you don't want to hang Harbi's picture in the neighborhood, Sousou?

That's right, I don't.

(A minute's silence) Very odd, because on my way here, you see, I saw pictures of these other guys but they were . . . How do I put it? They weren't unfamiliar to me.

They're Sika, Sayyid, and Sultan, ya hagg.

(He drifts. Glances sideways.) Very odd. The thugs?

(No answer. He's busy adjusting the pipe's pot of tobacco.)

They smoke hash from a sealed cup. They're both completely out of it.

Look here, Sousou. Don't go thinking Ali sent me to you.

There's no man can send you, ya hagg.

There's no man can send me. Quite right. You're quite right. It's Inshi, his wife, who sent me.

Inshi?

Inshi, Ali's wife.

(Waking up a little.) What's Inshi, Ali's wife, want then?

Sousou, she says she loves you and doesn't wish you ill.

(Dreamy) She loves me and doesn't wish me ill?

And she asks, for her sake, for a little less ill from your side.

(Focused) For her sake?

She's waiting for you to go to her and for you two to come to some agreement.

(Drifting) She's waiting for me to go to her?

The hurricane is raging through the city. Minna, Sousou's wife, suddenly opens the door, hair wild, a nightgown on, rage in her eyes. By the Good Lord, ya hagg, neither of us is going to shake hands with that piece of trash. If that husband of mine, that man there, goes to see them, I swear to God, he won't be a man in my eyes anymore. So tell me: how's he going to go now?

Minnatallah Mohamed Harbi: high-strung, stubborn, loved people, just so long as it didn't harm her own interests. She was the hidden factor behind the revival of the legends of the Three Esses and the presentation of the dark side of her father Mohamed Harbi—of whom she remembered nothing worth mentioning. She remembered him sitting smoking shisha in cotton underwear, remembered him beating her mother till she gave him twenty pounds to go and spend at the café, remembered him playing cards for money with his friends at home, taking a bottle of booze out of his gallabiya. In short, Minna did not have many positive memories of her father. But was that the motive for her attempt to smear his image, to portray him as a criminal and thug, and challenge his story with the stories of Sika, Sayyid, and Sultan? Not exactly. Perhaps it's a whole lot simpler than that. When a person goes to park his car somewhere and finds that someone else has gotten there first, well, he goes and parks it in another spot straightaway. No need for a big fuss and bother. It's a similar thing here. All there is to it is that Ali and Inji had bound themselves to Harbi's story, and challenging that bond had become an impossible task—a Mission Impossible—and so Minna had decided to park her car in another spot.

It all began with a little chat she had with Sousou. He told her that Ali, that scumbag, was trying to take advantage of her father, and she told him that Inji was no less of a scumbag, always hiding behind her portrait of Harbi the Pure. Well, I'll tell you about that Harbi. My father wasn't the man they say he was. I know all about him. He was one of those who'll go to hell even when they've told the truth. My father was a good man and everything, all right, but he was all sin. There was this one guy called Sultan who we used to hear about back in the day. He was twice the man Harbi was, I swear it.

Sousou started turning the matter over, examining it from all sides and recalling old stories, people he'd met, battles he'd seen, and battles he'd been involved in. He nosed and roamed and asked about and carried back an alternative history that he set about editing himself. Smiling, calm, assured, Sousou slept in his wife's arms.

For long years, Minna had gone on feeling grateful to Inji. Loved her with all her heart. Now she recalled that the first murder she ever committed had been for the sake of this woman. Right at the outset of her life, she'd killed a sheikh who had betrayed Inji. She had made up her mind to take revenge for her teacher, even if she ended up in prison as a result. It had all been going great at the time. Why then did what happened happen? No one can give you rational reasons for why people change. Interests aren't cause enough. Nor is jealousy, nor the desire for revenge. Everything happened suddenly. Minna felt that Inji was playing the fool with Sousou and, more important, that Sousou didn't mind, and, more important still, that Inji had it all: prestige, an excellent reputation, and the building that by rights was hers. Okay, so what to do? Nothing at all. Minna kept quiet, held it in her heart, and resolved that, just as she'd once gotten vengeance for her teacher, she would now revenge herself upon her.

Minna had no children and for years now there hadn't been the slightest hope she would. This destroyed her. She felt abandoned in the world, alone, without father, mother, or child, and as for her husband, despite years of love and longing and passion, she now wished she'd married someone else. The problem, of course, did not lie in Sousou himself—Sousou was better than most—but Minna, daughter of the Internet, online chat, and Facebook, dreamt of a marriage that would transport her away from the world of Karmouz—a rotten neighborhood, a worthless world—and yet every step she took only bound her tighter to the place. So it's like that, is it? It's all over? And Minna retreated into herself and wept: wept at the bitter loneliness, the faithlessness of her days and the betrayal of kith and kin, or those she'd thought her kith and kin. But she quickly rallied, got to her feet, brushed away her tears, and stood defiant, facing herself in the mirror and making up her mind: If this is the life she'd been dealt, then she would be strong. Be a wolf or the wolves of the forest will eat you up. Together with Sousou, Minna collected the tales told of Sika, Sayyid, and Sultan. She took on the job of collecting their pictures and enlarging them in a computer store. And in her mind she held a long conversation with Miallim Sultan.

For long years Minna would tell herself that there are people in our lives, either gone from our world or still alive, who we wish we could meet with one day to listen to them and to learn. Miallim Sultan was one of these people. And in her capacity as the woman responsible for running the Three Esses propaganda campaign she had hung on the walls his line, The lopped-off finger is never abscessed, in all its different iterations—"severed" for "lopped," "sores" for "abscesses"—you know, the variations you need if people aren't to lose interest; and alongside this slogan the image of an outstretched palm and a knife extending to the forefinger and cutting through it. A plan was growing in her mind: anyone who dealt with Ali and Inji, anyone who dealt with those who dealt with them, and anyone who dealt with that lot—the fate of them all would be the fate of the severed finger. Minna knew that the plan would be hard to implement at first, but everything in its time, and what was hard today would not be so tomorrow or the day after.

This coincided with the growth of a large sore on Minna's toe. In the beginning it was a little pimple, just a spot that was gone in two days. But the foolishness of man knows no limits. Minna worried at it with her finger. The spot grew into a great big sore. She tried popping it with her fingernails. The sore leaked a small quantity of white fluid and stayed there, full of some solid, unyielding mass. She left it alone for a couple of days and it shrank again. She couldn't allow things to end so easily. She went back to worrying at it with her fingers. It grew extremely large, till it had swollen so much that it pinched her to put on sandals. In the end a minor surgical procedure was required. The doctor injected the abscessed toe with a local anesthetic and began draining the pus. She was disgusted at herself, at her whole life, felt that the doctor was going to cut the toe off with his scalpel, and wished that he would to spare her this feeling. Suddenly, as though decreed by fate, the immortal line sounded in her head: "The severed finger is never abscessed." She smiled and dwelt on the wisdom of people back in the day. They had been prophesying.

Sultan's death was more than inspirational to Minna. Everyone joined against him—his men, his friends, the government, the terrorists—and when he was killed, no one knew who had done it and no one claimed his taar. They left his body in the street for a whole day and no one came forward to bury it. Even his wife and kids were afraid to approach it lest they be struck down by another bullet. Miallim Sultan, who'd killed more than twenty people with his own hands in the last weeks of his life for the sole purpose of purging the neighborhood of the police and those who dealt with them—was this his reward? Her whole life, Minna had hated populism and populists. She'd no time for them at all.

Minna pictured Miallim Sultan in his different states: eating, drinking, driving his car, having sex. She went to Qabbari to meet his wife. She drank tea with her and tried to make her spill the beans, and the lady didn't disappoint. At first she seemed shy, then offered some standard line about people not appreciating people who appear like candles in their lives—then she got into details. The miallim behaved appallingly at home. He was fine and good at first, but after he had his psychological episode he started to hate his wife and children. Night and day he'd sit there weighing things up—who'd met whom and who hadn't—and woe betide anyone who argued with him or asked him, Why did you do that? or said, You shouldn't have done that. One time his son Abdallah objected to the miallim killing a kid who studied with him at college. Father and son fell into a debate that ended with the miallim taking his pistol from his pocket and pulling the trigger, though luckily the magazine was empty. The miallim, he was fine and everything, the wife added, but he wasn't the type to worry about his kids and home, you know, and he didn't do right by them. Minna wrote down all these observations and drew her glittering conclusion: even the miallim's own wife and children hadn't understood him. Everything had conspired against him. And she thanked the Lord for the blessing of bearing no children, that she would not be burnt by the ingratitude of offspring as Sultan had been burnt before her, and continued her mission of brushing the dust of neglect from this perfectly formed and peerless man.

3

There are always nine ways to respond in the affirmative to a question like The afternoon prayer's yet to be called? You can say, Ah, you can say, Yes, you can give a slight and self-assured nod of the head, you can give a wavering, unconfident nod of the head, you can echo the question back in a decisive tone, The afternoon prayer *is* yet to be called, you can say, God willing, you can say, As God commands, you can say, As long as we have life, and you can say, As long as we have life, God willing the afternoon prayer will be called, as God commands. What we mean to say is that Ali, on entering the mosque that day and asking this question, had received these nine responses from nine worshipers sitting within. Each replied after his fashion and this, to Ali, had the quality of pure nightmare.

The nine responses were not all uttered at the same time. In turn, let us say. This one finished and that one begun, and were we to suppose that those sitting in the mosque numbered nine exactly (a sound supposition) and to suppose (soundly, too: no less so) that there were two worshipers sitting side by side before the minbar, two beside the south door, three by the north door, one in the very center of the room, and one by the fountain, and that these nine responses, issuing from locations far apart from one another, were uttered in raised tones without the speakers adjusting their positions, without them directing their gaze toward Ali, then we may easily comprehend the nightmarish quality Ali perceived in their responses. The nine responders were making light of Ali's question. The answers had a mocking tone or, at the very least, an indifferent one. And this was not the first time.

Ali, Sheikh Ali, Miallim Ali, Ali Basha: all these terms now seemed to belong to a past era, a golden era, an era in which great men basked in respect. What the government and his enemies had failed to do had been accomplished by a handful of wastrels lounging on street corners. To this extent, Ali's battle appeared to be with the values of the modern age, values that he—a sheikh now in his sixth decade of life—had never had to reckon with before. Sheikh Ali fought the present with all his might. Yet, "he didn't fit in," "he didn't acclimatize," "he didn't adjust to reality," are all gentle phrases that try to hide an uglier truth, a truth that Ali did not care to admit, even to himself—that his legend was steadily ebbing away. No one spoke this out loud. They thrust the thought away with all the strength they could muster. But from time to time it would peek out, in dreams and nightmares and slips of the tongue. This was Ali's private hell until, one day in Ramadan, what happened to him happened.

The tarawih, the prayers offered on Ramadan nights, have been performed. Ali's watching television with Inji by his side. He's eating a piece of basbousa and dragging on a shisha pipe. Inji's peeling an orange with her teeth and right hand and picking out a piece of kunafa with her left. Suddenly the title sequence of a fatwa show appears on the screen. Ali, weighed down with iftar, with sweets and fruit, with drink and tobacco smoke, isn't paying attention. The sheikh on TV is discussing a complaint from I.S., who says she no longer loves her husband. What should she do? Every one of Ali's senses pricks up. Out of the corner of his eye he looks at Inji, who places her orange and kunafa on a plate and goes into the kitchen. He starts to think. So you don't love me no more, Inshi, that's it? That's how it ends? You're complaining about me on TV? Piece by piece it started coming clear in his mind: the youngsters' manners aren't the problem anymore, nor are time and its changes responsible for people's lack of respect. Right now, his greatest foe is the one who calls herself Inji Suleiman Abdallah. She's the one who's leading the whispering campaign against him, the campaign that starts in Karmouz and runs all the way through to national television and beyond. He fixes on revenge.

We would be mistaken, deeply mistaken in fact, were we to think of Ali as being crazy. He might have gone a little overboard in his assumptions about the complainant I.S., it's true, but there's no smoke without fire. As he ruminated, Inji was elsewhere: in her office, writing a long and moving letter, four sheets of foolscap, to the editor of a new column in the *Al-Ahram* newspaper. The new column was entitled "Problem Solver" and filled the space left by an older column headlined "Friday Post." Inji followed the new column, with its problems and letters, its dilemmas, its torments, agonies, and yearnings, its moments of despair and divine deliverance, and for days and nights she considered becoming one of its heroines. She grew attached to the personality of the columnist and his answers and felt no shame in writing to him about her problem. Being cultured and well educated, she accorded great importance to these things, unlike Ali, who'd never opened a newspaper in his life. The papers were a part of her daily routine. Unlike the rest of the residents of this rotten neighborhood she didn't see them as a waste of time or empty words. She was perfectly calm, writing with a pencil, which she would sharpen and then throw the shavings into the wastepaper basket. She erased certain passages and rewrote them. She resolved to be more cautious than she'd ever been before. What she was writing now were not mere words, but destinies and fates intertwined, information that could ruin them all. She began:

Dear editor of the celebrated column "Problem Solver,"

Firstly, may I congratulate myself and you on the start of the blessed month of Ramadan. May God grant you a wonderful and blessed holiday. I pray to God that you and your beautiful family are as well as can be, and now I would like to tell you my story.

My story is such that were I to swear to you it was true ever so many times—and remember, we're in the blessed month of Ramadan—you still would not believe me. For it's a strange and wonderful tale, and stranger and more wonderful still, it happened to me alone, of all the people in the world.

Sometimes I find myself asking, Why me? Is there no one else but me on earth? The answer that comes back is just that this is the wisdom of our Lord, Almighty and On High, and that I, no matter how I strive to match His wisdom, will never attain it.

Now, I don't want to go on and on. I know you've got responsibilities and things to do. This tale of mine began many years ago, when I met a hardworking, ambitious young man and a smoldering passion was ignited between us. By chance, this young man was distantly related to me and so I surrendered myself to him and decided that he was the one the fates had chosen to be my shining knight—for I was always the epitome of the God-fearing, faithful wife. And now, some thirty years after God honored me with His call to don the niqab, I can say that I have always served Him and never strayed. The point is that this youth and I became entangled in a business that I do not wish to mention here, and we were compelled (she erases and rewrites it) were obliged to journey together to Alexandria, and in Alexandria the ocean of life, with its peaks and troughs, bore us up to the very heights then cast us down into the abyss. We were all at sea. What should we do? How do we face life? We were two youngsters, without any kind of experience.

Anyway, what I want to say is that my dear husband gave me the shock of my life. We were fighting one day about something and it ended with me deciding to leave the home where I had never, not once, felt at ease, and going to live some distance away in one of Alexandria's poorer neighborhoods. The years passed, however, and good folk interceded on both sides, until I returned to live with my dear husband once again, and it was then I discovered that he had become an entirely different person from the refined and well-brought-up young man I once knew. I discovered, dear sir, that he now gives little thought to his appearance and personal hygiene, so much so that he gives off a foul smell at all times, and there's not the slightest point in talking to him about this. And when I go out and leave him at home he doesn't think to clean up around the house, and when I come home nothing's where it should be. Even the fuchsia tracksuit I left behind when I was angry at him, I still don't know where it's got to. This is the state my husband's driven me to with his neglect and indifference.

Inji laid the pencil on the paper and went to the window. With great bitterness she thought back over her life and within her a single question echoed loudly: Why me? Why me? She noticed that the lamp she had told them to hang over the café door was leaning to one side, so she summoned an assistant and asked him to set it straight. She returned to her sheets of paper and wrote on:

> The point is, not to beat around the bush, that God blessed us with a little boy who compensated me for all the frustrations I feel and all the sadnesses and cares that have been my lot in this unhappy life. My husband and I committed ourselves to care for this child and now he has grown into a young man, strong and tall and full of life. But while the master of the house has been amusing himself, the child has grown up as careless as his father—and though we are now of considerable standing in Alexandria, masters of a great number of concerns and properties, and should be readying our beloved son to take charge of the same, my husband shows not the slightest interest. All he does is sit in front of the television and eat, so that he's reached a quite colossal weight—I'm positive he must be two hundred kilos or more—while I take care of my figure and my looks (even though I wear the niqab); not to mention his beard, which he leaves untended and hasn't cut for years, so that he looks perfectly horrible, even though appearance is a very important part of this profession of ours, which I would beg you not to ask me about, because it is of an exceptionally confidential kind.

Inji erased the word "confidential" and wrote "dangerous" in its place, then erased "dangerous" and wrote "confidential" again. Here, she saw that the paper had been worn through with all the erasing and pulled out a new sheet. She wrote out all the preceding paragraphs a second time, then continued:

> I am quite sure, dear sir, that you are dying to know who I am and are no doubt asking yourself, Who is this beautiful, anonymous woman who has burst into my life on this glorious day, to write me such a mysterious unsigned letter? I will respond by begging your pardon for not mentioning my name or any information that might hint at it, for to do so would

pose great danger both to myself and my beloved husband. But what I wish to say to you is, Be not amazed. Be not amazed that the lives of great people such as us also contain intimate details. Are we not humans in the end?

More than once, Inji considered deleting this paragraph. She wanted her letter to be condensed and focused, to speak to the point and nothing but the point. But she relented and decided to leave it in. Then she resumed her sad tale:

I won't hide from you, dear sir, that life with my husband has become quite unbearable: a hell. He is constantly peeling oranges and tossing the peel on the ground. And he does the same with seeds, not to mention cans of Pepsi and Mirinda, and when his clothes get dirty he leaves them in the wardrobe, not even troubling himself to throw them into the washbasin, so that they reek. And he fiddles around in his nose in a revolting way in front of our handsome boy, who's now a tall and strong young man, and he's always letting off foul-smelling gases. All this is deeply trying to me, as I come from an impeccably aristocratic family, while he is from what you might call a working-class family in Cairo—although we are distantly related—which makes me fear that our son may be influenced by such behavior. So, what do you advise me to do?

Inji filled the pages thus, then placed them in an envelope and sent a girl she kept in the house to post it. She had written neither name nor address, just her problem, set down on four sheets of paper wrapped around a two-hundred-pound note with the promise of a greater sum should her problem be published quickly. She knew the risks involved in giving her letter to another person to post, because the letter, with the information it contained, was dangerous—that's how she described it. No one must ever know who sent it. With her letter, Inji was hanging out the whole world's dirty laundry and exposing her little family to certain danger. Yet what can we do? In the end we're human. Humans have the energy to endure, but Inji ran out of hers a long time ago.

This is what Inji was up to. Ali, meanwhile, was taking his revenge. Ali was striking his most devastating blow, a blow he'd been planning ever since seeing that program on TV. Ali would later describe that period as the Ramadan of Surprises. The blows had rained down on him from quite unanticipated quarters and his responses struck where his opponents least expected. It seemed to him that we—all of us, not just himself and his family but all humanity—were floundering in some vast washing machine. The machine slams everyone inside it all about, what's above comes below, what's below comes above: the world's a washing machine from bottom to top, and at the end of it all, men come out. Washed well, it's true, but worn out, their colors faded, their sizes different from when they went in. Even the good-quality soap: the clothes that use it don't keep their old bright hues. Using this theory he not only deconstructed humanity in its entirety, but deconstructed television commercials too. Ali was at war with everyone and everything at that time, from the thing that makes a man a man, to the soap companies. At that time, he was the ideal of the Sufi philosopher, and the Sufi philosopher fears nothing so long as he has the conviction of his ideas.

Ali opened a store for his son Hamada next to Sousou's old abandoned one. He asked Hamada what kind of thing he wanted to do there and Hamada eagerly replied, Painting, Papa! So Ali set up a studio for Hamada, who christened it Arts and Colors. The studio adjoined the store Sousou had owned back in the day, which went by the name of Karantina Liver and which was officially rented out by an individual called Ramadan Maadoul, though in practice no one was using the place after Ali's men had attacked it and tipped the liver on the ground. And so, as time itself looked the other way, Hamada set about expanding his studio, bringing in men to run the two stores together in front of all and sundry, in open defiance of Sousou. He began work, painting pictures for people and selling a few sweets and cigarettes to children, all the while carrying on with his true project: sowing the seeds of the army with which he'd one day take on Sousou.

The men's enemy number one was, of course, Sousou, but there were other enemies as well. On Ramadan nights the chairs would be set out, the shutters drawn, and Ali would sit with his men in the store. He'd give them the family history, the history of Alexandria, then drop hints between the lines: for instance, was anyone aware that Inshi, Sheikha Inshi in her niqab, who prayed the full five prayers each day, ran a brothel out of the café? No one, of course. Okay then, so was anyone aware that this Inshi was a murderess as well? How many upstanding sons of Alexandria had she killed, for asking her, as politely and respectfully as you could wish, to put a stop to her activities? No one knew, either. Fine. Was anyone aware that once upon a time Inshi'd had a fling with a kindhearted sheikh called Khaled, that she'd given herself to him while she was still married to Ali, and that she was having another fling now with that filth Sousou? That she loved him and met with him in secret? That she loved him and met with him in secret (he repeated) after everything Sousou had done against them and against all Alexandria? Abu Amira whispered to Ali, That's enough hash for today, don't you think? and Ali pushed him away hard and shouted, Leave me be, ya hagg! Leave me be! You're just a nice guy who doesn't understand anything! At last, as usual, Abu Amira calls Hamada to prop his father up as he climbs up to the apartment. Ali can't see in front of him, and Abu Amira says, That's because of the hash, and Ali says, It's the dagger of treachery. The dagger of treachery is buried in his heart. It pierces him through—the sheikh who no longer wants anything from the world.

His words reached Inji. She sat and tried to write another letter to the columnist, but the tears overwhelmed her. Still fine of feeling, is Inji. She understands her husband's work is important and that their differences mustn't be put on display. She takes a photograph of Ali swallowing Viagra, a photograph of him with one of the whores, and sends the pictures off to the vice squad. For days and nights she sits there, waiting for him to be arrested, and no one makes a move. The fury's eating her alive. The whole country's crooked. She sits in the mosque giving lessons to ladies. She asks them, bless their hearts, how they can stand the biggest brothel in the history of mankind doing business in their neighborhood, and say nothing. Okay, so how is it the state knows about it and doesn't lift a finger? Isn't that a crooked country for you? And not one of them answers. One sighs, perhaps. Perhaps one nods her head. Inji is convinced that this country isn't deserving, that a true citizen has no place in this day and age, and she goes home to write another letter to the column's editor:

Dear editor of the celebrated column "Problem Solver,"
I've had it up to here. For hours now, I've been considering killing myself, but I tell myself I'm a God-fearing woman and I shouldn't do it. But life's gotten so hard, and my husband, or the man I thought was my husband, is saying disgusting things about me everywhere, and I don't want to give it back to him, because I'm a God-fearing woman. He says things you'll have to forgive me for not repeating here. But in this wonderful column, I say to him, as God's my witness, brother, you're as filthy a human being as they come. God be my comfort, you scum, you trash. Trash of trash.

She sends letter after letter and they are never published. Inji is a God-fearing woman, as she calls herself; she knows that there are many trials in life, that God shall recompense the patient in the life hereafter, so she does not despair. She weeps and with time, and much prayer, the tears of despair turn to tears of joy at God's imminent deliverance. Tears of love for the Lord.

The Ramadan of Surprises must end with the biggest surprise of all: Abu Amira died.

After the end of the tarawih prayers on Laylat al-Qadr, Abu Amira, full name Abdel Hamid Ragab Shehata, went home. He didn't stay out that night; he stayed at home, reading the Quran and performing his devotions. At last, at one in the morning, he ate his last meal, resolved to fast the following day, and slept. Then never got up.

This death, as we can see, is a most fitting end for a man who devoted himself to God his whole life long; a man who dedicated his days to the service of his fellow man and the remembrance of God. This, it seems, was the message the heavens sought to impress on the neighborhood's inhabitants: you've lost a righteous man and one of the true scholars of Islam. It is hard to guess at the reaction of family and friends to this passing, and above all that of Ali, who nurtured a love of a special kind for Abu Amira. He wept, perhaps, or screamed; perhaps he fell silent and privately savored the bitterness of the passing days. Those you love have gone, Ali, so you must either Be, or Not Be, there's no avoiding it.

At the aza, Ali met Sousou for the first time in a long while. In fact the situation required that they shake hands and join together in celebrating the life and deeds of the great man who'd departed. A single idea revolved in the mind of each man: the only one who held us together has gone. Now Ali could destroy Sousou if he so wished, and Sousou could respond with everything he had, and no one would force them to consider the feelings of the man who had once stood, a barrier, between them. Ali returned from the ceremony, his eyes swimming with tears.

And now, let us attempt together to review some of the achievements of the departed: Abdel Hamid was born in 1965 into a poor household in the neighborhood of Zananiri, the son of impoverished Southerners recently arrived from Sohag. His father worked as a doorman. Abdel Hamid inherited the trade from him, and other trades besides. He learnt how to sweet-talk a lady on her way up to some bachelor's apartment into paying him the greatest possible tip before mounting the stairs, and how to obtain a comparable sum from the young bachelor after she'd come down. After the death of his parents, after he'd become responsible for looking after and raising his brothers, he expanded the scope of his activities a little, with the consent, naturally, of the owners of the buildings where he worked. He never did anything without the owners' knowledge. While this was going on, he married Iman Hosni Abdallah, who was fated to become Umm Amira, and subsequently Umm Amira the Melon. He moved between Zamaniri, Ibrahimiya, and Chatby, until he finished up in Camp Cesar, where he had Amira, and where she died. Then, what he himself would later describe as the most important event of his life took place: he met Ali.

(Many claim that the friendship that blossomed between Ali and Abu Amira, and that lasted until the latter's death, was actuated by self-interest; that Abu Amira was well aware his interests lay with Ali and that he'd plotted the murder of Ali's brother to that end, so Ali might get his share of the inheritance and take Abu Amira with him to the top. In response to these people we say: that's incorrect. Sure, we don't possess sufficient information to refute the charge outright, but we do possess absolute conviction and a familiarity that requires no proof with the sublimity, the loftiness, of Abu Amira's moral code.)

Ali grew, and Abu Amira grew with him. The pair remained a rare instance of two loyal friends whom only death shall part. When Ali and Sousou had their final falling out, Abu Amira maintained neutrality. It was hard for him to watch all the effort he'd expended sowing the seeds of his fine, upstanding values being dashed by a quarrel over a few ephemeral possessions. Some say this hastened his end. Before he died, he told Ali that he had no desire to take part in any war between his brother and his best friend, but should circumstances compel him he would never find a better opportunity to punish his brother for his bad manners. Ali smiled, patted Abu Amira's shoulder, and took it as an endorsement. Truces are best, it's true, but it is up to each of us to maintain our standards.

Abu Amira died in 2037, after nearly seventy-two years on earth, and soared up, garlanded with glory, to the Supreme Companion, his soul entrusted to the trustiest hands of all. A prayer for his soul, O Muslims.

In the lives of nations there are periods of ascendancy and periods of decline. This is historical fact.

The lines ahead are hard going, hard to own, though owning the truth is part of our duty, as is delivering it—this truth—devoid of touch-ups, additions, or embellishment, to the hands of our dear reader, who will come to the truth sooner or later, whether it is we that speak it or some other in our stead. And so—and because the shortest route to certitude is honesty—we offer the picture in its entirety, objective and unbiased.

It would be difficult to claim that these were the finest years for Ali and Inji's empire. The 2030s were a period of decline for this pair, who had taken on their shoulders the task of founding an entire city from nothing. Following the Flourishing Twenties, during which the zealous couple had made impressive progress on the ground, the thirties had swept in with their melancholy opening act—Sousou driving naked men and women from the Karantina Café—and its corollary, people steering clear of such places for fear of certain scandal. Yet also, and more importantly, its corollary in the form of everyone doubting whether Ali and Inji were fully fit to grasp the Wheel of Change that Alexandrians had dreamed of for so long.

It was as though the two of them had grown old, or as though they'd given themselves over to their domestic wrangling and only with difficulty might either lift his head and look about him, at his neighborhood, his family, at his city's native sons. It was as though Alexandria were brushing from itself a beautiful dream that had held it captive for a while. At first, the people said that Ali and Inji were still the same, and that what seemed to be a period of decline was just a tactic. But the tactic went on and on, and the waiting with it. Gradually, the conviction grew that the beautiful time was coming to an end.

And early on, Hagga Nadia died. When she died, no one remembered who she was. Her death seemed a marginal affair. No one paid any mind to the passing of a woman who, once upon a time, had nearly become Harbi's wife. Harbi's family fell away. His brother, Sheikh Hassan, had died; Hagga Itemad, his wife, had died; and now Nadia, his lover and the person who'd been closest to him of all, had died too, while his daughter Minna had married Sousou and no one saw hide nor hair of her. Abu Amira's family was also on the slide. Umm Amira was dead. Abu Amira was dead. Sousou shut himself away and decided to work for himself. Adel left prison and traveled to Libya. Ali and Inji's family stood firm against death . . . but absurdly so. Ali sat at the café all day long, playing games on his phone and from time to time pulling a small pair of scissors from the top pocket of his gallabiya and snipping at nonexistent nose hairs. Inji grew ever more obsessed with reading the newspapers and magazines, clipping out pictures of stars and sheikhs and pasting them up in her office, then sitting down to pen letters to the column's editor. And Hamada painted people.

But nothing dies. Einstein taught us long ago that matter cannot be destroyed, it just takes other forms. Karantina's center of gravity shifted to Sousou's store and home; the happy couple, once Ali and Inji, were now Sousou and Minna; and Harbi's heroism morphed into the heroism of Sika, Sayyid, and Sultan. And all that went with this, the values of the past, the values of honor and trust, were transformed into the values of street smarts and guile, of your-wallet's-your-weapon.

Amid the civilizational collapse that struck Alexandria in the thirties, amid the civil wars that pitted the city's inhabitants one against the other, the police did not stand silently by. At all times of day, girls were escorted from the café, their johns in tow; drug charges were trumped up against the men of the neighborhood and some were tortured, too; plus, certain types of young men, the kind we saw a while ago failing to show sufficient respect to Ali, were entering the neighborhood, playing music at top volume, harassing passersby, and no one was standing up to them; there was no one with the spirit to stand up to them. Everyone's spirit was broken.

The decline began to pick up pace. The balance in Ali and Inji's bank accounts fell. They withdrew money recklessly without adding fresh sums. Inji proposed buying land in neighborhoods like Abu Talaat and elsewhere, but the project was constantly put off. Prices went through the roof, and it got so anyone who went out to buy a bit of cheese and pastrami with a thousand pounds in his pocket would return without the price of a taxi fare. And Ali loved pastrami, and had no love of buying land.

Back to square one, then. The past thirty years . . . as though they had never been. The people returned once more to their interests and affairs. The patriotic fervor that had roiled within them for years and years: stilled.

During the years that followed, the ancient chronicler set down his pen, went to make a cup of tea, returned and lit a cigarette, then turned a new leaf over and in a wavering, faint hand, wrote:

Has everything truly come to an end? Is this the final, terrible conclusion of one of the most dazzling pages in the history of Alexandria and the nation's modern era? Must we say farewell, never to meet again, to a beautiful dream that set up home in people's minds, then straightway died?

The chronicler feels tremendous pain as he writes on: There can be no doubt that the answer to these questions is yes. God is generous.

And so it was that the chronicler doused his lamps, and slept.

4

More than one hundred years before Abu Amira died, in 1933 to be precise, Tawfiq al-Hakim wrote a novel entitled *Return of the Spirit*. We could talk about this book for hours if we had to, but what concerns us here are a few paragraphs in which the author sets out a discussion between an English inspector of irrigation and a French archaeologist about the nature of the Egyptian people. The Englishman views them with disdain, with a blind prejudice against the civilizations of the Orient, whereas the Frenchman is enamored of the hidden essence shared by all Egyptians and is, moreover, more rational when he speaks.

We shall now cite a part of the conversation between the two—not, of course, the part that Abdel Nasser seized on when plotting his revolution. Calmly addressing his English colleague, the Frenchman says: "You may be confident, Mr. Black, that any corruption of morals is not native to Egypt, but was introduced here by other nations, the Bedouin or the Turk, for instance— and yet this does not affect their ever-present and unchanging essence." The Englishman—and we may picture him giving a whistle of surprise, striking his cap from his head to ruffle his hair as he absorbs the tidal bore of truth that now bears down upon him—answers him: "Tell me: What is this essence?" To which the Frenchman—and we picture a sage, untroubled smile upon his lips—replies: "You doubt my word! But I shall content myself with telling you, Beware! Beware of this people, for it harbors a terrible force of will!"

So it is that the Frenchman describes the essence of the Egyptian people, in wild and woolly phrases compounded of wisdom, conviction, force, and warning, all at one and the same time. But we cannot ignore, not for a moment, the fact that the author of these words was Tawfiq al-Hakim himself, who lived in Paris and admired its inhabitants and their ideas, and so, when he'd decided to create a character both wise and sympathetic to Egyptians, it was a Frenchman that first sprang to mind. And, just like al-Hakim, Hamada, too, loved Paris.

The tremendous force of will, possessed by all Egyptians and divined by Tawfiq al-Hakim some hundred years ago, seemed to find its clearest manifestation in the person of Hamada and his luxurious studio, which bore the name Arts and Colors. After all the symptoms of decline that we've detailed above, it was as though the ember of life had been transplanted to the studio, where Hamada tended it, sheltered it, kept it burning, in readiness for the day when it would appear before the eyes of all.

Strength and sensitivity were the two wings that held Hamada aloft. The strength came from the little army that he was raising in his studio to destroy Sousou, the sensitivity manifested itself in the canvases he painted: French in inspiration, refined, focused on the subjects' inner depths and not their trivial outer features. In a refined palette—orange, mauve, and turquoise, say—he created his most beautiful works. His best friend, Farouq, assisted him. He would prepare the paints for him, set up the canvases, lead people to his door. Hamada split the proceeds with him and would bestow on him looks of affection and encouragement. Farouq's a talented man, Hamada would tell himself. There's a great artist inside him and were things different I could be in his place, and he in mine. Hamada painted a huge canvas showing a tall and massive man alongside a short and scrawny fellow, then another, in which the same massive individual had transformed into the short one and the short one into the massive-and-tall. He gave the two pictures the title "Oh Cruel Fate!"

The forces of evil circling Hamada were plentiful and powerful. In those days, it was as if everyone was working in concert to convince him of a single fact: that Farouq was no more than an imaginary figure, with no basis in reality. Just a figment of his fancy. To answer these slurs, Hamada painted a picture of Farouq and himself greeting one another, with the sea and Qaitbey Fort in the background. Farouq appeared as he really was: skinny, eyes downcast, with something of what Hamada dubbed his "beautiful modesty." One fine day, Hamada drank coffee with his friend in a Sidi Bishr café, then drove him to Karmouz, to his studio. He opened the studio door and went in. He told Farouq he was going to see one of the greatest masterpieces of all time and whipped the drape from the canvas that he had worked on for a full two months. Farouq saw himself rendered by his artist friend's brush and was moved. So moved that he shook. Hamada lifted up the canvas and told his friend, This is a gift from me to you, and Farouq reached for his wallet to pay. Hamada grasped his hand. Shame on you, Farouq, he said. Shame. You're my friend and I'm a good guy. In an emotional, affecting scene, Hamada and Farouq embraced.

Hamada's most important customer by far during this period was Sabah, the girl he burned for till she had him wrapped right around her finger. The following took place one hot day in July. He was absorbed in some beautiful canvas when his phone rang in his pocket—*The companions are bemused, they mull things over, mutter back and forth*—accompanied by a powerful vibration. What was Hamada to do but curse those who disturb artists and cannot appreciate the gift of a sensitive soul? He pulled out the phone and answered, and got a shock: a female voice, uncertain, soft: Hello? Mr. Hamada? My name's Sabah. I work for Sheikh Ali in the café. I wondered if you might help me with something. When can I come to your studio?

Sabah. Sabah! The young man's heart beat hard. It's days like these that bring us the most precious gifts, that make up for the years of solitude and self-denial. He told her he'd be in the studio expecting her and feverishly began to set the place in order. He ran home, washed, put on scent, shaved, and dressed up smart—a full suit and tie in the boiling heat—then ran back down to the store. He set his phone to play a string of old-time Tamer Hosni songs and sat down to wait. Then he got up, took out the picture he'd been working on, took off his smart suit, donned his work clothes—a paint-spattered smock and beret—and started to paint, so she would find him engrossed in his art. Then he left the studio, dashed to the other end of Karmouz to buy a pipe, returned with the item and a bag of tobacco, and began trying to light it in the store. He failed once, twice, and made it on the third attempt. He was now the complete artist. After a few moments the image of the complete artist began to bore him. He removed the coat and beret and reclothed himself in suit and tie. He sat at the desk, opened *The Most Beautiful Poems of Nizar Qabbani*, and started to recite them in dreamy, though clearly audible, tones. After a bit he decided to go further. He set the open book on the easel and took his old guitar from the storeroom. He stood before the easel and began setting Nizar Qabbani's verse to music— *You, who are every woman in the world to me, love me; You, whom I loved till love was burnt to cinders, love me.* And Sabah appeared.

Basically, and without getting into a mass of complicating detail, Sabah wanted a portrait of herself. Those were tough days for anyone who worked a trade like hers, and the johns, how they'd fallen away. Sabah had prepared a series of framed portrait photographs of herself and decided to add an arty touch, a painting, brushes and oils—a mighty undertaking for which Hamada was the only viable candidate. She started laying it out to him and his heart beat violently. He could hardly hear her. In his mind he was readying what he'd say to her when she finished talking. His mind didn't help him out much: even him, king of tender word and romantic phrase. At last, or a little before, when it looked as though she'd stop talking, there sprang into his mind the most powerful response of all, a response that would shake the hearts of the strongest women. He begged her pardon, went to the storeroom, and emerged hefting a massive canvas. As he showed it to her he whispered: Leave it up to me, my lady.

For months on end Hamada worked on Sabah's portrait. He had obtained a photograph of her from her file at the café and started painting with its assistance. The picture was filled with little winged hearts; a light mauve dominated the color scheme. Everything about it was delicate, French, and Parisian, all at the same time. Sabah looked like another woman altogether: no freckles on her face, a slightly shorter nose, much longer eyelashes, her parted lips pure allure and romance. When Sabah had made this request of hers, Hamada had been sure that this was his golden moment. With this, he would later think to himself, he had gained one thing and lost another. His gain was that Sabah finally took note of his interest in her, and his loss was that she would not be coming to the studio time after time to ask how it was progressing. It was all wrapped up in a single visit.

But Sabah came a second time, and a third. She had just emerged from a stormy affair in which her boyfriend had taken advantage of her and she needed a shoulder to cry on. And Hamada put himself up for the role. She told him about the hard life she lived, about the people who craved her beauty in every corner of the world, about the boyfriend who had left her when she'd cheerfully told him certain details about her job, about his father (Sheikh Ali) and his mother (Hagga Inshi) who made her life hell whenever she took work outside the café. The whole world was conspiring against her, and Hamada, a knight in a knightless age, was volunteering to comfort her when she needed it. She told him that people like her—like her, Sabah— shouldn't have to work for anyone, that it wasn't in their nature, and that people like them—like her, Sabah, and like him, Hamada—shouldn't ever leave one another once they had been driven together. And he told her that the solution to these two problems was one solution. Inside him, the old dream had awoken: he would marry Sabah.

It would be difficult for us to claim that this decision on Hamada's part was met with open arms. Not all folk in Egypt are as forward thinking as Hamada. The customs and codes of the elite are not the customs and codes of the man in the street. At first, his mother didn't understand what he was on about. He said a great deal to her: for instance, that he was a grown man now, that the world had changed a lot, that our time's not like yours, Mama, that he had to enjoy his youth. His mother lit a cigarette. And just who, if you please, did you have in mind? Sabah, he said, and she smiled scornfully and went into her bedroom. He told his father and his father asked him if he loved Sabah the whore for being Sabah or for being a whore, and Hamada was flummoxed. He couldn't tell if this was a rejection or approval.

The next day he put the ball back in their court: he asked them both again. His mother went into her bedroom a second time. A second time, his father posed his question, reminding him that he hadn't answered him the day before. On the third day he put the ball back in their court, with one small addition: I'll kill myself if I don't marry Sabah. Kill yourself, his mother told him. Go to hell, said his father. And Hamada, well, he didn't know what to do. On the fourth day he informed them both that the men he'd assembled in the studio, the men who were earmarked to go to war with Sousou someday soon, God willing, that these men would not do so. That he had given them instructions to attack and kill Ali and Inji themselves that very week, and that he intended to visit Sousou tomorrow to make an offer of collaboration. Ali looked at him, spat a seed husk from his mouth and said nothing, and Inji got up and switched on the television. But Hamada flourished his phone. He dialed a number. Hello? Good morning, Miallim Sousou! I'm calling you about a very important matter, top secret. No, Sousou Bey, not on the phone. Ha ha ha . . . . What a big heart you have, miallim. Only with your permission . . . Inji went for Hamada's phone. She threw it on the floor, then bent down and switched it off. And so the discussion about Sabah could begin.

All arguments along the lines that Sabah was just a skivvy who worked for them and that in the end, however things turned out she wasn't the wife who would bring him honor and respect in his future life—all these arguments failed to bear fruit. Hamada had made up his mind and was at his most unmovable. He didn't answer, didn't debate, just stared unwaveringly into his parents' eyes and stayed silent. Not for a minute did he feel obliged to respond, to meet argument with argument. It was the first time Inji had seen this look in the eyes of her Hamada, her little chick: fixed, expressionless, stony, face cold and lips atremble as if on the point of exploding. Inji was frightened. The mother was frightened of her son. And Ali was frightened. And so it was that he married Sabah.

Hamada had never before embarked on any romantic adventures, of any kind. He had only loved with all his heart, and been sure that those he loved had loved him with all their hearts. But nothing more. For a long time now, Hamada had embraced the theory of body and soul: his soul stayed ardent and his body stood apart. Naturally, he practiced the secret habit. He'd read about it back in primary school and had done his best at the time. He'd tried squeezing his prick with both hands and nothing had come out. He'd become convinced that he was sexually impotent and surrendered to depression. In high school he had finally managed to produce a thinnish liquid that wetted the head of his cock. He rejoiced, thinking it the long-awaited elixir, and decided to treat himself to three burger combos. When he got home after this feast (which, incidentally, dealt a severe blow to the health regimen he was to follow, on and off, for his whole life), he tried masturbating again, and nothing happened. He didn't get upset. He patted his belly contentedly and told himself he'd come a bucketful already.

The real stuff took its time. It turned up when he was in college. He experimented with jiggling his cock, the pleasure mounting inside it and exploding. It was then that he became addicted to the habit, two or three times a day, and based on this imagined himself King Stud, the only man in whom was combined both delicacy of emotion and the unstoppable, virile surge. Until, that is, he slept with Sabah for the first time on their wedding night. Of course, there's no need for us to spell out that he couldn't get it up that first night. He gazed on Sabah's incredible body and felt some kind of stirring, but when it got to the kissing and groping, a sad question suddenly popped into his head. Deep down he wondered: Does a woman give birth to live young or lay eggs? He knew that she gives birth—he wasn't an idiot—but if she did, and didn't lay eggs, then why were ovaries called ovaries? He started thinking on this question and failed to notice his penis growing smaller and smaller. At last, just before the dawn prayer call sounded, he whispered to himself: It's because of the tiny eggs inside them . . . . Sabah was snoring. He repeated the sentence to himself a couple of times, to prove to himself that he hadn't failed to solve the riddle. Sabah awoke. Something wrong, Hamada? He kissed her brow. Sleep now, sweetheart. I'm thinking about something very big indeed. And Sabah went back to sleep.

Once, twice, thrice Hamada attempted entry, and on each occasion he would spend a little longer inside her and he would celebrate his victory with ever more burger combos. His weight grew and grew. He began to turn into a fully rounded human being: a sphere for a head over a larger sphere that was the belly, with two spheres tapering down beneath for legs—in addition, of course, to the two balls of his arms. Two months in, sex between them had become an operation of acute complexity. Because of his burgeoning size, to be exact. He would pant and sweat at every movement, would lie on top of her and his great weight would make her moan. One thing—her sucking on his nipples exactly as he sucked on hers—left him feeling slightly ashamed and, despite the fitness regime to which he'd committed himself some twelve years before, nothing had any effect. His terminal depression resumed, and with it, his habit of constantly reciting his poem, the poem whose one verse ran: *To see me, friend, you'd say, A killer, most uncouth, but I'm a poet of exquisite sensibility, and that's the truth.* Farouq was the one who saved him.

From the outset let us make it clear that Hamada's growth to new, unanticipated dimensions was not worrying in itself. What worried him were the scornful glances Sabah would cast at him from time to time, which he could feel piercing his belly and breasts. Hamada lost faith in everything, the value and importance of his own existence, Sabah's love for him, everything . . . until the day he met up with Farouq. The latter seemed to be going through some tremendous psychological crisis. Hamada asked him what was wrong and he did not reply. With the unshakable shyness, the delicate modesty that Hamada knew so well, he held his peace. Hamada looked at Farouq's rumpled clothes, the untucked shirt and wild hair. Bitterly, he said, You want to sleep with Sabah, don't you? Farouq gave no answer and Hamada went on: You tried to, didn't you? Farouq hung his head and stared at the floor, and Hamada began to address himself: Why? Why? Why does all this happen to me, Lord? He wheeled to face Farouq, who seemed to want to say something, to vehemently deny an accusation, to answer some other man's lies, to insist that the world was not so very cruel. Hamada understood. Farouq had tried to sleep with Sabah, but Sabah had knocked him back, rejected him with a full measure of cruelty, violence, and pride. Suddenly the sun came out again. Hamada leaned toward Farouq, gave him a hug, and kissed his cheek. You're a beautiful man, Farouq. I love you very much, Farouq. He went home to Sabah, a tray of basbousa in his hand. In that moment, it was like he wanted to take the whole world in his arms. And that was how Hamada became convinced of Sabah's love for him.

The ship of life bore Hamada and Sabah onward peacefully and trouble free. Life, at last, had turned to smile on the tormented youth. With his work in the studio, with his meetings with the men with whom, one day, he was due to fight Sousou, and with his fiery romance with Sabah, Hamada was now reaping the best of what life had to give. And when one day Sabah informed him that she was pregnant, the news was like the consummation of his happiness. That day Hamada did not eat a thing, not even burger combos. His soul had soared out of reach of base appetites.

Sabah gave birth. Gave birth to twins. Two beautiful girls. And as a poet, Hamada was not for one moment oblivious to the power of rhyme in a man's life. He gave his daughters two musical names: Yara and Lara. They, in addition to their mother, were the joy of his life back then. How often could Hamada be seen playing with them, lying on his back and perching them on his belly, the two girls laughing. He painted them dozens of pictures, wrote hundreds of poems about them, composed thousands of melodies. When he was alone he'd remember an old song, an old song that ran, *But I still fear the nights, You know their cruelty.* It struck him that this happiness might be a false happiness: that things might turn against him. The thought came to him in a flash and he quickly dismissed it. Perhaps that was the first tactical error Hamada committed in those days: he didn't plan for tomorrow.

The day Hamada found out that it was two girls that lurked in his wife's belly, he remained on edge, afflicted by depression, and lost his appetite. Let us not be hasty to pass judgment: Hamada was not one of those traditional types who grieve when they have daughters. Not at all. The fact is that if we're to understand his worry, we must go back a little, and many fathoms down, into the depths of his childhood fears. Hamada, with his plump body, had long believed himself to be a creature of uncertain identity, something halfway between male and female, and perhaps this was the cause for the constant, endless projects to reduce his weight. Once, as a boy, he'd raised a silkworm; watched as it transformed into a cocoon from which a butterfly emerged and flew away. In this way, he believed, would he transition from some sexless creature, flabby and amphibious, its time divided between the dust of Karmouz and the small pond circling the statue of the hen, into perfect femininity. Female hormones would continue to battle male hormones inside his body, the male hormones continuing to lose, retreating to strongholds that the female hormones would immediately take over, until the big bang came: his belly, breasts, and backside would explode and the perfect female would emerge from within, powerful, violent, capable of laying the whole world and its fixed ideas to waste. Nor did his imagination stop there: he pictured this female, as soon as she emerged from his body, brushing violently from her flesh the ghastly globs of fat that she'd once lived with in his belly, then grabbing a machine gun in either hand and firing off bullet after bullet, taking out all the pedestrians in the street as she capers on the rooftops, wearing—but of course—a short skirt, sheer black tights, and stilettos. A female who kisses every man in the street and kills them with her poisoned lips, a female who combines a fondness for cruelty with a passion to destroy the world.

A secret absolutely no one knows: As a kid, Hamada had asked his mother how a woman could tell she was pregnant; even once considering stopping in at the gynecologist for a checkup. He never went, but it remained his most deeply rooted fear: that he would turn into a female.

What we're saying is that what actually transpired—Sabah giving birth to Lara and Yara—was not so very different.

Sabah's life story can be seen as an object lesson in the cruelty of existence. She was born to a mother who sold tissues at Ramleh Station and to a father imprisoned on a drugs charge which he had confessed to in order to deflect it away from one of the big bosses, securing in return a reasonable future for his kids. Since she was small, Sabah had made her own way, from when she'd sold tissues with her mother till the time she found her way to the discotheques of Agami and started out along that shadowy trail termed "solicitation" in the world of Egyptian academia and "whoring" by normal folk. No one could approach her without her consent. She was assisted by a pair of thugs—hard men, criminals—their names don't matter: her brothers. They accompanied her everywhere, took care of her, and were, for her, the best possible substitutes for a jailbird father and ailing mother. By the time her father got out of prison after a twenty-five-year absence, broken, bony, renewing his addiction to alcohol after just one year on the outside, her brothers had taken control of the family. The family was no longer called by the name of its founder,

Hosni Abu Sabah, but by those of his two sons, Gaber Hosni and Amr Hosni, also known as Gaber the Vizier and Amr the Sheikh.

Following her marriage Sabah had been able—a gesture of gratitude—to introduce Hamada to the brothers who'd stood by her, and he decided to use their help in his coming war with Sousou. Each of the brothers had great experience in barricading streets, detaining passersby, and taking their due by force. At the outset of their acquaintance with each other Hamada asked them what they knew of Karantina's history and the pair rushed to recite what Sabah had made them memorize, beginning with Harbi and passing through Ali, Inji, and Abu Amira until they came to him, the man himself, Hamada, the latest incarnation of Alexandrian heroism, adding moving paragraphs about the vileness of Sousou, and about Minna who'd betrayed her father's memory. Hamada asked them if they were prepared to work with him to rid Karmouz of the likes of Sousou, and eagerly they both assented. After that, no one ever saw them outside Hamada's studio, debating the best ways to attack Gheit al-Enab. Both men, one with a cracked and ruined voice, the other hoarse, would dazzle Hamada with their extensive knowledge of Gheit al-Enab, Sousou's building, his store, and the kind of men he worked with. Both chose their words with care; both were alert to which side their bread was buttered. The name "Sousou" vanished from their lips. He was referred to by a number of descriptors—filthy, faggot, stinking—alongside fitting terms of respect for Karantina's bona fide heroes: Harbi, Abu Amira, Ali, Inji, and Itemad.

In those days one memory held sway over everybody: Sousou herding Karantina's men and women naked from the café. Another, less powerful, memory: Ali and Inji's men attacking Sousou's store, tipping the oil and liver onto the ground and chasing off its tenant. As could be expected, there were preparations in place for Sousou's revenge, but because attack is the best form of defense, Amr the Sheikh decided, We and the men need to burn down stinking Sousou's store, and how would it be, guys, if we killed him into the bargain? But Sousou's building was not to be had so easily. It was ringed by a number of stores all leased to Sousou's men, and even reaching this neighborhood was impossible for strangers. Anyone wishing to get there had to pass by eight stores, each filled with thugs and Sousou's eyes, then cross a broad patch of wasteland owned by Alexandria Petrochemicals, which no one ever crossed except to get to Sousou's building, which was itself, of course, only ever visited by five or six of his most loyal followers.

We need a double agent. Gaber the Vizier began his speech with utmost gravity, gesturing with his hands and staring into the eyes of Hamada and Amr the Sheikh. Okay then, listen up. It's no simple matter. We need a trusted figure who we can plant inside Gheit al-Enab, and that's a huge problem by itself. We all know that no one can get in there without passing through a number of tests: you take your life in your hands. Even worse, no one can live there other than those who work directly for Sousou. Amr the Sheikh looked at him, nodded his head, and continued where his brother had left off: We need a spy. A consummate operator. Someone who can walk through fire. A conman or, more precisely, a lovable rogue. No creed: you can't tell if he's Muslim, Christian, or Jewish. With a spy like that we'll be able to fuck his mother, God willing. Hamada, who'd been thinking deeply, leaned back against his headrest, gazed off into the distance, and murmured, as if conversing with himself: A spy, for sure, and what a spy!

The ideal candidate for this was Ramadan al-Maadoul. Ramadan worked for Sousou and rented out his store in Karantina, and he was the one who'd been beaten by Ali's men and whose liver they had tipped onto the ground. Al-Maadoul seemed ideal in one important respect: he worked for Sousou and so it would cost them nothing to plant him there. Plus, Ramadan al-Maadoul had always had dealings with the cops. Sousou knew this, Ali, Inji, and Hamada knew this; but no one else knew. Hamada had sufficient proof of his dealings with which to threaten him, but delicate and refined as he was, he preferred not to take the path of threats. The carrot's always better than the stick. Hamada announced that he would offer to paint a picture of Ramadan with his wife, a pretty souvenir to have when he grew old—something like that. Thus would he purchase his devotion.

The following day Hamada sat down with Ramadan. He asked about the money he got from Sousou. He offered him more, and also offered him the painting. On his phone, Hamada was watching footage of Ramadan meeting a captain from drug enforcement, but he said not a single word about this recording. He left it playing and continued talking to Ramadan—who got the message. Ramadan, who started sweating heavily as he watched himself on the cell phone so carelessly set down on the arm of the chair; Ramadan, who spent the entire conversation with a self-abasing, pleading expression in his eyes; Ramadan, who begged Hamada to consider him, from this day forth, his man, one of his men, and all the information about Sousou's neighborhood would be laid in his lap, piece by piece.

Hamada loved everybody, which is why everybody loved him.

In a matter of weeks Ramadan became one of his most important men. Ramadan never met with Hamada, Amr the Sheikh, or Gaber the Vizier within the bounds of Karmouz. They would always congregate in Bahari, Manshiya, or Ramleh Station. Al-Maadoul would tell them about the new defenses Sousou had introduced into his neighborhood, and about the secrets he'd spill during booze-fueled nights, but most important of all, Ramadan would tell them about those of Sousou's men who were promising candidates to come and work with them. And he'd make deals with these men, would bring some along to meet the group in person. As the days and nights flitted by it began to seem as though Gheit al-Enab's Karabantina was in their pocket.

Everyone was in a rush now. How many times did Amr the Sheikh and Gaber the Vizier tell Hamada to set a date, and soon! Everyone was straining to get a piece of the empire that Sousou had built, the empire of drugs and automatic weapons. Hamada, too, was in a rush. With his own hand he wished to inscribe the first line in the chronicle of his exploits, but he couldn't take a single step without his parents' say-so. His mother firmly rejected taking any action just then and deferred it to some unspecified date, and his father was busy with something else. One day he asked Hamada if he hadn't noticed anything strange about Inji recently. Hamada didn't understand and Ali went on mournfully: You know why your mother doesn't want to go ahead? She's frightened for Sousou. Last night she got home at eleven. She wasn't in the café, Hamada. I went down and looked.

Ali didn't reject taking action, nor did he defer it to some unspecified date, as Inji had. He only asked that it be put off until he could check his information regarding Inji and Sousou's relationship, and then Hamada could kill the pair of them, in each other's arms, in their underwear, and hang a great sign over the site of his crime on which would be written in blood, "This is the end of every traitor." Know how long your mother's known Sousou, my boy? A very long time. Remember the African snake, Hamada? Your mother wanted to kill us once, a long time ago, and speaking for myself, killing her has never so much as crossed my mind.

The situation, as we can see, is very complicated. Can Hamada stand such things to be said of his mother, and if he can, does he have the balls to kill her? To escape this tangled web of relationships, Hamada began to think along different lines. He would carry out the operation himself, with or without his father's consent. He wouldn't wait on anything. His father, who'd started, slowly but surely, to lose his mind, would have no say over his life from now on. My name is Hamada. My name's not Ali. I'm not Ali. I'm Hamada. Hamada. He repeated this over and over as, trustingly and transparently, he outlined all this complexity to his men. And by now the men, too, were burning to unite both halves of Karantina. Day by day, the call for speed gradually prevailed: a feeling—nationalist or patriotic with a revolutionary twist—that the decision was ours to make, that the matter is in our hands. The land belongs to he who plows it, not to the one who owns it.

Everyone's at Hamada's studio today—Amr the Sheikh, Gaber the Vizier, Sabah, and their men; even Ramadan al-Maadoul is there—getting ready for their dawn assault on Karabantina and Gheit al-Enab, in two hours' time. Hamada's on his way. The studio is locked from the outside. One of the men notices the absolutely filthy state the studio is in. They all set about cleaning it up. They pour benzene on the floor as they sing a new song that starts "hobba ya hobba," and forgetting the rest they laugh. Ramadan leans against the inside of the studio door and lights a cigarette. And throws the match on the floor. The match's flame sets the benzene ablaze. One of the men rushes to try to put it out and Ramadan stops him with a bullet from his pistol. Another dashes over, and Ramadan kills him too. There's no hiding the truth now from the men. As the fire devours her naked arm, Sabah screams, It was you, Ramadan! Ramadan, too, is burning before her eyes and they are all scrambling for the door in an attempt to open it, but the burning Ramadan does not let go of his pistol. He shoots them all, one after the other. A burning man fires on burning men. The fire's one undivided mass.

Half an hour later it's all over. Ramadan, Sabah, and ten of Alexandria's finest. By the time the people wake to screams at three in the morning, to the smoke rising from the studio, whatever it is that sent these two things spiraling into the air was well and truly finished. Fourteen charred bodies confront them. Hamada will get there twenty-four minutes later. He will see the scene before him: the bodies of thirteen charred men, some with holes in their heads; Ramadan's corpse propped upright to one side without a single hole and, cast down beside it, a pistol out of bullets.

Never before in his life, by good fortune or bad, had Hamada dreamt while he slept.

It was during these days that he dreamed for the first time. He learned what nightmares were. He saw Sabah trying to free herself from her burning clothes as she stretched out her hand toward the studio door. He saw Gaber, wrestling with Ramadan to get to the door. He saw Ramadan standing and smoking, a cigarette tucked carelessly in the corner of his mouth, and pulling out his phone to say, Everything's fine, ya basha. He saw Sabah leaving the building, laughing and joking with her brothers, and in her wake a cry echoing, a cry the dreaming Hamada did not understand, did not understand from whence it came, a strange cry, a cry from some strange time, Harbbbiiii, and Sabah is approaching the studio, she goes inside and the cry loops quicker, Harbi, Harbi, transforms into a whole sentence, intimate, hysterical, echoing through the dream as the studio door is locked from outside, and the smoke is rising from the studio and the cry has become one long line that soon scatters into the void, Haarrbbbiiiiii! Gradually the sentence dies. It burns.

Hamada saw his canvases in the dream, the pictures he'd spent five years painting; he saw the easels' uprights catch fire then collapse, the paintings falling face-first into the heart of the flames. Amid the burning bodies, amid the pictures he'd painted years before, he saw many faces: Abu Amira, Itemad, Nadia, Ali, Inji, even Umm Amira, even Mustafa, Ali's brother, even Inji's father Suleiman. All these Hamada saw sketched out on burning canvas; even Sika, Sayyid, and Sultan, even Sousou. He saw them stepping out of the canvases and taking drags on Ramadan's cigarette as he stands by the door, joking and embracing and nudging one another as they open fire on the others.

Hamada awakes in the dead of night. He checks on Yara and Lara, asleep on the bed beside him. He moves cautiously so as not to wake them. He demands to be brought the telephone. Dials Sheikh Pizza. Orders a large pizza with everything on it. It arrives and he eats it in ten minutes, tossing the pieces, saturated in greasy, congealed fat, into his mouth—the lumps of ground beef, sausage, salami, pastrami, and Turkish cheese. Then he calls another restaurant. Orders grilled chicken and fries. He eats and eats, and when the food is lying heavy on his stomach he tries to drink some beer and finds that there's no room left. He forces himself to down three bottles in a row and goes back to bed, pitching like a penguin. The instant he reaches his bed he bends to the ground. Throws up everything inside him. He doesn't wipe the vomit away. Throws himself into bed. In the morning the vomit has dried on the floor and its acid reek fills the room.

Yara and Lara cry all the time now.

Hamada embraced mysticism.

He let his beard grow out. He dressed in spattered, ragged clothes. He prayed the full five daily prayers at the mosque. He wept as he prayed. He wept and his body shook, and as he bent low he said in a loud voice like a shout, O Lord, I'm at Your door! He stopped drinking. He thought of paying Sousou a visit. He considered admonishing him in unruffled tones. He thought of giving it all up, of bringing it all to an end. O Lord, I'm too weak for all this, so do not torment me with one who has no mercy and does not let Your mercy descend. Hamada realized that the struggle called for another person altogether. He confronted himself with the fact that all this was than he could handle. He got to know a sheikh at the mosque by the name of Mohamed. The sheikh restored a degree of equilibrium to him. Together they attended Sufi gatherings and nights of chanting out God's names. More than once Hamada invited him over to eat at his parents' place, where he had gone to live with his two daughters. He'd seize chunks of meat from the fatta and give them to the sheikh and the sheikh would say, May God reward you well. He'd ladle rice and sauce onto his plate and the sheikh would pat his shoulder.

One day Ali asked him, What are you doing, Hamada? I'm taking care of Sheikh Mohamed, Papa. Hamada, there's no one here but your mother and me. Hamada looked at Sheikh Mohamed. He watched him smile his radiant smile as, slowly but surely, he faded away: the white skullcap, then the pale, white-bearded face, then the white gallabiya, then the brown sandals. Hamada grew depressed. He secretly cursed his father, then begged God's forgiveness. He lost his appetite and went downstairs to rejoin Farouq in the café.

This was just a phase. Gradually, with time, the veils of forgetfulness began to descend. The restoration of the studio was completed. Hamada shaved off his beard, took off the white gallabiya, and put on his old clothes and when he found them far too tight, he bought some new ones. He told himself that he'd lost much—his wife, her brothers, his men, his canvases— but that everything has a price. What Hamada had taken away from this incident was an acquaintance with a man of the caliber of Sheikh Mohamed. And so he'd gained a friend, and time would show that, alongside Farouq, the sheikh would be one of his most devoted companions.

Seven months after the incident, Hamada started to sow the seeds of another army: men whose only mission in life would be to kill Sousou.

5

One chilly day, Prince Rizq Bin Nayil was journeying through the desert wastes, alone. He was troubled and the cold pierced his bones. Victories no longer concerned him: vanity of vanities, all is vanity and clutching at the wind. The prince looks back over the past and cannot say what it is he has achieved. He gazes to the future and finds nothing: poverty, a sundering into as many grains as the desert sands, emptiness on emptiness on emptiness. What be the profit from worldly things, the battles, wars, and victories, if all must come to naught? The prince had grown old without bearing any children of his own, and his constant refrain was, Lord, my glory has gone from me and my head glows white with old age. The rest of the story we know. He heard God call out to him: To every man his lot, brother, to every man his share; Hearken to your God, Rizq, marry in Mecca the Fair. Rizq married, and sired the Champion of the Desert Arabs, Abu Zayd al-Hilali. Something of this kind happened here.

Sousou, like the prince, was a champion of the Arabs. He rubbed shoulders with the Bedouin, the pureblood Arabs of Abu Talaat Mountain, the number-one importers of hash into Alexandria and Cairo. He ate of their food, drank of their drink, and adopted their ways and, like the prince, Sousou reached the age of fifty with no child to bear his name. And this was a big problem for one of the Arabs' great leaders. At the very height of his victory over Ali and Inji's line, perfectly positioned to pounce upon their legacy, Sousou was sad. He went with Minna to a hundred doctors and every one confirmed that it was a question of time, nothing more, and time . . . there's nothing more plentiful than time. Sousou let time pass—and time passed—without any hope at all. This was the key to the profound and constant look of grief and sorrow in Sousou's eyes. Until what happened, happened.

Sousou is performing the dawn prayer at home. He has a terrible cold that prevents him going to the mosque. He's wearing a gallabiya with thick cotton underwear and over it a long robe, a sweater, and a shawl. As he bends down he registers that, in spite of all these defenses, a chilly breeze has wormed beneath his clothes. He rises and bows left and right to abort the prayer. He adjusts his clothes, wipes the leaking snot that smears his nose, then fetches a thick blanket, pulls it over him, and resumes his devotions. As he bends down this time he murmurs, Lord, grant me of Your grace a worthy progeny, wealth and sons. Then, hysterically: O Lord, a boy! O Lord, a boy! After a day hard at work and after two days in which Sousou had stayed awake without a wink of sleep, it's inevitable that he'll drop off as he kneels to pray. This is no nap, no fleeting drowsiness. Well, maybe at first, but Sousou soon rolls over on his side and starts to snore, to kick his legs in the blanket, and only wakes at noon the next day, after a most delightful dream: A blond child, ascending the minbar of al-Morsi Abul Abbas Mosque, and beneath his gaze the people lined in ranks proclaiming him amir of Alexandria, the city's ruler. Waking to the sound of the noon prayer call, he knows it to be a vision, a prophecy, or rather a portent: A boy shall be born unto him at last. Of course, the day before this prophecy arrived Minna had told him she was pregnant, and when he slept the vision came as confirmation. The anointed boy child would be born in mere months.

The boy child turned out not to be a boy. It was a girl. This was extremely frustrating to Sousou, but he didn't lose faith in his vision. He named his daughter Amira, instead of the Amir he'd seen in the dream. In this way did he hearken unto the call of God, and in this way, too, did he immortalize the memory of his brother's dead daughter and pave the way for his transformation into a second Abu Amira. Sousou decided to dedicate what remained of his life to Amira. What time remained was short and he himself knew not on what patch of God's earth he would meet his death. Sousou regarded his daughter—his single, post-term child—as his legacy, and he treated her accordingly. He passed on to her his ancient grudge: Ali and

Inji's treachery and their seizure of the building that belonged by rights to him and his wife—and after all he had done for them, after he'd murdered Ali's brother Mustafa, after his long exile in the South to take Ali's taar. And just as he passed on to her this ancient grudge, so too did he pass on a new one: Ali's men driving his man from his store and tipping his oil and liver on the ground. We serve people with all our heart and then they turn out to be scum of the earth: this was his grudge, neither ancient nor new, the grudge that transcended time.

Sousou's grudges were many, and each and every one required a revisiting of history. He gave his daughter Amira the whole story. Everything that comes from the Lord is good, he told her. God forbid we should ever complain, he told her. It's just that we ask ourselves, Why did what happened happen? It all began, he told her, when he took pity on his neighbor, a neighbor who'd been much mistreated by his people in the South. His kith and kin had mistreated him, and your Papa, Amira, my little Mira, my Mirmir, was the one who saw justice done. Minna was beside him, correcting him. A neighbor and his wife, ya hagg—and so he turned to Amira and whispered, A neighbor and his wife, ya hagg. I got justice for them. Am I to blame? And Minna added: You killed his brother, too, ya hagg, and that was before the business in the South. Then Sousou scratched his head and said, No, the South came first. Minna went on as though she hadn't heard him: And before the South, before his brother, you set him and his wife up and paid their bills. So Sousou turned away from his child. He buried his face in his hands, for five full minutes he covered his face with his hands, then he lifted his head and said: Look here. The South, then his brother, then we got them somewhere to live—and she said, No: his brother, then you set them up, then the South, then you killed the officer for their sake. And he corrected her: She's the one who killed the cop. And she replied, Who's she? Inshi, he answered. She said, Inji's a coward. Inji's filth. Inji doesn't do anything herself. I know her.

They get out a sheet of paper and a pen and try to set down the events in order. But there are too many events. They tear up sheet after sheet. They spend all night trying to set the events in order, but it's no use anymore. Minna leans in and whispers, Shall we ask him? He leans in and whispers back, Ask who, sister? She leans in and whispers, Ask Sheikh Ali—and he rises up and screams, Have you gone mad, woman! To hell with this and to hell with anyone who wants to work it out! She tries to bring him round—I've got his number here—and he pushes her away. He leaps on her. Then he pulls himself together. He goes out onto the balcony and smokes a cigarette. Even the lighter isn't lighting these days.

Adel returned.

Adel, the younger, absent brother of Sousou and the late Abu Amira, returned, dog tired and on his last legs after long years of hard knocks, first from prison, then from Libya, then from life itself. He searched for his brothers in Camp Cesar and didn't find them. He searched for them at the Karmouz Bridge and didn't find them. By the statue of the great hen he sat down and wept. A passerby saw him and asked what he wanted, so he told him he was searching for Abu Amira's house. No idea, the person told him, so he said, Okay then, Sousou? No idea, the person told him, so he said, Okay then, Sheikh Ali? The person pointed to Sheikh Ali's apartment and went on his way. This person spoke to another person and that person spoke to another, until word reached Hamada.

Hamada sat with his parents in Ali's apartment. He told them that Adel had returned at last and that two options now lay before them. The first was simple—expelling him from the neighborhood; the second less so—bringing him into the fold so he might act for them against Sousou ("bringing him into the fold" was the phrase Hamada employed). Ali seemed disgusted by all this nonsense. We'll cut him up and put him in the ground. Inji said, We'll leave him to freeze to death. And Hamada said, The most important thing at this stage is to win people over. From here on out, Adel belongs to me. And Hamada's view won the day. Slowly but surely, and with all due respect to the family's founding members, Hamada was turning into the decision maker.

Cold, water dripping from his old jacket, his shoes split at the seams and coated in mud, Adel entered Sheikh Ali's home. He drank down a cup of tea and spoke of Libya, of Sirte, and the tribesmen. He spoke of hashish and the desert. He spoke of his Libyan wife and two young children living in Benghazi. He said that he was out of touch with everything that had happened in Egypt, with the exception of scattered gossip. He'd heard that Ali was finished, that Hamada didn't know how to do anything, that Sousou had turned into something else entirely. (He spoke enthusiastically, meaning well, looking over at Hamada and Ali and chuckling innocently. Ali was disgusted. Inji spat. Hamada was furious. No one said a word.) These days, it's a day your way, the next against you. So what do you intend to do now, Sheikh Ali?

Ali looks at the man sitting before him in his torn clothes and mutters to himself: To stick a finger up your ass. Hamada interrupts: Look here, Adel. From now on you'll be staying here with us. We'll put you up in my apartment and you'll send for your wife and kids. We love you, Adel, and we want you to feel right at home and work with us. Adel agrees. He has no choice but to agree. Hamada gives a contented smile: Thank you, Adel. You may go now.

Two months later:
Adel? Who were the first people you met when you came back from Libya?
You lot were, Miallim Hamada.
And did you have any money on you, then?
No, miallim.
Briefly describe to me the state you were in when you arrived.
A complete mess, miallim.
And describe to me how you're doing now.
Blessed and contented.
And your wife and kids? Can anyone lay a finger on them?
No one would dare.
Adel. Who takes care of you?
You do, miallim.
I wonder, do we get anything out of it?
Just your heavenly reward and the satisfaction of good works, miallim.
Thank you Adel. You may go now.

Two months later:
Adel . . . what are you doing these days, Adel?
I'm not doing anything, Miallim Hamada.
So you're living on our charity, is that it?

That's right, Miallim Hamada.

And why's that, may I ask?

Because you told me you'd find me work, and you haven't.

And if I told you there was something?

Then I'd do it, miallim.

Thank you, Adel. You may go now.

Two months later:

Who's the filthiest human being on earth, Adel?

The Devil!

But the Devil's not a human being, Adel.

Who then?

I'm the one asking you. Who's filthier than the Devil?

No one, miallim.

Think hard. I wouldn't want you to upset me, now.

Stinking Sousou.

Thank you, Adel. You may go now.

Two months later, for the last time:

You're still not working, Adel, right?

Right, miallim.

Why's that?

Because you told me you'd find me work, and you haven't.

Who's right, Adel? Sheikh Ali or Sousou?

Sheikh Ali, miallim.

And is Miallim Hamada right, or is Sousou?

Miallim Hamada.

Right then.

Right then?

Right then. We want you to work with us.

What'll I do?

You'll be our eyes on Sousou. We'll plant you over there and you'll bring us his news.

. . .

Scared?

A little.

That's only natural.

Will I harm my brother?

No. You'll bring us his news and we'll get what's rightfully ours from him. Not a penny more.

So, you'll harm him, then?

Adel. Who takes care of you, Adel?

You do, Miallim Hamada.

Thank you, Adel. You may go now.

And so it was that the process of planting Adel in Sousou's empire began.

Adel's meeting with Sousou was replete with emotion and a surfeit of passion. Save me, brother, Adel said to Sousou: I come to you from heathen lands. Such hard times I've seen, my brother. And the tears flowed from Sousou's eyes. Where's your wife, Adel? Where's your son? And Adel said: I left them behind and came here. Okay, Sousou said, On my marriage vows, you'll stay here with me and nowhere else and you can send for the little woman and the boy. We're flesh and blood, my brother. Adel didn't tell him that he had another child and that this other child was staying with Hamada. One false move from Adel and the kid Ahmed would be sliced up. No joking around. Hamada had learned from past experience: never again would he permit himself to raise a double agent with divided loyalties.

Adel settled down at Sousou's. For three months he didn't leave the house. He sent for his son, Mohamed, and his wife, Fatima, and from the outset it was understood that Mohamed was to marry Sousou's daughter, Amira. The two children got behind this prophecy. They showed a noticeable interest in one another, and all beneath the gaze of the father, the uncle, and the women. Gradually, Adel recovered from his endless wanderings: prison, Libya, Hamada's home. He filled out a little and his cheeks grew rosy. But he never once forgot the reason he was there—to spy on his brother. Hamada's advice had been to concentrate on securing his position at first, to not attract attention, and then in time his brother would start to tell him about his plans. And that is what happened. Sousou's absolute faith in his family led him to back his brother to the hilt, to bring him along on his regular expeditions to the mountain and Wardiyan, even to Matrouh itself. Adel was silent most of the time: watching, absorbing, and saying nothing. It was only after he'd been living with his brother for six months that he met with Hamada in a café in Damanhur, far from prying eyes. He told him, Hamada, the situation's like this and an assault on the neighborhood will require this many men, and so on, and Hamada showed him video clips of his boy, recorded on the phone. The child's living in the lap of luxury, but any hint of treachery will ruin everything. Everything, Adel. I won't say it again. You may go now.

This time, Hamada was confident of victory. He'd regained his health, and his weight, which had ballooned to unprecedented levels, was down. He put up decorations in his neighborhood and ordered the Hen of Karantina to be repainted.

The truth is that this hen was more than a mere statue. For many years it had been the focus of the hopes and dreams of the neighborhood's native sons. The hen had been built in prosperous times. Back then there had only been one Karantina, belonging to its two indivisible leaders. Back then the hen had seemed full of strength, gazing heavenward, surveying the future, and many was the time its wings had sheltered lovers as they wandered past with hands entwined on their way to the casino. And the names on the four eggs had changed every day. Anyone who desired to record his or her name on the pages of Alexandria's history would write it on an egg. This signing of names was like a kind of longing to be recognized, the longing of two lovers to see their love endorsed. The image of the hen embracing her eggs stood at the head of newspaper articles about Karmouz or Karantina. Revolutionaries' dreams, the hopes of lovers, had converged upon it. But things were different now.

Battered by Alexandria's annual downpours, the statue had cracked in two. An icon, so it seemed, of an age whose heroes were falling one by one. And the hen, long a silent witness to the revolutionaries who climbed its sides to watch the police trucks drawing near, some of them exchanging gunfire from its wings, had shrugged off the memory of this time and its symbols. Only rarely now did anyone write anything upon its eggs, and its appearance, grown dismal with the years, was iconic no more.

Farouq was the first person to draw Hamada's attention to this fact. Pointing to the hen's head, he said, The hen's facing down a touch, Hamada, a pronouncement that was more than a little painful to the latter. The pronouncement came in the wake of the studio massacre, in the wake of the murders of Hamada's wife and brothers-in-law and of his men. Hamada took it as a subtle sneer directed at him. They were sitting at the café. Hamada turned: What do you mean, Farouq? And Farouq didn't answer. Out of the blue, the attacks of hysteria that had once plagued Hamada returned. He lifted the iron table and smashed it into Farouq's face, then thumped his shoe into Farouq's testicles. He bellowed: By God's glory, Farouq, if I have to speak to you again, I'll kill you! I'll kill you, Farouq! I'll kill you!

But Farouq was right. So Hamada thought to himself as he repaired to his bed that night. The hen really was collapsing, and perhaps the flagrant disrespect that his neighbors were showing him, his father, and his mother, was the result of this collapse, both actual and symbolic. For days and days Hamada considered repainting and restoring the hen, but these were not his best days, financially speaking. He asked his father about it and his father said, There's no money and there won't be any money. He asked his mother and she said, Your papa wants to kill me, Hamada. You have to protect me. Hamada remained despondent until the arrival of Adel and his employment as a spy on Sousou began. And then, well, the hearts of one and all were filled with hope for a prosperous future soon to come, it became possible to secure loans from the bank against the building, and the restoration got underway.

One of the workmen who came to paint the hen was called Gharib. A loyal young man, upright, who knew his history backward and was always repeating it in earshot of the men. The correct history, that is to say: history according to Ali and Inji, not Sousou and Minnatallah. Every day, Hamada would stop by the workmen and find him talking to them of the old days and how good the old days had been. Hamada approached him and asked him what he knew about Ali and Inji, and eagerly Gharib said that they were two young Alexandrians who'd built a mosque and a water fountain for the poor, then died, and that's why all the people loved them and prayed for their souls. This answer made Hamada happy, for all that it lacked a touch of historical accuracy, because it demonstrated the existence of a new generation that might be used to bring the empire of Karantina back to life. He invited Gharib for a cup of tea, which they drank at the café. And while they were at the café, Farouq and Sheikh Mohamed turned up.

Gharib did not stop talking the whole time, and Hamada, Farouq, and the sheikh seemed bewitched by what he had to say. The time to come, Gharib said, would be Hamada's time. He knew this because his father had told him so, and his father knew this because his father had told him. Thus is life. The glory might fade for a moment, for a moment or two, say three moments, brother, but class will out in the end. Hamada patted his shoulder. When they were done, Gharib asked that he might pay the check as a gesture of his gratitude for having met Hamada himself, but Hamada refused. And Gharib persisted, and Hamada persisted in his refusal. Gharib asked why and Hamada drew him aside. They stood next to the café's urinal. Hamada bent close to his ear and whispered, Listen up, brother. The miallim who owns this café is not going to believe that you exist. He might see you with own two eyes, but he'll turn his nose up and say, Nope! Your friend doesn't exist, you're just imagining him, and so on. Right to my face, mind you. Gharib smiled understandingly and Hamada patted him on the shoulder. At that moment, the miallim who ran the café walked by. He looked at Hamada and sneered, Talking to yourself, Hamada? Hamada didn't turn round. With a grin he whispered to Gharib: Didn't I tell you? See what I mean now?

This time, however, Gharib did not disappear before his eyes. Hamada smiled sagely and they went back to their seats. Just a short while later, Hamada would discover that his new friend had disappeared. He wasn't there anymore. He asked himself where he could have gotten to, then he continued his conversation with Farouq and Sheikh Mohamed.

A few days later Ali vanished. Without a trace. Hamada went round all the hospitals and couldn't find him. Inji lay in bed at home with a severe cold, glancing at her cell phone every other minute. Hamada got back at two in the morning, to inform her that not a trace of him remained. He saw her tears fall and spot the blanket. Inji said, Please, Hamada. Find out where he is for me, Hamada. I'm very ill, Hamada. And she gave a tremendous sneeze, releasing a flood of mucus, which drenched the blanket.

Next morning, the phone rang in the apartment. The caller asked if this was Ali Mohamed Sayyid's house and Hamada confirmed that it was. The voice coming down the line seemed to hesitate. It said that Ali had been found drowned in the Mahmoudiya Canal. It dictated the address to Hamada and Hamada rushed right over. There he saw his father's corpse. He cried a little and called his mother.

The mourning period quickly passed. Winter days are short and its nights are for sleeping. Later, this period would be entirely erased from Hamada's memory. He would recall scattered incidents, like the aza, which very few attended, chief among them Farouq, Gharib, and Sheikh Mohamed; he would recall a fight with the Quran reciter over his fee; he would recall one long night he spent awake, the rain lashing viciously outside and his mother sitting on the couch, sneezing and knitting a sweater, and abruptly asking, Hamada, you think I'm going to die any minute, don't you? Hamada didn't answer. Hamada! I'm not about to die, you mark my words, and you won't be inheriting this building. You'll die and I'll go on living, and this building will stay in my name till the last second of my life.

Another detail from that time, which Hamada recalled with absolute clarity: Lifting the covers from the hen, which had been repainted and restored as good as new. Hamada recalled this detail with such precision because the three simultaneous events—his father's death, the hen's unveiling, and the planting of Adel inside Sousou's empire—had left a single sentence burned into his brain. Hamada surveyed the scene and slowly said: Something dies, something is born, and something takes shape.

This is what life teaches us.

Nothing can stop the people of Karantina from reaching their goal. Even in the very depths of injustice, death, and destruction they did not turn aside from their rebuilding. Tawfiq al-Hakim had written, "Beware of this people, for it harbors a terrible force of will," and now the people of Karantina were bringing this lesson to life with their bodies. At all times, even in the cold days of mourning, Hamada would meet with Sousou's brother, Adel, in other, far-off provinces, in Damanhur and Tanta for example, and Adel would not hold back any piece of information he wanted to know. He'd hand him maps of the neighborhood, the names and characters of the men, the weak points in the well-secured fortress Sousou had built by the Gheit al-Enab Bridge.

It is worth wondering what Adel was feeling at this time. Did that young man, who had sampled the bitterness of exile and denial, of prison and police pursuit, now look at himself as a traitor—a traitor to his brother, first of all, but also to the man who had invited him into his home and given shelter to his wife and child? The fact is that direct evidence of any such feelings is hard to come by. We have no more than scattered hints. As Adel smokes hash with Sousou late at night, he tells him in a whisper: If I should die, forgive me, brother. Forgive him for what? Sousou wants to know, and gets no answer. Adel is only human: his conscience tortures him and, betraying the hand that reached out to him in his hour of need, sits badly with him. But he is a father before anything else, a father with a son held hostage and threatened with death should he back out of a mission that he convinced himself, in a moment of weakness, that he would carry out. Forgive me, brother, Adel tells Sousou, and in the latter's head a red light flicks on.

Another day. Mohamed, Adel's son, makes a misstep in front of Sousou. He describes the interior of Hamada's apartment. Sousou asks him when he had seen Hamada's home from the inside, and Adel changes the subject. Another day. Adel's wife Fatima is talking to Minna, Sousou's wife, and compares the hallway of Minna's apartment to the one in Inji's. Minna reports this to Sousou. The mistakes come thick and fast, and Sousou is sharp.

In a few short days Sousou managed to secure his own private entrance to Karabantina, move his men's posts, and appoint one of his men to follow Adel without Adel noticing. The man presented reports to Sousou on meetings that took place between his brother and Hamada in Kafr al-Dawwar.

Sousou started to pray more, as though seeking the assistance of his Lord through such terrible days, those that have passed and those yet to come. More than once he wept in Minna's arms at night, and more than once muttered feverishly in her hearing, My brother's betraying me, ya hagga. My brother, my father's son, has sold me to Satan. And she would wipe away his tears. Walking through the neighborhood with his hobble, which had become something of an overt lurch, with his bristling mustache grown white and the multiplying wrinkles on his face, Sousou looked as though he had aged dozens of years. No one knew what ailed Miallim Sousou. Miallim Sousou, the Fourth of the Three Esses, the one who would succeed where they had failed, the architect of the New Alexandria, was afflicted with a great pain that no one understood but Minna.

A week after the restored statue of the Hen of Karantina was unveiled, the inhabitants of the neighborhood were shocked to find the four eggs smeared with blood.

Everyone was asking where the blood had come from. Though the eggs were quickly cleaned and the hen returned to its original pristine condition, the question remained. Two days later, everyone found out. Adel's severed head was found dumped next to the statue, and boldly daubed in blood across the eggs: "Sousou—2/1/2044." Someone saw this and rushed to tell Hamada. Hamada saw it and trembled inside. The message was clear. Hamada went mad. He lost control. Beneath the rain, into the pure air up above, he screamed Ennnnough! and sprinted for the building. Inji was asleep and Yara and Lara were crying, and with them Ahmed, Adel's son. He didn't know what to do. He was screaming and pummeling the walls. Before his eyes many shapes, many figures, appeared, then vanished away. He forced his mother awake and wept in her arms as she sneezed and wiped her nose. He thought of throwing himself off the roof of the building as his father had thrown himself into the canal before him, but more figures rose up to distract him before they too returned to nothing. It took a whole hour before he calmed down. Sheikh Mohamed showed up and Hamada did as he was told. Together they went downstairs to the café. On the way the sheikh told him, Don't be sad, Hamada. He wasn't kith or kin. All it means is that the war must wait a little. Hamada looked at him and smiled. As they sat at the café he became calmer and calmer. For many minutes Hamada did not speak. He recalled something and smiled, and the sheikh said, Why are you smiling? Hamada said, Fancy a game of Monopoly, Sheikh?

They are playing now, surrounded by banknotes. Sheikh Hamada takes a city and Hamada takes two. The sheikh rents out a garage and Hamada rents out a market. And to the sound of the dice they cast upon the board, the pair start planning for a new round with Sousou.

I murdered my father's son. I murdered my mother's son. I betrayed my father and my mother and my brother's unsullied soul. I can forgive Hamada for killing my men, or trying to kill them, rather, but I'll never forgive him for making a murderer of me. I murdered my father's son. I murdered my mother's son. Sousou was writing in his journal. On another page he wrote: There are no winners in war. Everyone's a loser.

6

Cairo is the capital of Egypt.

After all the conflicts we've witnessed over the preceding decades, after the surging cataracts of gore, after the heroics, betrayals, and feuds, after history new and old has been written, after history new and old has been erased, after all that, Cairo, not Alexandria, remains the capital of Egypt.

The Alexandrian, my friend, stands in awe of two things: Cairo and the computer. Indeed, the Alexandrian—both before Ali and Inji appeared in his life and afterward—never gave up on his ancient dream: that Alexandria, his beloved city, its arms held wide to the free world of the North, should become the capital as it had been in its days of glory. Not Cairo.

We cannot separate this dream from the way in which Alexandrians embraced Ali and Inji in the first decades after they surfaced by the shore. As we have already pointed out, this surfacing had been accompanied by prophecies and omens of the return of this former glory to its rightful owners. But the days went by and control of Egypt passed into the hands of another ignorant dynasty who did not read history and cared not a jot for local culture. The new dynasty—consisting of an elder brother who sought to pass on power to a younger brother—was only interested in its internal conflicts, which played out in the two men's home town of Sheikh Zayid, and it did not perceive, or pretended not to perceive, the new history being born in Alexandria. All of which was most frustrating to your average citizen of Alexandria. Uncle Mustafa, a potato seller on the Corniche, told the *Voice of the Bay* newspaper (which started publishing in the early 2030s):

We're living like beggars, miss, no one thinks about us or asks after us. We're always going on about "Alexandria this" and "Alexandria that," but the fact is no one cares enough to speak to us or give us so much as a seat in parliament. Mahmoud Ragab Rihan, a fish seller from Bahari, had this to say to *Sea and Seagull*: The people who live in Alexandria, we're what you call a poor people, but the trouble starts when even the poor man doesn't get any respect. Let me tell you how it is, miss. When you've taken a beating once, twice, three times, the guy facing you is going to stop thinking of you as a human being, isn't he? No offence, don't get upset now, but it's like you're worthless. And he'll go on smacking you around whenever he feels like it. The pictures illustrating the report were of rocks along the Corniche, on which had been written: We want a revolution, O my country.

In the mid-forties a number of actors rose to prominence in Egypt. Suhair Naguib was the first of them, popularly known as the "Lady Boss," a homage to the nickname bestowed on that ancient star of the silver screen, Adel Imam. In her wake came a group of young actors who specialized in comedy roles—Mohamed Bekheit, Ayman Abdel Hamid, and Salama Salama; a movement dubbed the "New Fools." Critics condemned them for ushering in an era of moral turpitude, their vulgar wisecracks dominated by sexual innuendo. Even Suhair Naguib abandoned the dramatic roles that had accompanied her rise during the twenties and was whisked away on the currents of youth cinema. A critic of the time wondered: A new age has arrived, a featureless age: Is such depravity to be the stuff on which our children shall be raised in years to come?

The significance of this cannot be understood without reference to an important fact: that these actors—Naguib, Bekheit, Salama, and Abdel Hamid—all came from unambiguously Alexandrian stock, and from neighborhoods whose Alexandrian credentials could not be faulted—from Rushdi and Bakos and Sidi Gaber and Bahari and elsewhere. This phenomenon prompted one editor to rage in the editorial at the front of his monthly magazine: The Alexandrians are invading Egypt with their terrible depravity.

Therefore, and contrary to the effect one might suppose this phenomenon would have—to wit, the shifting of the center of Egyptian life to Alexandria—it in fact facilitated the very opposite: a gathering wave of xenophobia against Alexandria and Alexandrians, plus efforts to impede the progress of anyone making their way from there to Cairo. Someone signing himself Gamal al-Dowali—though it certainly was not him—wrote on the side of an Alexandrian tram: After Communismophobia and Islamophobia, now there's Alexandrophobia, and scrawled a smiley underneath.

We cannot, in truth, separate Sousou and Hamada's struggles from this new wave of blind hatred toward all things Alexandrian. The fact is that the feud in Karantina was exploited in the papers to highlight the barbarity of Alexandrians. Something along the lines of, Look! These are the inheritors of Greek civilization and enlightenment, the people that gave us Khaled Said, the revolution, and the million martyrs. They're slaughtering one another and the police stand helplessly by! Even your average citizen, unmoved by political loyalties of any kind, regarded Alexandria as a vast jungle inhabited exclusively by feral villains. The number of summer visitors to the city fell dramatically, and as a result many cafés that subsisted on local tourism had closed their doors. This, coupled with successive governors' neglect of the city, in whose streets the trash piled higher day by day and brutal murders multiplied, plus the emigration of many Alexandrians away from their city to Cairo, but also to other places like Damanhur, Benha, and Qalyubiya, even to the cities of the South—all this led to the very result with which we began this chapter: After all these expansive dreams, Cairo was still the capital of Egypt. And that was very sad.

There are people who can confirm that Sousou was essentially no different from Ali. Like Ali, Sousou had built up a vast empire. And just as Ali relied on a (legally) proscribed activity—namely prostitution—so Sousou relied on drugs. And just as Ali had deliberately murdered his brother, Mustafa, so Sousou had set about murdering his brother, Adel. Only one thing differentiated the two of them: Sousou had no national vision for Alexandria.

Sousou, no more than a market boy after all, sought salvation in a savage capitalist world and set up a vast business. Unlike his predecessor, he was never interested in ushering in a new dawn for Alexandria. Even the stories of Sika, Sayyid, and Sultan that he had brought back into circulation were just a gambit to take on the mighty tale that Ali brought back to life, the tale of the martyr Harbi. In any case, we don't claim to be objective. There's no such thing as objectivity in this world. We are reporting history from Ali and Inji's point of view. We are biased toward Ali and Inji.

Days after killing his brother, Sousou began plotting his most devastating blow: an assault on Hamada's Karantina, killing Inji and Hamada, and seizing the vast inheritance that belonged, in his view, to him and his wife. Sousou planted men everywhere and got his hands on enough weaponry to blow all of Alexandria sky-high. The conflict was at its most intense. Now that Hamada had forced him to murder his brother, Adel, there was no room left for forbearance and forgiveness.

Karmouz's heart beats faster. The bell tolls. The reckoner makes his reckoning.

Hamada didn't lose hope. Among the new men now helping Sousou, Hamada planted a man who belonged to him. With time, and the failure to uncover this individual, he planted another, then a third. This time he didn't meet with them himself. He gave his men the job of meeting them, in provinces far, far away this time, in Cairo, Beni Suef, and Minya, for example. He had his hands on every piece of information concerning Sousou, but what use was this information if it all led to the same gloomy conclusion: Hamada, you just aren't capable of attacking Sousou's Karabantina right now, and worse still, Sousou's plotting to attack your neighborhood and there's nothing you can do to stop him. Sousou has guns coming out of his ears, he has armored vehicles, he has—so it was rumored at the time—a helicopter. Hamada's spies confined themselves to corroborating the date on which Karantina would be crushed, and Hamada just had to sit there like a woman, waiting for the inevitable.

In those days Hamada was busy with something important, the most important thing of his life. He'd tried art and he'd tried mysticism, and neither had brought solace to his confused and tormented soul. He was busy with a final project, which would occupy what space remained in his life: the attainment of wisdom.

As he waited for Sousou's crushing assault on Karantina, Hamada took to perching on the wall of the hen statue each day, sunbathing, or so it seemed, though in fact he wasn't sunbathing at all. He was trying to penetrate the secret of existence. Hamada did not move from his position for days at a time. By night he received the squalls of rain on his head, and the icy winds by day, his face turned ever to the statue, eyes cast down at the statue's basin full of rainwater, contemplating the fry that swam there and asking himself what species of fish they were. He pondered on the life of each tiny sprat and tried to listen to all the varied sounds of existence. He looked as if he'd aged dozens of years: him, a man just turned forty. His beard sprouted and he rapidly lost weight. His body was melting away.

He drank more during this period than at any other time of his life. Once a day he would ascend to the apartment and, carrying three or four loaves of bread, a bottle of water, and bottles of brandy and whiskey, would descend once more and assume his position on the statue's wall. He would open the bag of bread, dip loaf after loaf in the water, and swallow them down. Then he would begin to down the booze, and when he'd finished it would dispatch one of the neighborhood kids to bring him more. He would gaze at the water and at the tiny creatures in the water. All the time, just gazing at the water and the tiny creatures in the water beneath his feet, and thinking. To attain wisdom one must contemplate, and Hamada did not stint: he would contemplate every particle of the water beneath him. I wonder, does this tiny creature have a life, like ours? I wonder, are there people who are bigger than us, gazing at us as we gaze at these fry, laughing at us and belittling us, and indifferent to our stories? And I wonder, can we look at ourselves as we look at these fry, you know, are we able to know our true selves, like the bigger creatures know us? We are fry, Hamada said and swallowed a mouthful of brandy. He let out a short whistle, then went back to gazing at the water.

From afar, Hamada looked like one of those vagrants, their minds gone, who are found in all places and all times: his filth-caked clothes, his pungent black beard, his long hair that had begun to breed the insects that grazed upon his nape. He ate by the hen and drank there and when he needed to piss he'd stand up, take down his trousers, pull out his penis and let the urine gutter down into the water. But all this was just appearance, nothing more, and if the price of attaining wisdom is to appear mad, Hamada would declare, then how cheap the price. From his post up on the wall, he would beckon to the children. At first they were afraid, then bit by bit they started to come closer, and Hamada would talk to them about the water, about the hen, and about the world. This world is a book, he once told one of the kids, and you're its idea. Tell me, what does that mean? The kid didn't answer. Hamada looked down for a long time, then said: It means that this world, the world in which we live, is a book . . . and you are its idea. He half rose in order to make himself more comfortable, and the kid couldn't stop himself: he gave Hamada's asshole a swift jab and fled.

One day, in order to protect his position, to guard against the waves of children who bombarded him with bricks and mocked him all day long, Hamada went upstairs to his apartment. This time the loaves of bread and water were not enough. He stopped at the couch in his bedroom, opened the chest, and pulled out his pistol. Then he went down into the street.

At first he shot into the air whenever the children crowded around him. But one time, one of the kids provoked him and didn't flee. Hamada fired a second shot into the air and the kid, insufferably, stayed where he was in front of him. So Hamada gathered himself and shot him in the shoulder. The kid screamed and galloped away. Hamada, on the other hand, ran into the building. He took a machine gun from beneath the chest and carried it downstairs and, facing the local residents enraged at the wounding of one of their children, he brandished his gun and threatened to kill anyone who came near.

That day Hamada learnt an important lesson. Wisdom might be a creature with a mind of fire, all well and good, but its body was weak. Wisdom was in constant need of someone who could defend it; who could defend it and who could bring it to the people. Threatening them with his machine gun, Hamada was able to herd a group of children to his seat by the statue and talk to them about wisdom, existence, death, and birth.

He speaks slowly now, like someone trying to get to the truth, emphasizing every word, long pauses while he thinks, and never looking his interlocutor in the eye as he goes on, but always at the fry swimming in the water. He crafts short sentences along the lines of Wealth comes and goes but morals are the Crown of Man, or, The bird has two wings, but love and contentment with one's lot are Man's Two Wings, or, Success doesn't just happen. He delivers this proverbial wisdom, glances at the seated children out of the corner of his eye, checks his gun, and then goes back to gazing at the water. After a while he raises his head and asks the children to think hard about what he has said, as he'll be testing them on it tomorrow.

The world's first school for the imparting of wisdom. This is how Hamada viewed it, contentedly, back then. And being a school for wisdom, the curriculum it taught was of a different order. Hamada didn't ask the children what he had said to them yesterday, but rather what they'd understood of life's wisdom over the course of the day before, and every one of them would volunteer an answer as Hamada patted his gun and smiled. But the children, who at first had been frightened of the gun, soon went back to mocking him. One day, Hamada decided that he needed to impose his authority again. He asked one of the children what life wisdom he'd acquired the previous day and the child said he had learned that anger's bad. Hamada bowed his head. A poor answer, he mused. And he pulled his gun out and shot the boy in the head. The boy died.

The days to come would prove difficult. Killing a child's not the breeze it used to be. Hamada ringed his post with butane canisters. He carried a pistol in his back pocket and a machine gun on his arm and every day would tip gasoline into the statue's basin, threatening anyone who approached him that he'd send the whole neighborhood up in flames. I've got nothing left to live for, but those who want to fight me do. A lot to live for.

He's sitting in an impenetrable fortress now. By day he ventures out, grabs two or three or four young kids and, under threat of arms, herds them before him. He opens the door in the ring of butane canisters. Shepherds them inside. Closes the door. Seats them around him and, silent, careworn, sunk in thought, starts contemplating existence. And when one of the children asks him what he's thinking about he gestures at him to be quiet, and a little while later, in ponderous tones, says something like, The world's become simply intolerable. Then he turns to the child and starts explaining himself in detail, with long interludes of silence between each word and the next. One time, it takes him fully seven minutes and thirty seconds to deliver one paragraph, which runs as follows:

I told her, sister, you're not up to these people. Watch out for them. They're serious operators and you're just a fifty-pound-a-trick whore. But they lit the fire and sent her head in a box, right here, to my feet. Why haven't you come, Farouq? Or you, Sheikh Mohamed? Why don't you come? Won't you come? As he said to the actress! Hee hee hee! So many things I just can't cope with anymore. You know, to be honest, I was a little tired there for a while. Mentally, I mean. I'm fine now. Not tired like I was before. But the whole world's telling me, Go easy on yourself, you're worn out. Honestly, is that any way to talk? I mean, what's the good of that?

Hamada only ate the barest minimum back then, just a few loaves of bread and cheese per day, washed down with oceans of adulterated liquor. From dawn to dusk he drank. At the start of the day, at ten or eleven in the morning, his speech was fluent. As time went on, his head would start to sag against his shoulder and he'd mutter. He'd question a child about the things he was saying, go on muttering, then lift his head and proclaim, for instance, All people are lovely in the eyes of the lovely!—then park his head on his shoulder. Sometimes he'd vomit briskly into the basin, and his eyelids would continue to sag lower. He lost a lot of weight back then. All that was left was a round face, two still-protuberant breasts, and a small potbelly. And he was forever scratching at his crotch and armpits, and muttering the words that were formerly his ringtone: The companions are bemused; Who are you, my love, who are you?

Inji caught wind of what was happening. She wasn't happy. She, too, was suffering back then, afflicted with the curse of reliving everything, from the very beginning to the present day. But Inji could face down anything, memories included. And she too—like Hamada—knew that the end was just a matter of time. She knew that Sousou was coming with his tanks to wipe the neighborhood from the map, but she, unlike Hamada, would not accept that her only option was to wait.

Once, as the dawn prayer was being called, she went downstairs, leaning on a stick and wrapped in a thick shawl. Hamada was asleep, snoring by the statue's pedestal. She made an opening in the ring of canisters and went inside, Hamada still snoring and dead to the world. She slapped him lightly on the cheek until he awoke. As he came to she sat down beside him. You don't care for your mother anymore, Hamada? You don't like her because she makes people laugh at us? Don't you ever think of the woman who gave birth to you and worked so hard to raise you? A foul stench was seeping from every centimeter of his body, and one fouler still was seeping from his crotch. Even so, Inji bent down over his thighs, sank her face into his lap, and began to talk, as if she were talking to herself: I mean, when my own son treats me like that, what will strangers do? Out here, Hamada, instead of considering me and saying, My mother's an old lady and needs me by her side? Out here instead of raising your children, Hamada? Instead of going to visit your father in his grave? My heart aches, Hamada. Am I not your mother? She was murmuring these words in an almost inaudible voice even as she tried to flake the filth from his trousers with her fingernails. She'd spit on her finger and rub it on the cloth and, of course, nothing would come off.

The moon is high and full, the weather mild. We're in spring now. Suddenly, Hamada springs up and wriggles away. Get back! he screams, I'll kill you, Mama, I'll kill you. I swear to God, I'll kill you. He brandishes his gun and fires off shots into the air, one after the other. Inji leaps up. Runs back to the building. He shoots after her. She manages to get up to the apartment and bolt the door behind her. Hamada tucks the gun behind his back and goes back to sleep. A little while later the sound of his snoring rises into the air.

One of Sousou's men was killed during a dispute in Bahari.

Of the many incidents that made up the feuds over Karantina, this one met with particular attention, not because it lay behind Sousou's belated decision to attack Ali and Inji's Karantina, but because it prompted him to go to Karantina himself, to attend the assault in person, having previously intended to put the entire operation under the control of one of his men. The blood boiled in Sousou's veins, convinced as he was that the murder of his man in Bahari had been Hamada's doing. He resolved to take revenge and kill Hamada with his own two hands.

Sousou readied his men and arms and set out. Two trucks loaded with men burst into the neighborhood. The men got out. They were met by feeble, scattered bands, incapable of holding them off for long. Then, all of a sudden, other men appeared at the windows of Karantina's buildings, pouring heavy fire on Sousou's men. Without warning, hell flared up about them. One of the victims was a fruit seller stacking his wares in the street. Before his eyes he saw the oranges and tangerines tango in the hail of bullets, their acid juice spattering out and drenching his gallabiya. Some of Sousou's men fell, but trucks carrying yet more rolled in unendingly, and out of one of them stepped Sousou himself. Preceded by a clutch of his men who cleared his path and screened him, he ascended the Karantina building. He walked in on Inji, who was sitting next to Umm Salah the maid, the pair of them watching the proceedings through a window left ajar.

Inji looked at Sousou and he at her. She smiled. You haven't changed much, Sousou my boy. His eyes turned earthward. You know, the dear departed was always on your case. He really hated you.

Can time have done all this? Sousou marvels, as he stares into Inji's wrinkled, uncovered face. He thinks back to another Inji, forty years ago: pale and beautiful, with dainty glasses, and half her words in English. The old lady leans into him coquettishly, running her hand over his chest and saying: Because he thought I was in love with you. Her finger reaches his nipple, pinches it lightly, and she moans like a bitch in heat. She winks at him with her left eye and the skin around it crinkles. She says, In love with you? What kind of talk is that? You're my little brother. Then she stares into his eyes and smiles. What's up, my boy? Why so hot and bothered? He thrusts her away suddenly. Go to hell, woman! He runs to the balcony, from where he spies Hamada, asleep and snoring, ringed round by canisters of butane. He shoots the canisters and they explode. Hamada is now in the very heart of the fire, which quickly ignites the gasoline poured into the statue's basin. Hamada, who used fire and butane and gasoline to prevent anyone approaching him, will now meet his fate by this same fire and butane and gasoline.

It wakes him. In a matter of seconds he has grasped the situation. He reaches for his gun and opens fire on Sousou standing on the balcony. Sousou topples from the balcony. Hamada runs, ablaze, flames clinging to his clothes. He breaks through the ring of canisters and drags Sousou along the ground. He throws him into the heart of the fire. And Sousou struggles.

He pulls Hamada by his trousers. Hamada, who for an instant seems like some flaming god, strips off all his clothes. He does this quickly, skillfully, unafraid of the fire against his fingers, which unhitch the buttons of his shirt and unzip his fly. He strips off all his clothes and takes off. He mounts the stairs at a gallop, bursts into the apartment, and starts shooting wildly at Sousou's men who are dispersed about the place. Naked, sweating, bearded, filthy, he fires at everyone indiscriminately. And afterward he goes into the bedroom of the two little girls, Yara and Lara, and carries them in his arms — along with Ahmed, Adel's son. He sets them down next to his mother, who is hiding in her bedroom with Umm Salah the maid. He peers down from the balcony. He cannot believe what he sees. The miracle is there before his eyes. His men are tossing Sousou's men into the fire. Sousou himself is but a charred corpse now. The gunfire falls off dramatically. Victory is assured for Hamada and his men. Fate has had its fun.

Hamada smiles contentedly. He surveys Karantina, ablaze beneath him. Runs his hands over his injured, bleeding body. They come away smeared with blood and sweat and soil. He looks into the distance. Feels a faint dizziness. He notices one of Sousou's men stir down below. With infinite difficulty he pulls out his gun. Tries to draw a bead on him but his balance deserts him. He topples to the bare earth of Karantina.

Hamada dies: naked, bleeding, aflame, filthy, still young, potbellied, but also crowned, with a halo of splendor that history will long remember.

For the fortnight that followed, an unbroken calm descended on Karmouz. The sounds of squabbles or conversations, the laughter of young men, were rarely heard. Even the chickens and ducks were quiet. No sound in Karmouz now but calls to prayer and tolling bells embracing, fused together, from the church and mosque that Ali and Inji had built upon some distant day. At last Karmouz is free to write its history and honor its heroes, calmly and free from distraction.

It seemed to everyone that they were on the threshold of a new era, an era in which everything would be rebuilt from scratch. After the slayings of Sousou, Hamada, and Adel, after Ali's suicide, after the death of Abu Amira, after all these things, it seemed as if Karmouz were shrugging off the weight of its history and returning to how it had been before. All were calm and sleepy, biddable as children. And during these same nights, the Interior Ministry slept on serenely, now that Sousou, the emperor of West Alexandria, had finally been disposed of; after the many months it had spent cultivating cadres in Karantina to dispose of Sousou when he launched his final assault on the neighborhood.

The days that followed brought wind and dust clouds that hid all of Alexandria from sight. Then came the gigantic bulldozers. They razed the statue of the hen to the ground, brought it down before stunned residents, and likewise leveled a few unlicensed buildings. As for the four floors of the Karantina building where Inji lived with her two granddaughters, the bulldozers did not approach it. The building and its legend still held sway.

In the days that followed, Umm Salah the maid swept up Ahmed, Adel's son, and took him off to Sousou's Karabantina. She handed the child to Minna, Sousou's widow, who smiled and made her lunch and tea. They did not talk about anything. They ignored the seas of blood and tears and drank their tea. Minna said that she was taking on the job of raising Ahmed and Mohamed, the sons of the traitor Adel, alongside her daughter Amira. They've done no wrong. Hagg Sousou was a God-fearing man and he knew that no man carries another's sin. She took a sip of tea and continued: That bitch, Adel's wife? I chucked her out. A filthy whore.

As Umm Salah made her way back to Inji's apartment, along the road that ran through what was once Sousou's Karabantina, she felt that it was harmless now, that this neighborhood would never again be a refuge for scum, as Ali had been fond of calling it. She felt free, and she gazed at the leveled buildings and the trucks busy asphalting the streets, and laughed. She started to really laugh, like someone who had at long last been set free. Days earlier, the police had conducted a purge here too, and just as in the original Karantina, Sousou's building—Harbi's old building, burdened with its grim and heavy history of struggle—had been spared. Umm Salah laughed, laughed and pranced in the street like a bear.

And because, as the proverb tells us, forgetting is the bane of our alley, the details of this struggle were wiped from the minds of the inhabitants of Karmouz. Isolated images remained, foremost among them the image of Hamada, naked and ablaze on the balcony, ridding the neighborhood of evildoers with his machine gun, of Hamada squatting like Buddha beside the hen, swigging cheap booze and every five minutes delivering a pithy dictum on the secrets of life and death, then returning to his contemplation of the fry swimming in the rainwater. And many other images besides.

The years before had all been full of blood, but this year stood apart as a festival of murder, all these icons perishing so close together: Ali, Hamada, Sousou, Adel, and more. For this reason, for many reasons, the forty-fourth year of the second millennium after the birth of Christ was the most crucial in the history of the neighborhood, with no year that followed more so.

FEMALE EMPOWERMENT

Seven women who ruled the world.

1

In the late thirties the Shanghai Tunnel was opened, an event that captured the attention of the whole world.

"Shanghai Tunnel" was the name given to a huge project on which work first began sometime around 2028: a long borehole excavated through the earth, starting from Shanghai and surfacing on the far side of the planet, in the Atlantic Ocean off Argentina's coast. Obviously, the project aimed to reduce the distance between Asia and Latin America, but its primary goal was to entertain wealthy individuals who wished to view our planet from within. It was overseen by an American travel company. Not only did this company drill out the tunnel, it also designed vessels made of a reinforced glass capable of withstanding the intense heat and pressure beneath the earth's surface, and these vessels began making daily journeys along the tunnel's six lanes, back and forth between Shanghai and the Atlantic Ocean. The price of a journey was set at three million dollars, which enabled the company to cover the costs of the project inside two months.

The company, which was called Beneath and whose slogan ran, "We look beneath our feet," managed to make the whole world turn its gaze from the heavens earthward. Where the twentieth century's craze had been for outer space and other planets, the twenty-first century was wild about Planet Earth itself.

The company brought out a television series about two children who took a ride through the Shanghai Tunnel. Their glass vessel blows up en route but they, somewhat miraculously, survive, and decide to spend the rest of their lives underground. Dressed in their heat- and pressure-resistant suits they discover a whole world inside our planet, meet all manner of different creatures, and every episode saw them embark on zany new adventures. The series ran on endlessly and the whole world sat down to watch it. Reservations for the Shanghai Tunnel's vessels went up.

Almost without exception, that is how people were thinking by the early forties. Everyone watched the series, and cutting more tunnels through the planet was every country's ultimate aspiration. An Egyptian tycoon declared that he was determined to be the first man to bring the miracle to Egypt. He designed a logo for his company that showed a planet riddled with tunnels, the oceans leaking from the holes, and over it the phrase "That's our goal!" Everyone was quite dazzled by the Sino-American miracle and a planet like a colander was an almost sexual fantasy shared by all the nations of the earth.

Egypt was not out of the loop, then. A flood of Egyptian films and TV series attempted to imitate the American original, and it can be confidently asserted that some of them were genuinely successful and well made. What was lacking was the miracle itself. The miracle of seeing what lay beneath, the miracle of penetrating the planet's crust. Bit by bit it began to look like the dream might come true on Egyptian soil, and specifically in its northernmost metropolis, in Alexandria.

On November 13, 2048, the Alexandrian Metro Company opened its new line.

The opening was filmed and footage broadcast of the Minister of Transport standing next to the Governor of Alexandria, the children of the neighborhood surrounding them. The neighborhood welcoming committee included two girls who laughed away as the minister took the scissors and snipped the tape. The minister noticed their laughter, and when he had finished the cutting he looked at them, waved the scissors in their faces, and laughed himself. They looked shyly at the ground and went on laughing.

The minister and the governor, along with the other officials and the children, descended into the Metro tunnel and rode the first train to Maamoura. The cameras that came along for the ride caught the following heartwarming scene: the governor pulling silly faces at the two girls seated opposite. One of the girls came closer and asked: Uncle, are we going back? You want to go back? the governor said and she replied, Because Teta's all by herself and my sister and I have English homework. Her sister, who was hovering in the background, plucked up her courage and stepped forward. The governor, the minister, all those watching at home, observed how exactly the twin sisters resembled one another. What's your name? the governor asked the girl and she replied, I'm Yara and that's Lara. Lara screamed, No! She's a retard, don't believe her! We have science homework, not English. And Yara, well, she frowned, and after a moment's hesitation, said: English for me and Science for her.

For years afterward, thanks to this footage, which would be repeated over and over on Egyptian television, the twins would be known as "the Karmouz Metro girls." Wherever the girls went, the people of Alexandria would recognize them and call out, English for me and Science for her. This amused the two girls, who had lost both their parents and lived a dull life with their grandmother, a life devoid of any pleasure or distraction.

English for me and Science for her. To this day, Yara and Lara smile whenever they recall this phrase, and to this day the two radiant young women dissolve into giggles if someone reminds them of "the Karmouz Metro girls."

The destruction of the statue of the hen in 2044 was not destruction for its own sake—not entirely. One year later, it had become clear that a Metro station was to be built on that very spot, facing the building that had once belonged to Ali and Inji and that was now home to no one save Inji, the aged grandmother, her two granddaughters, and Umm Salah the maid, in addition to a number of short-term tenants. There was a station outside Ali and Inji's building and a second in Gheit al-Enab, near the home of the late Sousou. The first was called Karantina and the second, at the end of the line, was Karabantina. The two stations were close to one another and every day people would get on at the one and get off at the other, and the other way around.

The barrier between the two neighborhoods had come down. It had become part of history.

Umm Salah had gotten to know Ali and Inji when they were both starting out. She worked for them for a while. She'd had some tough times. Back then she was a strapping young woman called Ghada. She left Ali and Inji once she'd managed to open a little shop of her own selling fish in Kom al-Dikka, where she married, bore a son, Salah, and gave up working in Karantina. But life didn't let her go. Her husband was put in prison and she was forced to turn once more to Inji. She asked that Inji take her current situation into consideration, to respect the fact that she was a wife and mother. She went to stay with her. She scrubbed and swept and cooked, and when Ali and Hamada died, she became nanny to the two girls, Yara and Lara. The woman with a past had escaped her own black history.

The story of Umm Salah's life is a sad one. She lived through wars, and from the start she knew on which side good lay and on which side evil. She was educated: a degree in commerce from Alexandria University. No one could accuse her of being ignorant. So it was she came to play an active part in managing the conflict. Her part was small but crucial. With the advice she dropped in Hamada's ear, the lullabies she crooned to Yara and Lara in their cots, and the small talk she swapped with Ali and Inji, Umm Salah became a figure of pivotal importance in the house. But the slaughter of 2044 brought change. With everything at an end, with Hamada killed and Sousou killed, Umm Salah made her way home from Minna's, and it was then that the veil was lifted from her eyes, if the expression serves. She saw everything with greater clarity than before and her soul soared up above the world and its petty cares. She scented freedom; felt that anyone might roam where they pleased. Felt, too, that nothing and nobody deserved all this trouble. That day the sun shone down after days of dust-filled winds. The sun could still shine, life was still good, so what was everyone fighting for? From that moment on, Umm Salah chose amnesia, a purposeful forgetting of all that had happened in the decades before. Now she spoke, like everybody else, about rising prices, about how hard it was to get by, about the overcrowded buses. And she transferred this amnesia of hers to Inji, who seemed cleansed by the slaughter. Inji was now a wise old lady in her mid-fifties. And now that she'd attained respectability she at last took off the niqab and her pale and wrinkled face, her still-beautiful smile, appeared for all to see. Her face now glowed with the light of God.

Nor was this all. The residents of Karmouz seemed to have forgotten—or were trying to forget—the difficult days of the past. Even the portraits of Abu Amira, Hagga Itemad, and Madame Nadia were taken down from the entrance to the Karantina building. The neighborhood was like a man who has lost his memory, and it was better that way. And when the new Metro line was opened and a station materialized outside the building, their lives changed utterly, a process aided by the growing incidence of this amnesia. Only the government, it seemed, did not forget. It was the government that named the station Karantina and thereby determined the fate of the neighborhood and its future identity. In any case, there is no such thing as absolute amnesia in this world of ours, nor total recall. Things always sit between two poles. Well, mostly.

On the other hand, there is only one phrase to describe the years that followed 2044: the miracle of motherhood. Minna had certainly shown she was worthy of the sacred honor of motherhood. She'd given her daughter Amira the best upbringing a child could have, had sent her to the best schools and turned a blind eye to all the grudges of the past. Amira grew up as gossamer and unencumbered as a butterfly. Were we to describe her upbringing, we should choose no other term but "happy childhood" to do so. Happy childhood: also the name of her school.

Amira, like Hamada's girls Yara and Lara, and Ahmed and Mohamed, Adel's two sons—all of whom attended Happy Childhood Primary—never showed any interest in knowing anything about her late father. All she cared about was drinking the maximum number of sodas in the shortest time possible. Amira had become addicted to soda, just like Yara, who was a touch fatter than her twin sister. The twins, too, had little interest in their dead father. Plus, that image of Hamada, which was engraved in the memories of the neighborhood's inhabitants, contained little by way of important information. Hamada was always referred to as a hero, but heroism is usually on behalf of one lot of people and against another. Only Hamada's heroism was absolute, without friends or enemies. The devil didn't lie in the details, because there were no details to begin with.

215

The five of them would meet up on their way to and from the school. Merriment and joy were the dominant themes at this stage. They laughed constantly, threw bricks at people, hurled bags of kushari into the faces of others, and swapped winsome, girlish insults that began with mothers and ran on through and beyond reproductive organs and religion. Affection and tenderness drew them together and the War of the Sugarcane and Lizards broke them apart.

Like all children, our five heroes drank sugarcane juice out of plastic bags. Yara was the first to sample the yellow liquid, which she'd glug down at the stall surrounded on all sides by bottles of Pepsi and Coca-Cola. She called herself "the cane-juice connoisseur"—the first cane-juice connoisseur in Egypt, in the world, in Africa and Asia and the Americas. She started buying two bags every morning, drinking one on her way to school and putting the other in her satchel. Lara found out about this and starting sneaking sips from the second bag when her sister wasn't watching the satchel. Then Ahmed, Mohamed, and Amira joined her. And when Yara discovered that her yellow liquid was disappearing, the others made sure to spill a little into the satchel and claim that the shortfall was due to leakage. Yara received this news first with anger, then by cutting the others dead. Lara, however, was the sharpest of the lot. She took Yara aside and informed her that she'd seen Amira drinking the juice and that Ahmed and Mohamed had joined in. Yara had complete faith in her twin sister and the pair of them decided to play a diabolical prank: to fill the bag with piss instead of juice.

The satchel was left lying on its own. They stood nearby and watched to see what would happen.

It was Mohamed, or Humma as he was known, who sprang the trap. He took a sip, spat it out violently, and wept, rinsing his mouth out dozens of times. When he saw Yara and Lara giggling at him he understood. He grabbed the two girls and started thumping them with his little fists. He bent over Lara and grabbed Yara by the legs when she tried to wriggle free. He was joined by his brother Ahmed and his cousin Amira. The three of them took the girls by their arms and hauled them over the sand and sharp gravel that covered the playground. Faggots! the girls screamed. We'll fuck you up! By the Book, we'll fuck you up! But they showed them no mercy. They dragged them out of the school gates, the girls kicking their legs and their smudged and filthy underwear showing, while Amira cackled and taunted each in turn: You and your mucky panties! The three dumped them by the entrance to their building and ran home, and Yara and Lara walked up to their apartment in tears. They rushed toward their grandmother and in a single breath told her what had happened.

Inji, with an old scene—an old, old scene—flaring in her mind's eye, of Abu Amira dragging a woman she could not recall along a street she could not recall, told herself that this filthy family were all the same, and spoke with Minna on the phone. She jumped down Minna's throat: It wouldn't do. If she had something against her, then she should say it to her, not set the kids on each other. And Minna was scared. She came to see Inji the next day, for the first time in many years, and kissed her head. She said that she had given the kids a roasting. That in the end, Yara and Lara were like sisters to her lot. Minna said that she remembered, even if Inji did not. That if Inji forgot, she did not. It was Inji who had taught her English, and everything else besides, she said. The two girls eavesdropped on this meeting from behind the door and it seems they took this fledgling truce as some kind of betrayal of their cause. They did not react immediately. They waited a while. They readied the ground for their personal vengeance.

For years now, Ali and Inji's apartment had teemed with all manner of insects. This went back to those distant days in which Hamada had tried to raise insects and lizards at home. The project had ended in failure, due to the shortsightedness of his parents who couldn't get their heads around what he was trying to do, but the creepy-crawlies remained. In every corner of the apartment grazed lizards and geckos of every shape and size, leaping from kitchen dressers, roaming under couches, popping out of plugholes, and the women of the house had learned to live with them. The lizards had become part of the apartment's culture, and now they became the weapon by which the two girls were able to revenge this affront to their dignity. The day after the meeting, before the end of the school day, they filled Mohamed's satchel with lizards they had brought with them in a plastic bag, then moved on to Ahmed and Amira, and when the three of them got home the lizards scattered out into the apartment. The day after, a lizard emerged from Ahmed's satchel and the twins rushed to put another in Amira's hair. The whole class laughed and Yara and Lara gazed at one another in mutual adoration.

Although everything had been forgotten, or was on the verge of being forgotten, there was one thing that Inji remained conscious of: the need to secure the girls' future—and the lesson that the years had left etched in her mind was that the future was secured by money, and nothing else. Hamada's old studio, Arts and Colors, was converted into a vast kushari outlet into which Inji poured all her savings. The kushari place bore the names of the two girls, Yara and Lara, in Arabic and English. Standing directly opposite the Metro station, the restaurant gradually became one of the most popular hangouts in Karmouz. Karantina's golden age began to make a comeback and suddenly there was hope that history hadn't ended in 2044, that there were chapters yet to come that might be more splendid, or more grim. What matters is that the wheel keeps turning.

Over the entrance to the restaurant a big picture was hung of the two girls hugging the governor, smiling the smile that all the inhabitants of Alexandria knew so well. Beneath it, beneath the legend Yara and Lara, ran the words: Deluxe and Everyday Kushari—A gift from the children of Hamada.

A person's childhood is an indivisible part of his present and future. The characteristics we acquire in childhood are, of necessity, those that accompany us in adolescence and early adulthood. The exact opposite happened here. Yara and Lara grew up, Amira grew up, Ahmed and Mohamed grew up, and the War of the Sugarcane and Lizards was forgotten. Indeed, there was enough room for a mild romance between Mohamed—Humma—and Yara. A plump young lady, with wide eyes, a faint mustache, and a line of hairs joining her eyebrows, she was the girl who captured Humma's eye in high school. He bet himself that he could make her shave off her mustache in a matter of months. He didn't ask her directly; he was careful to slip his pleas between the lines. He said, By the way, your sister looks fucking awful. Like my brother. Why don't you tell her to shave off her mustache? His words stirred Yara's femininity. She said, You're on the money, Humma. My sister's turned into a man. But I'm nothing like her. That day, in the restrooms of the Metro station, they shared a long kiss, which she would break off every other second with a gasping squeal: Oh Humma! Oh yes!

Inji observed the romance blossoming between the boy and girl with a tolerant eye. She did not stand between them. Perhaps she thought that it would end in marriage, that Sousou's legacy would be joined with hers, and that in this way the two families might, after making peace, come to form a new, combined empire, avoiding the errors of their wretched past. Inji asked her granddaughter if the kid didn't want to visit them at home. And Humma came, ate fish and prawns with them, and not only avoided any mention of a shared future for himself and Yara, but when Inji asked him to make sure he took care of the girl, he told her that he thought of Yara as his sister and he knew his duty. Yara took this statement to heart. Afterward, she asked him: I'm your sister now, is that it? So when you kissed me you were kissing me like a sister? He gave her a pat and said, Come on girl, don't be such an idiot. I've been preparing the most amazing surprise for you . . . .

What was this surprise? Humma's gift to Yara was certainly without equal. At three in the morning he called her on the phone and said, Where are you? and she told him she was at home. He told her he was coming up to see her. He wanted to have a word in her ear. He told her he knew her sister was away in Fayoum on a school trip and that the old lady had been asleep for hours, thus blocking off all her avenues of retreat. Hesitantly, she opened the door for him and he marched straight through to her bedroom, where he swept her into a powerful embrace and whispered: What? I tell you I'm coming up and you're going to say no? So you don't want me now, girl? She placed her finger over his lips to stop him going on and whispered back: Rub my chest for me, Humma. He mashed it furiously, then extracted her right breast from her pyjama top and proceeded to lick and bite her nipple, one hand playing with the long, sweaty hair in her armpit and the other pushed into her panties, where it too played deftly. She felt his prick stiffen and pictured it dividing her in two. Oh you dog! she whispered in his ear, You stud!

Humma loved Yara with all his heart. At night, he'd sit and write her lines of verse and compose songs for her. He had no desire to come clean to his brother about this, nor to his uncle's wife. It stayed cocooned in his heart: a coal ready to burst into flame. His only worry at this stage was the girl's indifference to her appearance, since to him appearance was important. He adored her body, full without being fat, and the promise of gold in her hair. And he liked the way she talked as well, the way she said to him, Oh Humma! Of course, however you look at it, Yara, like her sister Lara, was a revolting young woman, but let us not leave Humma's age out of our reckonings. Humma was fifteen years old, and adolescence is a perilous stage.

It was at this perilous stage that Humma decided he would marry Yara. And like Hamada before him, he decided that nothing would prevent him marrying the one he loved. It is true that he lacked Hamada's iron will, and true too that his perspective on Life and Existence and Fate was a little out of kilter, and it is true, furthermore, that he fell head over heels with any girl he laid his eyes on (the polar opposite of Hamada's unbending devotion to Sabah), but love fashions miracles—of that he was certain.

Humma spoke to his uncle's wife about marrying Yara. Minna said nothing. She was thinking about Amira and her terrible luck. Suddenly she looked at him and said, And what's wrong with my girl, boy? For a few moments he racked his brains for a suitable answer to this, then told her that Amira was amazing and everything . . . it was just that she was like a sister to him and he worried about her like a brother. She was silent and said nothing. After a while she told him, You're young, Humma. Go and do something worth your while. Play sports. Find yourself a nice game and play it.

This wasn't the end of Humma and Yara's stormy romance. It ran on in various guises: him coming up to the apartment, the pair of them going out to Montazah together, sampling hot chickpea soup and harisa by the sea, him rubbing up against her in the public lavatories on Glym beach, and other things besides. Humma told Yara a strange tale. Once upon a time, any guy was free to feel up his girl, to sleep with her even, and it all took place close to home. Very close to home. Right over your heads. The apartment above yours, Yara. Yara had no idea what Humma was talking about and she asked her grandmother. Her grandmother had no idea, so she went asking people in the streets and at school, and they had no idea.

During the long nights, Yara would tell Lara about Humma, how tender and gallant he was with her. She would quote him. Humma talked about you for two hours straight. He says you don't take care of your appearance. He says he can't tell you apart from his brother Ahmed. And Lara, who regarded herself as the prettier of the pair, would bury her head in her empty pillow, bite her tongue, and say nothing. It was her misfortune in those days to discover her body: a terrible ache in her back, blood bursting out of her and drenching her clothes, a tiny chest swelling out, sore nipples. But what can we say? It's no little thing to be a woman: it hurts; it has its trials. Lara now saw herself as the most feminine female in Alexandria and began, for the first time in her life, to remove her mustache, the thick hairs that sprouted over her lips. She heaped tons of makeup onto her face. Selected a profusion of colors for the coverings she layered atop her head. Not in deference to Humma's wishes, but following her own private desire.

Lara began by taking advantage of her sister. Once in the street, she asked Humma, Why don't you ever talk to me, Humma? You're my sister's fiancé. Do I make you shy? That day they spoke together at length. He told her about his family home, about his father and mother—one of them murdered, the other in Libya—and he told her about his uncle, Sousou the Martyr—and in return she told him about Hamada the Hero, and about the kushari place, and about old Teta. For two hours they talked, and only when they were almost done did he utter the thing that he'd been choking back so long: her sister Yara wasn't enough of a woman. She was hard. Tough, you know? And she had a mustache. Just make her understand, sister. Drop a hint. Lara smiled.

Lara and Humma's romance began that very day. Lara, the girl of many and joyful colors, resolved to follow this road to its end and crush the twin sister who'd always hinted that she and Humma were engaged in a passion-ate sexual relationship. Fine. If that's how it is then two can play that game. For his part, Humma was much taken by the idea of being a lover to two sisters at the same time. Don Juan the First: King of the Night, Lord of All Ladies. And, just as he'd done with Yara, he told Lara the story of the old place, directly over their apartment, where any young man who wanted to give his girl one could go. Humma slept with her in the kushari joint's kitchen, Lara locking it up from inside after the workers had gone home and giving him a ring on his phone, and him, slipping in to join her. They would spend the night kissing and embracing. Lara was a virgin and she told him she wanted to stay that way. At first, no one noticed their relationship. Later on, a forty-year-old man by the name of Yehya Burkan, who waited tables at the outlet, took it upon himself to tell her that some people had noticed Humma's repeated visits to see her in the restaurant.

Lara took note and notified Humma that they should change venues, but Yehya Burkan, who wanted the best for the two sisters, told Yara. And Yara said nothing. She hid her wound; took refuge in noble silence. Only now did Yara become convinced of the need to remove the hair on her lip and between her eyebrows. She began to turn into a carbon copy of her sister—a vivid covering for her head, a riot of color on her face—and once again the twins were identical. She hung around the restaurant a lot, watching the comers and goers, and when Humma failed to show, when she'd spent a solid three months lying in wait for him, only then did she send a message from her phone: Humma, I have to see you today, urgently.

They met up in Montazah. She told him she'd never dreamed that he would do what he'd done, that she expected trickery and treachery from everybody, but not from those closest to her. What trickery, what treachery? he asked, astonished. She fell silent and he clasped her in his arms and whispered, I'm cheating on you, is that it? You're saying you've been treated badly? You? She tried to squirm out of his embrace but he held her tight, so she brought her hand up to his face and stroked him. So you still love me, Humma? I've never loved anyone else. In his arms, she felt his prick stiffen, and she looked at him and smiled flirtatiously. A flirt: that was Yara. A flirt to end all flirts.

So it was that Humma managed to square the circle: to keep his relationships with Yara and Lara going at the same time. He needed no more than a honeyed word and batted eyelash, and the girls no more than his warm embrace. Over the years he managed to maintain both the quality and the coziness of the embraces he extended to the sisters, finishing up at college and visiting each one in turn at the kushari place (when free of workers) and the apartment (when free of their grandmother) and in the restrooms of the Metro station (when free of those who had to go). Each was aware of the relationship that bound him to the other, but neither spoke of it. They were content with their lot, with their designated portion.

Inji refused to send her granddaughters to college. Inji, child of the venerable Cairene bourgeoisie whose creed was that education was the best investment one could make in life, refused to let the two girls complete their education. She said that education was worthless. Look at Hamada. He'd had the best education, had become a great philosopher, and in the end he'd died in the dirt like a stray dog. Education hadn't done him any good. So the girls made do with their high school certificate and took over the running of the kushari outlet. Love was their substitute for higher education. The love that fashions miracles; the love in which each one found herself, her future, and the meaning of her life so far. By night, watching porn together, the idea of group sex most definitely crossed the mind of each girl. Each girl would look over at the other, would take a breath, would prepare to speak the words, but the words would snag on their lips, trapped, and would never be spoken. The offer might have come had things continued on their natural course, but the wind never blows to catch the sail.

Humma graduated with a degree in law: the bright hope of his family, the sure deliverer of his brother Ahmed (from jail, where he'd been thrown after an—unjust—conviction for dealing). Humma was a handsome young man with honey-colored eyes and fair hair, a cultured man, a good citizen, who knew his rights and his duties to his country. If he managed to get a job with a big-shot lawyer, Minna promised him, she'd give him his own office in the building. And so the lad secured his future. Minna's next step was to visit Inji. She asked her—I beg you, for Hamada's sake—to keep the girls away from her nephew. I mean no offence, Inshi, but the boy needs to look to his future now. And anyway, we decided long ago that Humma's going to marry Amira, and I'm getting ready to open an office for him in our building for when they get engaged. The truth never upset anyone, right? Inji swallowed the insult. Who's this scumbag Humma that my girls are all into? And she was silent. And after she'd been silent, she went even further: Minna spoke the truth, she conceded, and the truth never upset anybody.

But Minna was a nag, in every sense of the word. She had achieved through nagging what violence never could. She kept on at her nephew, kept on at her daughter. She dressed her daughter herself, picked out her clothes and, just as she picked out her clothes, she picked the Faculty of Law for her to study at and asked Humma to give her lessons at home, thus providing him with yet more hours to sit alone with his future bride now he had moved out of his uncle's apartment to set up in a room on the roof of the building. Minna watched as everything took shape before her eyes.

For days on end, Yara and Lara tried to contact Humma, and the response they got every time was that the number they had dialed was unavailable. Humma had switched phones. This was deeply wounding to the sisters' feelings, and they sought their grandmother's advice. And Inji, for the first time in years, abandoned diplomacy. She was slicing tomatoes for a salad. She buried the knife in a tomato and said, By my faith and worship, that boy's going to marry one of you and no one else. The tomato's innards splattered across the girls' clothes. Each looked at the other and an almost identical thought sprang into their heads: He doesn't have to marry just one of us. We can share him. They'd done it before and they were ready to do it again. If the hope of all lovers is to be by their lovers' sides, then their hope in loving Humma was love itself.

The moment was not long in coming. Minna called Inji to invite her to a little party, just a few people, you know, to celebrate Mohamed's—Humma's—engagement to Amira. The grandmother passed on the news to her granddaughters and asked them what they were going to do. Yara leaned against the couch. She mused. Lara lit a cigarette and mused. The silence was broken by Inji.

Inji: That boy's always been a bastard. Always. (She takes a sip of tea.)

Yara: He was always stealing sandwiches and telling tales to teacher.

Lara: Just sandwiches, you fool?

Yara: And cane juice.

Inji: No, I'm not talking about that. That boy's a bastard and he was born that way. It goes back to his father's day.

Lara: What about his father, Teta?

Inji: His father? What about his father? His father was a lovely man. If only he'd turned out like his father! His uncle was the bastard. His uncle's where he gets it from.

(Yara and Lara look at one another.)

Inji: I'm an old woman now. I've grown old. I bet you think I've lost my marbles too. Go on, why don't you just say so? You're filth, the pair of you. But you have to do something.

Yara: Like what, Grandma?

Inji: Like something. Maybe now's not the time for me to talk, but go and ask that woman Minna. Ask her how her husband died. And when she's told you, come back to me, and I'll tell you how your father died.

This conversation was cut off from what came before it and what came after. Like a dream. A cry in the darkness. Like the impatient traveler who drives his horse so hard that it can carry him no farther, and he is left stranded in the wilderness. It did not give the girls much in the way of hard and fast facts, but because matter (as we've said before) is neither created nor destroyed, the impact of this sentence lingered on in the minds of both.

The next day Yara sat with Yehya Burkan, the kushari waiter. You happy about all this, Uncle Yehya? she asked him. And he said, Look here, Miss Yara. You're a good girl, and I've known that boy since he was knee high, and I knew his father and his uncle. They don't come any worse. I wanted to warn you, to be honest, but I saw that the boy had gotten under your skin, so I couldn't say anything. Yara trembled and Yehya patted her on the shoulder. So she flung herself against his breast and began to weep. Weeping's good. It makes things better.

The date for the engagement was set, the twenty-seventh day of March, and to drive home the humiliation Amira called the sisters to invite them. They were united in their response: Of course, sweetie! Your happiness is mine! Yara added, Don't you go thinking I'm upset; I'm so happy for you, I swear it. At the end of her call, Lara choked up, and when Amira asked her what was wrong, she said, Tears of joy, sister, I just can't believe it! That same day, the two sisters sat down together and each looked at the other. They were thinking the same thought: they would go down to the sea together and there they would sit awhile. So they went downstairs and caught the Metro.

So far, so conventional. Absolutely run-of-the-mill: some little shit making love to three girls at the same time. Less conventional was the form the vengeance took.

2

There's this old TV drama series where the husband, Tamer, threatens to throw himself into a volcano. His wife, Shawqiya, continues to eat her food, unmoved, and advises him to wear a parachute. For an instant the husband is silent; then he asks her with a sneer what she thinks she means. Does she want him to roast slowly, for example? A nice slow grilling? Then he interrupts his question with another, more pertinent query about what she thinks a volcano is, anyway. The wife clearly believes a volcano to be some massive pit, some rock-bound ravine with thundering waterfalls, but not a bit of it. The fact is that the volcano is the most terrible thing known to man. It is the third and final stage of nature's wrath. The volcano is fire and storm.

Now, the name by which Yehya Abdallah Sultan was known in Karmouz was Yehya Burkan, which is to say: Yehya Volcano. Given his impressive physical strength, the name seemed fitting, but no one knew just when and how he'd gotten it. Not that this mattered. A colossal man in his forties, no flab, all muscle, with a massive mustache, always dressed in a vest and dark-gray tracksuit trousers, with the sole addition of a combat jacket in winter. No one knew anything about his past. There was some secret in Yehya Volcano's life, so said they all, but no one tried to find it. And for his part, he said nothing. Perfectly silent, was Yehya Volcano.

He did not excel at anything in particular. When he first appeared in Karmouz, it was at a lathe in a workshop at the bottom of Sousou's building in Karabantina. The sight of him toiling amid steel and fire, with his filthy vest, his hairy chest, his sweat, and his silence like the silence of some god, stirred desire in the breasts of the neighborhood's young ladies, the girls from the schools, from the college, from the institute. He didn't pay them any mind, though. He was always busy with his work. And when, one time, the workshop's owner provoked him, and Yehya was driven to lift the lathe aloft and lay the man's head open, it became a seminal component of his legend, for what it said about his moral fibre, but also, as evidence that he was a seriously sexy guy.

Yehya left Sousou's Karabantina and got work at another turnery close by Inji's building, but the turnery's owner soon threw him out when he heard of his gory prior offense at the other workshop. It was around this time that the kushari joint belonging to Hamada's girls opened its doors. He went to work there as a busboy, clearing and laying tables. He accepted this fate. Had no desire to change it. And at night, when he got back to his room beneath the stairs, he'd give thanks to God for everything. If you knew what lay around the corner you'd take what you've got, he would sigh, and sleep.

Yehya Volcano, the time has come to reveal, was the grandson of Miallim Sultan, the miallim who rose to power in Qabbari all those decades ago, said to have been a drug dealer, said to have been a philanthropist, and forgotten by the very Alexandrians who had so described him. Like his grandfather and father before him, Yehya Volcano worked in the drug trade for a while. Spent years behind bars, then got out. He returned to Qabbari and encountered other miallims who made it impossible for him to deal and who squeezed him out of the market. It was said, too, that he was the target of assassination attempts. One dawn he prayed and saw a white light telling him to make an honest living, and he decamped for Karmouz.

These weren't Yehya's only qualifications. Straight after high school he'd volunteered for the army and joined the commandos. It was there that he displayed a special talent. His fellow soldiers tell of the unearthly skill with which he passed all training courses and tests, a skill born of his tremendous strength and bull-like body. And when he was wounded in the shoulder, he was handed his papers and he left the army with the rank of sergeant. He went back to drugs, following in the footsteps of his father and grandfather, but every so often the memories of his time in the army would return like some friendly ghost—when he was in prison, when he was working a lathe in Karabantina, when he was clearing kushari from tables. His current existence, his life of stability and steadiness and calm, did not seem right for Yehya Volcano, no matter that he'd convinced himself of the opposite.

Yehya Volcano came late to drink and gambling, while he was in Karmouz. It made up for his creeping suspicion that he was no longer serious about his life. After finishing work, he'd spend the rest of the night playing cards at the café with his friends and knocking back the booze. He was a skillful player. He won a lot, enough to buy the booze and go on playing. Drink made his soul more delicate. For all his terrifying appearance, the muscles that bulged from every part of his body, Yehya Volcano had the soul of a child. He wept to see a slaughtered hen, so what of a human being unjustly treated? Plus the drink also lent his soul a greater purity. So it was that he observed Humma and Yara's romance from afar, then Humma and Lara's affair, and when Humma decided to do the dirty on the two girls, this hurt him deeply. He comforted Yara. He promised her that he would take revenge. And he was confident it was a promise he'd fulfill.

Everyone who saw Yara and Lara when they were young assumed Yara was older, and when one of them would explain that they were twins, the onlooker would conclude that Yara must have come out first. Yara had wisdom and a forceful character, unlike Lara, who'd been unable to develop any kind of personality independent of her sister. Which of you was born first? Which of you got all the love? This was the playful and frequently heard question that the sisters had to field.

In addition to fashioning their own future and exacting revenge on Humma, Amira, and Minnatallah, the two girls had one sacred mission: to restore their mother's good name in the neighborhood. Everyone had forgotten everything, it seemed, everything except the fact that Yara and Lara's father was Hamada the Hero and their mother was Sabah the Whore. Hamada the Hero needed no defending. The problem was with Sabah. The mission was Yara's and she was well suited for the task, however complex it might appear. It's no easy matter to defend yourself against accusations that your mom's a whore, especially if it's true, and no easier to defend someone whose life you know nothing about. No one spoke about those days, or the things that had gone on back then. Inji wasn't talking, nor was Umm Salah the maid, and those who were, knew nothing. But while this made her mission more complicated, it was also the cornerstone of Yara's defense: Do you know the first thing about her? Do you have any idea who she was or where she came from? We Egyptians just love our opinions, don't we? Everyone's got something to say! The Arab Republic of Unsolicited Advice, that's us! And Lara would add: Yeah! We all just love opinions! For a while this defense worked. At first. Later, there was no choice but to fight. So Yara stood in the center of the kushari restaurant, screaming, By the Prophet, sister, why don't you mind your own business? at female customers, then turning her attention to the men: Anyone breathes a word about my mother I'll fuck him up in front of everyone here. If there's a man among you, show yourself! Another time she got into a fight with another customer, a university student most likely: dainty, glasses, jeans, a short-sleeved T-shirt. Yara was standing around keeping an eye on the restaurant when she noticed this particular girl pointing at her and winking to her friend. Whether Sabah was the subject of the wink—which was probably the case—or not, Yara descended on the scene. Later, all the girl could recall was a woman materializing over her head and declaiming, in a bellow that echoed through the place: You scum, you trash! Yara knocked her off the chair, threw her down, and kneeled over her, lashing out at her and biting her arm: Trash! Filth! Bitch! The girl's boyfriend tried to intervene. He was terrified, from time to time crying out: Madame, that won't do! Madame, for shame! Miss! The girl, in an attempt to save her spectacles, had raised her hands in front of her face, leaving Yara no option but to attack the interlocking fingers, wrench the glasses from her, and set about squashing and mangling them as she screamed hysterically: Ha! Call these glasses? Trash! Scum! Before the girl and her squire could leave the restaurant they were forced to pay for the breakage, a sum to restore Yara's injured dignity, and a sum to compensate the restaurant for the damage sustained to its reputation, plus—of course—the cost of the meal they had ordered.

This is what people saw. Secretly, though, Yara had come to sympathize with the person her mother had been, even though she might not know much about her. For reasons unknown, her mother had become linked in her mind with one specific image: a woman dressed in brightly colored feathers, like a parrot. She never heard the name Sabah without that image leaping to mind: on her head, feathers like a squaw and, when she stripped off her clothes, colored feathers stuck to her belly, shoulders, and breasts. And when Sabah would speak she'd say nothing for herself, but merely repeat the last words she'd heard. To her daughter, Sabah had come to represent the very picture of the female parrot, and this just made her sympathize even more. She would visit her grave each Friday and recite the Fatiha, would decorate the tomb with money from her pocket, and on her behalf would enter into battle against her grandmother, Inji. Yara moved out for two whole weeks, enraged at something Inji had said, and when she came back, she came back with conditions: My mother was the finest woman in the whole wide world, and anyone who says different, they're the one that'll move out. It was Yara that fought these battles, not her sister.

The battle over their father was also fought by Yara. The pictures of Hamada scattered through the apartment displeased her. She was quite certain her father hadn't been so fat; that the pictures had been photoshopped by those who hated him, to destroy his image. Her reasoning had logic: How could someone as fat as that be capable of destroying his enemies? With this line of argument, she was able to persuade her sister to begin a campaign to rewrite history from another point of view. The two sisters dwelt on memories in which they were both with their father, who was tall and broad, his body swollen with muscles.

Fine, so if that was how it was, then how come there are pictures that show him like that? Yara had her answer ready: My dear fellow, you must be aware that he was an artist. The man photographed and painted everyone in the neighborhood and he never let anyone do the same to him. He'd tell me: Yara my girl, no one would ever be able to capture me the way I capture other people. Whoever draws me, I want them to draw me using my style, not his. This was why every attempt to take Hamada's photo unawares failed, leading to the creation of doctored images of the man who changed the history of the whole neighborhood. Lara would be following the conversation and nodding her head to lend emphasis to her sister's words.

Both sisters suffered from Humma's treachery, but Yara took it hardest, and it was she who convinced her sister of the necessity of revenge. The reasons she cited could be described as purely feminist. He's not going to get away with thinking we're idiots just because we're girls. No, sweetheart. He's going to get a taste of what these girls can do to him soon enough. And Lara, the sister who seemed younger, did not interrupt. But when Yara had finished talking, the pair of them lying on their shared bed in the wan glow of the bedside light, Lara would whisper: Know what I'd really like, sister? For every one of that lot to learn their place, and for Papa to come back so they could see how silly they were. We've put up with enough, sister.

What Lara did not say was that the night before, she had seen her father in a dream. He was sitting with his best friend Farouq and Farouq was pointing at Hamada and saying to her: History will show, with evidence to prove it, that you all let this good man slip through your fingers. I mean it, Lara: you lost a great deal. Exactly how much I couldn't say, but I do know that you lost a lot: millions of pounds, about. Perhaps a tiny bit more—or less.

The girls went down to catch the Metro. On the way they met Yehya Volcano. He told them that he was going to Manshiya, so they went through the stiles together. Inside the station, Yara went to the bathroom. There she thought back to her red-hot encounters with Humma, and it seems that she was somewhat affected by this, so much so that her eyes positively shone from a sudden access of tenderness. When she emerged, Yehya Volcano asked her what was wrong and she burst into tears. She said, Forgive me, Uncle Yehya. I'm just so torn up by what's happened. Lara pressed against his shoulder and asked him: Why is this world so cruel, Uncle Yehya? And Uncle Yehya could not bear all this. His feelings overflowed and were it not for the shame and the people watching he would have wept himself. They all got on the train.

Halfway between Karantina and Manshiya the Metro broke down. It shuddered violently and came to a complete halt. For a quarter of an hour it stood there. The atmosphere inside was stifling. It's early spring, remember, in a pitch-black tunnel, and the airconditioning's out of order, as usual. Men flapped at their faces with newspapers, fat women slumped to the floor

231

to await a deliverance that might never come, children were crying. A pregnant woman was screaming, from the pain, from lack of air. Yehya Volcano decided to open the carriage door with his bare hands. Again and again his powerful muscles strained at the door, but the door would not budge. At last it sprang open. A breeze blew in. The children stopped their crying, the pregnant woman her screaming, the men their flapping, and the fat women stood up. Yehya Volcano leaned down and whispered in Yara's ear: Let's walk to the next station. Walking in the tunnel's dangerous, she told him, but he'd had enough of not being able to breathe and all this shit. He said he was going and he went. Yara and Lara followed him, and then the other passengers came too.

Traversing the length of the tunnel toward Manshiya Station was a momentous experience in the lives of the three friends, who used their illuminated cell phones to help them see. The three of them laughed and giggled as they walked a road they had never dreamed they would tread, for all that it lay so close by. The other passengers spread out on either side, over the two lines: the tracks going out and the tracks leading back. They felt fine about the line leading out, with the train silent as the dead behind them and seemingly motionless. It was the line leading back that was frightening. Down the narrow stretches of the tunnel's twisting length a speeding train might come and crush them all. Lara heard a sound far off and screamed, then realized it was the sound of a child crying. She laughed and everyone laughed with her.

Then, suddenly, without warning, the train was approaching. The squeal of its wheels against the rails, the blast of its horn, and in an eyeblink it was over. A short while later the train came to a halt. All those standing on its line had died, crushed beneath its wheels. Yara and Lara and Yehya Volcano saw it all.

The driver got down. Just these three, and two other men. The driver's face was haggard—so it appeared by their cell phones' glow—and his voice was hoarse. He was disoriented and didn't know what to do. Yehya Volcano shouted: Get back in, brother! Keep on going. You were going along minding your own business and there was a bunch of people standing in your way. What were you supposed to do, eh? You've got nothing to blame yourself for, my friend. The driver returned to his train, the train moved off, and Lara shrank up against the tunnel wall and sobbed, her sister at her side, comforting her and sobbing too, while Yehya Volcano sat himself down some inches away. He took a bottle from his jacket pocket and drank from it, and sobbed. He polished off three-quarters of the brandy. Neat. And nothing to nibble on the side. He tried standing up and lost his balance. He slumped back down beside the sisters, and slept. Yara looked at the body sprawled out beside her and tried to rouse him. Uncle Yehya! Uncle Yehya! Please wake up! We'll be killed as well! No use. In the end she grabbed the bottle of brandy and started drinking, gave a sip or two to her sister, and the pair of them curled up around the body of Yehya Volcano.

Maybe Yara and Lara slept, maybe they just dozed, but either way it wasn't for long. Ten minutes later, Yehya Volcano woke up. He hauled the girls up by their arms and continued to pick his way toward the lights of Manshiya. When he reached the station's entrance he was feeling a little more awake. Swaying slightly, with the reek of alcohol on his breath, he leaned into Yara and whispered: The kid Humma's going to die. He'll be killed the way you saw back there, like those people who died just now. His voice carried to Lara. The sisters looked at one another, then at Yehya Volcano. They suppressed the smile of triumph that was trying to leap to their lips.

A nation without memory and history is a nation without a future.

What had happened to the residents of Karmouz? Everyone, it seemed, had surrendered to forgetting. No one remembered anything that had taken place before. Everyone refused to remember, and if they remembered they refused to speak. And so new generations grew up who knew nothing of their past, immersed in their distorted present and refusing to see anything else. For years, for about fifteen years, Yara and Lara had remained totally ignorant about the feud between the two families, between Sousou's family and Ali's. Only now did they decide to break the barrier of silence.

One moonlit night the two girls sat with Umm Salah the maid, smoking hash, on the balcony that had once seen Hamada plummet to the street and die a martyr. Yara and Lara were wide awake, careful not to overdo it. The smoking bowl stayed by Umm Salah's side all the while. Tell us about Sousou, Umm Salah. So Umm Salah told them. My girls—sweethearts—once upon a time there was a mighty man, a veritable giant, and his name was Sousou. He was an infidel. He bowed his head to no god. And your father, girls, was a good man. He couldn't stand injustice. Your father was lovely. My goodness, was he ever. I saw everything. I saw the slaughter. Explosions and gunfire. I saw your father die a martyr, just because he said no to injustice's face. Sousou wasn't having that. Who's this telling me no? Me, the mighty monarch, the richest fellow alive, beneath whose feet the rivers flow? Bring this man who tells me no! And everyone knew your father. They said to Sousou, Ya miallim, this is a strong and righteous man, but Sousou couldn't be moved. They fought, one in the right, one in the wrong, and here, my girls, here in this sacred place, your father died a martyr. I saw him die and I wept. And beneath us, down there in the street, Sousou died. He killed your father, and then he died.

But Umm Salah, why didn't you tell us this before? Because the truth is hard. Because you're girls, and girls these days are powerless. Because you won't do a thing. I was a girl like you and I know. I've had my troubles. I've seen it all. (Here, her voice grows choked.) The truth has wrung me out. I know people. Do they know me? Not a bit of it, they don't know me at all. I'm worn out from my memories, worn out from talking, worn out from hash. I'm going to bed. She stands and leans against the balcony wall. Lara helps her in. Now the two girls are sitting together. They look at one another. Umm Salah might be worn out but they are not done yet. They will carry history forward. Their arms may be weak but their will is of iron. Silent, intent, unshakable, and sunk in thought, they pass the hash bowl back and forth between them.

Humma was busy at the time preparing for his engagement. He bought the rings and turned his attention to Amira's engagement present. He got a loan from Minna, went window-shopping with Amira, and picked out some jewelry. Everything was going swimmingly. He'd gotten work with a big-shot lawyer in Ramleh Station and was just waiting to open his own practice — assuming Minna kept her promise.

The question now was where, amid all this happiness, were Yara and Lara? The question was posed to him by Amira, his intended. She asked him if he had ever loved them. He quashed this line of thought. He smiled. Said:

Love? What are you talking about? Then he told her that the two sisters used to pester him at every opportunity. And after all, I was a kid. Anyone in my place would have done the same. Yara, I swear to you, I hated it. Amira met this mispronunciation of her name with a smile, while he grew flustered. She patted his shoulder and said, Never mind, Humma. We all make mistakes. And he didn't understand exactly what mistake she meant, and he smiled too.

Amira had never borne a grudge toward the sisters. She had always operated with the mindset of the victor, which has no time for petty concerns. She really blossomed in those days. She chose her own trousers and jackets and scarves, and in a single session plucked every rogue hair from her face. She started choosing her words carefully, peppering her conversation with "my fiancé told me," or complaining about the difficulty she had choosing her engagement present: If I'd known it would be this hard I would never have agreed to get married! And Humma at her side, nodding at her claims and lending them legitimacy. Amira insisted to him on more than one occasion that the name Humma didn't suit him. She asked him to go back to who he was. To Mohamed. He had no idea how he would accomplish this. She helped him. She stopped referring to him as Humma. My fiancé Mohamed just loves this color. My fiancé Mohamed gets so jealous about me! I wouldn't want to make Mohamed cross. And so on. And people went along with it. They didn't mind. She was perfectly charming to everyone around her, and she never ever bore a grudge toward the sisters. She was the closest thing to an angel back then.

The resemblance between the two twin sisters was not absolute. Why then had Humma loved them both at the same time? The question arises in the context of another romance. Back in high school, Lara had fallen for a boy in her class. For a long time he would just gape at her and pass her his test answers, until one day he confessed to loving her. She was, like, so embarrassed, and went to complain to Miss. Miss called the boy forward and bawled him out in front of all the other students, Yara and Lara among them. Miss screamed, You're molesting the girl and her sister? Lara turned to Yara, who informed her that the boy had been constantly on at her, too, telling her he loved her. In the evening, the sisters talked of their shared hurt. They discovered that the same things had been said to both of them.

History repeats itself, once as tragedy and again as farce. By the end of that night they had reached farce. They roared with laughter as they discovered more and more repetitions.

Love held them together. Love and the little details. Yara would think of something and Lara would think the same thing at the very same time. Sometimes they would say the same thing simultaneously. And bitterness bound them, too. Following Humma's betrayal they both resumed their indifference to their appearance. The bristles on their lips and brows grew back, they wore whatever came to hand, and they kept company with no one but their grandmother and Umm Salah the maid.

Umm Salah would tell them everything. She told them about history from the point of view of one who'd seen it and hadn't taken part. There was just one little incident that the Umm Salah of old had played a part in, back when her name had still been Ghada, and she told the sisters all about it: Now girls, your great-great-great-grandfather was a man called Bekheit, and I found out all about him. He was what you might call the family's founder. I traveled to the South myself, I asked around, I listened, and I found out. Your great-great-great-grandfather was a Southerner. Like an umda. A good man. So, in the South I met Umm Amira. (The girls break in: Auntie Minna?) No, girls. No. Never. Not a chance. This was another woman, a good woman, too, just like Bekheit. She wanted good for people. Now, she had seen your great-great-great-grandfather. She was a member of your family, one of your cousins or something. Anyway, she told me about Bekheit. That's right. She told me all about him. Bekheit was King of the South, she said. Magnificent and mighty and something else that means magnificent, but he never harmed a hair on anybody's head. He killed tons of people, sure, but that was justice: they were the ones who wanted to murder him, wanted to steal from him, wanted to cheat him. That's your great-great-great-grandfather, girls, and that's his story.

March 27 draws near. Exactly one week to go. Humma is on his way to Maamoura. He bumps into Yehya Volcano. They catch the train together. At Manshiya the carriage fills up with passengers. Humma is sweating. Yehya Volcano hands him a newspaper and says, Fan yourself, brother. The heat's unbearable. And then the train stops, suddenly, midway between Ramleh and Azareeta. For a quarter of an hour the train just sits there, until at last Yehya Volcano manages to force open the steel door, just as he did before. They get out together, along with a number of other passengers. They walk down the tunnel toward Azareeta Station. Humma notices that the train can't move because of a huge log laid across the tracks. A group of men are trying to move it out of the way. He suggests to Yehya Volcano that they join them and Yehya cries: Why bother, friend? Two minutes and we'll be at the station, then we catch a ferry from the street. So they walk on. There's a lot of crowding, men jostling one another. Some of the men are walking along the tracks leading out, some on the tracks leading back, and when the approaching train blows its horn, then suddenly, whoa!, quick as a flash, Yehya Volcano shoves Humma into its path. And just like that, along with a few others, Humma is transformed into a memory of a man: flesh clinging to the rails, blood blotted up by the gravel.

Yehya Volcano returns to the world above. He tells everyone he sees about his best friend, martyred beneath the wheels of the train. He was right beside me. By the life of the Prophet he was with me every step of the way. He died and I'm still here. He weeps. He rains curses on the head of whoever it was that put that log in front of the train and glued it to the rails. He seems to everyone like a man emerging from some state of nervous shock, its aftereffects lingering on. Everyone sympathizes. His sadness makes them sad; they weep for his tears. And when he disappears into his apartment for a whole week and stops going to work, they come to visit. He is weeping. He died and I'm still here. I'm the one who killed him. I'm the one who told him let's get down and walk. They pat him on the back and say to him, And what more could you have done, Yehya? It's fate. Their words bring him no comfort. For a long time he is silent, staring at the wall. He pulls out a bottle.

For two months an air of mourning hangs over Minna's house. Amira silent, unspeaking, and her mother trying to comfort her, without success. Yara and Lara come calling, apologizing for the absence of their grandmother, so old and tired, and Minna responds scornfully, Tired? Hope she gets better. Then, looking daggers: The old lady's happy now, isn't she? Yara looks at the floor, and then says firmly: Shame on you, Auntie. And Lara adds: For shame! In a lifeless tone Amira says, My mother speaks how she pleases. The girls leave and on the way home complain to one another about the ingratitude. We come to see them with the best of intentions and they can't even find a civil word for us. As if someone would ever get a kick out of another person dying!

Minna was a sensitive person, despite her occasional bursts of temper. She still remembered those good people—now gone—who had stood by her, and the people—now gone—whom she had stood by. The latter group had included Miallim Sultan, God rest his soul. Minna remembered going to visit his widow and comforting her, and trying to reconstruct the life story of the woman's departed husband. She recalled the phrase "the severed finger is never abscessed," which she had taken upon herself to hang up in the neighborhood accompanied by Miallim Sultan's portrait and a short text on the man's life. And when some upstanding citizen informed her of Yehya Volcano's connection, the sole surviving grandson of Miallim Sultan, she felt a dagger of flame run her through from behind. She did not discount the possibility of Yehya Volcano's involvement in the death of her daughter's husband-to-be. Not only did she not discount it, she was certain of it, which was why she took a decisive step and went to visit him in his apartment. She asked him for a detailed account of what he'd seen as the train ran over Humma.

Yehya is silent. The grief is killing him. He describes the incident to her with absolute fidelity, without altering a single detail. Save one, of course: the part where he pushed Humma onto the rails. Minna picks up the brandy and takes a swig, then says: People saw you, Yehya. Saw you push the boy. He doesn't answer. He is sad, or stunned. And she shows him no mercy. And there are people who saw you the night before cutting down the tree outside the kushari place. He denies it. She keeps on with her questions. Then who was it that cut the tree down, Yehya? He starts to babble. His nerves go again and he starts to weep hot tears: He's dead, and I'm still here. I feel like I'm the one who killed him, hagga. To which the hagga sternly replies: No, you don't feel it, Yehya. You really killed him. Look, Yehya . . . I haven't come here to sit and chat. I just want you to think about one thing. Your grandfather. Your grandfather, who died in the street and no one would go near the body. People were afraid to. I'm the one who made a hero of him. I'm the one who reminded people who he was, who told them that there was once a man here by the name of Miallim Sultan, a man they should show respect to, a man they should treat properly and remember, because he was a proper man. Because he knew God and knew that the most precious things in life are truth and justice.

Very faintly, Yehya Volcano says, You didn't make a hero of anyone. He was a hero anyway. Only now does Minna scream. She throws the bottle at his head. Don't answer back when I'm talking to you, faggot. The man you call a hero was trash. I met your grandmother and we talked when you were just a speck of shit. Years and years before you were even born. Yehya Volcano does not duck out of the bottle's path. He wipes his forehead and his hand comes away covered with blood. And she goes on. When a couple of scheming little sluts come up to you and say, Kill so-and-so for us, you should be asking, Who's so-and-so, you skank? You should know who his people are and where he comes from.

Look, Yehya . . . I'm not going to bring the police into it. I won't be speaking to anyone from the government. I know some pretty serious people, mind you, but I won't be speaking to a soul. Not because I'm a nice person. No. Ask around. You'll discover that I'm a bitch. They'll all tell you. She's a piece of filth and she always gets her due, no matter from who. That's how I am. God made me that way. She is silent for a moment, then, calmly: Yehya, just know that you're in my debt and you've got no grounds for complaint.

Minna leaves. She slams the wooden door behind her and it comes off the hinges. We are still in the early days of spring. The cold weather has not yet gone for good. Asleep, Yehya is tormented by nightmares, by the volleys of chill air admitted by the broken door.

Perhaps to avoid the cold, Yehya Volcano decided not to sleep at home. He asked Yara if he might stay over in the kitchen of the kushari joint once its metal door had been bolted shut, and she granted him permission. He slept but found no peace. For two nights straight he tried to sleep, but the cold, the nightmares, and Minna's strident voice assailed him. No one knows just when the idea first came to him, nor why, nor how. Perhaps it was prompted by his restless nights, or by his guilty conscience toward the woman who'd revived the memory of his late grandfather. What matters is that at two a.m.

one night Yehya Volcano gathered up his blankets and bottles of brandy, and made for the entrance of the Metro station. He descended the stairs, vaulted the metal barrier, and walked, weighed down by the three blankets that swaddled every inch of his body but his eyes. He climbed down into the tunnel. Kept his lighter lit all the way to beat back the waves of darkness that surrounded him, and midway between Karantina and Manshiya he sat down. He pulled out the brandy, took three straight swallows, and closed his eyes. Yehya Volcano slept deeper than on any previous night of his miserable life. He woke at five-thirty in the morning, walked back the way he had come, and as the first train began to move he was already back home. There he slept some more, having discovered the cure to his chronic insomnia.

So it was that Yehya Volcano took to sleeping in the tunnel. Became addicted to it—alongside the booze and gambling. In fact, he brought along his friends from the café to play cards with him down there, beneath the ground, where no one could bother him, where he owed no one anything. They would play as they pleased, sleep an hour or two, and then, before the first train set off, they would depart, each to his home. And so it went on, regular as clockwork, until the bloody assassination attempt.

A group of men emerged from a hiding place that had escaped Yehya Volcano's attention and opened fire on the players. Sudden and fierce as wildfire. But Yeyha Volcano was not to be taken in by a childish ploy like this. From beneath his blanket he pulled out a machine gun and met fire with fire, rattling off an order to the men around him to make for the fissures in the tunnel wall where they would be safe from the flying bullets. All except one, who whipped a pistol from his jacket pocket and started shooting back as well. At last the gunfire died down. Yehya Volcano cautiously approached the spot, his gun in his right hand, to find the bodies of two young men. He searched every inch of the tunnel, all the way to Karabantina Station at the end of the line, and finding no one else he handed his weapon to one of his men and told him to stand guard over the bodies. Like you're on guard duty. Don't move a muscle till I give you the word, and if anyone shows up, tell him to stop where he is, then shoot him. I want you to wing him, Huda, not kill him. Don't kill anyone. I'm going up to get the guns, and I'm telling you now, if anyone dies down here I'll kill you myself. So Yehya Volcano departed and Huda remained behind, alone, guarding the two bodies. And when Yehya returned with the guns everything was how he had left it. Two hours later they all went their separate ways. The bodies were interred beneath the gravel and Huda spent the day sitting on the platform in Karabantina Station watching to see if anyone went down into the tunnel, while over in Karantina Station sat someone else, each carrying a sword and an automatic beneath their clothes. And at twelve minutes past midnight both jumped down into the tunnel. Yehya Volcano showed up with a mob of his men. No drinking today. Just cards. And everyone keeps his eyes in the back of his head.

Waiting is hard. Yehya Volcano was confident that Minna's men would return in the days ahead, at the very least to find out what had become of their men, at most to retrieve the bodies, and so he stayed on high alert. He didn't relax. He spent the day with Yara and Lara at the restaurant, and went round to Inji in the evening, keeping the three women apprised of current developments. His voice trembled and he became excited, waving his hands all over the place. Yara gazed at him in admiration, at his body, solid as a wall, at his filthy vest and his short, unkempt black beard, at the hair on his arms and neck, the hair on his chest, at the chest itself, which rose and fell as he became more exercised. Yara was smitten. And that was nothing to be ashamed of. Nothing wrong with that at all. Yehya Volcano deserved to have women be smitten with him. And he began to dwell on his glory years: the commandos, the combat operations, the Bedouin, bullets flying everywhere, the struggle against the government. The friendly ghost was back, teeth bared this time. Happy days, Yehya, he was constantly murmuring to himself.

It was five days before three men came down to look for the two missing bodies, only to be met by the artillery of Yehya Volcano and his comrades. It was just before dawn.

The first train is getting ready to depart. The battle is raging. The first train's on the move now. One of Yehya's men opens fire on the train driver. The windshield disintegrates and the driver falls to the floor of his cab, dead. The battle ends with Minna's three men being bound hand and foot and laid on the tunnel's floor at gunpoint, with Yehya Volcano's wild dash to the station's control booth where he orders the controller to set the trains running to Manshiya. Send all trains to Manshiya and from there you'll move them off. We've taken over the Karantina tunnel, from Gheit al-Enab through to Manshiya. Any train that stays behind will be ours. We'll break it up and sell it for scrap. The trains set off. Neither the drivers nor the station controllers can do anything in the face of the guns that sprout from every nook and cranny along the tunnel to menace them. Once all the Metro employees have left, Yehya and two his men ascend to bar the station's steel gate.

So the trains set off for Manshiya. One train stayed behind. The train whose driver had been killed stood in the station. The spoils of war, thought Yehya Volcano, and decided to open its doors to his men so that they could keep warm, eat, and shelter from the cold, damp winter. For those brief moments, Yehya conducted himself with the high drama of a military commander, well aware that history was recording his name, aware that any escalation on his part would result in the deaths of him and his men, but with one eye on glory, on the chance that the final moments in the lives of him and his men might be inscribed in letters of gold.

Did Yehya Volcano have a death wish? Absolutely not. He was a sensitive individual who wanted the best for other people, whose heart was stirred by any affecting scene or snatch of music. And yet, for all that, he wanted a glorious life. Quite what shape it would take he didn't know, but he did know that when the day came he would know it. That night, following their takeover of the Karantina and Karabantina stations, he dined with Inji, the two girls, and Umm Salah the maid, wordlessly balling up wads of rice and popping them in his mouth. Silent, sunk in thought, dipping bread in the bowl of mulukhiya, and staring into the distance. Suddenly, he turned to Inji. Know what, hagga? Before all this I was living as though I wasn't alive at all. Like a farmyard animal: eating, drinking, and sleeping. Just like an animal. But today I can say that I've done something. I swear on this gift from God (he holds the mulukhiya-moistened crust aloft) that I won't sleep a wink, won't rest easy, till I've repaid all you've done for me, dear lady. Inji gave a contented smile and ladled more mulukhiya onto his plate. She made him promise to eat a whole half chicken.

Yehya Volcano was looking for a meaning to his life, and everything in those days was telling him he had found it.

3

Over the course of history, in the cause of brevity, Egyptians have worked hard to devise a number of alternative vocal renderings for such unwieldy, yet popular, lines as, "And upon you be peace and the mercy of God and His blessings." The heroic Egyptian people have set such excessive verbiage at defiance, with innovations like "Ponyoubepeaceamlessins," or "Ponyaeessings," or even "Peessings." Nor is the phrase "Peace be upon you"—to which the line above is the proper response—an exception. "Peace be upon you" is frequently found as "Peassonyou" or "Psonyou," all the way through to "Pyoo." Only Amira stood apart. Amira alone would say slowly and firmly and deliberately, "Peace be upon you," "Upon you be peace and the mercy of God and His blessings," every last syllable, every last letter, every last dash and dot in place. Her name was Amira—princess—and it fit her like a glove.

Like Yehya Volcano, Amira, too, was searching for a meaning to her life, but unlike Yehya, she had not found it. As a child she'd had a minor squabble with Yara and Lara at school. She was sitting next to the girls, who were whispering to one another. Maybe they said, "Samira," maybe something about "Khamira," but Amira was stricken by a suspicion that they were talking about her. She turned round and the girls brought their conversation to an abrupt end, grinning. Amira was filled with rage. I heard you, she said. I heard you talking about me. Actually, Yara and Lara had not been talking about her, but Amira was blinded by rage. With a violent jerk of her arm she flung Yara's notebook to the floor and ran home. Where she started to cry.

There are sentences that stay with us. This happens at certain periods in our lives. The sentence, with its unique tone, bounces around our mind incessantly. We picture ourselves saying it and we invent, oh yes, we invent, we are at it all the time, inventing the perfect setting that will allow us to utter the line intact, with its tone violent or mocking or smug or flirtatious, depending. The sentence "I heard you talking about me" wouldn't leave Amira be. She had no idea just when she had first strung it together in her mind, nor why this sentence, above all others, continued to echo in her mind with such clarity. A sentence like this sheds light on the personality of Amira—the superstar, as she saw herself. Everyone was talking about her and she, like any star, wasn't overly concerned whether they spoke good or ill. What mattered was that people were talking. Ever since she was little Amira had viewed her future with considerable trepidation. Another line she was always repeating: "I want to be something." And what something did Amira want to be? No one knew, not even her, but beyond doubt she saw herself being something big, something important—given the chance. She graduated from the Faculty of Law with mediocre grades, and so she ruled out the possibility that she would become something in the legal world; her fiancé died in a tragic accident and she ruled out the possibility that the something important would be being a wife. And she sat around at home. She propped her cheek against her hand and it seemed to her that life was never going to grant her the chance to be something. And this is why, taking the confidence reflected in the way Amira said, "And upon you be peace and the mercy of God and His blessings," and the lack of confidence reflected in a line like, "I want to be something" or else, "I heard you talking about me," we have no difficulty in describing Amira as a woman who subsisted on contradictions. And this, we shall see, is no exaggeration.

Once, and she'd told no one of this, Amira had tried her hand at acting. She fell in with a group of extras who hung out at a café in Bahari, but she got bored. She was engaged at the time, and all her efforts went into show-ing her fiancé that she was the model bride-to-be: polite and bright and chic and cultured. And when her fiancé died she abandoned her footlight dreams. She went back home, tears on her cheeks, and patiently endured her mother's consoling words. But the dreams did not abandon her. She drifted through daydreams. Saw herself walking through Karmouz and everyone bowing down before her. Everyone, including—or rather, first and foremost—Yara and Lara and Inji. It could be that these daydreams were Amira's main incentive to go on taking care of her appearance: the fortnightly trips to the hairdresser, the manicures and pedicures, the latest creams for removing unwanted hair. This alone gave her comfort.

Her mother Minna was uneasy about all this. She tried striking up conversations about everything and nothing, but Amira stayed stony-faced. What's on your mind, Amira? Nothing, Mama. Won't you eat something, Amira? I'm not hungry, Mama. And so on, every time. Two weeks went by after Humma's death with Amira sitting at the window, watching the passersby. One evening she was sitting up late, watching the street outside, a group of drunk young men standing beneath her window. One of them whispered something to his friend, who shouted out, Don't be upset, now, miss! And Amira was sure they were talking about her. She shut the window and retreated into the depths of the apartment. She opened the door to the living room, the door that was always closed, and there she sat, where no one could see her or sense her presence. Hers was the kind of depression that kills.

Amira sat in the living room for days on end. She ate and drank and slept there. Her mother tried to get her to come out every way she could, but all her efforts ended in abject failure. Something had to be done, felt Minna, not on Amira's behalf, but with her help. She felt that someone would have to be killed in the days ahead, and that someone's name might be Inshi, might be Yara or Lara, or Yehya Volcano. The point was that it would be impossible without Amira's help, not because Minna lacked experience in such matters. No, indeed. Minna was a woman worth a hundred men. She'd been raised by Sousou and she knew how wars are fought. It was the psychological angle, you see? I won't be able to kill anyone without my girl being in the picture. She's the one who'll see it through. Plus, Amira's depression was making her depressed, until the day the girl emerged from the living room and dined with her mother, where she uttered her first proper sentence in weeks. Mama? What did my grandfather do, exactly? Your grandfather, Amira? Grandfather Harbi, Mama. She spoke determinedly and looked her mother straight in the eye.

All right, then. Minna put two and two together: the living room, where Amira had been holed up for weeks, was the room that long ago, oh so long ago, back when the world was young (if we might so describe the very distant past), had belonged to Harbi; the very room that Harbi's lover had given them—given Sousou and Minna—at the start of their married life. The room had been through many ups and downs: once a barbarous expanse, savage and forbidding, a sword or knife or bag of weed wherever you looked, it had become a cozy living room. What had Amira found in the room? The answer, of course, isn't important. Minna's eyes shone and she began to talk.

For an hour and a half Minna talked about her father, about Harbi the Hero, the man who'd once saved Alexandria from the blackest fate; about—call a spade a spade—the people who were his enemies, Ali and Inshi and Hamada; and about the worthless fools who hijacked his revolution, Sayyid and Sika and Sultan. That Sultan was the grandfather of Yehya Volcano, the man who murdered Humma, your fiancé. And she spoke of the prophecy Harbi made before he died. As he was closing his eyes, readying himself to meet his Maker, Harbi said, Take care of my daughter, Minna. It's Minna and her girl who'll return what's mine to me. Minna's voice shook as she told her tale. Her eyes shone, she choked up, and she laid her hand on her daughter's shoulder. And Amira was silent all the while, her gaze fixed on her mother like an iron band and her heart rejoicing. The mother was reminiscing about her roots and the daughter was discovering them. I was just a little girl— little, sure, but I understood everything. I saw my father die before my eyes, Amira, and when you were born I knew that the good Lord had blessed me. Amira wept. For the first time in the conversation, she wept. And she made a pledge. She pledged to take revenge for her grandfather. Revenge was the word. Revenge on those who had besmirched his name and killed her fiancé, on those who hated her and wished her and her mother ill. The list of Amira's grievances was long indeed.

Concerning Amira: this girl with the black hair and pale eyes was not her mother's darling, as it might appear from the scene above. The truth was that in more than one place and on more than one occasion, Minnatallah had stated that Amira was the reason for her sorry lot in life.

Many things had paved the painful route to this confession. For example, Amira had insisted, despite her mother's repeated warnings, on going about the apartment barefoot, without slippers on, and on drinking directly from the tap, without using a glass, just as she insisted on leaving the light on when she went to sleep, although she knew that her mother had to pay for it. Her old mother, sixty-eight years old, with aches in her knees and aches in her back, spent her days wandering the apartment and howling lamentations along the lines of, Do you want to kill me? Am I some servant girl your father bought for you? I'm leaving the apartment to you and I'm off. Happy now? Of course, it didn't stop there. During one of these battles Amira screamed, God! I just don't want to live anymore! I've had enough of you! And her mother screeched back, Well, kill yourself then, sister. Why don't you kill yourself and give me a rest? Amira thundered over to the kitchen dresser screaming that she'd pour benzene over herself so her mother could have her rest. She opened the dresser and couldn't find the benzene. Her mother, now out of her mind with rage, left no stone unturned in helping her daughter. She pulled the benzene out from under the sink and handed it over with a challenge in her eyes. Amira hesitated for a moment, but before she could take it her mother had slopped the benzene all over her. She sparked a lighter and held it up to her daughter's sopping clothes. Amira gazed at her mother in terror, ran for her room, and bolted herself inside. That night, when the two had calmed down, Minna kissed Amira on the top of her head. Don't you go getting upset with me, Mirmir. I only want what's best for you. The girl clung to her mother and kissed her cheek.

Another frequent source of tension: Amira's hair-removal cream, which would stick to the bottom of the washbowl. Minna decided she would throw herself off the balcony. She pushed back the balcony's wire screen and lifted her leg. Amira, next to her, was trying to heave her into the street by her buttocks. Suddenly, Minna thrust her daughter aside. She sat with her back against the balcony wall and began to sob softly. And Amira started stroking her and smiling. All of sudden she said, You see, Mama, if you want to jump to your death it's not going to work. Her mother looked at her. We're on the ground floor, Mama. Minna was silent for a while, then her sobs turned to impassioned weeping. She slapped her face and screamed, Lord! Take me, Lord! I'm weary, Lord!

All this was an obstacle to Amira, who was eager for her life to have some great meaning, a meaning that was forever being put off. Only—and we can make this claim with some confidence—only when this meaning suddenly appeared out of the blue, when Amira realized that her existence from here on out was to be bound up with revenge on those who had once harmed her and her mother; only then would the girl and her mother stop their bickering. The two were now united. They forgot their ancient quarrels and started planning for what would happen in the days ahead.

Like all the girls, Amira had been much taken by Yehya Volcano, and it's certain that she had been visited by sexual fantasies involving him; fantasies that had visited her at a former stage of her life, in adolescence, when with fingernail and fingertip she'd indulged her secret habit as she dwelt on images of him working at the lathe.

What was it, then, that had turned her infatuation into disgust? Amira was revolted by everything about him, by his sweat, his stink, his coarse voice—keeping in mind that this volte-face took place a long time before the death of her fiancé, meaning that her feelings were unconnected with her desire for revenge. Most likely, Amira had grown up. She had started to become attached to Humma, the handsome, educated, cultured young man, and was sketching out for herself an image quite beyond the reach of Yehya Volcano, of a university girl who'd get the marriage she deserved and hold her head high before the denizens of her stinking neighborhood. And after her fiancé was murdered and she had shut herself up in the living room surrounded by the memories of her father and his heroic past, the nightmares had started to visit her every time she closed her eyes, day and night and afternoon. She's walking down the street and hears the sound of footsteps following her. She turns to find a man with a big beard, whom she recognizes as none other than Volcano. She tries to flee but he blocks her way and grins his savage grin, uncovering a scattered profusion of blackened teeth. Or she's in the women's carriage on the Metro, buried in a hell of sweating female flesh, and suddenly she realizes that all the women around her are clones of Yehya Volcano. The carriage rocks, like it's about to tip on its side, and she wakes.

When at last she emerged from the living room and her mother confronted her with her grandfather's illustrious history, she had taken the decision to kill Yehya Volcano, and knew that this would only be the first step. The Karantina of Ali and Inji, the Karantina of Yara and Lara and Hamada, antique, ancient Karantina, charged with symbolism, would be blown to smithereens and the whole foul lineage plucked out by the root.

The site of the battle was not of her choosing, nor her mother's. The site of the battle was chosen for them: the Metro tunnel. Around this time, her mother began calling up her late husband's men, Sousou's old lions and his cubs, or rather, those who had been cubs back in 2044, and who were now seasoned predators, each and every one, and, what is more, all harboring the darkest memories of Hamada and Ali and Inji. In 2044 the neighborhood had been razed to the ground and anyone who owned a kiosk or workshop or phone store was turned out onto the streets with his children—and all because of Ali. Every man and woman born and raised in Karabantina knew their history. True, no one had brought this history up for years, which gave the impression that everything had been forgotten, but far from it. The spark caught, bitter memories leapt to the surface, and men thirsting for blood whetted their unsheathed blades.

Minna's home was filled with men of every kind, strewn over the chairs in the living room and hallway, and in the hand of every one a cigarette and cup of tea prepared by Amira, who scurried back and forth between them. Yehya Volcano was the target, everyone agreed, and killing Yehya Volcano would not take much. Three men to go into the tunnel while he was drunk and bring the whole thing down on his fucking head. Less clear was what would happen next: taking on the government; taking on Inji and those two granddaughters of hers who would never let it lie. All we need from you, ma'am, is money. Don't bother your head about the guns. And Minnatallah met all suggestions with a confident smile. God bless you, men. That's perfect. Amira! More tea for the men! And Amira was learning to live all over again.

A man is not aware of all he wishes for. The wind never blows to catch the sail. The men who set out to assassinate Yehya Volcano in the tunnel did not return. Volcano and his men defeated them.

But Minnatallah was not to be frustrated so easily. It was around this time that she got to know a fish seller, a lady she prayed with at the mosque. The fish seller, who went by the name Sheikha Salha, was a cheerful woman. Never before had Minna felt the peace of mind that she felt with her. Once, after Sheikha Salha had led her in the afternoon prayer, the two talked together. Sheikha Salha told Minna that she knew all about her and urged her to observe the full five prayers. Minna was mystified. She had never in her life done anything to anger God, and, moreover, she performed her prayers punctiliously. Sheikha Salha told her that she needed to draw nearer to God. The woman's smile, her cheerfulness, her face aglow with the light of God, all this prevented Minna taking against her.

Again she spoke with her, and again and again, and Minna took to visiting the sheikha at home. She wanted to hear more from her. And she started to involve her in the details of her life. Little things at first, then she began to talk about it all, about the murder of the men who'd gone to assassinate Yehya Volcano, and about the families of her men, who'd gone to retrieve the bodies of the men who'd gone to assassinate Yehya Volcano. And Sheikha Salha knew about it all, as did everyone in the neighborhood. Her friendly advice was to the point—one thing, and one thing only: Don't force it, Umm Amira. Nothing works by force. Keep God in your mind and it'll come. Minna asked her what she meant and Sheikha Salha opened the window. Look at those people. Look at all those people walking the street. They are all God's creatures, and so are you. God, may He be praised and exalted, told us that He shall create on Earth an heir. Well, we're all heirs here. I want you to think about that. When you're looking someone in the eye, I want you to remember that that's one of God's creatures, just like you.

So Minna found the spiritual regimen that she was to observe in the days ahead. She took to watching people, examining God's image in each and every one, and thinking of God whenever she saw a fellow human being. Her soul became serene. She prayed more. She invited her daughter, Amira, to come and listen to the sermons Sheikha Salha delivered between the sunset and evening prayers every Monday and Thursday. Amira was much taken with the sheikha too. She made sure she knew her phone number and took to calling her at all times of the day to inquire about all sorts of trivial things that might cross her mind. The men who came to Minnatallah's house back then were entranced by the light that shone from her eyes. After their comrades were killed they plucked up the courage to ask, What'll we do now, ma'am? And she replied, Leave it to God. He alone would provide. She set the date for the assault on the tunnel—since occupied and annexed by Yehya Volcano—for two weeks from now. How and when and where? Neither Minna nor Amira gave much thought to the details. Both firmly believed that if they devoted their cause to God, He would come to their aid. And Sheikha Salha backed them up. She rallied the girl and her mother, told them: Leave it in God's hands now. And they left it in God's hands. They gave no thought to the morrow. Tomorrow belongs to the Lord.

And the miracle was not slow in coming. When Minna and Amira finished the evening prayer in the mosque, Sheikh Salha greeted them. She smiled and told them that patience brings its reward and that she had seen a vision of them both as she was praying. And as they reached the entrance to the mosque, about to return home, one of the men approached them and said that the plan had worked. The men had assaulted the tunnel and opened fire. They had killed three of Yehya's men and brought their bodies back with them, and they had retrieved the bodies of their two men as well. More men, heavily armed, had gone down into Karabantina Station and set up camp there. Heavily armed, ma'am. Anyone goes near them now, they'll chop him up and throw him to the cats. Minna smiled; was filled with a profound inner joy. But she did not allow the euphoria of victory to blind her. With her daughter she retraced her steps into the mosque and together they gave a prayer of thanks and ordered that a sheep be slaughtered for the poor.

For the first time in memory a party was held in Sousou's Karabantina: songs and weed and hash and beer and meat till sunup; dancing girls and pipes-a-playing. And that was not all: there was a lottery for the residents of the neighborhood. The man whose ticket came up had Umm Amira's pledge to marry him off, if he was single, or to marry off his children, if he was married. Minna attempted to give Sheikha Salha a gift, anything. Anything you ask for is yours, ya sheikha. But Sheikha Salha refused politely: My gift is that you and your girl are happy, Umm Amira. Minna bent over her hand, and kissed it.

Amira's soul was pellucid, serene and sparkling. She was convinced that she had put her foot on the path that would turn her into something, something important. Sure, people didn't bow down to her when she passed by as she'd once dreamed, but in their eyes she made out a love for her and for her mother.

She sits by the window. The drunk kids catcall every girl that passes but at her, at her alone, they stop. They lower their eyes, ashamed of their drunkenness and the stink of booze that swirls about them.

Amira has the air of a queen anointed: class, bearing, respect, but also her grandfather's distinguished history. She starts talking to people about Harbi, who killed himself for their sake, that they might live a better kind of life. And the people had not forgotten Harbi. Not for one second. They brought him up all the time and spoke nothing but good about his daughter Minnatallah and his daughter's daughter, Amira. Amira took it upon herself to hang pictures of Harbi up in the neighborhood: pictures of him sitting at the café smoking shisha, waving a switchblade at his daughter perched up on his shoulder and grimacing comically, driving a herd of goats that he'd managed to liberate from quarantine, alone in his deck chair on the Corniche with the speeding cars miraculously avoiding him, plus that picture of him fishing in the sea, a net in his right hand and a bottle of brandy in his left. Many new faces had come into the neighborhood since 2044. The young men housed in low-rent residential blocks by the Ministry of Housing had had children of their own and their children were now young men themselves, but the stories were passed down from generation to generation, and after long years that had left no one who could remember what Harbi looked like, these photographed portraits were the best possible reminder of the glorious past that these new residents and their children could hope for.

The tale was born anew. It surged and swelled and no one could stop it, the tale that bestowed legitimacy on those subterranean creatures currently winning victory after victory beneath the ground. At night, the men camping out in the tunnel would mount sorties against Yehya Volcano's men, stealing weapons and returning to their posts. Word of this reached Minna and Amira, as did other, less happy, news: for instance, Minna discovered that some of the men were selling off spare guns, and this she strongly objected to. Any spare guns should be put in storage. Who knows what the days ahead might have in store. She tried confronting them with this, and failed. Later, she accepted it and made excuses for her men: You know, a guy finds himself five thousand short, he'll do what he has to do. Better than stealing from me. Unable to control this black-market trade she turned a blind eye, like any canny ruler.

But when all was said and done, Minna was human. She complained of many aches and pains, in her back and in her legs. In recent years she'd been unable to go to the bathroom without her laxative tablets. About to embark on her seventieth year, she was weary, and the weariness showed. Amira assumed her duties, meeting the men and drawing up plans for their assaults, assaults that were all still preliminary and would remain so as long as Yehya Volcano and Inshi and Yara and Lara kept out of the firing line.

Man's share of happiness endureth not: One day, Amira went to pay Sheikha Salha a visit while her mother stayed at home to take a bath. When Amira returned she was surprised to find the bathroom door wide open and her mother lying naked on the floor, muttering unintelligibly. Minnatallah had slipped in the bathroom and there had been no one to come to her aid. Amira called Sheikha Salha right away and Sheikha Salha was there in fifteen minutes. She recited the Quran over the old lady's head and called the doctor and the doctor coldly gave his diagnosis: paralysis of the brain.

Amira was running on three brains at once: one for her ailing mother, one for the men in the tunnel, and one for Sheikha Salha. The sheikha came round every day. She'd recite the Quran, talk to Amira, and direct meaningless phrases at the mother laid out on the bed, who would respond with her unintelligible mumblings. The sheikha said to Amira one time, When your mother's up and about . . . and didn't complete her sentence. Amira said, My mother's not getting up, Sheikha. Forget it. And she turned her face away. The sheikha trembled at the implied lack of faith in the Lord's mercy. She told Amira it wasn't right to speak that way. But Amira did not answer. And time proved that she was in the right.

The sheikha recites the Quran over the old lady's head. *Speak, O ye who believe! Despair not of* . . . and Minnatallah mumbles in response, this time intelligibly: . . . *the mercy of God*. And the sheikha smiles. She senses the beginnings of an improvement in the woman's condition and departs full of hope. Two hours later Amira calls and says: She's gone. The sheikha clearly recalls Minna's last words in which she expressed her feelings as her end drew nigh. She prays mercy for the soul of the departed. The aza lasts three days.

These weren't the best of times for Amira, naturally; not just because of her mother's death, but also because of Yehya Volcano's men, who were taking liberties with her underground, and aboveground too. One of her men was mugged as he walked along the street in the heart of Sousou's Karabantina. Unknown assailants took his ID card and the five hundred pounds that he had on him, and there were other little incidents of that nature. The men themselves resented being ordered around by a woman like Amira, a little girl who knew nothing of the world and acted as though she'd been born yesterday. Amira was no longer in control. She tried, it's true, but the world was stronger. The men would sit around her hallway, walking in with their shoes where once they had respectfully slipped them off at the front door, and Amira, as obsessed with cleanliness as her mother, locked it in her heart and did not speak. The men would stub their cigarettes out on the carpet, swap filthy jokes, curse each others' mothers, the lot, and Amira could not keep them in check.

It was around then that Amira's nerves went. She decided to withdraw and go to her room. Once inside, she bolted the door behind her and tried to go to sleep, but couldn't. She started to eavesdrop on the men outside. Suddenly she flung the door open. Her eyes were red, her hair wild and uncovered. What were you just saying about me? she screamed at them. The men were asleep, laid low by the brandy whose bottles lay everywhere about them. One of them looked up at her with half-closed eyes. He moved his arm and tried to say something, but gave up. His arm slumped back by his side and he went to sleep again. Hysterically, she screamed: I heard you talking about me! No one answered. She grabbed a big vase and threw it on

254

the floor; the men stirred. Go on, get out now! Get out, you animals! Not one of them moved. Completely out of it, the lot of them. She picked up a shard of broken vase and pressed it to the neck of the nearest man. She nicked his neck: I'll kill you! Only then did the man take notice. He got to his feet, gave her two slaps to the face, followed by a series of blows to her shoulders and belly. Amira shook. She dashed into her bedroom. The man tried to follow her in. She bolted the door. The man hammered away for a while, then slumped, then slept. She took refuge in the bedsheet. For two hours she trembled. She fell off the bed and beneath it found a full bottle of whiskey. So the men had been drinking in her room as well. She continued to tremble as she opened the bottle and took a sniff, then as she took the first sip of her life, then a second, then a third. Three-quarters of the bottle finished. She drank it neat. Then everything swirled together before her eyes. She forgot it all, and smiled. And slept like the dead.

It's July. The weather's hot and the humidity unbearable.

Amira made an attempt to go down into the tunnel. At the entrance one of the men blocked her way. Where are you going, miss? To see the men, she replied. Forbidden, the man shot back tonelessly. She raised her voice. Forbidden? It's forbidden, miss, he repeated forcefully, I'm telling you. She raised her voice louder and louder. At this juncture another man emerged from the tunnel and shouted at the first, Forbidden, you animal? That's Miss Amira, fool. To Amira he said courteously, Please, miss, you're most welcome to come inside. Just an ID check, if you'd be so kind. Amira gave him her ID card. Hang this round your neck, he said, so no one bothers you. He handed her a badge on which was written Abdo the Prince. She hung it round her neck and down she went.

The atmosphere underground was stifling, especially then, with July's humidity at its height. At first Amira couldn't take it, then she adjusted. Men everywhere, on every side. She was the only woman. The men—children, middle-aged types, and youths—were sitting and playing cards together. And there was this terrible, choking stench. Lumps of shit lay everywhere, alongside pools of piss and hovering clouds of flies. Amira tried avoiding them, then saw how pointless it was to try, and plunged right in. Every eye was on her. One man approached. His gaze lingered at her breasts, but he backed off when he saw the badge. He went back to his friends and they all whispered back and forth. She was convinced she was the subject of their conversation, but she ignored them. On and on she went until she came to a large metal barrier and there she saw a sign hung up, on which was printed "The End" and handwritten tags: "Amir and Rasha—Eternal Love— 5/6/2063"; "The Ghosts of Karabantina: al-Masri, Mesilhi, and Karawana"; "No ceasefire"; "This is our life and we live it; We are here, our enemies are over there." And more. Amira retraced her steps. She was revolted and her nerves were in a terrible state. At the entrance to the tunnel she gave the badge to the guard and retrieved her ID. Before leaving, she asked who Abdo the Prince was. He smiled. Abdo the Prince is nothing. There's no one called Abdo the Prince. It's just a code the men use so they know who's with us and who's not. Those others (pointing into the distance, at Yehya Volcano and the inhabitants of Inji's Karantina) are convinced there's some- one called Abdo the Prince. Only we know the truth. She smiled in relief. She had been terrified that someone by that name had taken control of the tunnel without the knowledge of her or her mother. Once home, she went to bed, a soothing thought in her mind: things were still under control.

Was that right? Were things really still under control? Yes, and no. If we're being honest, then there was this one rumor, frequently heard at the time. Everyone was saying that Amira was finished. She'd lost control of her men and the battle. But this was a rumor, and like any rumor it lacked accuracy. Amira had a healthy balance in her bank account, monthly salaries were still paid out to the men, and from time to time bonuses as well— smaller than they'd been before Minnatallah died, but the men still needed them. She still held all the cards, then. And she still had her resolve, which is no little thing for a woman in her circumstances.

Amira was on her way back from the tunnel when she heard the noon call for prayer, and she remembered that it had been ages since she had last visited Sheikha Salha. Sheikha Salha was another card she had yet to play, she told herself, with her formidable spiritual power and the smile of hope that was her gift in the most trying of circumstances. She went to her at night, and spilled her heart out to her, and wept. She told her that she'd drunk alcohol just days before; that she had been disgusted with herself, but that she'd drunk it anyway; that she had the feeling God was angry with her because of this. Sheikha Salha made no comment. She only smiled, and spoke the very words that Amira, at this trying time, was most in need of: Don't fear, sweetheart. God is with you.

4

War is give and take. A day your way, a day against you. Yehya Volcano had always held this to be true.

One day, the communist and, more recently, elected government of China—with the agreement of the Argentinian government—decided to nationalize the Shanghai Tunnel. The decision came as a total shock to the U.S.-based Beneath Corporation, which had overseen the digging of the tunnel and the running of the glass vessels back and forth between China and the Atlantic. Making an enemy of Beneath was no laughing matter. The corporation owned a considerable number of shares in the U.S. government. That's how things are now. Standard procedure. We're talking about the post-post-capitalist era. The Americans were not slow to respond. They stockpiled their missiles in Pakistan and Mexico—two allied states—and for years war raged between Asia and the Americas. Two strikes in the North and two in the South: America was shaken, no mistake, and the world looked on. Yehya Volcano would read the news and ponder his own personal problem: Karantina.

When Minnatallah's men had occupied the Karabantina tunnel he hadn't been annoyed. The days we live in! he'd said, and smiled. And when he and his men had been rocked by defeat after defeat, he'd left it in God's hands as well. War beneath the ground was no game. Anyone who wants to play had better know that it's kill or be killed, with a third, rarely trodden path: be killed today and return to kill tomorrow. This third path is the one that Yehya Volcano chose.

Yehya wasn't required to sell his successes to Inji. She understood. Thanks to her extensive military experience, she knew that early victories only mean tougher times ahead. Plus something else: Inji had long cared for Sousou's family. Didn't love them, but neither did she hate them with uncontrolled loathing. The endless war between her family and theirs had created a kind of bond. Sometimes she had the feeling that her existence was dependent on that of Minnatallah and Amira. This can happen, and every student of political thought in times of war knows it, but what happened here was more than just a bond based on a decades-long feud; the families were united by happy memories as well. Inji had strong memories of giving the young Minnatallah English lessons; memories of Sousou sticking up for her and her husband in the neighborhood; memories of Sousou with his knife, slaughtering those who'd killed members of her family; and, of most interest to us here, memories of Sousou talking to her on the phone and telling her the story of Bekheit, her great-great-grandfather. For all these reasons, Inji was not overly keen to hit Minnatallah hard. She took the side of the doves in the underground war, while Yehya Volcano and Yara and Lara played the hawks.

All of which led to the scenes outlined above. When Inji heard the news of Minnatallah's death she couldn't believe it. She asked her granddaughters to accompany her to the aza and the two of them refused outright. And so did Yehya Volcano. What'll people say about us, hagga? But the hagga was unmoved by cautious counsel. One night she awoke at two a.m. and moved through the apartment. The sound of her footsteps woke Lara. She switched on the light and, dazzled, Inji hid her eyes. Where are you off to, Teta? asked Lara and she replied, To the aza at Minna's. Now Lara was well aware that no aza was ever held at two in the morning, but Inji was not. The girl led her grandmother back to bed. Tomorrow we'll go and pay our respects and do everything you want. Inji resisted. She pushed her granddaughter away and said she had to go now. No one's going to stop me. Lara tumbled to the floor and Yara woke up. Inji suddenly went wild. Neither girl could cope. They called Yehya. Teta's gone nuts. Come and help us. They tried to tie her up but some tremendous strength was surging though the old lady's body. She sprang toward the bathroom, went inside, came out, then it was through the kitchen door and back out again. All of sudden she looked up at the two girls and asked, Where's the front door? and crashed to the floor. She started muttering, I'm the one who killed her. I threw her under the train and she died. I killed her in Ramses. Her vision was playing tricks. She saw the faces of the two girls bathed in blood. But I didn't mean to, she said: She was bothering Sheikh Ali, sitting on his lap and flirting. I don't want to say any more. She was muttering, her gaze fixed on the girls, then she drifted off. When Yehya arrived she was asleep, a smile upon her lips.

One time she locked herself up in the bathroom for an hour and a half and when she emerged she called the girls. She sat them down in front of her and said that she'd tried to commit suicide in the bathroom. She'd smashed her head against the wall a few times and hadn't died. In the bathroom, directly over the sink, were spots of blood. Lara wiped them away and told her sister that from now on the front door to the apartment had to be locked, with the key. Inji found out and decided to stay in her bedroom talking to herself. She's the one who wanted to kill me, she said. She put an African snake in the room and stole my tracksuit, and when I found it, it was covered in nasty stuff. I've got no problem with the nasty stuff, swear to God. It's the other way round. It was her who always had a problem with the nasty stuff. And it was her who hid the key from me. Umm Salah the maid gave her shots of tranquilizer, and she slept. And woke, at dawn, to hunt for the front door. Minna, my girl! she screamed. You upset with your Auntie Inshi, girl? I swear to God I didn't mean it. Don't you be upset, now. She tried to open the screen door to the balcony and failed. She tried again and succeeded. You'd be a real idiot to be upset with me! Have I ever wanted anything but the best for you? She stepped onto the balcony and a thread of blood flowed from her and stained the tiles. Have you forgotten who taught you to say *Sank yoo*, and *Mersey bore votter komblimon*, my girl? Wasn't it your Auntie Inshi? And who was it got you what you were owed? She lifted a leg over the wall. She closed her eyes and did not hesitate. She threw herself off the balcony.

It was Umm Salah who woke the girls. She told them that their grandmother had chucked herself out of the window. The girls rushed downstairs and found her there, a motionless corpse, a smile on her lips, and across her right wrist a knife gash topped with congealed blood. The mourning ceremony was held the next day. The apartment was filled with people of every kind. Yehya Volcano received the men's condolences in the mosque, and the girls received the women's condolences at home. It's down to you now, the women whispered to Yara and Lara, and to Yehya the men said the same. There was a general sense that one age had come to an end, for another to take its place. That evening, Yara took her sister aside and told her she wanted to go into the tunnel. We haven't been once and now we've got to carry the burden ourselves. The old lady who took the load for us is gone. What to do? And Lara said, Either we shoulder the responsibility together, or we sit at home, our heads in our hands. The two of them agreed to shoulder the responsibility.

The Egyptian state was not out of touch with what was going on in the tunnel. It was watching from afar and it was dragging the conflict out. The Karantina tunnel file was given an airing every time the corruption of the Minister of Transport, the Minister of the Interior, and the Governor of Alexandria was probed. Their men had taken kickbacks from the two warring parties beneath the ground. But any attempt to sideline these three men would result in a slaughter whose size the two ministers and the governor would not care to guess at. Sure, the Egyptian state was a quagmire of corruption, if that's how you want to put it, but it was corruption of a kind impossible to avoid. The budget was being spent on development in the South and in northern Sinai, and Alexandria slipped back to last place on the list of priorities. All of which made the tunnel seem like a complete and functioning society.

By the time Yara and Lara descended to the Karantina tunnel, reality was far outpacing imagination. They went down with Yehya Volcano, their tourist guide to the netherworld. He told them that there was a truce on. Morale was low on both sides due to their leaders dying in quick succession. But that didn't stop there being skirmishes from time to time (he smiled): a little gunfire at the border if you like. Your grandmother was down here every day or so and the men took heart from her. Now I'm doing all the work myself and that's more of a curse than a blessing. He led them to the operations room, as he referred to it: one of the stripped-down train carriages where he and three of his aides would sit and draw up battle plans.

Just as Amira had, on her tour around the tunnel, the two girls read numerous signs suspended from the walls: "Plant a resistance beneath the earth"; "No to healing the divide!"; "The severed finger . . . what of it?"; "Kama Sutra salutes you!" And more. Regarding the last sign, Yehya introduced them both to Kama Sutra—whom he also referred to as Gamasa: a fifteen-year-old kid with a machine gun slung over his shoulder. A bubbly kid, jolly and joking and always singing Hindi hits.

"Ashni Patchi Khan Allah Akbar"—something like that—then with a final "Akbar" he brought the mournful ballad to an end and perched on the carriage door. Suddenly, his glum show done, he transformed into a clown. He smiled over at the two girls and hopped down. And now, ladies, after that beautiful musical interlude, time for a test of the little gray cells. We shall ask you both a question and whoever can provide the answer is surely the true daughter of Hamada. The girls looked at one another. He went on: Who is both a girl's father and her uncle? Neither answered and he jumped in, stern and theatrical: Wrong! Wrong as it gets. Your answer is . . . wrong. Wrong. Wroooong. Then he returned to the carriage and held the muzzle of his rifle to his mouth like a microphone: Esteemed guest, to be a girl's father and uncle at one and the same time, we do not ask much. Our demand is simple, easy, perfectly lovely: you must sire . . . Amira! The test is over, and now for another turn! Despite themselves the girls smiled and thought of Sousou, Amira's father, who'd also been brother to Abu Amira, the original father of Amira, back in the day.

This was the sunny side of life in the tunnel. But the tunnel had other faces. One of the men started talking. It's fine here, no one says otherwise, but when Miallim Yehya told us to come down here, we were told they'd build us shacks. No one's asking for a palace, but just look around you, miss. The folk here are at the bottom of the heap. We're sleeping out on the street. If people need to relieve themselves, it has to be out here in front of everyone. Not a sight for your eyes, miss. And there's the stink, the filth, the lack of air.

As soon as Yehya Volcano had taken over the tunnel he'd made it known throughout the neighborhood that anyone who needed somewhere to live—not a palace, mind, not a villa, just somewhere to make do—could come and stay in the tunnel. Mobs of the homeless and gangsters swarmed down and occupied the tunnel—with the exception of women, children, the elderly, and disabled. The numbers weren't overwhelming, by any means: at the height of the boom the Karantina tunnel hosted no more than fifty individuals. But there was one condition: that anyone who came to live there must learn to use a gun, if only the basic principles, the simplest steps, for self-defense. So Yehya had ruled.

It's fine here, but the problem is the flies, begins one. The flies are everywhere now, and they're big and aggressive. Remember the flies back in the day? You'd tell them, Shoo! miss, and they'd shoo. But now? No way. (The man standing next to him laughs, so the fellow looks up at him and restates his position.) Don't believe me? (A mocking grin) These days it's the flies that shoo the people. I'm telling you.

Wherever the two girls went, the flies went with them. Even they, raised among cockroaches and lizards, were exasperated beyond measure. For an instant it seemed to Yara that the flies were watching her. She said, The flies are looking at us, and Lara added, They really are. They squatted against the tunnel wall and Yara leaned her head on Yehya Volcano's shoulder. She looked at him and teased, You don't want to marry me then, Uncle Yehya? and he stammered and said in a flustered voice, Be an honor, miss. The miss was satisfied with this answer. She draped her arm round Yehya Volcano's shoulders and closed her eyes. Her twin sister was busy scrutinizing the physiology of a large cockroach that had started staring at her and wiggling its whiskers. She flipped it on its back, watched it legs dancing in the air, and laughed.

From afar, the thing looked ridiculous. A man by the name of Sameh Kazarouna had managed to conceal a five-hundred-pound note beneath the mattress he slept on and when he awoke it wasn't there. The tunnel was up in arms. Sameh himself went over to complain to Yehya in front of the two girls, and Yehya bellowed that he didn't have time for this and that no one could pester him into doing their dirty work for them. The man became threatening. Like that, is it? Okay then, fine. Fine, Mr. Yehya the Volcano, I'll go and take what's mine from the lion's mouth. But don't complain if you don't like it. The man went to retrieve his five hundred pounds from the tunnel's inhabitants. One by one he talked to them all, circling and scurrying like an idiot. He began his interrogation by going on the attack. Give me my five hundred pounds, Afriqi. I saw you yesterday, Arabi, I saw you take it. Don't waste my time. Hey, Ashraf Zimbabwewi! My money goes back in my pocket right now. I won't ask you twice.

The kid Gamasa (Kama Sutra) was looking on from a distance. He started trailing Sameh Kazarouna around, drumming his hands on the butt of his rifle. When Kazarouna had had enough of this he grabbed his arm and twisted it back hard, then gripped him by the neck and dragged him over to the barrier, where he pushed his face into a pile of shit. Gamasa heaved himself upright. He looked angrily at Kazarouna. It's like that is it, Sameh? Just don't you forget it. And he walked away.

Hey, Gamasa!
What is it, Sameh?
Did you get upset with me today?
I don't get upset, Sameh. You know that.
So why the frown then?
I wasn't upset with you, I was upset for you.
You were upset for me?
Yeah. You were irritating me and I made everyone laugh at you. Made you look a real idiot.
(Angrily) You're a faggot anyway. You're not even worth teaching a lesson.

Yehya Volcano!
What?
Run along now, Volcano.
I touch your mother or something?
A little respect, Volcano, I'm telling you. Don't make me get upset with you.

So, when those people attack us . . . .
What people?
The people over on the other side, brother.

What about them?

When they attack us . . . .

What will they do?

I'm the one asking, brother.

Then ask.

Forget it. I don't feel like it anymore.

Miss!

Yes?

Are you really Hamada's daughter?

Yes.

And Hamada was a hero just like everyone says?

What do you know about Hamada?

I know he was a hero.

(Another man approaches, playful) Honestly now, miss: is he nicer or am I?

(Smiling) You're both nice.

(Angrily) No one tells me I'm like anyone. I'm Afriqi. I'm Afriqi! (He thumps his fist against his chest. He looks around. He laughs.) The one and only. I'm Afriqi! Afriqi forever! Afriqi stares down time itself! Afriqi über alles! Afriqi says to his enemies: Eat your heart out! (He starts chanting, waving his hands in mock defiance, aping a scene from an old film, an ancient joke on an ancient commercial.) Give us Riri baby food! Riri for us! The revolutionaries won't settle for less!

The day after their visit, Yara and Lara requested a meeting with Yehya Volcano. They told him that the situation in the tunnel was insupportable. Filth everywhere. Back in the day, Uncle Yehya, everyone would praise Karantina for its cleanliness. Now, the moment we expand and take a slice of tunnel from the government, it gets as filthy as this? I'm not happy about this situation and the way I see it something has to be done. It's a joke. A big joke, Lara added.

Uncle Yehya . . . you're the leader and all that down below. God knows I've nothing against that. No one's trying to ruin anybody's life here. But there's nothing wrong with cleaning up now and again. Just assign a team to come and clean up every day. It's not like I'm talking to a stranger here, Yehya, and to be quite frank the sight of it makes my skin crawl.

It was Yara who said this, and she curled her lip in disgust.

Yehya Volcano took things like this to heart. He was desperately sensitive regarding any observations directed his way, particularly those observations that related to the way he did his job and his management of matters underground, and particularly when those observations came from Yara. All right, then. We find ourselves obliged to confess that in Yehya's heart a tenderness had taken root, for Yara, his current boss and the granddaughter of his former. It wasn't that Yara was throwing herself at him. Maybe that's how it was at first, but when he settled himself down to sleep in the carriage, he'd talk to himself: I'm Yehya Volcano, a strapping Egyptian youth two years the wrong side of forty and yet to marry because my mind's always been on my work and I've never had time for such things. Now I spend all my time thinking about my future bride, the dream girl whose world I'll make a paradise, with God's help. My friend, I won't conceal from you (remember: Yehya Volcano is talking to himself) that there is this one lady who's been trying to turn my head for years now. And I'm interested in her too. Is it fate's decree that we shall be joined together in happy fellowship and righteous amity? (Thus ends his soliloquy.)

Yehya Volcano was a man. He took himself seriously. No man could tell him what to do (the result of his sensitivity over Yara's admonitions). And so it was that he decided to take the initiative. His phone calls to Yara got longer. He told her the latest jokes, would check to see she'd gotten home safe each night, and made sure to end each nocturnal call with, Sleep well, dear lady. And Yara met this gift from the heavens with affection of her own. Prepared his food herself, visited him in the tunnel every day, until he confessed—Forgive me, dear girl—that he felt something for her. I'm scared to step out of line. Yara's hand upon his thigh, her questing fingers, told him there was no line there. But Yehya Volcano was a man. He did things properly.

Maybe I'm not the most important man to love you, nor the best . . . .
(She smiles indulgently, graciously.)

(Silence)

(She looks at him in astonishment.) Why don't you finish? But what . . . ?

What do you mean, But what?

What do you want to say?

That maybe I'm not the most important man to love you, nor the best. That's it?

That's it.

I don't understand, I . . . just a moment. (She is silent for a long time. Then she makes up her mind. She pats him on the shoulder.) No, Yehya. Don't let me hear you say that again. You're just fine, Yehya.

Yara's status down in the tunnel was soon established. True, she was the only woman there, and true, too, that despite the bristles on her brows and lip, despite the repellent stench of her sweat, she was the dream of every man down there, but she was constantly accompanied by the supreme leader, the man the tunnel's denizens knew as Yehya Volcano, and was under his protection. No one was able to approach her, and even were we to set aside this immunity, Yara had a powerful personality of her own that allowed her to impose her point of view on the men. Now, it is true that one of them had been less than respectful at first, but he quickly learned that this wasn't just any woman. A woman of fire and steel: that was Yara.

Each day Yara would prepare Yehya Volcano's dinner in the carriage where he chose to sleep. Serve him dinner, then go home. Never once did she try to stay on after the food was served and never once did he try to make her stay. Yehya Volcano was a man. The world might have given me plenty of knocks, Dr. Yara (she'd told him more than once to drop the "Dr." but he couldn't bring himself to), but I've never done wrong. I've never done anything to make anyone upset with me. As God's my witness, it's not me people are upset with. There are people who'll tell you Yehya Volcano's really upset us, people who'll tell you he's killing our children and the rest of it, but I've always acted with the best of intentions. My circumstances haven't been the easiest but a fellow's got to have good intentions at all times. Yara leaned over and printed a kiss upon his cheek. The only kiss since he had confessed his love to her. Their relationship was clean, spotlessly clean. If there was anyone who wanted their relationship to stray over the border into filth, well that someone wasn't Yehya Volcano, because Yehya Volcano was a man. A man of the first water.

The proposal came from Yehya. She was eating a fuul sandwich down in the tunnel. He told her he was frightened to say what he was about to say but that circumstances compelled him to say it. I'm an old man. Over forty, I mean. And you're still a lovely young madmoozel. But I swear to God I've never had an unworthy thought about you; you've always been like a sister to me, and I've taken care of you like you're my own flesh and blood. He stopped and looked into her eyes, and she looked into his. They stayed like that, staring into each other's eyes, until he summoned his courage. I've been thinking. If God were to bring us together, then I'd have found a good woman who'd care about me and look after me when I'm older, and you and your sister Lara would be under the protection of your man. People are merciless, my lady. Yara smiled. She tried to say something romantic, but instead she sneezed, a tremendous sneeze that resulted in her pulling a handkerchief from her pocket and wiping away her snot. She was just recovering from a particularly unpleasant cold. He looked at her, unsure of where he stood, but she was just a mess of hanky, snot, and a chain of little sneezes that she ripped off like shots from a machine gun. Amid the sneezes she noticed that he was looking at her and said, I'll–*tchoo*–marry–*tchoo*–you. She gave a final sneeze and laughed and, laughing, was overwhelmed by a coughing fit. She sprayed him liberally and, confused, he brushed the specks of bean from his shirt.

Yara's dowry wasn't to be cash, or an apartment, or a car. There's only one thing I want. I want you to clean the tunnel for me. The cleanliness that Yara had in mind was not just a physical cleanliness; it was above all a spiritual one, and that was more important than anything. She was well aware that there were plenty of useless people living down in the tunnel, and that Yehya collected his share from them, just as she knew that he traded weapons, along with hash and special narcotic cocktails, like they did on the other side of the barrier. We're no different from them, right? She wanted all this to stop. You and me, we're going to be one, God willing, and the restaurant brings in all we need and more. There's no need for all these dirty dealings. Yehya Volcano promised to expel the useless and just keep the ones who were fit to fight; to dedicate his men to restoring what had been stolen from its rightful owners. I had a piece of land here and they took it from me by force, no manners. If they'd just come and said, We'd like that piece of land, Uncle Yehya, I would have given it to them on the spot. But bad manners I can't stand. Everything will be set right and everyone here will learn his place. Here before you, before the Lord of the Worlds, I give my word. Yara said nothing. She gazed at him with a gaze of profound gratitude.

Yet Yehya Volcano did not turn them out. True, he loved Yara more than he loved himself, but he had absolutely no faith in the future. His life to date had taught him that good times don't last, and that whatever could be made from the tunnel belonged by rights to him and his children after him, God willing.

Yara observed the presence of these ghastly people in the tunnel every time she went down there. These people, with their repellent manners, were in her view the very ones who were hastening the end of the underground kingdom that she and the others had built with the sweat of their brows. If we turn the tunnel into a beautiful, civilized showcase for Alexandria, then nobody can say anything to us, not the government, not anybody. She spoke to him about it more than once, and every time he promised her that he'd sort it out soon, but as time went on it started to really annoy her. For three whole days she stopped visiting the tunnel. He tried calling her and she didn't answer. He spoke to her sister Lara, and asked why she wasn't coming, and via her sister, Yara gave her angry reply: She's not upset with you, Uncle Yehya. She says she's upset for you. Look, my sister loves you, all right? She's a sweet-hearted girl, you know? She hemmed and hawed, then said, She's given me a message to pass on to you, Uncle Yehya, and like the Good Book tells us, the duty of the messenger is to give a clear account. She says she's set you up and supported you for all these years and she says, well, something I'm embarrassed to repeat. She says she's got no problem supporting you in the years to come, you know, you don't need to worry about where the money's coming from. Then she just swore a bit, you know.

269

The next day saw two men ejected from the tunnel. Yehya shouted at them that the soup kitchen was shut and dragged them along the tunnel's gravel floor, each by his arm, toward the exit. Yara watched this scene from a window in her apartment. She smiled and sent him a text: My heart forgives you, Yehya. Come and have lunch with us today. And a charming little smiley.

Yara's next visit to the tunnel went almost perfectly. We say *almost* because there is nothing perfect on God's earth or beneath it, but also because the following scene took place:

As Yara said goodbye to Yehya, signaling her imminent return home, her attention was caught by an assortment of noises emanating from the carriage next to them. She asked him about these noises and he did not answer. She sprang into the carriage, where she was confronted by a series of curtains partitioning off the seats. She drew one back to find a girl sitting on a young man's lap. The girl's hijab had slipped off her hair, her breasts were in the young man's hands, and he was sucking on a nipple. The boy and girl looked at her. They didn't seem surprised. A quantity of bottles lay around them. She closed the curtain and opened another. A man inserting his penis between the buttocks of a fat woman. Yara looked at Yehya Volcano and he turned his eyes to the floor. What's this, Yehya? He lifted his head and smiled shyly. That's right, my dear! So we can't make a few pennies for ourselves? She smiled to see his smile. She relaxed. So make them, Yehya, but not like this. It's not becoming.

They walk together. He defends himself. Says he can't make promises he can't keep, that he needs money for his pocket, that he doesn't want to be a burden on her. She quite understands, but it's not like she shortchanges him. My dear, I know. Did anyone say anything about shortchanging? Suddenly she stops. He breaks off. He follows the line of her gaze. A young man in his twenties pissing against the wall, his gun lying on the ground half a yard away. It's too much! she screams. I can't take it anymore. He tries to soothe her but he can't. She runs for the exit. Trips. Picks herself up. Keeps on running.

They've got their reasons, too, my dear.

Yehya! I'm warning you, don't irritate me. What do you mean they've got their reasons?

Well, put yourself in their place. Down in the tunnel twenty-four hours a day? They're going to have to go.

He can go outside and piss as he pleases, brother. The mosque's right next to the stairs.

And the elderly? The ones who can't manage?

The elderly and the ones who can't manage, you said you'd thrown them out. Or were you lying to me?

I've never lied to you in my life, but I can't turn out an old man who depends on me.

Yehya!

(He looks at the ground.) I'm sorry, Yara. Forgive me. I can't throw out a man my father's age.

You asking me or telling me? Don't irritate me, now . . . . (With an effort she restrains herself.) They can go to hell, Yehya, and they will.

(Slowly, gazing into the distance) I'm sorry. I can't.

This was the second strain on Yara and Yehya's relationship. Yara went away in a rage and he stayed on in the carriage, thinking about her. He thought of calling her but his pride prevented him. And all around him people were talking, going on and on with their insinuations and forced cheer. He was extremely angry and didn't know where to direct his anger and, in the end, the anger was turned on Kama Sutra, on the kid called Gamasa.

Gamasa came up to him and said, Forgive me for what I'm about to say to you, Yehya. Yehya was on a hair trigger. He looked at Gamasa and said nothing. And the kid went on. It's just Miss Yara. With all due respect, I just feel that she's taking advantage of you. Taking advantage of me how? Well, to be honest she's not a nice person, and you're like a chief down here, a commander, and she knows that if it wasn't for you she'd be finished by now. What do you want? Well, I might be younger than you, Yehya, but you should think of me as your little brother—who's seen his fair share of life. Aren't those Sabah the whore's girls? Let her go, Yehya. Let her go and spare yourself the headache. Upon hearing these words, Yehya Volcano rose to his feet. Grabbed the kid. Pulled out his bayonet and buried it in his arm. He was screaming like a man possessed: Have you forgotten yourself, you faggot? Forgotten who scraped you off the street and made you fit for company? He shoved the kid toward the exit. The kid began to run as Yehya bombarded him with half bricks. By my mother's womb, if I see you again, I'll kill you, faggot.

So Kama Sutra left the tunnel. In the space of seconds his world had collapsed about his ears. The tunnel had been his Paradise, his Dream, his Everything, and he had been cast out like a stray. He sat on the station wall gazing longingly at the tunnel. A tear fell from his eye. And away he went. But this was not the end of his tale. Like those before him, like all those who had been cast out of the tunnel before him, Kama Sutra was not defeated. He pulled himself together, gave himself over to God's tender care, and set out for the building where dwelt Amira, Sousou's daughter. Once there, he told her: Consider me your devoted servant, to do with as you will. Amira finished her prayers. She saluted the angels seated at her right hand and her left. She smiled. And tenderly she patted him on the head.

5

One night Lara saw herself in a dream, alone. She is alone and comfortless, walking down a shadowy road, and abruptly everything is illuminated. She sees Hamada in the distance, sitting with his friends, Farouq and Sheikh Mohamed. She approaches, and Hamada folds away the Monopoly board on which he's been playing and strokes her hair. He kisses her forehead and asks her, Why so upset? She is about to speak when he shudders and slaps her face. Farouq tries to calm him, but to no avail. Suddenly, Farouq pulls a switchblade from his pocket and slashes Hamada's face. There's a machine gun in the dream now, a machine gun raining fire on everyone. The café's chairs tip over, the tables sway, and Hamada falls to the ground, and then his body starts to swell; it swells to unprecedented proportions, until he fills the frame, spills over even, and Sheikh Mohamed's standing on a chair threatening all present that if they don't go home he'll rape them one by one, and playing with the cock that's jutting fiercely beneath his gallabiya. Lara awoke, sweating and scared.

It was the days following Yara's marriage to Yehya Volcano. Lara wasn't sleeping. She would hear them having sex, quite openly, without the slightest shame, and it is not hard to deduce that she was burning with desire and envy at one and the same time. It was around then that she got close to Umm Salah the maid. She'd hear the sounds of sex, decamp from her bedroom, and repair to the maid's, who would sense her presence and hold her as she slept. This one time, Lara found her gone, out with relatives. Downcast, Lara went back to her room and decided to call her. She told her she wanted to talk to her about something very important and that she was coming over to see her, now, in her apartment in Kom al-Dikka.

All the way to Kom al-Dikka Lara wracked her brains for something to say to Umm Salah. She had no idea. She was scared, that was all. Umm Salah greeted her with a smile. She made her a cup of tea and did not speak, and neither did Lara. And then Umm Salah broke the silence. Men have become a real handful. She did not explain. Lara went to her and laid her head in her lap. Umm Salah began to talk. Know what the problem is? The problem is that all the first-rate folk are gone: died, killed, locked up. My own husband's been behind bars for God knows how long. All that's left are the younger generation, and the young don't know anything.

And what is it that the young are supposed to know? Umm Salah had no clearly defined answer to this. Her monologue ran on and on without her pausing to draw breath. Men back then weren't like that. There were tender ones, there were kind ones, there were some absolute bastards too, it's true, but these days only the bad ones are left. I mean, not all men are bad; the majority, let's say. The best thing is that there aren't that many of them anymore. Look here (she starts counting on her fingers): There's you, there's your sister, there's Amira, there's Inshi, God have mercy on her soul—and another one who died is Minna, Amira's mother. Then there's the original Umm Amira, the old one. The men are finished, they hardly count. (Lara looks at her, like she's about to say something.) No, no, my girl. I don't count Yehya Volcano as a man. Not because he's bad. Because without you two he'd be nothing. Yehya was raised by your grandmother and now he's your sister's husband—your turn next, God willing. In other words we made him and we keep him.

This, more or less, was just the preface to the tale that Umm Salah wanted to tell. The meat of the story came only after the tea had been drunk and the tobacco plugs fixed atop the shisha. Her tale was the tale of two women who once upon a time had left Alexandria reeling. The police had been unable to catch them; they played with men like they'd played with dolls as girls. I want you to really pay attention here, because one day you and your sister might be able to achieve what those two ladies achieved back in the day. I want you to get close to your sister. Don't hate her and don't resent her happiness. Remember those two ladies and remember what they managed to achieve when they loved and cared for one another. Their names were Nadia and Itemad.

Umm Salah took a pull on the pipe, passed it to Lara, and began to tell her tale. This all took place a long time ago. In those days, it was easy for any man who wanted to sleep with a girl to do so, anywhere in Alexandria. Everyone was at it. There were locations known to those who wanted to pick a girl and pluck her. Your grandmother made a living out of it. Don't get upset with me, my girl: everyone was doing it. It was perfectly normal, you see, and no one minded. People thought of it as a creature comfort, a way to let your hair down, you might say.

Lara didn't feel insulted. She had heard this piece of information, with differing degrees of frankness, from a multitude of sources. The point is that Nadia and Itemad were working for Inshi. They weren't beauties, but with the right clothes and the right makeup they could look the part, and they appealed to certain types of young men—old ones too. Middle class and lower; a very important category of customer for Inshi, who wasn't concerned with the richest so much as with the neediest. But even such lofty principles as these were powerless before the demands of the market. Nadia and Itemad's want of beauty was the direct cause of their coming off the game and devoting their efforts to pulling the customers in, to laying out the advantages their casino had over the others, as well as recruiting the right kind of girl to come and work there.

Nadia and Itemad were sisters, vegetable sellers from Zananiri, Umm Salah said. They started working for Ali and Inji when they were still young, in about 2015. Inji met them at the market. She took their phone numbers and gave them a call the following day. Invited them over for tea. She inquired after their circumstances and offered them a job with her. They thought about it for a bit. Both were married, and Itemad had a little girl. But times were very hard.

We women have to think very hard before taking a step like that, my girl. The way I see it, if a woman's married with kids she's better off staying at home. Take me, for instance. I got married, had my children, and told myself I'd never go on the game. When I was younger everything was fine and dandy. These days, not so much. But I'm ahead of myself. I wanted to say that people aren't all alike. These two gave it a lot of thought and they asked around and took advice. Lots of folk told them not to, but there were some who encouraged them. There were whores everywhere back then. It was so you couldn't tell who was a whore and who was a God-fearing woman.

With the encouragement of the encouraging few, Itemad began working at the Karantina Casino, while Nadia turned it down. Naturally, Itemad didn't inform her husband of her decision. She told him she'd met a nice lady who taught the Quran at the mosque and that she went to visit her every day. And this was her cover. A year passed, then two, then three, and Itemad bought herself a car on deposit, upgraded from Cleopatras to Marlboros, and kitted out her apartment from top to bottom. And Nadia was watching all of this, the envy eating her alive. She dropped in to see her sister, who lived in the apartment above hers in Seven Girls Street in Labban, and looked on as, in front of both her sister and her husband, she applied her makeup, slipped into a tank top with built-in support and a miniskirt that showed off her thighs, then draped a long black robe over the lot. At this point she became convinced that her sister's husband had found out the truth. She went home and spoke to her husband about her sister's life, about the new furniture and the way she spoke, which had changed considerably. She told him that God had certainly heard her prayers. She paused for a long time, then said that her sister was working for Inji. She was a waitress, she said: she fetched the customers their orders. But her husband wasn't taken in. He knew who Inji was, who Ali was. He was silent. He said, And you're not thinking of going to work for them as well? She confessed that she was, and he confessed that he was fine with it.

Umm Salah emphasized her point: Everyone was doing it. It was perfectly normal. People thought of it as letting your hair down, you might say. She warmed a lump of hash, pressed it down into a cigarette, slid the cigarette into a sealed cup, and continued with her tale:

Itemad and Nadia pulled in the young men of Karmouz, and as time went on Inji came to rely on them more than ever before. The product sold and both women learned the secrets of the trade. They learned where the penniless customers could be found and where the rich johns gathered and they focused their attentions on the latter, though the latter, sadly, were in short supply in Karmouz. There wasn't much cash for their sweat. They spoke to Inji about it and she smiled and said that what was true for them was true for her, her husband, and her son. She took no more than they. This is our trade, people, and this is what we make. Our customers are just getting by. Itemad and Nadia were happy with this explanation, but the demands of home life were many and people are forced by circumstance to do things they would rather not.

Umm Salah was meandering from the hash. As she talked she would hand the cup to Lara, pause as she held the smoke in, squeeze her eyes tight shut, then give a cough or two and go on talking. And Lara was listening, remembering things she'd heard as a child, so long ago, about two women called Nadia and Itemad. She'd never known who they were or what their story was, and now all the stories were being freed from Pandora's box.

Itemad and Nadia fought with your grandmother. A real blowup. They didn't like what they saw: they thought their sweat was stocking her larder. They told her to her face: You're a thief. We're giving everything we've got and all we get from you is crumbs. And your grandmother was one tough old woman. She didn't let a word go to waste. Truth be told she was straight as a die; she didn't stand for any messing about. Fine, she tells them. Find yourself work elsewhere. I raise you, I teach you, and you want to take off and leave me. Fine by me. I won't beat around the bush. Good riddance.

Nadia and Itemad started working out of their building in Labban. The customers were better there. They joined their two apartments together, knocked through the ceiling that separated them, and installed a flight of stairs. In just a few months their home was reeling in the men of the neighborhood, and when the burden became too much for them to bear they had to recruit. It was their two husbands who took on this role, first of all because their wives were swamped as it was, but also because of their expressed unhappiness with the way the building's residents were looking at their women. They were quite firm on this point. Over a stormy supper they both agreed that they were not going to stand for their wives being subjected to the mudslinging of any worthless bastard. And there was a third reason, which both husbands were well aware of, but which neither stated openly.

They were convinced the place would do better with other women, more attractive than their wives. They hung a sign on the building, advertising The Freedom Casino within, then the two men began searching for women and customers, first in West Alexandria, which they knew best, then in the East.

Everything went swimmingly, my girl. People were content and no one asked about a thing. There were a few that gave them trouble, but that's how it goes. When you live in a building, my dear, you've the right to ask who's coming and going. But no one ever *said a word*. Or at least, a word might be said, but just a word and never harshly spoken, and then everything would be back to normal. But then there's greed, Lara. Greed's the worst thing in the world, my girl. I want you and your sister to keep your eyes peeled for greed. It never brings anything good.

What did Umm Salah mean by greed? And how did greed bring about Nadia and Itemad's tragic end? Umm Salah talked on. It was winter, and as was usual in winter the customers were few, while Alexandria's reputation was sliding into the mud, victim of the feuds between Ali's and Sousou's families, and people cowered at home. Rent was due and deposits on everything they owned were left unpaid. Itemad's husband was a violent man. The most violent and least cautious of them all. He brought an Emirati businessman to the apartment. Led him to a bedroom at the back, where the man bedded one of the girls, and at that point, with the businessman naked, his buttocks cocked in mid-air (Umm Salah held her hands apart and added with a smile: And what an ass he had on him, good Lord!), the husband burst in. He photographed him with his camera phone, then demanded he hand over every penny he had, plus his Visa card and the keys to his car and apartment. The Emirati refused. He refused in the strongest terms and tried to strike the husband. There was a fight, and when the Emirati started to scream the husband clamped his hand over the man's mouth. After a few minutes of this, the Emirati slumped lifeless to the floor before the girl's terrified eyes.

Umm Salah is high as a kite now. She slumps to the floor. Lara approaches her. After a minute she comes to, shakes violently, and continues:

Once, twice, three times and that lot had the move down pat. They started bringing in wealthy clients and murdering them. Itemad wasn't happy. Always saying, Hasaballah, we were doing fine. Why are we getting involved in this now? (She pauses; digresses.) Hasaballah was her husband. His name was Ahmed Hasaballah and they called him Hasaballah. Nadia's husband was Abdel Aal: Mohamed Abdel Aal. It was the men who started it, but the women didn't object, if you see what I mean. And anyway, the two ladies were helping out: they'd bring people round, customers and suchlike, take their money, make them sign over their things, and then they'd murder them. It was a huge deal at the time. Everybody knew about it.

Was Umm Salah raving under the influence of the hash? Lara couldn't tell exactly. Most likely, the general outline of the story was true, but the details were debatable. In the days that followed, some people told Lara that Hasaballah had been Nadia's husband, not Itemad's, and that Abdel Aal had been married to Itemad, not Nadia, and some people said that Nadia had never been married, and that Itemad had a husband called Bekheit who was from Sohag. Whatever the case, the names didn't matter; what mattered right then was what took place, to wit: that Karantina was not the only well-spring of revolutionary fervor in Alexandria. Never! Who said such a thing? Umm Salah went on. The whole of Alexandria was up in arms, from Miami to Bahari, from Agami all the way down to Maamoura. The government in Cairo was tearing its hair. Who are these people? Who are these people setting the whole world on fire like this? Who are these people, all manliness and toughness? Alexandrians are no pushovers, my girl. And they're an ancient people too, with a beautiful culture that we're all so proud of.

The Freedom Casino in Labban claimed four victims: two men and two women. Fifty-fifty: we don't discriminate (a smile). The police were really dragging their feet, which gave Nadia and Itemad time to take precautions. They sold the two apartments, which they'd gone and bought outright, and moved with their husbands to Mansoura. And there they picked up where they'd left off, a career in which murder rubbed shoulders with prostitution, with the wails of the baffled and the bereaved, with mothers' tears.

Umm Salah tells another tale: Hasaballah and Abdel Aal—with the assistance of a third thug, by the name of Arabi—started to put pressure on Nadia and Itemad. Their demands grew, even though they weren't pulling their weight. The two ladies considered getting rid of them. Nadia lost her nerve and Itemad kept at her, trying to convince her. Nadia was a coward, a drunk, and she vacillated. Itemad was strong; feared no one but her Maker. In the end they reached a compromise: they would poison Arabi, and this would send a stern message to Hasaballah and Abdel Aal. And so it was. Arabi was eating fish with them and all of a sudden he was curled up on the floor, screaming. Hasaballah looked at Abdel Aal—they got it—and as if instinctively the two women and their husbands dropped to their knees to stifle his screams. When the life was gone out of him for good, they set about stripping him bare: a nine-millimeter automatic, three thousand pounds, a Visa credit card, a cell phone, a leather jacket, gallabiya, shoes, and an expensive watch. Together they carried him away to dump him in the wasteground beneath the building.

That night the husbands would sit with their wives in the apartment, Hasaballah despondently rolling a joint and gazing up at the ceiling from time to time and muttering, The dead men down below, the dead men down below, while Abdel Aal buried his face in his hands, crying like a baby, the words coming indistinctly from the back of his throat, something like, It'll all come out. And all night long they looked over at their wives mistrustfully. The message had hit home.

Nadia and Itemad. Two names that filled the skies over Alexandria, over the whole world, when investigations with relatives of the missing started to point to them. They were arrested just months after Hasaballah's first murder. And the investigations uncovered more: a far-flung criminal network, the deliberate policy of marginalization to which the two men, Hasaballah and Abdel Aal, had been subjected by their wives, leaving Nadia and Itemad to run the show, luring in the johns, killing them, and taking possession of their cash and assets, and leading, eventually, to these same husbands giving evidence against their wives. Men envy women, Lara; they don't love them and they wish them ill. It was their husbands who brought Nadia and Itemad down, no one else. Here Umm Salah came to the end of her story, to the moral of her tale: Left to their own devices women can achieve whatever they want, and that's why I don't want you or your sister to worry. You're only girls, it's true, but girls these days are something to be reckoned with. The Good Lord, may He be praised and glorified, says that girls are the glory of this lower world.

These last few lines came out disjointed. Umm Salah was practically asleep when she delivered them. She dozed off briefly, then came to and finished her thought. Lara could see the state she was in. She fetched her a blanket, covered her up, and left the building. It was nine-thirty in the morning. The traders were opening their stores, the sun beamed down on all and sundry, and Lara felt that she was strong. Strong and free and capable of anything.

These were the best days of Yara's life, no doubt about it. She lived in her own building, under the protection of the man she loved; her men churned out victories over the men of Amira, Minnatallah's daughter; and everyone treated her with the respect she deserved. We'd be telling a lie if we said that the thought of marriage had never occurred to Yara before. The truth was, she'd thought of nothing else. Take her bed, mute witness to her incessant masturbation, or the porn sites where she boned up with bated breath. Now Yara: she had achieved everything she longed for; she lacked for nothing—except the part of the tunnel annexed by Amira's men. That was not going to be easy. It was worrying, especially in light of reports of renewed attacks on her men, of the vast quantities of weapons owned by the enemy. Yara began to fret. From the window she looked for Yehya Volcano and saw him sitting at the café with his friends, drinking and playing for money, for very large sums of money. A fear flitted through Yara's mind, faint and alarming: she felt that she was alone in the world. These were the worst days of Yara's life, no doubt about it.

Lara was supportive. She told her the tale of Nadia and Itemad. She said that Nadia and Itemad had been two women, sure, but that hadn't prevented them achieving a great deal. Were it not for their husbands' treachery they would have gone on working for years and years. The sisters were silent; then Lara said, Do you think Yehya might betray us? Yara returned her gaze to the window and said, Betrayal's written in the stars. I just pray to God that he'll come to his senses. The thought occupying Yara was that Yehya had become a full-blown alcoholic. That he couldn't live without the booze.

The lesson they took from Nadia and Itemad's tale was that Yehya Volcano should be sidelined, in view of the fact that he was incapable of managing the war, and because, were he to become capable, he would promptly betray them just as Nadia and Itemad's husbands had done. In circumstances such as these, caution was a duty. Yara and Lara went down into the tunnel without him, they went down again and again and again, and on each visit they would meet other men, all fit to run the war. The same man occurred to both sisters simultaneously: Afriqi. A guy in his late twenties. Witty, handy with a gun, a natural leader. Lara sat with him. She said, We want you, Afriqi. We want you to be our right-hand man. What about Yehya Volcano? he asked her. Her reply, to the letter: Forget about Yehya Volcano. He's only your leader because we allow it, and we want you to be leader now.

Alcohol is bad. No coincidence that Our Lord, may He be praised and glorified, describes it as the mother of all mischief. We've seen it destroy Hamada in previous decades, and now we are watching it destroy Yehya Volcano. Yehya Volcano spends all his time sitting with his friends and drinking, only rarely venturing down into the tunnel, his pocket fat with cash from a number of little schemes he's got running belowground, from hard candy, falafel sandwiches, and automatic weapons all the way through to the stolen hours of pleasure in the train carriage he rents out to the men and their women. The cash never leaves his pocket. He drinks and gambles and his business takes care of itself. But this has its dangers—above all, to his image. He was spotted puking in a darkened street in Bahari, and he was spotted lying on the sidewalk in Abu Suleiman, unable to get up. Yara's heart is being torn apart.

She tried talking to him, and he spat on the floor and went to bed. When she went after him he slapped her face. Yara was pregnant. With his child in her belly, the blow filled her with pain. Yara was storing everything away. She didn't forget.

No one had a clear idea of what was going through Yehya Volcano's mind back then. Did he feel that the empire he'd built by force of arms was on the verge of collapse? Did he feel revolted by himself, or was it the other way round? Was he proud? No one knew. The byways of Yehya's psyche were hard to access, particularly if we take into account his poker face and clipped speech. But we can deduce that he spent each day tormented by the contemptuous expressions with which many people had started to greet him and which he was unable to meet. He was impotent. His speech was as it always had been, ditto his expression; the difference was that he was now unable to do anything. Even after he learned that his wife and her sister had turned to Afriqi to lead the battle beneath the earth, he couldn't summon even a single word of reproach. He only asked her, as they lay in bed together: So is Afriqi in charge of the tunnel now? She nodded coldly, and he turned his face away and switched out the light.

The days that followed saw a severe decline in conditions down in the tunnel. For two whole days Amira's men kept up a steady stream of fire. The men were exhausted. Many were wounded, some died, and they were forced back some meters; meters that Amira's men soon occupied. Afriqi dined with Yara and Lara in their apartment, and told them that the response would be harsh, and indeed, the tunnel was to tremble from the assault of Yara and Lara's men upon Amira's. Molotov cocktails lay strewn on every side; shell casings, empty cartridges, slingshots. Yara's men managed to reclaim the few meters they had lost and Yara's faith in Afriqi grew. She gave him greater powers and she and her sister formally declared him to be their military commander down in the tunnel in place of Yehya Volcano, who at that very moment was retching in the street like a dog.

None of this took place in isolation. The eyes of the whole world were locked on Karantina and its feuds. Media interest in the city began when an American journalist visited Karantina. With her cell phone she managed to capture images of the war in the tunnels, and she sat down with Yara and Lara, Amira and Yehya Volcano to conduct interviews with them in her flawless Palestinian-accented Arabic. Her five-page article on the city was published by *The New York Times* with the headline "Alexandria: The Story of Seven Women Who Rule the World," and opened, thrillingly: "Even as man digs down to the very core of our planet, to the center of gravity itself, Egypt is not far behind. While major world powers such as Argentina, China, and the United States fight for possession of Earth's bowels, Egyptians are conducting their own, remarkably similar feuds." The report included pictures of Yara and Lara, Inji, Minnatallah, and Amira, with a biography of each and an explanation of their role in the story. Also included was a little box of text that recounted the tale the city's inhabitants told—its historical accuracy unverified—of two woman who took up prostitution and killed their customers, two women who went by the names of Nadia and Itemad. A second page displayed pictures from the tunnel and talked about the juvenile fighters who carried out the orders of their female bosses. The report struck the Arab media like an earthquake. Correspondents descended on the region in droves. A few Arab channels managed to broadcast short documentary films on Karantina before access was denied. Local residents grilled strangers about what they wanted and searched them top to toe.

Entering the neighborhood was nigh on impossible now, forcing the state media to use its imagination to try and fill the gaps in the story told by *The New York Times* and the Arab satellite stations. For instance, what could all those men and women be getting up to down there if not sex? What on earth were the neighborhood's residents doing, if not carrying out some fiendish plot to smear the reputation of the Bride of the Mediterranean? Enraged, one journalist wrote about Devil-sent creatures, who had snuck unnoticed into our world to wreak havoc on our lives, while the Egyptian state was busy "developing" the South. Well! One fine day we would realize that they had laid to waste decades and decades worth of work to revive the city that had once been a beacon of learning and liberation to the entire Orient. Another drew attention to a peculiarity shared by the seven women: that they were all ugly, a look of terrible evil in their eyes, including that one in the niqab (he was referring to Inji) who appeared to be their leader, the one who pulled the strings.

All of which had its effect on the collective consciousness of Egyptians. Alexandria became synonymous with the bestial epithets applied to its inhabitants. One cartoonist specialized in depicting Alexandrians with tails; another always colored them green. An anthropologist wrote the following of the Alexandrian character: "The Alexandrian is an individual who loves blood and violence. War drums are sweeter to his ear than the delicate strains of classical music and guns dearer to his heart than hymns to peace. By his nature, the Alexandrian only appreciates jokes told against his enemies, and can only enjoy works of art that belittle others and glorify himself.

There is no one cause around which Alexandrians are united, no principle that inspires them all. Indeed, one might say that every Alexandrian has a cause and principle that is his and his alone. It is their blind and blood-thirsty fanaticism for all these various causes and principles that unites them. Reports from psychologists' clinics inform us that Alexandrians suffer from sadomasochism, an illness in which delight in torturing the self and the other are evenly matched. Of course, we have no desire to engage in sweeping generalizations. We have no doubt that there exists a minority of decent Alexandrians whose voices are most unfortunately swamped by the barbarous, vengeful, and primitive hordes."

This modest paragraph was the most widely circulated piece of psycho-logical analysis of the day. It was quoted in all the papers and everyone knew it. They would recite it, adding analyses of their own. The 2060s were the worst decade as far as Alexandria's reputation was concerned.

The impact this had on the Egyptian state—as represented by the Inte-rior Ministry—was clear to see. The minister had frequently come under fire for tolerating the existence of Karantina, with all the threats it posed to the peaceable and kind-hearted national character, and equally frequently the governor had stepped in to reassure the world that they were drawing up plans to do away with the cesspool (the officially approved moniker for Karantina), but no one did a thing. Then, without warning, in an unprece-dented move by the president, the minister and governor were both sacked. The residents of the neighborhood noted a certain escalation in tone. Karantina was encircled by a number of banners bearing the signature of the Interior Minister himself. The message they conveyed was unambigu-ous: "Respect the police"; "You will destroy the cesspool with your own hands." Plus a poem:

The first fruits dangle down
When January the twenty-fifth rolls around
Year in, year out
We love the police
We fear the police
And we do just what we're told.

So it was that the new minister and the new governor began their terms in office. Both pledged to get rid of Karantina once and for all. Their tone was violent and spoke of patience worn thin. Indeed—in a snippet subsequently leaked on the Internet—the Minister of the Interior slammed his hand on the table and screamed, That fucking place needs to know its limits!

The explanation above is vital if we are to understand what followed. On March 14, 2064, an advertisement was published in all the Egyptian newspapers, the text of which ran as follows:

Dear citizens,
We wish to inform you that in two weeks from now, on March 28, 2064, the neighborhood of Karantina in the Karmouz district of the governorate of Alexandria will be cleared. All citizens resident in this neighborhood will be transported directly to temporary shelter until such time as the housing units in Mohamediya have been made ready for their arrival. We ask all citizens to refrain from obstructing our troops, officers, and police units, who will clear the area by force if necessary. The Egyptian state disclaims all responsibility for any casualties that might arise in the event of force being used against decent policemen who are devotedly and selflessly doing their duty for their country.

Success comes from God alone,
The Karmouz Municipality

6

Alone in the darkness at one in the morning, a woman in a niqab walked down the street from Sousou's Karabantina to Ali and Inji's Karantina.

No one could tell what she was thinking, especially given her covered face, nor why she was abroad at this late hour, nor how—more importantly—she managed to cross the checkpoints that divided the two Karantinas with such assurance, untroubled by the search committees installed in no man's land.

A munaqqaba in a billowing black robe, striding past the sleepless youth and encountering a checkpoint, proceeding on her way without answering the men who beckoned her over. A munaqqaba, walking alone until she came to a kushari joint—Hamada's Daughters—about to close its doors. She stands outside until someone comes out and asks for her order. She says she wants to speak to Madame Yara about something important. This is what she asks for and refuses to say a syllable more unless Yara comes in person. Yara comes outside. How are you, Yara? says the woman, simply. I'm Amira, your Auntie Minna's girl. I want to talk to you about an urgent matter.

In the apartment, Yara made tea for Amira, who had taken off her niqab. Lara woke up and joined them. Three women, none more than midway through their third decade, but bearing on their shoulders the responsibility of fashioning a world—and in the belly of one, in Yara, a fetus in its fourth month. You will have to excuse us for reproducing their conversation in its entirety, but no single extract allows us to understand what was going on, nor to appreciate the tremendous tension that filled the air. We beg indulgence, compelled as we are to bring you every word, every syllable spoken, for without the details the thing is meaningless. The three women drank tea and each scrutinized the others. The visit came as a surprise to Yara and Lara both, but its purpose was clear all the same. The same thought had occurred to all three women two days before—the thought it now fell to Amira to explain: The Interior said they'd clear the neighborhood by force.

Yara muttered, They won't be able to.

Lara added, If they wanted to clear it they'd have done it long ago, and she looked at her sister.

Amira said the day's papers had reports of some secret plan to attack Karantina, and that the president had come on TV not long ago to say that the people living there had better find themselves somewhere else to stay, or else the government wouldn't be responsible for what happened. Yara and Lara looked at each other. They knew, and they were worried.

Amira: I don't want to scare you guys. We're in the right, after all. We're the ones who live here and we know what's best for ourselves better than anyone else. And God's on our side, not theirs. God is great.

Yara and Lara were silent. This side of Amira was new to them: a side dripping with faith in God and confidence in the righteous soul's ability to overcome all obstacles. A side set straight by Sheikha Salha; a side the two girls did not know so well. A side with a prayer bruise the size of a pancake slap-bang in the center of its forehead. Yara tried to head off this spiritual assault. She said, They didn't bother with us until you and those goons of yours started shooting. The spiritual assault didn't flag for a second. Amira fixed the sisters with a stare and said: Maybe I've done you wrong, and God will hold me to account for every wrong I've done those who never harmed me. All I want is for Him to forgive us all. I'm asking that we stand together now against the Interior, the Friday after next. That's all. And afterward we can do as we please. Kill each other, even, why not? She worried at the corner of a fingernail, then went on: If we unite, stand hand in hand, no one will be able to touch us. We don't want trouble for trouble's sake. Each of us thinks she's in the right, but if we fight among ourselves then we'll lose the lot and they'll pack us off to those shitty housing projects. I've been to those Mohamediya projects and I've seen for myself. Filth and squalor: as bad as it gets.

Now you two might think I'm weak for coming here and asking to stop the war between us, but no. I swear by the Good Lord, if I wanted to I could blow the whole neighborhood sky-high and nothing could stop me. You ask folk in Karabantina.

Yara leaned toward Lara. Whispered something. Maybe she said Amira still thought she was the Amira of old. And Lara laughed. Amira looked at them both. Coldly, she asked Lara, Something funny, Lara? And Lara replied, No, not at all. I just thought of something.

The tension began to show in Amira's voice, the tension the two sisters knew well. Shame on you, acting like that. Shame on you, laughing at me when I've come all this way to see you. Yara and Lara looked at each other, and Amira started to scream. That's right! I came all this way because I'm worried about you, but as God's my witness I can stop the Interior Ministry and the president himself in their tracks singlehanded! I'm to blame, though, for doing the right thing.

Yara was provoked beyond measure. The words that came from her mouth were like bullets: Stop them in their tracks how, sister? Show us. (Receiving no answer from Amira, she stood up and waved her arms.) Amira! Sweetheart! If my sister and I weren't so well brought up you'd have been dead and buried long ago. And not just you, my girl, but all those useless men you've got as well.

Lara: Yeah. All of them. From the youngest to the oldest.

For a while, Amira said nothing. She seemed to be undergoing some ghastly nervous collapse. She ground her teeth. Looked at the sisters. Then, in a faint voice, she said: And Yehya Volcano?

What about Yehya Volcano?

Amira decided to reveal her terrible secret: That Yehya Volcano happens to be my husband, dear. Married me ages ago. Just after he married you. And to be honest the man's never shortchanged me. Brings the guns to my men in person. And your news. Tells me all about it, every last morsel. You going to kill him too, sweetheart? Amira fell silent again. Decided to introduce a more human note into her discourse. Her face turned to the floor. She added: And I'm pregnant by Yehya Volcano, by the way. There's that. You'd kill Yehya and leave his child an orphan? Yara stared at the belly of her enemy. She was shaking.

Yara sat down. She stared at Amira in silence, her eyes full of defiance. Amira had something to say. Amira had bumped into Yehya Volcano after his marriage to Yara. And as before, she was much taken by his appearance and his muscles, but as a God-fearing woman, a woman who valued her friendships, she did not breathe a word to him. Not before he did. He flirted with her once, then again, then his hands started wandering, and she, as a God-fearing woman, was careful to make it quite clear that they could never be together outside the divinely sanctioned bond of marriage, unless he divorced Yara as soon as circumstances permitted. Amira laid all this out, cold-bloodedly, along with a few other little surprises. Yehya Volcano sold guns to the men in the tunnel. Yara knew that he sold guns to her men, and Amira knew that he sold guns to her men, but what neither of them knew was that he was selling guns to both sides and that he was leaking information about both sides to the other in return for cash. This is what the two women discovered during the course of their conversation.

The conversation ended at around six in the morning, Yara pale and exhausted, Amira looking as though a great weight had been lifted from her, and Lara on the verge of saying something, but saying nothing. Only at the very end did Yara say a few halting words, her voice almost inaudible:

So that's how it is. Even if you're telling the truth, let Yehya stand with us when the police come on Friday. We'll stand together and afterward we'll rip each other to pieces. There's only one thing to do now. Either we shoulder the responsibility together or we sit at home, heads in our hands.

And the three of them agreed to shoulder the responsibility.

That night we might fairly term The Night With No End. As soon as Amira left, Yara went off to try to get some sleep. Half an hour later, Lara came over. She patted her sister, and Yara looked up. Lara said what she had been unable to say earlier: Now don't be upset with me for what I'm about to tell you. Yehya Volcano's a filthy human being. I know him. (She fell silent for a few seconds.) Always trying to get me into bed.

(Expressionless) Trying to get you into bed or got you into bed?

(Looking at the floor) Got me into bed. Three times. When you weren't around. I tried to tell him no, but I didn't know how.

Yara turned away from her sister, without answering. She closed her eyes. Lara noticed that her sister's body was trembling violently and heard the sound of muffled sobs.

From this we might conclude—tentatively, no guarantees we're right—that Yara, bundled up in her tear-soaked blanket, was thinking two thoughts at once: the first concerned the curse of female enemies, of girls who made enemies of each other and were loved by one man—one man, it was always one man, not two or three—who left them to stumble along, living out the worst of all existences; and the second, a song from the distant past, now echoing round her mind, the tune, the rhythm, the beat, the moves, she can't remember where she heard it or who sang it or why she memorized it, the song whose opening line ran, *If my finger were snipped off, it would never hurt me again; I'd never suffer any pain, never, never, never again.* Only when she remembered the words did the drowsiness start to steal over her eyes. Peace of mind.

Before going up to her apartment, Amira called on Sheikha Salha.

On the way she thought hundreds of thoughts. She thought that now, with half a lifetime behind her, she had finally achieved her heart's desire. Her whole life she had yearned to be something and now she was something, and something important too. Amira wasn't bragging; she had dropped any tendency she had to brag since getting to know Sheikha Salha. She only spoke the truth: that now she was something very important—in the neighborhood, in the city, in the state of Egypt—but the knife thrust of treachery . . . this is the hardest thing of all, and we might fairly say that it was this knife thrust of treachery that had robbed her existence of the very meaning she had been searching for her whole life long. Amira was a woman whose life had no meaning.

With tears in her eyes, Amira told her woes to Sheikha Salha. She told her she had thought she could make Yehya Volcano change; that he'd divorce Yara and be hers alone. I never denied him anything, Sheikha Salha, everything he wanted he got. Why, Yehya? Why? Sheikha Salha dried her tears. For a few seconds Amira lay in her arms, then immediately sprang up again. What do Yara and her sister want from me? Just think of it, Sheikha, just think: he was sleeping with that Lara too. Her sister sent me a message to let me know. What do they want from me? Who was it helped them with their homework when they were little? Who lent them money when they were in need? Wasn't it me? Why, Yara? Lara, why? Oh my darlings, why oh why?

In the face of Amira's tears, all Sheikha Salha could do was call for tolerance and love. We're all God's creatures, Amira. All of us, no exceptions, and you're no better than any one of them. Remember that well. No one's better than anyone else. Amira looked at her for a long time. Thought about what she'd said. She decided to take her words as her guide in the days to come. No one's better than anyone else.

When Amira came in to Sheikha Salha's apartment, she didn't say Peace be upon you. It was something like Pissonyou, and from our earlier discussion on this subject, we know what that signifies to her—and to us. Without fear of exaggeration, we can state that Amira was in pieces, no longer the spiritual Amira she was before—not just because of Yara and Lara, but also, but mainly, because of Yehya Volcano. The subject of Yehya Volcano was the last to arise in her meeting with the sheikha. Her gaze was unwavering, fixed on the sheikha's shoulder, and it never moved. She had come to the brink of total nervous breakdown. Despite her unvarying, mechanical tone, the softness of her voice, the unbroken fixity of her gaze, Amira was destroyed. Every cell in her body destroyed, every syllable of her speech destroyed. Why, do you think? Why didn't he fancy me? You know? He never slept with me once, can you believe it? Every day he'd come over from Yara's and say, I'm tired, and, We'll do it tomorrow. He didn't even sleep with me on our wedding night. Imagine! You don't believe me. Fine, well, for your information that was our agreement. He tells me, I'll marry you because I know you want a man to look after you and take care of your business, but I won't sleep with you, he says—because he doesn't want to cheat on his wife. And that's all nonsense. You know why? Because afterward I hear that he's sleeping with the woman's sister. Don't believe me? It's like I'm telling you, swear to God. Yara and Lara, sure, but Amira? No way. Amira's ugly. Amira wears her khimar down to her knees and she's all God-this and the Prophet-that and believes there are things that aren't right and proper between a man and his wife. Amira's a bore. (Sneering) What, and those two are so much fun? (Her expression grows harder, less forgiving.) Just imagine, I'm still a virgin. That's right. Why so surprised? Still a virgin. I've never done anything wrong in my life and that's why I'm waiting for God to make it up to me, make it up to me good. Is there a God or isn't there? (She hides her face in her hands. Her body begins to tremble.) But I told her I was pregnant. I want that so much. I wish my belly would get big like hers. Lord, I wish my belly would get so very big.

Only Lara did not weep. But weeping is not just tears: the heart can weep too. Inside, she was in pieces, just like the other two: Lara, who'd betrayed her sister, then been betrayed by the man she'd betrayed her with. In the days that followed she couldn't summon the courage to look Yara in the eye. She felt ashamed. She felt very small, as small as small could be, imperceptible to the naked eye. And she did not weep. She didn't weep until the fifth day.

She watched a scene from an Arabic soap in which the heroine confessed to her lover that she had left him for reasons only God might know and begged his forgiveness, and her lover gave a bitter smile and told her that the body's sufferings were written in the stars, but who could compel the soul to suffer? Lara wept fiercely. She rocked and slapped her face and screamed, Forgive me, sister. There was no one else at home at the time. It was like she was talking to herself, and certainly she longed for her sister to come in at that very moment and see her in this state, but her sister was far away. No one knew where Yara was.

Lara turned to the tale of Nadia and Itemad, and to the lesson it contained: that women, on their own, can do anything. Given the chance, women can do the impossible. And there was another lesson. One night, Lara decided to cross the line and go and pay Sheikha Salha a visit.

She knocked on the door of the apartment and said, It's Lara. If you want to spit in my face, go ahead and spit, but I'm so, so tired, and I won't be at peace until I've spoken to you. Sheikha Salha greeted her with a smile. She wafted incense around her and recited *I seek refuge with the Lord of the Dawn* and *I seek refuge with the Lord of Mankind*. When she had calmed down a little, Lara sat. She said, I was tired. I'm just a woman and I got tired like women do. And I did wrong, God forgive me. But God bless you, Sheikha,

I'm not leaving till you've told me something to ease my soul. Sheikh Salha told her something to ease her soul. She told her that she was no different from her sister and Amira. We are all the same before the Lord. This was the second lesson Lara learned.

Lara took herself off to see Afriqi, the man who ran her and Yara's war down in the tunnel. She set out the details of the plan that had been laid for next Friday: the barriers between the two tunnels would be torn down and everybody would gather down there. Everybody meaning everybody, meaning Lara and Yara and Amira and Yehya Volcano and Afriqi, and even Kama Sutra, Amira's commander in her section of the tunnel. We'll defend ourselves with everything we've got: hatchets and swords, Molotovs and machine guns. We're all together now, there's no differences between us. The young kids will stay up top by the entrance to Karantina. They'll mine the entrance to the neighborhood. Any vehicle belonging to the Interior will be blown to bits if it comes in. The women will be up on the rooftops with bottles of acid that they'll chuck at anyone who enters. This tunnel, brother: this'll be something like a command center. We'll run the battle from here. I want you to set up a big screen so we can watch what's happening aboveground. Have you got it, Afriqi?

Afriqi had got it, of course. Afriqi had memorized every detail of the plan. It had already been explained to him by Amira, and before that by Yara, each in a private meeting of their own.

These were the stated details of the plan, the details the three women had agreed on between themselves. In her private meeting, Lara appended some other details. She told Afriqi that she couldn't take this life any longer. It cheated people, and then they cheated you, like we're all in some kind of jungle. I'm not better than anyone, and no one's better than me. The Good Lord says, You are all equal. I want to bring this whole story to an end. I've had enough.

Lara's plan to bring this whole story to an end was a simple one. Afriqi would lay dynamite in the tunnel, a ton of dynamite. Then he'd get out, and when Lara called him on his phone he'd send it all sky-high, and her with it; her, and Amira and Yehya Volcano, and Yara. This would take place after victory over the Interior had been achieved, after the ministry's trucks had been blown up one by one, and after Afriqi had made sure that the neighborhood was secure and no one would ever dare to attack or destroy it again. Lara leaned against Afriqi. Like she was in a trance. Don't think I'm happy about all this, she said. Don't think me and my sister want to kill people and turn them out of their homes. Every single one of us, even Amira, even my mother, God have mercy on her soul, wanted to get out of this story. God hadn't shown us the way. But he's showing me now. I want my sister to get out of the mess she's in, and Amira, too. Amira's a sister to me, boy, and it's hard for me to see her like this. Maybe when we die, God will show us mercy. No one knows where God's mercy will fall. Lara promised him the Karantina building when they were gone. It'll all be over. No one will be left to inherit anything. I'll sign over everything I own to you. Afriqi tried patting her on the shoulder, but she swept his hand away and smiled. I'm not crazy, boy. Don't go thinking I've gone crazy. God showed me what to do yesterday, while I was praying for guidance.

What Afriqi did not tell her—out of consideration for her feelings—was that Yara had paid him a visit the day before and made the same request, phrased more or less identically, and nor did he tell her—out of ignorance—that Amira would be paying a visit to her second-in-command Kama Sutra tomorrow, and would make the same request, also phrased more or less identically, nor that he and Kama Sutra would sit down next Friday and confide in one another. Afriqi lit a cigarette and gave it to her. He embraced her and said that everything would go just fine, God willing. And she gave in to his embrace. In his arms, she seemed delicate as a bird.

Sheikha Salha led the women through the Friday prayers.

In his sermon, the sheikh spoke of the importance of sticking to one's principles in difficult times. He would return to this thought throughout the sermon. This is the hour of holding firm, my brothers. I swear by God, the hour of martyrdom is upon us.

After prayers, Sheikha Salha sat with the women, her formidable spiritual energy pulsing from her eyes. Many things had taken place in the neighborhood, she said. People had hated one another and killed one another and women and children had been put out onto the street as a result. And for what, sisters? Because people did not love each other. Everyone secretly believed that the Lord favored them over everyone else. Now, does God stand for that? Did God tell us anyone is better than anyone else, or did he say that no one is privileged over his brother, that no one is better than anyone? During the lesson, Yara was looking at Lara and Lara was looking at Yara and Amira. On the lips of both lay a smile of contentment and peace. The joint betrayal they had suffered had softened their hearts: the first thought of each of them had not been to revenge themselves on the others for betraying them; their first thought had been to kill themselves. Everyone was equal now. History had proved itself to be just.

Half an hour later the police begin to shout through their bullhorns, calling on all residents to vacate the neighborhood immediately. The neighborhood would be cleared by force. The three women are down in the tunnel, Afriqi and Kama Sutra by their side. Up above, the neighborhood is up in arms. The tear gas trickles down into the dark below, men fall before the squalls of lead, the troopers too. And Afriqi and Kama Sutra direct the women standing on the rooftops: they issue orders, where to throw the bottles of searing acid, where to lob the Molotovs; and they direct the men as well, instruct them how best to provoke the armored vehicles into driving their tank tracks over the mined front lines, and one after the other the vehicles are destroyed. Police officers are snatched and taken into Karantina. We're sitting pretty. Afriqi looks over at the women and smiles. And they smile back. They watch as the stones fly out toward the troops, blinding them forever. The big screen down in the tunnel shows everything, everything. Better than Al Jazeera, better than CNN.

As the battle rages, Amira comes up to Yara. Says, Forgive me, sister, you know how much I love you, and Yara pats her hair. Amira gets down on her knees and kisses Yara's bulging belly. She trills happily, My little chick, my little dear. My sweetheart. What a darling. With tears in her eyes, she looks at Yara and asks, What will you call him, sister? and Yara says, Abdallah, then points at Amira's belly and says, And you'll be blessing us all with his little sister in no time.

Afriqi is sitting on the ground beside Lara. He says, With God's help, sister, no one will be able to get near us. We're nice and safe. And Lara grasps his hand and kisses his fingers one by one, then looks at him and says, Why are you so lovely? My boy, don't make me fall for you now. And they laugh.

The sunset prayer is called and the Interior's armored trucks, or what remains of them, gather up the corpses of the soldiers that litter their flatbeds, and withdraw. Yara and Lara and Amira are alone in the tunnel, now that Afriqi and Kama Sutra have left. When the last truck has disappeared for good, each looks at the others, and all together, all at once, they pull out their phones and dial. It's impossible not to notice. Each looks at the others and they all smile at the same time, at the very same time, as the place where they stand rocks with a mighty explosion, as each of them throws herself down on the gravel and tries to crawl anywhere and everywhere, as down in the tunnel the blood of four people flows, the blood of three women and an unborn child. Suddenly, a woman's scream rings out: God grant me victory over you both, you pair of scumbags . . . . Which of the three women gave this cry, no one knows or cares. Why should they? A dying person doesn't care about details of this kind.

Sheikha Salha performs the evening prayer with the women in the mosque, then the prayer for the souls of the martyrs who fell in battle. She leaves the mosque with Umm Salah the maid. The neighborhood is utterly destroyed. The tunnel gapes, its roof caved in by the six massive explosive charges sown along its length. For the first time in a long time, the residents can see the tunnel underground, exposed to the air above.

Sheikha Salha notices the corpse of a dog next to the ruined tunnel. She picks it up in her hands and tosses it into the pit. Smiling, she turns to Umm Salah. Even the animals, ya hagga: they intercede for our souls if they're buried properly.

They walk on together, Sheikha Salha and Umm Salah, into the heart of Karantina, formerly Sousou's Karabantina. God have mercy on their souls, Umm Salah whispers and Sheikha Salha replies, A thousand times over. They gave comfort and were comforted. Yehya Volcano is wandering off along the road from the mosque to the café. The only one to be spared the slaughter. Umm Salah considers, then nudges Sheikha Salha. Sheikha Salha looks at him and twists her lips. Climbing the stairs to Sheikha Salha's apartment,

Umm Salah feels that she has been set free, that a vast load has been lifted from her shoulders. She feels weightless, feels a desire to soar over the rubble of Karantina. She hasn't felt this way for twenty years, she thinks, since 2044, when Hamda died, and Sousou, and the men. She smiles at a sudden shameful thought: that she's reveling in the misfortune of others. She looks over at the sheikha and finds her smiling contentedly as well. Asks, Haven't we got a conscience, or what, ya sheikha? And the sheikha laughs. Upstairs in the apartment, with the Quran's *Verse of the Cow* playing in the background, steam rising from their cups of scalding tea, Sheikha Salha whispers, The Lord is kind to those who serve Him.

Together they drink their tea and ponder the inner peace that has descended, without warning, over the whole world.

GLOSSARY

aza: Roughly analogous to a wake, where friends and relatives gather to pay their condolences to the bereaved family.

basbousa: Flat, dense cake of baked semolina soaked in sweet syrup.

basha: Arabic rendering of the Turkish term pasha, formerly denoting high rank, but used here as an informal term of respect. Appended to a name (i.e. Ali Basha) it conveys a slightly more formal sense of social superiority.

bashmuhandis: Literally "chief engineer," the term is most often used as an all-purpose term of respect in the same manner as basha.

bey: Another Arabic rendering of a Turkish title, bey derives from beg, but is once again a term of respect often appended to a person's name.

Fatiha: The first chapter of the Quran, customarily read as a preliminary to concluding a deal or partnership, and to seal an engagement. The term is also used of prayers said for the dead.

fatta: The Egyptian dish of this name consists of rice and beef or lamb layered with crisped bread and cooked in vinegar and a garlicky tomato sauce.

fuul: Properly fuul midammis, this is a pungent broad bean stew.

gallabiya: The classic Egyptian full-length robe. The gallabiya has working-class and rural overtones, often positive ones associated with ideas of authenticity and traditional values.

hagg/hagga: Literally meaning someone who has been on pilgrimage to Mecca, hagg (or hagga for women) is a term of respect that acknowledges seniority in years and social status.

harisa: Cake-like sweets made with flour, butter, and sugar.

iftar: The meal eaten after a day of fasting during the month of Ramadan.

khimar: One of the more extensive veils for women, covering the head and shoulders and at least the upper chest area.

kunafa: A flat dish made of fine noodles cooked in butter and then soaked in syrup and topped with nuts.

kushari: An Egyptian staple of lentils, pasta, and rice, topped with tomato and garlic sauces and fried onions.

Laylat al-Qadr: "The night of power," on which the first verses of the Quran were revealed to Mohamed, it falls at the end of Ramadan every year. Referred to as "better than a thousand months" in the Quran, prayers offered on this night are supposed to be more effective.

mabrouk: "Congratulations."

mulukhiya: A soup-like stew made from chopped mulukhiya leaves (tossa jute, or Jew's mallow), cooked in broth and served with meat and rice.

munaqqaba: A woman wearing the niqab.

niqab: A veil that covers the head and face, except the eyes, a symbol of overt piety.

umda: A village or local "headman" or mayor.

rakaa: Here, the term refers to the set of actions that constitute a single "unit" of Islamic prayer.

saagh: An obsolete military or police rank roughly equivalent to "major."

taar: A debt of honor calling for vengeance.

Teta: An affectionate term for grandmother.

yuzbashi: Another obsolete rank, one below saagh and roughly equivalent to "captain."

Modern Arabic Literature

The American University in Cairo Press is the world's leading publisher of Arabic literature in translation.

For a full list of available titles, please go to:

mal.aucpress.com